Finding Forever: The Doctor's Surprise Gift

MAGGIE KINGSLEY

SARAH MORGAN

ALISON ROBERTS

MILLS & BOON

First Published in Great Britain 2022
by Mills & Boon, an imprint of HarperCollins*Publishers* Ltd,
1 London Bridge Street, London, SE1 9GF

www.harpercollins.co.uk

HarperCollins*Publishers*
1st Floor, Watermarque Building,
Ringsend Road, Dublin 4, Ireland

FINDING FOREVER: THE DOCTOR'S SURPRISE GIFT © 2022
Harlequin Books S.A.

St Piran's: Tiny Miracle Twins © 2012 Harlequin Books S.A.
St Piran's: Prince on the Children's Ward © 2012 Harlequin Books S.A.
St. Piran's: The Wedding! © 2013 Harlequin Books S.A.

Special thanks and acknowledgement are given to Maggie Kingsley for her contribution to the *St. Piran's Hospital* series.
Special thanks and acknowledgement are given to Sarah Morgan for her contribution to the *St. Piran's Hospital* series.
Special thanks and acknowledgement are given to Alison Roberts for her contribution to the *St. Piran's Hospital* series

ISBN: 978-0-263-30423-7

MIX
Paper from
responsible sources
FSC™ C007454

Maggie Kingsley decided that she wanted to be a writer when she was eight. That dream stayed with ... when sh... her – ordinary people – didn't write books, and so she trained to be a teacher instead. But it was only after working in various other jobs that her family nagged and dared and finally persuaded her to take up her pen. And the rest, as they say, is history!

Sarah Morgan is a *USA Today* and *Sunday Times* bestselling author of contemporary romance and women's fiction. She has sold more than twenty-one million copies of her books and her trademark humour and warmth have gained her fans across the globe. Sarah lives with her family near London, England, where the rain frequently keeps her trapped in her office. Visit her at www.sarahmorgan.com

New Zealander **Alison Roberts** has written more than eighty romance novels for Mills & Boon. She has also worked as a primary school teacher, a cardiology research technician and a paramedic. Currently, she is living her dream of living – and writing – in a gorgeous village in the south of France.

Finding Forever

December 2021
An Unexpected Bride

January 2022
Falling for the Rebel

February 2022
The Doctor's Surprise Gift

March 2022
Surprise by Sunrise

April 2022
Saying I do

May 2022
A Passionate Proposal

ST PIRAN'S: TINY MIRACLE TWINS

MAGGIE KINGSLEY

I often wonder how my sister Elizabeth puts up with my many crises of confidence when I'm writing, without ever saying to me, 'Maggie, get a grip!' or strangling me, but she does. So thank you, little sister. This book is dedicated to you, for your patience, forbearance and all the times you've listened to me when I've said, 'Okay, do you think this would be better?' without running screaming from the room.

CHAPTER ONE

People say time heals everything but it doesn't, not completely, never totally. Sometimes all it takes is the overheard fragment of a song, a whispered comment, or an unexpected meeting, and the scab that time has so carefully placed over the old wound begins to come apart, leaving the pain just as acute as it ever was, just as raw.

'So, the rumours are true, then,' Sister Brianna Flannigan observed as she sipped her coffee in the canteen of St Piran's. 'A troubleshooter really is coming to the hospital to see which departments should be closed?'

'And not just coming, I'm afraid.' Megan Phillips sighed. 'He's actually arriving some time today if the grapevine is correct.'

'But this is a good hospital,' Brianna protested. 'The staff are dedicated, the quality of surgery is second to none, and it provides a much-needed medical resource for the people who live in this part of Cornwall.'

'Agreed.' Jess Corezzi nodded glumly. 'But, according to the board, we're leaking money like a sieve, and…' She held up her hands and made pretend speech marks. '"Something Has to be Done".'

'But surely that doesn't have to mean ward or—heaven

forbid—complete department closures?' Brianna demanded. 'There must be some other way to save money.'

'Canning my job will probably be the first thing on this auditor's list,' Jess said ruefully. 'Counselling patients, and their families, as I do...' She shook her head. 'I can't see him regarding that as necessary.'

'But your job is vitally important,' Brianna protested, her large brown eyes troubled. 'The parents of my babies in NICU need you—'

'As do the parents, and kids in Paeds,' Megan chipped in, but Jess didn't look convinced, and Brianna could understand why.

If the auditor had been drafted in to make economies he was bound to look at the non-nursing staff first, and though she and Megan might think Jess's counselling role essential she had a horrible suspicion this money man would not.

'What does Gio think?' Brianna asked, thinking of Jess's handsome Italian husband, a neurosurgeon who had arrived at St Piran's the previous autumn and swept her friend off her feet.

'He thinks like you, that the auditor will recognise how valuable my work is and recommend shelving the new specialist paediatric burns unit instead, but frankly...' Jess shrugged. 'I can't see that happening. There is a need for that unit, plus the building is almost complete, and Admin have already asked that foreign prince to perform the grand opening in a couple of months.'

Brianna didn't think Gio's suggestion likely, either, and neither did Megan, judging by her expression.

'At least both your departments will be safe,' Jess continued bracingly. 'No one in their right mind would shut down a neonatal intensive care unit or a paediatric ward.'

Brianna could think of one man who would. One man

to whom statistics and efficiency had always been more important than people, and she shivered involuntarily.

'You OK?' Megan asked with a slight frown, and Brianna forced a smile.

'I just don't like all this talk of department closures. This hospital has been my...' She came to a halt. She had been about to say 'refuge', but though she, Jess and Megan had become friends during the two years she'd been at St Piran's there were areas of her life that were strictly off limits, and her past was one of them. 'I've been so very happy here,' she said instead.

'Me, too,' Jess replied, and Megan nodded in agreement.

'Look, do we know anything about this man?' Brianna asked. 'Where he's from, what other hospitals he's been to?'

'All we know is he's from London,' Jess replied, and the shiver Brianna had felt earlier became more pronounced.

'London?' she echoed. 'Jess—'

The insistent bleep of a pager brought her to a halt. All three women instantly reached for theirs, but it was Megan who got to her feet with a groan.

'Nothing wrong in Paeds, I hope?' Brianna said, and Megan shook her head.

'It's Admin. They've got themselves in a real flap about this visitation. Yesterday they wanted everything in duplicate. Now they've decided they want everything in triplicate.'

With a rueful smile the paediatric specialist registrar headed off towards the canteen exit but, as Brianna and Jess watched her, the door suddenly opened and Josh O'Hara, the consultant from A and E, appeared. He clearly said something to Megan, actually put out his hand to stay her, but she pushed past him without a word, and Brianna and Jess exchanged glances.

'The atmosphere's not getting any better between those two, is it?' Brianna said, and Jess sighed.

'I guess it can't. Not when Josh is married to Rebecca, and Megan's most certainly not a home-wrecker.'

'Has...?' Brianna cleared her throat awkwardly. 'Has she said anything to you about him?'

'I only know there's a past history there, not what it is, and I wouldn't dream of asking,' Jess replied. 'My guess is they were an item years ago, before Josh got married, but as to what happened or why they split up...' The hospital counsellor lifted her shoulders helplessly. 'I just wish he hadn't taken the consultant's job in A and E. OK, so he didn't know Megan would be working at St Piran's, but can you imagine how awful it must be, having someone you once loved reappear in your life like this?'

Brianna could. She didn't want to imagine it, but she could, all too vividly.

Secrets, she thought as she watched Josh walk slowly across the canteen then stare unenthusiastically at the lunch menu. She, Jess and Megan, all of them had secrets. Maybe that's what had drawn them together, made them friends. That, and the fact they never pried into one another's private lives so she'd had no idea until a few months ago that Jess had HIV, or that Megan was nursing a badly broken heart, while neither of them knew she...

Don't go there, Brianna, she told herself. *Don't go there, not ever.*

'The annoying thing is, I like him,' Jess continued as Josh picked up a doughnut and coffee, then morosely went to sit at an empty table near the back of the canteen. 'Whatever happened between him and Megan in the past, I still think he's one of the good guys.'

'And does your husband know you consider Josh "one of the good guys"?' Brianna asked, her brown eyes dancing, and the counsellor laughed.

'Gio knows I only have eyes for him,' she replied. 'I just wish…this situation between Megan and Josh… I just wish there was something I could do to help.'

Brianna wished she could, too, as she and Jess left the canteen and went their separate ways. She'd liked Josh O'Hara from the very first minute she'd met him. For sure he'd teased her when he'd discovered she was from Ireland as he was, had said that with her long, auburn hair she reminded him of the 1940s Hollywood actress, Maureen O'Hara, but she knew he hadn't been hitting on her. He was just a natural-born charmer, adept at making people feel at ease. Unless, of course, that person was Megan Phillips, she thought with a deep sigh.

And she could have done with Josh at her side, dispensing a whole bucketload of his charm, she decided as she swiped her ID card to gain entry to NICU, only to walk straight into Rita, NICU's ward clerk, and her least favourite member of staff in the hospital.

'I'm not late back from lunch, Rita,' Brianna said, consulting her watch pointedly, 'the unit doesn't appear to be on fire, I'm sure you would have paged me if any of the babies was giving cause for concern, so can I assume you want to report one of the nursing staff for some petty infringement?'

'He's here,' the NICU ward clerk hissed. 'The auditor. He arrived half an hour ago, and I've got him in my office, looking at some files, but I don't know how long I can keep him there.'

'Have you considered chains, manacles, possibly a straitjacket?'

'This is not a laughing matter, Sister Flannigan,' Rita retorted. 'Mr Brooke is still in Theatre—'

'Which is probably just as well,' Brianna interrupted. 'Letting Babbling loose amongst walking, healthy people…' She shook her head. 'Not a good idea.'

'Neither is referring to our head of department by that stupid nickname,' Rita protested, apparently conveniently forgetting that she called their consultant Mr Brooke 'Babbling' just as often as the rest of the staff in NICU did.

'Rita—'

'First impressions count, Sister, and we've already got off to a bad one with Mr Brooke not being here to meet the VIP.'

'Yes, it really was *very* inconsiderate of little Amy Renwick to get so sick, wasn't it?' Brianna said dryly, but her sarcasm was lost on the ward clerk.

'It certainly couldn't have happened at a worse time,' Rita agreed. 'I only have two years left to work before I retire and the last thing I want is the unit closing down before I'm ready to go.'

Yeah, and you're all heart, Rita, Brianna thought, but she didn't say that.

'I very much doubt anyone would ever contemplate shutting down a neonatal intensive care unit,' she said, deliberately echoing Jess's optimistic words, but Rita wasn't placated.

'We're grossly understaffed,' the ward clerk declared, her tightly permed grey curls practically bristling with indignation, 'and this auditor is bound to notice. Lord knows, I'm not one to complain—'

You never do anything but, Brianna thought irritably. In fact, it would be a red-letter, stop-press, post-it-to-the-world-on-Twitter day if Rita managed to get through one day without complaining.

'And no-one can say I'm not doing my best,' Rita continued, 'but, without a nurse unit manager, I'm fighting an uphill battle.'

Brianna was sorely tempted to tell the woman she might find her job considerably easier if she didn't spend half her time prying into everyone else's business and the other half spreading gossip, but the trouble was the ward clerk was right. They *were* finding it tough without a nurse unit manager, and though Admin had promised to advertise the post after Diego Ramirez returned to Spain, there had been no sign yet of them doing anything.

'I'm sure the auditor will make allowances for us,' she declared, 'and now, if you'll excuse me—'

'Selfish, that's what I call it,' Rita continued. 'Mr Ramirez leaving us all in the lurch. In my day people had a sense of duty, a sense of responsibility, but nobody cares about standards nowadays. Look at all the unmarried mothers we get in NICU. Feckless, the lot of them. In my day—'

'I'm sure every family behaved like the Waltons, and nothing bad ever happened,' Brianna interrupted tersely, 'but right now, if you're so anxious about making a good impression, wouldn't it be better if you simply got on with your job?'

Rita's mouth fell open, she looked as though she'd dearly like to say something extremely cutting, then she strode away with a very audible sniff, and Brianna gritted her teeth.

She would undoubtedly pay later for what she'd said— Rita would make sure of that—but the ward clerk had caught her on the raw today. Actually, if she was honest,

Rita always caught her on the raw with her 'holier than thou' attitude to life.

'Walk a mile in my moccasins.'

It was one of her mother's favourite sayings, and her mother was right, Brianna thought as she washed her hands thoroughly then applied some antiseptic gel to ensure she didn't carry any bacteria into the unit, except…

She bit her lip as she caught sight of her reflection in the small mirror over the sink. 'The country mouse'. That was what her colleagues had called her when she'd been a student nurse, but that had been fourteen years ago. She wasn't a country mouse any more. She was thirty-two years old, the senior sister in a neonatal intensive care unit, and time and life had changed her. Especially the last two years.

Don't, Brianna, she told herself as she felt her heart twist inside her. *Don't start looking back, you can't, you mustn't, not now, not ever.*

And normally she didn't, she thought as she took a steadying breath before tucking a stray strand of her auburn hair back into its neat plait, only to realise her hand was shaking. Normally she lived in the now, determinedly refusing to look back, or forward, and it was all the fault of this damned auditor. His arrival was upsetting everyone, turning what had been her refuge into a place of uncertainty, and she didn't want uncertainty. She wanted the hospital to stay exactly as it was. Her haven, her sanctuary, her escape from all that had happened.

'Blasted number-cruncher,' she muttered as she used her elbow to push open the door leading into the NICU ward. 'Why can't he just go away and play on a motorway?'

'You wouldn't be talking about our esteemed visitor, would you?' Chris, her senior staff nurse, chuckled, clearly overhearing her.

'Got it in one,' Brianna replied, feeling herself beginning

to relax as the familiar heat in the unit enveloped her, and she heard the comforting, steady sound of beeping monitors and ventilators. 'Anything happen over lunch I should know about?'

'Mr Brooke's not back from Theatre yet and neither is Amy Renwick.'

'So Rita told me,' Brianna replied. 'It looks as though he's had to remove part of Amy's intestine after all.'

It was what they'd all been hoping the consultant wouldn't have to do. Amy Renwick had been born twelve weeks premature, and scarcely a month later she'd been diagnosed with necrotising enterocolitis. The condition wasn't uncommon in premature babies—their intestines were frequently insufficiently developed to handle digestion—but generally it could be controlled with antibiotics. In Amy's case, however, the antibiotics hadn't worked. Mr Brooke had thought he might only have to drain the infected fluid from her stomach, but, from the length of time he'd been in Theatre, it looked very much as though that solution hadn't proved to be an option.

'Is Mrs Renwick here?' Brianna asked, and the staff nurse nodded.

'She's in the parents' restroom—very upset, of course—but her family's with her.'

And they'd been a tower of strength over the past few weeks for Naomi and her husband, Brianna thought as she lifted a file from the nurses' station. Not all of their parents were so lucky. Some families lived too far away to provide emotional support, while other families simply couldn't deal with the constant up-and-down pressures of having a very premature baby.

And sometimes the people, the person, you were so sure you could depend on let you down, she thought with a sudden, unwanted, shaft of pain.

'You OK, Brianna?'

The staff nurse was gazing uncertainly at her, and Brianna manufactured a smile.

'You're the second person to ask me that today, and I'm fine,' she replied. 'I've just got a bad attack of Monday blues, not helped by the imminent arrival of this blasted auditor—'

'Who, if I'm not very much mistaken, has just arrived with Babbling and Rita,' the staff nurse warned in an undertone. 'And, if that *is* him, he looks scary. Good looking in a designer-suited, high-powered sort of way, but most definitely scary.'

Quickly, Brianna glanced over her shoulder, and in that split second her world stood still. Dimly, she heard their NICU consultant introduce the man at his side as Connor Monahan, but she didn't need the introduction. The six-foot-one rangy frame, the thick black hair and startling blue eyes, the expensive city suit and equally top-of-the-range laptop that he was carrying... It was the man she hadn't thought about—had refused to allow herself think about—for the past two years, and the file she'd been holding slipped from her nerveless fingers and landed on the floor with a clatter.

From beside her she heard Chris's small gasp of surprise at her unusual clumsiness, saw Mr Brooke's glare of irritation, but what pierced her to the core as she quickly retrieved the file then straightened up was the way the familiar blue eyes had flashed instantly from recognition to anger. How those same blue eyes were now boring deep into her, tearing her heart apart just as it had been torn apart two years ago.

'I can assure you my staff are not normally so clumsy, Mr Monahan,' she heard Mr Brooke declare, and saw Connor shake his head dismissively.

'Accidents happen,' he replied, 'and, please, everyone, call me Connor. I'm not here to judge anyone. My visit to this hospital is merely as an observer, to find out how a hospital like this serves its local community.'

'Yeah, right,' Chris muttered. 'And like we don't all know that he's been sent in to find out which department should be closed, so he can give up on the "let's all be friends" routine. And, oh, Lord, Mr Brooke is now insisting on introducing everyone,' the staff nurse continued, rolling her eyes heavenwards. 'What's the bet he won't remember half our names?'

Brianna didn't care if the middle-aged consultant did or not. She was too busy keeping her eyes fixed firmly on the file in her hand, wishing she was anywhere but here, but, out of the corner of her eye, she could see the inexorable approach of a pair of mirror-bright black shoes, could smell an all-too-distinctive sandalwood aftershave, and she sucked in an uneven breath, willing this moment to be over.

'And this is Sister Flannigan,' Mr Brooke announced when he drew level with her.

'Sister Flannigan,' Connor repeated slowly, and Brianna winced as she reluctantly raised her head to look up at him.

Never would she have imagined anyone could put quite so much sarcasm into her surname, but Connor just had.

'She's only been with us for two years,' Mr Brooke continued, clearly completely oblivious to the atmosphere, 'but since then she's become an indispensable member of the team.'

At any other time Brianna would have savoured the praise from the portly consultant, who never gave anyone any, but not today, not when she saw Connor's left eyebrow rise.

'So, you've been living here in Cornwall for the last two years, have you, Sister Flannigan?' he said with deliberate emphasis, and Brianna clasped the file in her hands even tighter.

Don't, she wanted to say. *Please, don't. Not here, not in front of everyone.* But she couldn't say anything, not with her boss listening, not with Rita's eyes darting avidly between her and Connor, her mind clearly already whirring away with speculation.

'Yes, I've been here for two years,' she muttered, 'and now if you'll excuse me…'

'Oh, absolutely not,' Connor declared, his voice ice-cold and implacable. 'In fact, I *insist* you stay.'

Had he always been quite so tall, so intimidating? she wondered as she involuntarily took a step back. Of course he had. He couldn't possibly have grown since she'd last seen him, and he'd always possessed an air of authority and power, and yet she felt transported back in time to the little country mouse she'd once been, and she hated feeling that way.

'I'm afraid you really will have to excuse me,' she said, putting as much defiance into her voice as she could muster. 'I have babies to attend to, and I also need to talk to the mother of one of our patients. Her daughter has just undergone major surgery—'

'From which we are hopeful she will make a full recovery,' Mr Brooke interrupted. 'Of course, the next few days will be critical, as I will explain to Mrs Renwick myself.'

Which is exactly what I *don't* want you to do, Brianna thought unhappily. Of course, all operations carried risks, but not for nothing had the nursing staff in NICU nicknamed their consultant 'Babbling' Brooke. Brilliant surgeon though he might be, he would persist in constantly—and at great length—giving parents the worst-case scenario possible, terrifying them witless in the process. Megan would have handled Naomi Renwick so much better, but Megan wasn't here.

'It would be no trouble for me to talk to Mrs Renwick, Mr Brooke,' she said desperately. 'I could go now—'

'Not running away from me, are you, Sister Flannigan?' Connor said, and she bit her lip savagely.

Had she been the only one in the unit who had heard the unspoken word *again* in his comment? She hoped she was, she prayed she was.

'Of course not,' she replied. 'I just… I know Mrs Renwick very well… I'm her daughter's primary carer—'

'And I'm her daughter's surgeon, and head of this department, so I will speak to her,' Mr Brooke interrupted with a finality that told Brianna there was no point in arguing. 'Now, Connor, I'm sure our ward clerk will be only too happy to let you examine more of our files—'

'Which I'm sure would be absolutely fascinating,' Connor interrupted, 'but I'm only going to be in St Piran's for the next six weeks so what I'd like to do in NICU, over the next few days, is interview all of your staff individually. Form an idea from them of how they think they fit into this unit, what their duties are, gain the bigger picture, if you like.'

Six weeks? Brianna thought, glancing from Connor to Mr Brooke with ill-disguised horror. Connor was going to be in the hospital for *six weeks*? Even if he only spent a few days in NICU, it was going to be a few days too many and Mr Brooke clearly thought the same.

'I really don't see why there's any need for you to interview my staff when I can give you the bigger picture immediately,' he said. 'Sick babies come in here, my nursing staff and I attempt to make them better. End of story.'

Brianna could have kissed the consultant, but Connor

merely smiled the smile of a man who had no intention of having his intentions thwarted.

'I still want to speak to your staff,' he insisted evenly. 'My interviews will take no longer than half an hour, and after that I will simply be a silent observer. In fact, I doubt you'll even notice I'm here.'

I'll notice, Brianna thought, desperately praying their consultant would feel the same but, to her dismay, he had clearly become bored with the conversation and simply shrugged.

'Fine—whatever,' he said. 'Just don't get in my way, or the way of my staff. So, who do you want to interview first?'

Connor made a show of glancing over the assembled nurses, but Brianna knew who he was going to choose, just as she knew Connor knew it, too.

'I'm sure Sister Flannigan and I will find a lot to talk about,' he declared with a smile that didn't even remotely suggest it would ever reach his eyes. 'Mr Brooke, do you have an office or room I could use as a base while I'm here at the hospital?'

He wanted to use NICU as his base? Even when he was assessing other departments he would keep returning to NICU as his base? *No*, Brianna thought desperately, dear heavens, *no*.

'I'll get Maintenance to clear out the nurse unit manager's office for you,' the consultant replied vaguely. 'It's not in use at the moment, but there are confidential files in it that will have to be secured, so in the meantime you could use the nurses' staffroom if you want.'

Connor nodded.

'Sounds good to me,' he said.

It didn't sound good to Brianna, and neither did the way Connor shadowed her all the way out of the ward and down the corridor as though he was convinced she might bolt. And she would have bolted, she thought, if she hadn't known that a pair of five-foot-two-inch legs could never have outrun the six-foot-one-inch legs of the man at her side.

'Would you like some tea, coffee?' she said, walking quickly over to the kettle as soon as they entered the staff-room, desperate to delay the inevitable for as long as possible. 'There's some herbal tea here, too, though I can't vouch for it being drinkable, and hot chocolate—'

'So, is it still *Brianna* Flannigan,' he interrupted, 'or did you change your Christian name as well as your surname?'

She stared at the cork board which one of the nurses had affixed to the wall above the kettle and cups. Postcards from far-away places were pinned to it, along with old birthday cards and congratulation cards, and there was also a whole array of cartoons that should have been funny but she had never felt less like laughing.

'I…I kept my Christian name,' she muttered, mechanically switching on the kettle and spooning some coffee into a cup, though she didn't really want anything. 'Flannigan was my mother's maiden name.'

'But not yours,' he said. 'You do realise I could get you fired for working at this hospital under a false name?'

He could, she knew he could, but suddenly she didn't care. Suddenly she felt cornered, and defeated, and wearily she turned to face him.

'OK, get me fired,' she said. 'If that's what you want to do, then go ahead and do it.'

'Of course that's not what I want!' he exclaimed, tossing his laptop onto the nearest seat. 'What do you take me for?'

I don't know, she thought as she gazed up into his cold,

rigid face. *I don't know because I feel like I don't know you any more, and I'm wondering now if I ever did.*

'Look, can we sit down?' she said. 'You standing there—looming over me like some spectre of doom—isn't helping.'

With a muttered oath he sat down, and, after a moment's hesitation she abandoned the kettle and took the seat opposite him.

'You really were determined I wouldn't find you, weren't you?' he said, his blue eyes fixed on her, daring her to contradict him. 'Changing your surname, moving to a one-horse town in the back of beyond in Cornwall.'

'Connor, it wasn't like that—'

'Wasn't it?' he interrupted, his voice dripping sarcasm. 'So how—exactly—would you interpret it?'

'I wanted…' Oh, but this was so hard to explain, and she wanted to explain, for him to understand. 'I just wanted…' Her voice broke slightly despite her best efforts to keep it level. 'Some peace. All I wanted was some peace.'

'And to get that you had to walk out on me?' he said incredulously. 'Walk out without a word?'

'I left you a letter,' she protested, and saw his lip curl with derision.

'"I need to be on my own for a while,"' he quoted. '"I need some space, some time to get myself together". That's hardly an "I'm leaving you, and I'm never coming back", dear-John letter, is it?'

'Connor—'

'You applied for this job without telling me, didn't you?' he said. 'You applied for it, and got it, and yet you never said a word to me about what you were planning to do.'

She swallowed hard. 'Yes.'

'So that's why you only ever took three hundred pounds out of our joint bank account,' he declared, fury deepening his voice. 'You didn't need any more money because you had this job to come to.'

'Yes,' she whispered.

'Why, Brianna, *why*?' he demanded, thrusting his fingers through his black hair, anger, hurt and bewilderment plain on his face. 'I thought we were happy, I thought you loved me.'

'Things…things haven't been right between us for a long time, Connor,' she replied, 'you know they haven't—'

'That's nonsense,' he retorted, and she clasped her hands together tightly, desperately trying to find the words that would make him understand.

'I was going under, Connor,' she cried. 'After what happened—you wouldn't talk to me, you wouldn't let me talk, and I knew—if I didn't get away—I was going to slide further and further into the black pit I'd fallen into, and if I kept on falling…' She took an uneven breath. 'I was scared—so scared—that I would never be able to get myself out again.'

'And me—what about me?' he exclaimed, his blue eyes blazing. '*Two years*, Brianna, it's been *two years* since you left and in all that time you never once lifted the phone to tell me you were OK, never once even sent me a scribbled postcard to say you were alive.'

'I was going to write, to tell you where I was,' she declared defensively, but had she really been going to? It wasn't something she wanted to think about, far less face. It was enough of a shock to see him sitting there in front of her. 'Connor—'

'You left your phone behind, the house keys, the police wouldn't help me—'

'You went to the police?' She gasped, her eyes large with dismay, and he threw her a look that made her shrink back into her seat.

'What the hell did you expect me to do? Did you think I'd simply stay home in our flat, night after night, watching TV, thinking, Well, I expect Brianna will come back eventually? *Of course* I went to the police. I thought…' He closed his eyes for a second, and when he spoke again his voice was rough. 'I thought you might have done something…stupid, but they said as you'd left a note, and your parents knew you were safe, it wasn't a police matter but a domestic one.'

'I'm sorry,' she murmured. 'I didn't realise—I never imagined you'd go to the police—'

'Can you imagine how that made me feel?' he said, his lips curving into a bitter travesty of a smile. 'When the police told me your parents knew where you were, but I didn't? I went back to Ireland, to your parents' farm in Killarney, thinking you might have gone there, and, when I discovered you hadn't, I begged them to give me your address, even your phone number, so I could at least hear your voice, know you truly were safe, but they wouldn't give me either. They said you'd made them promise not to tell me anything, that you would contact me when you were ready.'

'I'm sorry, so sorry,' she repeated, willing him to believe her. 'I didn't…' She shook her head blindly. 'I wasn't thinking clearly, not then. I just…'

'Had to get away from me,' he finished for her bitterly, and she bit her lip hard.

'Connor, listen to me—'

'Every time I heard on the news that a body had been found in some secluded spot I feared it was you,' he continued as though she hadn't spoken. 'Every time someone was pulled out of the Thames I thought, Please, don't let it be Brianna, but, as time went on, God help me, I sometimes…' He took a breath. 'Sometimes I hoped it *was* you because at least then the waiting would be over. All I needed…all I wanted…was to know you really were safe, and yet you denied me even that, Brianna.'

'I would have called you, I would have talked to you,' she said, her voice trembling, 'but I knew talking to you wouldn't help, that you wouldn't listen.'

'How can you say that?' he demanded angrily. 'Of course I would have talked, of course I would have listened!'

'You didn't before when I needed you to,' she said before she could stop herself. 'All you ever did was cut me off, change the subject, or you'd ask me…' She swallowed convulsively, hearing the tears in her voice, and she didn't want to cry…she so didn't want to cry. 'You kept asking me what was wrong, and I thought I'd go mad if you asked me that one more time because it was so obvious to me that everything was always going to be wrong, that it was never going to be right.'

'You're not making any sense—'

'Because you're not *listening*, just like you always don't,' she flared. 'Whenever I try to talk to you, you never ever *listen*.'

'Well, I want to talk now,' he countered. 'To talk properly with no lies, deception or half-truths, only honesty.'

She knew he was right, but talking honestly meant resurrecting everything that had happened, meant having to face it again. She hadn't forgotten, she never would, but over the past two years she'd managed to come to a kind of acceptance, and to talk about it now… She didn't think her heart could take that, and she shook her head.

'Connor, this isn't the time, or the place.'

'Then *when*, Brianna?' he exclaimed, and there was such a lacerating fury in his blue eyes that she winced. 'When will be the time, or the place?'

She wanted to say, *Never—nowhere*. She wanted even

more to say she wished he had never come, had never found her, but she didn't have the courage.

'I don't know,' she said wretchedly. 'I don't—'

She bit off the rest of what she had been about to say. The door of the nurses' staffroom had opened, and Megan's head had appeared hesitantly round it.

'I'm really sorry,' the paediatric specialist registrar began, glancing from Brianna to Connor, then back again, 'but I'm afraid Brianna is needed in the unit.'

Brianna was hurrying towards Megan before she had even finished speaking, but when she reached the door she heard Connor clear his throat.

'We have to talk, Brianna, and talk soon,' he said.

She thought she nodded, but she couldn't be sure. All she knew was she had to get away from him, and she was halfway down the corridor before Megan caught up with her.

'Brianna—'

'Is it Amy Renwick? Is she back from Recovery, and there's a problem, or—?'

'Actually, I'm afraid I lied, and you're not needed in the unit at all,' Megan interrupted, looking shamefaced. 'It's just…I was passing the nurses' staffroom and I heard the auditor yelling at you. I wasn't eavesdropping, honestly I wasn't,' she continued as Brianna stared at her in alarm. 'It's just the walls in this place are so thin, and you sounded… Well, you sounded really upset, and in need of rescue.'

'I did—I was,' Brianna said with a small smile.

'I think you should make a formal complaint,' Megan declared angrily. 'It's one thing to inspect a unit, to ask the staff questions about how it's run, but harassing someone…' She shook her head. 'That's completely out of order.'

'Megan, I don't want to make a complaint,' Brianna

replied. 'My interview is over, done with, so let's just leave it, OK?'

'Not on your life,' the paediatric registrar insisted. 'If this Connor whatever his name is—'

'Monahan. His name's Connor Monahan.'

'Thinks he can ride roughshod over the nursing staff, upset them, then he can think again. I can understand why you might be reluctant to make a complaint, but I'm not. I'm more than willing to march up to Admin right now, and tell them they'd better warn him to back off or they'll have the nurses' union on their doorstep.'

Megan would do it, too, Brianna thought, seeing the fury in her friend's face, and it was the last thing she wanted. It was hard enough for her to deal with Connor's reappearance in her life without having the staff in Admin gossiping about it after they'd been told all the facts, and she would have to tell them all the facts.

'Megan, it's got nothing to do with the nursing staff, or the unit,' she said unhappily. 'It's me. It's to do with me. You see, Connor Monahan and I... We know one another.'

Her friend gazed at her blankly for a second, then a look of horrified realisation appeared on her face.

'Oh, lord, he's not an ex-boyfriend of yours, is he?' she exclaimed. 'Oh, Brianna, I'm so sorry, what a nightmare for you.'

'A nightmare, for sure.' Brianna nodded. 'But you see...' She took a deep breath. 'The trouble is, Connor isn't an ex-boyfriend. He...he's my husband.'

CHAPTER TWO

'BUT Mr Brooke said yesterday—after Amy's operation—that she might need another operation,' Naomi Renwick said, her eyes dark with fear. 'He said he wouldn't know for the next seventy-two hours whether he'd successfully removed all of the infection, so you'd be keeping a very careful eye on her.'

'Which I would be doing whether Amy had been operated on or not,' Brianna replied, wishing the ever-pessimistic consultant to the darkest reaches of hell. 'Naomi, your daughter is doing very well. We have no reason to think she will require another operation—'

'But if she does... She's so little, Sister, so very little, and if she needs another operation...'

'We'll deal with it just as we've dealt with all the other problems Amy has faced since she was born a month ago. Naomi, listen to me,' Brianna continued, as Amy's mother made to interrupt. 'I can't give you any guarantees—no one can, but, please, *please*, don't go looking for bridges to cross. Amy's temperature's normal, her colour's good. In fact,' she added, 'just look at her.'

Naomi Renwick gazed down into the incubator where her daughter was vigorously kicking her little legs despite the fine line of sutures across her stomach, and her lips curved into a shaky smile.

'She's beautiful, isn't she?' she said, and Brianna nodded.

'She is, and right now she's in the best possible place, getting the best possible care, so hold onto that, OK?'

Brianna hoped Naomi Renwick would, but she wished even more, as she turned to discover Connor standing behind her, that her husband would dog some other nurse's footsteps, if only for a little while.

Twenty-four hours, she thought as she began walking down the ward, all too conscious he was following her. Just twenty-four hours ago her life might not exactly have been perfect, but at least she hadn't felt permanently besieged. Now she felt cornered, under attack, and it wasn't just by his presence, or his continual questions about the unit. It was the way he managed to somehow incorporate so many barbed comments into what he was saying that was wearing her down, little by little, bit by bit.

'How many incubators does the NICU at Plymouth have?' he asked, and she came to a weary halt.

'Twelve,' she replied, 'which is double our capacity, but their hospital covers a far greater area and population than St Piran's, so it's bound to be bigger.'

'I also notice from your ward clerk's files that every baby has a primary carer,' he continued. 'That doesn't seem to be a very efficient system in terms of time or personnel.'

'Not everything can be measured in terms of time management, or personnel distribution,' she said acidly. 'Especially the care of very vulnerable babies.'

'I see,' he said, but she doubted whether he did as she watched him type something into his state-of-the-art phone, which could probably have made him a cup of coffee if he'd asked it to.

Figures, statistics had always been his passion, not people, and he didn't seem to have changed.

'Connor—'

'Does this unit normally have quite so many unused incubators?' he asked, gesturing towards the two empty ones at the end of the ward.

'There's no such thing as "normal" in NICU,' she protested. 'We've had occasions when only three of our incubators have been in use, times when we were at full capacity, and last Christmas we were so busy we had to send babies to Plymouth because we just couldn't accommodate them. It was tough for everyone, especially the families.'

'It would be.' He nodded. 'Christmas being the time when most families like to be together.'

And you've missed two with me. He didn't say those words—he didn't need to—but she heard them loud and clear.

'Things don't always work out the way we planned,' she muttered, 'and babies can't be expected to arrive exactly when you want them to.'

'Not babies, no. Grown-ups, on the other hand,' he added, his eyes catching and holding hers, 'have a choice.'

And you chose to walk away from me. That was what he was really saying, and she swallowed painfully.

'Connor, please,' she said with difficulty. 'This is a good unit, an efficient unit. Please don't make this personal.'

His eyebrows rose. 'You think that's what I'm doing?'

'I *know* it is,' she cried. 'Look, I can understand you being angry—'

'I'm sorry to interrupt,' Rita interrupted, looking anything but as she joined them, 'but I'm afraid we've had a complaint about your car, Sister Flannigan.'

'A complaint?' Brianna echoed in confusion, and Rita smiled.

A smile that was every bit as false as the sympathetic sigh with which she followed it.

'You've parked it in the consultants' side of the car park today instead of the nurses'. Easily done, of course, when you're stressed—'

'I'm not stressed—'

'Of course you are, my dear,' Rita declared, her face all solicitous concern, but her eyes, Brianna noticed, were speculative, calculating. 'How can you possibly not be when you're doing two jobs?'

'Sister Flannigan has two jobs?' Connor frowned, and Rita nodded.

'Our nurse unit manager returned to Spain a few months back, and, as Admin haven't yet appointed his replacement, Sister Flannigan has had to temporarily step into the breach, which is probably why we're not as efficient as we should be.'

'I can't say I've noticed any inefficiency on Sister Flannigan's part,' Connor replied, attempting to walk on, but Rita was not about to be rebuffed.

'Oh, please don't think I'm suggesting Sister Flannigan is inefficient—'

Yeah, right, Rita, Brianna thought angrily, and this is clearly payback time because I chewed your head off yesterday.

'But when you're as much of a perfectionist as I am,' the ward clerk continued, all honeyed sweetness, 'I do like everything to be just so.'

'Which makes me wonder why you're still standing here,' Connor declared, 'and not back in your office, dotting some i's and crossing some t's.'

The ward clerk's mouth opened and closed soundlessly for a second, then she clamped her lips together tightly.

'Well, no one can ever accuse me of remaining where

I'm not wanted,' she said, before stomping away, and Brianna sighed.

'Which, unfortunately, isn't true.' She glanced up at Connor hesitantly. 'Thanks for saying what you did, for backing me up.'

For a moment he said nothing, then his lips twisted into something like a smile. 'I thought I always did. I thought we were a team.'

They had been once, she remembered. There had been a time when she couldn't have imagined her life without him, and then, little by little, things had changed, and two years ago…

'I'm sorry, Connor,' she murmured, 'so sorry.'

'Sorry you left, or sorry I found you?'

His eyes were fixed on her, and the awful truth was she couldn't give him an answer, not without hurting him, and she backed away from him, afraid he would realise it.

'The car,' she said haltingly. 'I have to…I need to move my car.'

She was gone before he could stop her and, when the ward door clattered shut behind her, Connor clenched his fists until his knuckles showed white.

She hadn't answered him. He'd asked her a simple, easy-to-answer question, and yet she hadn't answered him, and he needed—wanted—answers.

Dammit, she owed him that at least, he thought furiously. When he'd first seen her yesterday, his initial reaction had been to thank God she was safe, his Brianna was safe, but then anger had consumed him. A blazing, blinding, irrational anger that she could be standing in front of him looking better than he'd seen her look in a long time, had been living happily in Cornwall for the last two years, when he'd been to hell and back, fearing the worst. And she'd disappear out of his life again in an instant given half a chance. He'd seen it in her dark brown eyes, in the way she looked at him.

Well, she wasn't going to walk away from him a second time, he decided. This time he wanted answers, proper answers, and not some nonsense about him never talking to her, never listening, and he headed for the ward door to follow her.

'I'm really very sorry about this, Sister Flannigan,' Sid, the hospital handyman, said uncomfortably after she'd moved her car out of the consultants' bay and into the nurses' part of the car park. 'To be honest, I don't think there should be any divisions in the car park, but some consultants…' He shook his head. 'It's a status thing for them, you see.'

'It's all right, Sid, truly it is,' Brianna said quickly. 'I don't know where my brain was this morning…' Well, she did know—it was on Connor, she'd been thinking about Connor, and how she didn't want to meet him again, but she wasn't about to share that even with someone as nice as their handyman. 'So could you please tell whoever it was who complained that it won't happen again?'

The middle-aged handyman didn't look any happier. In fact, she could hear him muttering under his breath, 'Officious twit…that's what he is,' as he walked away, and she smiled, but, as she closed her car door, her smile vanished.

It would be so easy to simply get back into her car, and drive away. No one would miss her for a while, and if she kept on driving, and driving, she might eventually reach a place where Connor would never find her. She could start again, change her name again, and—

'Don't, Brianna,' a feminine voice said gently. 'I know what you're thinking, and it won't solve anything.'

'It might,' Brianna muttered, as she turned to see Jess watching her.

'Megan told me about Connor being your husband. She wouldn't normally break a confidence—you know she wouldn't,' the counsellor added quickly as Brianna stared at her in alarm, 'but she's worried about you.'

'I know, but...' Brianna shook her head. 'Jess, have you ever wanted to run away? To just run away, leave everything behind, and start all over?'

'I did—I have,' the counsellor replied. 'When the staff at the hospital I worked in before I came to St Piran's found out about me having HIV...a lot of them cut me dead, crossed the street to avoid me—'

'Oh, Jess!'

'And I couldn't bear it so I ran, and then...' She sighed, a low, sad sigh. 'Well, you know what happened. That reporter from the *Penhally Gazette* broadcast my condition all over his newspaper, and I wanted to run again, but I knew if I did, I would be leaving behind the people, the hospital I felt I'd become such a part of.'

'And Gio,' Brianna murmured. 'You would have been leaving him behind, too.'

'I had no guarantees he would stand by me when he found out the truth, Brianna. He could have walked away and, if he had, then I...' Jess managed a watery smile. 'I would just have to have lived with it.'

Brianna stared down at the car keys in her hand.

'I don't know if I'm as strong as you are.'

'I think you are,' Jess said softly, 'but it's your choice, Brianna. You can stay and confront your fear, or you can run, but if you do run don't forget that whatever you're scared of won't go away. It will always be there, like a dark shadow hanging over you.'

Her friend was right, she knew she was. Running wasn't

the answer, but to stay and try to get Connor to talk to her, to really talk…

'Jess…' she began, only to look sharply round with a frown. 'Did you hear that?'

'Hear what?' Jess said in confusion. 'I can hear the traffic, the birds in the trees—'

'It's a baby. A baby in distress, and it's close by.'

Jess stared at her as though she was suddenly having grave doubts about her mental stability but, having worked with babies for most of her adult life, Brianna could recognise a baby's cry from five hundred paces, and this baby was in trouble. Big trouble.

'Maybe it's a cat,' Jess observed, following Brianna as she headed back to the consultants' part of the car park. 'Cats and kittens often make a sound like a baby.'

But it wasn't a kitten or a cat. It was a baby who hadn't been there when Brianna had moved her car just a few minutes ago. A baby lying wrapped in a white shawl beside Jess's husband's glossy Aston Martin. A baby whose face was blue, and who was breathing in tiny, rasping gasps.

'Oh, my God!' Jess exclaimed, as Brianna swiftly lifted the tiny bundle into her arms and cradled its head against her breast. 'Who on earth would leave a baby here?'

'It doesn't matter who,' Brianna replied. 'This baby needs attention, and it needs it now.'

She was off and running before Jess could reply. Running so single-mindedly she didn't see the tall figure walking towards her until she almost collided with him.

'Brianna, we need to…' Connor looked down, then up at her incredulously. 'That's a baby.'

'Ten out of ten for observation,' she replied, 'and now can you please get out of my way because it needs help.'

NICU was the obvious place to go, she realised as she ran on with Jess and Connor following her, but she didn't know if the bundle in her arms would make it that far, so she sighed with relief when she saw Josh walking across the entrance foyer of the hospital.

'Hello, gorgeous, where's the fire?' He grinned as she raced towards him.

'No fire,' she replied breathlessly. 'It's a newborn, I found it in the car park, and it's floppy, blue and breathing oddly.'

All Josh's amusement disappeared in a second.

'Jess, can you page Mr Brooke and tell him to come down to A and E immediately? And, if you can't get him,' he added as the counsellor turned to go, 'page Megan. Brianna—you and the baby—A and E—now.'

'My guess is respiratory distress syndrome,' Brianna said as she hurried into A and E and placed the baby on one of the examination tables. 'See how his skin and muscles are being pulled in every time he takes a breath?' she added, carefully unwrapping the shawl. 'How tight his abdomen is?'

'It's a boy?' Connor said, his voice sounding slightly constricted, and Josh frowned at him.

'Who are you?' he demanded. 'The baby's father?'

'I'm Connor Monahan, the hospital auditor.'

'Which doesn't explain why you're here, so I suggest you go and audit something. OK, I wants sats, a ventilator, an umbilical line and a cardio-respiratory monitor,' Josh told his staff. 'And a face mask—the tiniest we've got.'

'BP low, heart rate too high,' one of the A and E nurses declared. 'This baby is going to go into shock if we're not careful.'

'Not on my watch, he won't,' Josh said grimly. 'Where's that umbilical line?'

'Josh, can't you hurry up and stabilise him?' Brianna

said, her eyes fixed anxiously on the baby boy. 'He needs the resources we have in NICU.'

'Agreed, my beautiful colleen,' Josh replied as he began to insert the umbilical line, 'but, as you know very well, stabilising can't be rushed. Poor little mite,' he continued as he checked the cardio-respiratory monitor. 'He can't be more than a couple of days old, which means his mother must need medical attention, too.'

'Yes—yes—whatever,' Brianna said quickly, 'but hurry, Josh, please, hurry.'

'This respiratory distress thing,' Connor said, 'can it be cured?'

Josh looked round at him with irritation.

'Why the hell are you still here? Run out of departments to audit already?'

'I asked a question, and I'd like an answer,' Connor declared, his voice every bit as hard as Josh's, and a small smile curved the A and E consultant's lips.

'Are you quite sure you're not the baby's father? OK—OK,' Josh continued as Brianna threw him an impatient look. 'Yes, Mr Monahan, RDS can be cured. Premature, and very underweight, babies often don't produce enough surfactant in their lungs to help them breathe, but we can give it to them artificially through a breathing tube.'

'But only in NICU,' Megan declared as she swept into A and E, pushing an incubator, 'so can we have a little less chat and a lot more action?'

'I'm simply answering Mr Monahan's question, Megan,' Josh answered mildly, but the paediatric specialist registrar was clearly not about to be placated.

'A question we don't have time for,' she retorted.

'Oh, I always have time for questions,' he countered. 'I don't always give the right answers—'

'Now, there's a surprise—*not*,' Megan replied, her voice cold. 'Perhaps if you spent less time—'

'Look, could the two of you park whatever problem you have with one another and concentrate on this baby?' Brianna exclaimed, then flushed scarlet when she saw Megan's hurt expression and Josh's eyebrows shoot up. 'I'm sorry—I shouldn't have said that—I'm just…'

'Worried.' Josh nodded. 'Understood. OK,' he added as he carefully lifted the baby boy and placed him gently into the incubator, 'this tiny tot is good to go.'

Brianna instantly began pushing the incubator out of A and E towards NICU but it didn't make her feel any better. She'd hurt Megan, she knew she had, and it wasn't as though she hadn't known Megan and Josh had some sort of history so to say what she had…

'Megan, I'm sorry,' she murmured when they reached the unit and Chris began hooking the baby to their monitors. 'What I said—'

'Forget it,' Megan interrupted tightly. 'OK, I want an ultrasound scan, more X-rays and the ophthalmologist.'

'Do you want me to check the sats again?' Brianna said uncertainly. 'Josh's staff did them in A and E, but…'

'Double-check them. Josh's staff aren't specialists, we are.'

'He is going to be all right, isn't he?' Connor asked as he hovered beside them. 'That doctor in A and E—the one who was flirting with Brianna—seemed to think he would be.'

'The doctor's name is Josh O'Hara, and he wasn't flirting with me,' Brianna said swiftly, seeing Megan's head snap up. 'He was just being pleasant.'

'Was he indeed,' Connor murmured dryly, and Brianna could have kicked him for the dark shadow that suddenly appeared in Megan's eyes.

'Look, Connor, why don't you wait outside?' she said abruptly. 'All you're doing is getting in the way.'

'I'll stay,' he said firmly, and, when she turned back to the baby with a shrug, he took a shallow breath.

He couldn't leave, and it wasn't just because he was genuinely concerned about the baby Brianna had found. When she'd almost collided with him outside the hospital he'd been unable to believe what she'd been carrying. The little form so motionless, the shock of thick black hair… For a moment it was as though the last two years had never happened, and then he'd blinked, had seen Brianna's blue uniform, and the two years had rolled back again, bringing with them all the old pain and heartbreak.

He'd told himself that all he wanted from her was answers. He'd told himself she deserved to be punished for what she'd put him through, but he'd seen the pain in her eyes when that A and E consultant had been examining the baby. She was still in her own private hell, just as he was, and lashing out at her wasn't the solution, not if he wanted her back. And he did want her back, he realised, feeling his heart twist inside him as he saw her gently touch the little boy's cheek, because without her… Without her he had nothing.

'Shouldn't the police be alerted?' he said. 'If this baby is only days old, won't his mother need help, too?'

'Good point,' Megan declared. 'Did you see anyone hanging about the car park, Brianna?'

'To be honest, I wasn't looking,' she replied.

In fact, Brianna thought with dawning horror, if Jess hadn't turned up when she had, she would probably have been halfway up the motorway by now, and God knows when this baby would have been found.

'Damn,' Megan muttered. 'Chris, could you try paging Mr Brooke again, see if we can track him down?'

'There's something wrong?' Brianna said, her eyes flying to the baby in the incubator, and Megan shook her head.

'"Wrong" is too strong a word. I'd just be a lot happier if this little chap wasn't quite so inactive. Jess said he was crying when you found him, and yet now...'

'Maybe he's just cold?' Brianna suggested hopefully, and Megan frowned.

'Maybe, but I'd really like Mr Brooke to take a look at this little one. Which reminds me,' she continued, 'we can't keep calling him "little chap" or "little one", until his mother comes forward.'

'How about Patrick?' Chris suggested. 'It's March the seventeenth soon, St Patrick's Day, and you're Irish, Brianna, so I vote we call him Patrick.'

Brianna stared down at the baby boy in the incubator. He was so small, so very small, scarcely 5 pounds in weight, and, gently, she adjusted the pulse oximeter taped to his little foot.

'Harry,' she said softly. 'I'd like...I want to call him Harry.'

She heard Connor's sharp intake of breath, knew what he was thinking, but she didn't turn round, didn't acknowledge him, and Chris shrugged.

'Personally, I still like Patrick, but, as you found him, Brianna, if you want to call him Harry, then Harry he is.'

Just until his mother comes forward, Brianna told herself as she carefully slipped a hat over the baby's head to make sure he didn't lose any more heat. He would only be Harry until his mother claimed him, she knew that, and the mother would come forward, she was sure she would, but until then… Until then she would make sure this little Harry always had someone to care for him, to watch out for him.

It was a very long afternoon. Mr Brooke might eventually have arrived, and announced that in his opinion little Harry was most definitely suffering from respiratory distress syndrome, but he departed again with the observation that he also couldn't rule out the possibility of bronchopulmonary dysplasia.

'Remind me never to be on a sinking ship with that man,' Brianna observed with feeling, and Megan laughed.

'Yeah, he's a regular little ray of sunshine, isn't he?' She glanced down at her watch, and gasped. 'Hey, shouldn't you have been off duty hours ago?'

'I know, I just wanted…' Brianna shrugged helplessly. 'I wanted to stay until I was sure little Harry was OK.'

'Well, in the time-honoured hospital jargon,' Megan replied, 'he's doing as well as can be expected, and to be honest that's about as much as we can expect in the circumstances.'

'How old do you think he is?' Brianna asked, and Megan frowned.

'I'd say a day—two days at most. We're still waiting for the results of the scans to confirm his gestational age, but I don't think he's premature, just very small, which would suggest his mother probably wasn't eating properly.'

'And she's out there somewhere, needing help.' Brianna sighed. 'And I don't have the faintest idea what she looks like. If I'd only kept my wits about me, looked about before I rushed her son into the hospital…'

'Hey, don't beat yourself up over it—Jess didn't see anyone either,' Megan replied, then glanced over her shoulder and lowered her voice. 'How's it going with Connor?'

Brianna grimaced. 'What do you think?'

'At least he seems to have finally left for the day,' Megan observed, 'or maybe he's just annoying the hell out of the staff in some other department. Whichever it is, I'd cut and run if I were you. And, yes, I'll phone you at home if there's any change in Harry,' she continued as Brianna made to interrupt, 'so go, will you?'

Brianna laughed and nodded, but, as she turned to leave, she paused.

'Megan, what I said this afternoon in A and E… If I could take it back, I would. If I could reverse the clock, I'd do it in a minute. What I said was so thoughtless—'

'But correct,' the paediatric specialist registrar interrupted. 'Josh and I should have been concentrating on little Harry. It's just… I'm afraid the two of us only have to be in the same room together now and…' She smiled a little unevenly. 'Let's just say it's not good.'

Brianna knew exactly what Megan meant as she left the unit and drove home, but the trouble was she didn't even have to be in the same room with Connor for her nerves to be on edge. Even when she got home to her cottage in the small fishing village of Penhally, and had changed into a pair of jeans and a sweatshirt, she couldn't relax, couldn't stop thinking about him.

Diversion, she thought as she picked up a book, only to just as quickly discard it. If she'd reached home at her normal time she would have gone for a walk on the beach to try to calm herself, but it was too dark for that now. What she needed was something—or someone—to channel her thoughts elsewhere, so, when her doorbell rang, a little after nine o'clock, she hastened to answer it. With luck it might be Jess who sometimes stopped by to discuss how the parents of a baby in NICU were—or weren't—coping, and they could have a cup of coffee, and chat, but it wasn't Jess on her doorstep, it was Connor.

'If you're here to talk to me about the unit,' she said quickly, 'it's late, it's been a long day, and I'm tired.'

'I haven't come to talk to you about the unit,' he replied, putting out his hand to stop her as she began to close the door on him. 'I've come to see you.'

And he had a suitcase with him, she noticed with dawning dismay. A suitcase that could only mean one thing.

'Connor, you can't think…' She dragged her gaze away from the suitcase, and back to him. 'You're not expecting to move in here with me, are you?'

'I figured it was stupid to keep staying in a hotel when you have a house within easy driving distance of St Piran, so I checked out of my hotel this evening.'

'But you can't,' she protested. 'People will talk. They'll say—'

'That a husband is living with his wife?' he suggested, and she flushed, and regrouped hurriedly.

'But won't your impartiality be compromised if you stay with me?' she exclaimed. 'I know you would never shut down an NICU but people could think—might suggest—I had exerted undue influence upon your report.'

'Then people would be wrong, wouldn't they?' he replied smoothly. 'So, are you going to leave me standing on the doorstep, or let me in?'

He'd backed her into a corner. Her only way out would be to tell him the truth, that she didn't want him in her home, prodding and poking at old wounds, but though he had asked her for honesty she knew she couldn't be quite that honest with him.

'You'd better come in,' she said in defeat.

'Nice house,' he observed as he followed her down the

narrow hallway into her sitting room, having to duck to avoid hitting his head on the old oak beams across the ceiling. 'Very…compact.'

'Tiny, you mean,' she said. 'I suppose it is, but I like it.'

'And this is where you've been living for the last two years?' he said, putting his suitcase down by the coffee table, and she nodded.

'I lived in nurses' accommodation at the hospital for a few weeks when I first came to Cornwall, but I wanted somewhere to call home so I rented this.'

'You have a home,' he reminded her, 'in London. Our flat.'

But it isn't mine, she thought. It never was mine, but I don't think I'll ever get you to understand that.

'Would you like something to eat?' she said, deliberately changing the subject. 'I was just about to raid my kitchen.'

'That would be nice.'

She didn't know if it would be nice, but eating something would certainly be preferable to them simply staring at one another in awkward silence for the rest of the evening, or, even worse, talking about things she didn't want to talk about.

'Chilli, lasagne or beef casserole?' she asked as she went into the kitchen and opened the freezer.

'Lasagne was always my favourite.'

It had been. She couldn't recall how many times she'd made it for him in the past but that had been then, this was now.

'Lasagne it is,' she said, and, as she placed it in the microwave, she prayed he would eat it quickly so she could retreat to the safety of her bedroom.

But he didn't eat quickly. In fact, he seemed to be in no hurry at all.

'This is lovely,' he declared as he forked some lasagne into his mouth. 'Every bit as good as I remember.'

'I'm glad,' she said, pushing her own lasagne around the plate without enthusiasm. 'Would you like some wine to go with your meal?' she continued, half rising to her feet, only to sit down again as he shook his head. 'Connor…' *Get it out,* she thought, *just say it.* 'Why have you really come?'

'Because we need to talk, and there's never any opportunity at the hospital.'

Which was fair enough, but that didn't mean she had to like it.

'That doctor at the hospital,' he continued, 'the A and E one who was flirting with you—'

'How many times do I have to tell you he wasn't flirting with me?' she interrupted with a huff of impatience. 'Josh is from Ireland, as you and I are, and the way he talks… It's just his style. He does it with every woman he meets, whether she's nine or ninety. And anyway,' she added for good measure, 'he's married.'

'So are you,' Connor observed, staring pointedly at her left hand, 'and yet you're not wearing your wedding ring.'

Damn, she'd forgotten about that, and she felt a warm flush of colour creep across her cheeks.

'I took it off when I came here,' she said uncomfortably. 'I thought…I felt it would be easier, would mean I wouldn't have to explain anything, or answer any awkward questions.'

'And is that what I am for you now—an awkwardness?' he said, putting down his knife and fork. 'Someone it's better not to think about, someone who can be jettisoned as easily as pulling off a ring?'

She could see the hurt in his blue eyes, but what could she say? Wasn't that exactly how she regarded his reappearance in her life? As something she'd far rather not deal with, someone she wished hadn't reappeared? And yet the man sitting in front of her was her husband, the man she had once pledged to love for the rest of her life.

'Connor, I know you want answers—and you're entitled to them,' she said unhappily, 'but I can't deal with this right now. I'm sorry—'

'You keep saying that as though it somehow makes everything all right,' he retorted, and she bit her lip.

'I know it doesn't make everything all right. I know it's not enough, but…' She took a breath, and it sounded unsteady even to her own ears. 'Can't you see this is hard for me?'

'And you think it's easy for me?' he exclaimed. 'Easy for me to sit at a table with my wife, knowing she doesn't want me here? Easy for me, today in the unit, when you named that baby Harry? You should never have done that, Brianna, *never.*'

She stretched out her hand to him, half in apology, half in a plea for understanding, but he pulled away from her.

'Connor, he hasn't got anyone, not right now,' she said with difficulty. 'He's all alone, and he…he's so very little, so fragile, and he reminded me so much of our son.'

'But he isn't our son,' he retorted, pain clear in his eyes. 'He isn't our Harry, Brianna.'

'I know,' she said. 'I know he has a mother, that she'll come back for him eventually, but until then—'

'You can pretend he's Harry?' he finished for her, his eyes fixed on her, daring her to contradict him. 'You can pretend we didn't lose our son—is that what you're saying?'

'No— Yes—' She shook her head. 'I don't know. All I know is this baby needs me right now, Connor.'

'*I* need you!' he exclaimed. 'I'm here, and *I* need you.'

'But when I needed you, you weren't there for me,' she blurted out, and saw his face contort with disbelief.

'How can you say that?' he demanded. 'I was always there for you, and our son. *Always!*'

'Not enough to let me cry for him after he died,' she threw back at him. 'Whenever I cried you'd say, "Don't cry, Brianna. You mustn't cry."'

'You were making yourself ill—'

'And whenever I tried to talk about him you changed the subject. My parents—my friends—because Harry died twelve hours after he was born—they never saw him, so he wasn't...' She swallowed hard. 'He wasn't real to them. They had no memories of him, only you and I did, but you... You just seemed to want to airbrush him out of our lives.'

'That is an unforgivable thing to say,' he replied, his voice raw. 'He was my son, too.'

'A son you would never talk about—a son you never cried over!'

'Brianna, if talking would have brought Harry back, I would have talked myself hoarse,' he protested, 'but talking wouldn't have changed anything, you know it wouldn't.'

'It would have kept him alive for me,' she said, tears thickening her voice. 'It would have kept him alive, and with us, but you... It was like you'd decided it was better to pretend he'd never lived, had never been.'

'Brianna—'

'All through the funeral you just sat there as though what was happening...what the priest was saying...was nothing to do with you while I... I kept thinking he'll wake up, Harry's going to wake up, and cry, and they'll realise they've made a mistake, and then I can take him home, and I so...' She let out a small sob. 'I so wanted to take him home.'

'Brianna, please—'

'You want to know how I really felt before I left you?' she continued, dashing a hand across her eyes. 'I wanted to die, Connor. All I wanted was to die, so I could be with Harry, and then he...' Her voice broke. 'He wouldn't be alone, and I couldn't bear the thought of him being alone, in the dark, with no one to hold him.'

'Brianna, *don't*,' he said, his voice cracking. 'Please, *don't*.'

'See—you're doing it again,' she cried. 'You say you want us to talk, but every time I try, you cut me off.'

'Because I can't bear to see you upset,' he said hoarsely. 'I can't bear to see you suffer like this.'

'Connor—'

'You're right,' he said, abruptly getting to his feet. 'It's been a long day, and we're both tired, and I still need to unpack.'

His face was closed and tight. It was the expression she'd grown used to seeing before she'd left him. The one that told her he didn't want to listen to her, didn't want to hear what she was saying, and she stood up, too, in defeat.

'What about the dishes?' he continued as she walked past him towards the kitchen door. 'You could wash, and I could dry, just like we used to.'

'Leave them,' she muttered. 'I'll do them later.'

'But—'

But nothing, she thought, walking determinedly into the sitting room, then up the narrow staircase to the first floor, leaving him with nothing to do but follow her. She didn't want to play happy couples with him in the kitchen, pretending that everything was all right over the washing-up. They weren't a happy couple. They hadn't been one for a very long time.

'The bathroom's in here,' she said as she opened the first door on the landing. 'It has both a bath and a shower so you can have whichever you want.'

'Looks good,' he replied with a smile, which she didn't return.

'I hope you'll be comfortable in here,' she said, walking into the next room. 'There's a double bed so you shouldn't feel cramped, and plenty of hanging space for your clothes—'

'But it's not your room.'

It was a statement, not a question, and she smoothed down the duvet, which didn't need smoothing, and deliberately avoided his eyes.

'The room faces south so you'll get the sun in the morning,' she continued, 'and there's a lovely view of Penhally bay and the harbour—'

'Brianna, when I said I needed you, I meant every word.'

His voice was soft, entreating, and she forced herself to look up at him. He was the man she had married, the man she'd fallen in love with all those years ago, and yet now… She knew she should feel something, ought to feel something, but it was as though her heart was frozen, and where there should have been love for him there was nothing but pain.

'Connor, I can't just go back to the way we were before Harry died,' she said haltingly. 'I can't pretend everything's all right between us, or forget, or—'

'Share my bed.'

She shook her head, unable to speak.

'Would…?' He took a deep breath. 'Would you rather I just left?'

'Yes' would have been her honest answer, but she knew she couldn't say that. She'd accused him of never talking, of never telling her what he was thinking and maybe, if he stayed, maybe he might talk, maybe he might listen, and she had to at least give him that opportunity.

'You have every right to be here,' she said.

Which wasn't what he wanted to hear, he thought as she left the room. He didn't want to hear he had a 'right' to be there by virtue of being her husband. He wanted her to say she wanted him there, but she hadn't.

Why had he come? he wondered as he sat down heavily on the bed. He should never have come, except…

He'd told himself he wanted answers. He still wanted them, but he wanted more than that. He didn't want to lose her, not again. He didn't want her to just slip away from him, and she was slipping away, he knew she was.

With a sigh he stood up and walked over to the window and gazed out. It was too cloudy tonight for stars, but he could see a light in the distance. A light that went on and off rhythmically. A lighthouse, his brain registered. A lighthouse, which gave hope to sailors lost at sea, and hope was all he had right now. A hope that was much fainter than the lighthouse's bright beam, but he would hold onto it because there was nothing else he could do.

CHAPTER THREE

'I JUST wish I could have been more help to the police yesterday,' Brianna said as she checked the cardio monitor above Amy Renwick's incubator. 'They were so kind, so patient—even offered to bring in their face-imaging expert, to see if I could re-create an image of Harry's mother— but I honestly and truly don't remember seeing anyone in the car park.'

'Neither did Sid, or Jess, so you're not the only one,' Megan said soothingly. 'Have the police had any luck identifying where Harry's shawl might have been bought?'

Brianna shook her head.

'Apparently it can be bought in lots of high-street shops, which means the mother could have come from anywhere.'

'She'll be some local, unmarried teenager.' Rita sniffed as she appeared, clutching a sheaf of forms. 'You know the sort—the airhead kind who think having a baby will be fun until they're presented with the reality. I'd wager my next pay cheque we'll never see her again.'

'Of course we'll see her,' Brianna said, hearing Megan's sharp intake of breath. 'She'll realise she's made a mistake, and come forward to claim her son. What mother wouldn't?'

'The irresponsible sort,' Rita declared. 'The sort whose

families have never given them any proper values, or a decent upbringing. *My* daughters waited until they had a wedding ring on their finger before they hopped into bed with the first man who paid them any attention.'

'Girls—women—become pregnant for all sorts of reasons,' Brianna said stiffly, 'and I don't think we—as medical staff—should set ourselves up as either judge or jury.'

'Too right,' Megan said, her voice ice-cold. 'Are those forms for me?' she continued, gazing pointedly at the papers in Rita's hand.

'They're admission slips for the babies who came in last night,' the ward clerk replied. 'You have to sign them in triplicate.'

'Bureaucracy gone mad,' Megan muttered. 'What's the stats for the new admissions?'

'Both full term,' Brianna replied. 'One has severe jaundice, the other congenital hypothyroidism. Mr Brooke started the jaundiced baby on phototherapy last night, and the CH baby is being given oral thyroid hormone.'

'Good.' Megan nodded, then frowned as she gazed out over the ward. 'Unfortunately that means we're now at full capacity, so let's hope we don't get hit by another emergency admission.'

'And that would be a problem?'

Connor had joined them, his phone poised and ready in his hand, and Brianna gritted her teeth at the sight of it, and him.

'We have six incubators, which now have six babies in them,' she replied. 'Do the maths, Connor.'

'I can count as well as you can,' he replied mildly, 'but I understood you had an arrangement with the hospital in Plymouth to take any babies you were unable to admit?'

Out of the corner of her eye, Brianna could see Megan

determinedly shepherding Rita towards the ward door, but she didn't give a damn whether Rita stayed and eavesdropped or not.

'We do,' she declared, 'but, as I explained to you yesterday—though you clearly weren't listening—sending babies so far from their homes is upsetting for everyone.'

'I hardly think a thirty—or thirty-five—minute drive could be considered particularly stressful,' Connor observed, and Brianna gritted her teeth until they hurt.

'I wonder how stress-free you'd find that journey if you received a phone call in the middle of the night telling you your baby's condition had deteriorated?' she demanded. 'Or how stress-free you'd be if you arrived to discover your son, or daughter, had died? Not all babies leave NICU alive, Connor.' She met his gaze. 'You should know that.'

It had been a low blow, and she knew it, as she saw all colour drain from his face, but she'd had enough of him today. If she was going to be honest, she'd had more than enough of him by the time they'd shared an excruciatingly awkward breakfast in her home this morning, and the last thing she needed was him dogging her every step, making stupid comments.

'Sister Flannigan?'

Brianna glanced over her shoulder to see Naomi Renwick hovering uncertainly by the ward door, clearly unsure as to whether she should approach or not, and hitched a smile to her lips.

'What can I do for you, Naomi?'

'Nothing, really. It's just…' Amy's mother flushed. 'Experience has taught me that if more than one person is clustered round my daughter's incubator, something's wrong.'

'Far from it,' Brianna insisted. 'I completed Amy's obs about half an hour ago, and there was no sign of any post-op infection, and her sats are perfect. Of course, we're going to have to wait and see what happens when we start feeding her orally instead of through an IV line, but at the moment I'd say everything's looking pretty good.'

'Thank you, Sister, thank you so much,' Naomi said, letting out the breath Brianna knew she'd been holding. 'I know it's silly to always suspect the worst, but sometimes—'

'It seems as though all you've done, since Amy was born, is take one step forward and two steps back,' Brianna finished for her. 'I do understand, but try not to worry, OK?'

'I'll try,' Naomi promised, and, when Brianna hurried across the ward in answer to Megan's beckoning wave, she smiled up at Connor. 'Sister Flannigan is always so encouraging, isn't she?'

'She would appear to be,' he replied noncommittally.

'Are you a doctor, Mr…Mr…?'

'Monahan. Connor Monahan,' he said, 'and, no, I'm not a doctor. I'm…' His lips curved a little ruefully. 'I guess you could call me a glorified accountant.'

'Right.' Naomi nodded, clearly none the wiser. 'This is my daughter, Amy,' she continued, gently touching the incubator. 'She was born two months premature.'

And I don't want to know this, Connor thought, half turning to go, but Mrs Renwick wasn't finished.

'All the nursing staff here are really wonderful,' she continued, 'but Sister Flannigan… She's something special, you know?'

He did know, he thought as he noticed Brianna's brow begin to furrow at whatever Megan was saying. He'd known it from the very first moment they'd met, when he'd been twenty-two, and Brianna had been twenty-one. All it had taken was one shy smile from her, across the dance floor in her home town of Killarney, and he'd fallen for her completely.

'It's like she somehow knows how all we parents feel,' Naomi observed. 'That she's not simply mouthing words of sympathy, but really understands what it's like to worry, and to fear.'

They had both known worry, and fear, Connor thought, feeling his stomach clench as memories surfaced in his mind, memories which were as bitter as they were unwanted. When Harry had been born, one month early, he'd known so little, been so naive. What's a month? he had asked himself. Babies of less than twenty-eight weeks survived, so a one-month-early baby was nothing, but then the hospital consultant had dropped his bombshell.

'Everyone says Mr Brooke is an excellent surgeon,' Naomi continued, 'and I'm sure he is, but he is a little…a little…'

'Brusque?' Connor suggested, and Naomi chuckled.

'Downright depressing would be closer to the truth. I know he has to be honest, but…'

'You'd prefer a little less honesty, and a bit more hope?'

Naomi nodded. 'Dr Phillips is always very upbeat— she's nice, too. In fact, I'm surprised a pretty woman like her isn't married, but then neither is Sister Flannigan, and I think she's just lovely.'

She was, Connor thought, glancing across the ward at Brianna. With hair the colour of burnished autumn leaves, large brown eyes and a smile that had always made his heart beat faster, she looked again like the girl he had married ten years ago rather than the skeletally thin woman who had left him. Over and over again he had begged and pleaded with her to eat, but she'd simply stared back at him with eyes that seemed to have grown too big for her small face. Now she'd regained some of the weight she'd lost, and he could not help but wonder what—or who—had finally persuaded her to eat.

'I understand… Sister Flannigan…I believe she's quite close to that A and E doctor—Josh O'Hara?' Connor commented, despising himself for asking, but needing to know nevertheless.

'Oh, no,' Naomi replied. 'He does come into the unit occasionally, and he certainly makes her laugh, but he's married, and, even if he wasn't, I wouldn't say he was Sister Flannigan's type.'

'You wouldn't?' Connor said hopefully, and Naomi shook her head.

'If you want my opinion, I'd say Dr O'Hara and Dr Phillips would be better suited. They just sort of look right together, if you know what I mean, though, of course, people do say it's often opposites who attract.'

Everyone in Killarney had wondered what Brianna had seen in him, Connor recalled wryly—she with her gift of always being able to talk to anyone, and he so very reserved unless he was discussing a balance sheet—but they'd been happy, they'd loved one another, and then Harry had been born.

'It's so sad about Harry.'

Connor's eyes shot to Mrs Renwick, wondering for one awful moment if she could possibly have read his mind, but she wasn't talking about his son. She was gazing at the incubator nearest the wall, and his forehead creased with foreboding.

'His condition has worsened?'

'Oh, no—at least, I don't think it has,' Mrs Renwick said quickly. 'I meant it's very sad that his mother abandoned him like that, but at least he's got Sister Flannigan.'

And Connor wished the child hadn't as he watched

Brianna walk away from Megan to the little boy's incubator. God knows, he meant the child no harm but, after just one day of looking after him, he knew Brianna was getting too close, and if this child died…

He closed his eyes tightly, but it didn't help. Nothing would ever erase the memory of that day when they'd come home from the hospital, after it was all over. Never had he heard anyone cry the way Brianna had cried, like an animal racked with pain, and he never wanted to hear that sound again, but the longer this baby's mother didn't come forward the more involved Brianna would become, and all he could see was heartbreak ahead for her no matter what happened.

'Are you all right, Mr Monahan?'

He opened his eyes to see Naomi gazing up at him with concern, and manufactured a smile.

'I'm fine. It's just…wards like this… You never know what's going to happen next, and I find that…unsettling.'

'My husband's the same.' Naomi nodded. 'He likes certainty, too, but I keep telling him, think positive, it's the only thing you can do.'

And Connor was positive something had just gone very wrong as he saw Megan join Brianna at Harry's incubator, and his wife begin to shake her head angrily.

'I'm afraid you'll have to excuse me, Mrs Renwick…'

He was vaguely aware that Amy's mother said something in reply, but he couldn't have said what. His eyes were fixed on Brianna. She looked upset now as well as angry, and whether she wanted him at her side was immaterial. He was going to be there.

'Problem?' he said as he approached her, and saw Megan bite her lip.

'There's a reporter outside in the corridor from the *Penhally Gazette*,' the paediatric specialist registrar replied.

'He wants to interview Brianna for his newspaper, and Admin think it would be an excellent way to give Harry more exposure, and perhaps encourage his mother to come forward.'

'And Admin can whistle Dixie as far as I'm concerned because I know damn fine that the only exposure Vermin would give Harry is the muckraking kind,' Brianna said tartly.

'Vermin?' Connor echoed, his eyebrows rising.

'His actual name is Kennie Vernon,' Megan replied, 'but he's known as Vermin for a very good reason. Not only does he work on the principle of never letting the truth get in the way of a good story, he's also the man who told the world—or at least the St Piran and Penhally part of it—that Jess has—'

The paediatric specialist registrar came to a sudden, red-cheeked halt, clearly deeply mortified by what she had almost said, and Connor glanced from her to Brianna, his eyebrows raised.

'Jess Corezzi has what?' he asked, and saw Brianna grimace.

'She has HIV, Connor,' she said in a low undertone. 'And before you say anything—'

'All I was going to say was, so what?' he replied, and Brianna sighed.

'Unfortunately that wasn't most people's reaction when Vernon splashed her condition all over the front page of the *Penhally Gazette*. I will never, ever forgive him for the way he crucified her, Connor, and for Admin to think I'd be willing to even be in the same room as that man, far less give him an interview...'

'Look, would it help if I sat in with you?' he said. 'I wouldn't interfere, I promise I wouldn't,' he added as Brianna began to shake her head, 'but I do have a lot of experience in dealing with the press through my work, and, whether you like it or not, Admin is right. The more press exposure the hospital can generate about this baby, the better.'

Megan caught Brianna's gaze.

'He's right,' she said reluctantly. 'I know you don't want to do it—I wouldn't want to either—but if Connor is there as back-up…?'

'I don't need back-up,' Brianna said, annoyance plain in her voice. 'I'm a big girl. I don't need my hand held.'

'No one is suggesting you do,' Connor said gently. 'But don't ever underestimate the press, Brianna, and sometimes two heads are better than one when it comes to dealing with the enemy.'

For a moment Brianna said nothing, then she let out a small, grudging sigh.

'OK. All right. I'll do it. Where is the little toad?'

Megan grinned.

'I told him to wait outside in the corridor. I also made him thoroughly scrub and disinfect his hands. He wasn't very happy about either.'

'Good,' Brianna declared. 'OK, Connor, let's you and I go and slaughter the little jumped-up slimeball.'

Wrong, Brianna, Connor thought as he followed her out of the ward and he saw the man waiting for them at the end of the corridor. Kennie Vernon might look like a refugee from a very bad eighties pop video, with his goatee beard and ponytail, but the muddy brown eyes that watched them walking towards him were calculating and shrewd. This was not a man to underestimate. This was a man who would use anyone, and anything, to get himself out of the *Penhally Gazette* and into one of the big London newspapers, and Connor instinctively moved closed to his wife.

'Sister Flannigan,' Kennie declared with a smile that

was every bit as false as the replica Rolex on his wrist 'How very pleasant to meet you.'

'I'm afraid I can't the say the same,' she replied. 'I'm not that big a hypocrite.'

Kennie's smile didn't slip at all as he transferred his gaze to Connor.

'And you are…?'

'He's…' Brianna came to a dead halt. How on earth was she supposed to introduce Connor? If she said he was her husband, Vermin would dig deeper, and if she said Connor was an auditor, that would give the reporter an even bigger story for the *Penhally Gazette*. 'He's—'

'Connor Monahan. Sister Flannigan's PR adviser,' Connor announced, and it wasn't only Brianna's jaw that dropped.

'You have a public relations adviser?' Kennie said to Brianna, but again it was Connor who answered.

'Naturally,' he said, in a tone that suggested only complete losers didn't. 'Now, I'm sure you don't want to conduct this interview in a corridor,' he continued, 'so shall we adjourn to my office?'

He opened the door of the nurse unit manager's office pointedly, and Kennie Vernon walked into it without a word, but as Connor made to follow him, Brianna caught hold of his arm.

'Why the hell did you say that?' she hissed. 'About you being my PR adviser?'

Connor shrugged. 'I had a sort of flash of inspiration.'

'Yeah, right,' she replied. 'Well, try not to have too many more of them, OK?'

And he smiled. A smile that made her heart clench because it suddenly transported her right back to that night in Killarney when her eyes had met his over the crowded dance floor. She'd known immediately that he wasn't local, and so had all the other girls.

'He's here on holiday,' someone had whispered. 'From Dublin.'

And her friends had all giggled, and nudged one another, because, to them, Dublin was somewhere exotic, somewhere exciting. He'd looked so out of place in the village hall, dressed in his crisp white shirt, blue tie and smart black trousers, while all the other young men had been wearing jeans and T-shirts, but when he hadn't reacted to her friends' giggles, or their fluttering eyelashes, they'd all muttered, 'Stuck-up prat,' and dismissed him, but she'd hadn't.

She'd kept sneaking curious glances at him, and his eyes had eventually met hers, and he'd smiled. The same half crooked, half self-deprecating, smile he was smiling now, and she hadn't seen that smile in such a long time.

'What?' he asked as she stared up at him, and she shook her head.

'Nothing. It's…nothing.'

But it was, she thought as she went into the nurse unit manager's office. It was a painful reminder of how she'd once felt about the man at her side. A bitter-sweet reminder that she'd once loved him more than life, and had thought nothing would ever separate them.

'I understand Jessica Corezzi was with you when you found this baby?' Kennie declared, sitting down and instantly flipping open his notebook, pen poised.

'Yes, she was,' Brianna replied, deliberately remaining standing.

'She married a consultant at the hospital recently, didn't she?' Kennie murmured. 'Which is somewhat surprising given the circumstances.'

Because Jess has HIV, Brianna thought angrily. That's

what you're saying, you horrible little man. That you're amazed she could actually find someone willing to marry her, and she wasn't about to let him get away with that.

'Now, just one minute,' she began, only to pause when Connor shook his head warningly at her.

'Both Jess Corezzi and Sister Flannigan found the baby together,' Connor said smoothly, 'but, unfortunately, neither of them saw the mother. Or the father, come to that,' he added with a smile. 'After all, why be sexist, why assume it was the mother who left the baby there?'

'Right.' Kennie Vernon nodded, looking slightly bemused, but he wasn't finished. Not by a long shot. 'It's strange, don't you think, Sister Flannigan, that the baby should be found in the consultants' car park?'

'Strange?' she repeated, puzzled. 'I'm sorry, but I don't understand what you mean.'

'I was just wondering whether the unfortunate mother might perhaps have had a relationship with one of the consultants in the hospital,' Kennie said, 'and she left the baby where he would find it because he'd dumped her.'

And you know exactly whose car little Harry was found next to, Brianna thought furiously. It was Gio Corezzi's car. Jess's husband.

'Mr Vernon,' she began, but Connor cut across her again.

'I fear you may have been reading far too many trashy novelettes, Mr Vernon,' he drawled. 'Surely the most plausible explanation is that the mother left her baby in that particular car park because it was the furthest from the road and she wanted to ensure her child didn't become…' He frowned in apparent concentration. 'Now, what's the word I'm looking for… Ah, yes. Road kill.'

Road kill? Brianna thought, shooting her husband an

appalled glance, and could almost have sworn she saw him wink back at her.

'I think the term you were searching for, Mr Monahan, is road fatality,' Kennie Vernon said stiffly, then flipped over a page of his notebook. 'Colour of hair and eyes of this child, and does he have any distinguishing features like a birthmark or a mole?'

'Harry has black hair, and blue eyes,' Brianna replied, 'but no birthmarks or moles.'

'Harry?'

'We didn't want to keep calling him Baby X,' Brianna replied uncomfortably, 'so we decided to name him Harry until his mother comes forward.'

'I'd like to take a photograph—'

'No, absolutely not,' Brianna interrupted. 'I can take a photograph of him for your newspaper if you want one, but I cannot allow you into the ward because of the risk of infection.'

Kennie leant back in his seat, and smiled at her with a smile she did not care for.

'Are you always this obstructive, Sister Flannigan?' he asked, and she saw Connor move forward a step.

'Sister Flannigan is merely stating hospital policy,' her husband replied in a tone that suggested arguing would be most unwise, but that did not prevent the reporter from trying.

'I'd like to remind both of you of the rights of the press—'

'Which I do not think would ever include endangering the life of a very vulnerable baby,' Connor declared.

'But—'

'You could, of course, apply for a court order,' Connor continued smoothly, 'but I think that would be…unwise.

Unless you wish to be front-page news yourself for harassing a minor?'

Kennie shot Connor a look that was positively venomous, then snapped his notebook shut.

'Thank you for your time,' he said as he stood up. 'That will be all.'

'No, it won't.' Brianna sighed as the reporter strode out the office without a backward glance. 'He'll be back.'

'Undoubtedly,' Connor agreed. 'But round one to us, I think.'

'I'm just very glad you were on my side,' Brianna said with feeling, and Connor smiled, a slightly lopsided smile.

'I always was, I always will be,' he said simply.

There was no answer to that except one, which she knew would hurt him immeasurably, so she opted to change the subject.

'Road kill, Connor?' she said as she led the way into the corridor. *'Road kill?'*

'I had a momentary memory lapse, couldn't remember the correct phrase.' He grinned, and she shook her head at him and chuckled.

'Yeah, right,' she said. 'And like I would ever believe that. You never forget anything.'

'Except, it seems, the things that really matter,' he murmured.

His eyes were troubled, but what could she say to him when she knew he'd spoken the truth?

'Have you seen our graduation board?' she asked, trying to change the subject.

'Your what?' he said with an effort, and she pointed to the board on the corridor wall, which was covered with baby pictures.

'It started shortly after the unit was opened,' she said.

'Parents of babies who had left the unit, gone home, began putting up pictures of their children to give other parents encouragement, to let them see there was light at the end of the tunnel, and it sort of snowballed.'

He grimaced slightly. 'I see. Brianna—'

'Hands,' she said. 'If you're going back into the ward you need to thoroughly scrub and disinfect your hands.'

'Oh. Right. Sorry,' he replied, but after he'd thoroughly scrubbed his hands, and she had, too, he turned to her uncertainly. 'How can you bear to work here after losing Harry? Don't you find it incredibly stressful to be constantly surrounded by very ill babies?'

'It can certainly be challenging, and upsetting at times,' she agreed as she pushed open the ward door, 'but…you see…with Harry…' She took a steadying breath. 'There was nothing I could do, nothing anyone would let me do, but working as a nurse in here, I know there are times when I can make a difference, times when my skills matter, and I can help.'

'Yes, but even so, don't you—?'

'Oh, *hell*.'

For a second, Connor was completely bewildered by her exclamation, but as he looked past her, into the ward, he saw what she had. Megan was standing at the top of the ward, her eyes fixed firmly on one of the monitors, while Josh was ostensibly deeply in conversation with Mr Brooke, but only a fool wouldn't have noticed that the A and E consultant's eyes kept darting in the direction of the paediatric specialist registrar.

'What gives between those two?' Connor asked in an undertone. 'Every time they meet I swear Megan's back couldn't get any stiffer if she had a poker strapped to it, and yet Josh constantly seems to be trying to gain her attention.'

'It's none of my business,' Brianna replied firmly, 'or yours.'

'Fair point,' Connor conceded, 'but it's odd.'

It *was* odd, Brianna thought as Mr Brooke bore Connor off to interview some of the nurses in Gynae, and she saw Josh make an attempt to talk to Megan, an attempt she very quickly rebuffed. Normally, Josh didn't seek Megan out. They might occasionally meet because of their work, but he had never actively attempted to get her to talk to him so this was different, and puzzling.

'You OK?' she said to Megan when Josh finally left.

The paediatric specialist registrar faked a smile.

'Shouldn't that be my question?' she said. 'After all, you were the one who was being interviewed by horrible Vermin, so how did it go?'

Which was as neat a way as any of avoiding answering, Brianna thought, but who was she to point the finger?

'He was his usual obnoxious self,' she said, 'but Connor took no prisoners.'

Megan nodded.

'Connor…' she began carefully '…he seems…nice. Maybe a bit of a statistic obsessive—'

'A bit?'

'OK, a lot,' Megan agreed with a small chuckle, then her face grew serious. 'Look, Brianna, I guess, what I'm trying to say—very badly—is, if you want to—you know—talk at any time, I'm a good listener.'

'Me, too, if you ever want to talk—you know—about Josh,' Brianna replied.

'Yeah, well, Josh and I…' Megan gave a dismissive smile that didn't fool Brianna for a second. 'That ship sailed a long time ago.'

Had Connor and her ship sailed, too? Brianna wondered as the rest of the day sped by in a round of obs, X-rays and scans. She didn't know, but neither did she want to answer the other question of whether she actually wanted to still be on board.

But it was a question that wasn't going to go away, she realised when her shift ended, and she drove home to find Connor's Range Rover already parked outside her house. It was a question she was ultimately going to have to face, but not now, she decided as she got out of her car, grabbed her jacket, and determinedly took the rocky path that led down to the beach.

Except the walk had been a very bad idea, she realised when she reached the shore and recognised a familiar figure standing there, gazing out to sea. A figure who saw her just as soon as she saw him, giving her no chance to slip away.

'I thought I'd get some air,' he said as she slowly walked towards him.

'Me, too,' she replied. 'I often walk here after work. I find it helps if…' She had been going to say, 'If I'm stressed,' but that didn't seem the kindest thing to say in the circumstances. 'I find it clears away the cobwebs.'

A bracing March wind was blowing across the beach, whipping the slate-grey sea into frothy white breakers, and sending dark clouds scudding across the sky, and Connor smiled wryly.

'I can believe that,' he said, and an involuntary chuckle broke from her.

'You hate it here, don't you?'

'Not hate, exactly,' he replied as she began walking along the beach, and he fell into step beside her, 'but…' He waved his hand towards the small cottages dotted along the hill-side, the rows of houses nestling further down around the bay that made up the town of Penhally. 'Don't you find it incredibly claustrophobic? All those net curtains constantly twitching, the way everyone knows everyone else's business, and what they don't know they make up?'

'People can only know what you choose to tell them,' she replied. 'For sure they can speculate, gossip, but you'll find gossips everywhere.'

'But Penhally—and St Piran—they're both so far from civilisation,' he insisted, and she smiled.

'When I first came here I heard a holidaymaker say that to one of the old fishermen, and he said, "It all depends on what you mean by 'civilisation'". Of course we don't have big shops, and there's no cinema, or any sort of nightclub, but if you need help it's always given. Actually, it reminds me a lot of home.'

'But it's nothing like London,' he protested, and she blinked.

'I meant Killarney. London was never my home.'

'Brianna, we lived in London for nine years,' he replied with ill-disguised irritation. 'It was most definitely our home.'

'Maybe for you,' she muttered, but he heard her, and came to a halt, forcing her to stop, too.

'All right, explain,' he demanded, and she opened her mouth, then closed it again to marshal her thoughts.

'Do you remember the flat we rented in Killarney when we first got married?' she said, and he groaned.

'Do I ever? It was so small, and dingy, and whenever I had a bath every damn pipe in the place rattled.'

'OK,' she conceded, with a small gurgle of laughter, 'so the plumbing wasn't the greatest—'

'And the mice…' He rolled his eyes heavenwards. 'Brianna, the place was overrun with mice, and you'd never let me kill any of them so I was constantly catching them in those humane boxes, and taking them outside, until Mr Fitzgerald told us that unless I took them at least six miles away they'd find their own way back.'

'So you used to load up the car every weekend, and drive them out to the country,' she chuckled, remembering, and he shook his head ruefully.

'A proper eejit I looked, too, emptying all of those boxes into a field like some sort of Pied Piper.'

And his Irish accent was coming back, she noticed, the accent he had so carefully excised from his voice because he didn't want to be thought provincial by all the big shots in London.

'And don't forget Mrs O'Leary in the flat next door,' he continued. 'Always wanting to tell us how much the flats had gone downhill since her husband died, and that bright red wig she wore—'

'Oh, I'd forgotten all about her wig,' Brianna declared, starting to laugh, 'and her hats—do you remember the hats she used to wear—all those feathers, and ribbons, and bows?'

'Brianna, I swear those hats will remain scarred on my psyche for ever,' Connor said with a shudder.

And she laughed out loud, and it was so good to hear her laugh, had been so long since he'd heard her laugh, and her cheeks were flushed with the wind, and her eyes were sparkling with a life and a vibrancy he hadn't seen in them since they'd lost Harry, and, without thinking, he reached out and touched her cheek, only to see her step back and the light in her face instantly disappear.

'It's beginning to get dark,' she said, half turning. 'We ought to start heading back.'

'Oh, I'm sure we can risk a few more minutes,' he said quickly, wanting so much to recapture her laughter, not wanting to return to her cottage where he knew she would shut him out again. 'What made you think of our flat in Killarney?'

'I guess…' She looked out to sea. The breakers were much higher now, the clouds more louring. 'I guess it's because even though it wasn't the greatest flat in the world, it was our home, and I was so happy there.'

'You never objected when I started applying for jobs in England,' he said, pointedly, and she sighed.

'I was so young when we got married, Connor, and my mother said a wife should always follow her husband wherever he wanted to go, and I didn't question that. I know different now. I know it should have been a joint decision.'

'But why did you never tell me you were unhappy?' he demanded. 'Why did you never say, "Connor, this isn't the life I want"?'

'I wasn't unhappy. Unhappy…' She shook her head help-lessly. 'Unhappy makes it sound as though I was crying in secret, miserable all the time, and I wasn't. I just felt… detached. As though my life was on hold while I was in London, but eventually I'd start living again.'

He gazed at her uncomprehendingly.

'But, every time I went for a promotion, you were always solidly behind me, saying, "Go for it." Every time I found us a nicer flat, a bigger flat, you seemed so happy, and when I decided to go it alone, to set up my own business, you were thrilled to bits.'

'Because you were,' she admitted. 'I shouldn't have pretended—I see that now—but you were so determined to make it big in England, and money—status—they always mattered much more to you than they did to me. All I ever wanted was enough money for us to get by, a nice place to live in, and…and a family. I would have been more than happy to stay in Killarney, with you working at the local accountant's office, and me in the hospital there.'

'But my career…my own business…' He dragged his fingers through his hair, his eyes bewildered. 'Brianna, I did it all for you, so you wouldn't ever end up like my mother.'

'Your mother?' she echoed in confusion. 'There was nothing wrong with your mother. She was a lovely lady—'

'Who I watched grow old before her time, trying to put enough food on the table to feed myself and my dad, and my three brothers,' Connor said bitterly. 'All her married life she had to scrimp and save, and she never…' He shook his head. 'Brianna, she never got anything pretty, or silly, or frivolous, and I vowed when I watched her, sitting up to all hours of the night, trying to find enough money to pay for the food, and rent, and electricity, that my wife would never have to do that.'

'Connor, it wasn't your father's fault that the only work he could get was occasional because he had emphysema—'

'I know that,' he said impatiently. 'I don't blame him.'

'And your mother *loved* your father,' she insisted. 'Even though they never had much money, there was always laughter in your house, and your mother wanted your father, not the things he could buy her, just as I only ever wanted you and not the fancy flats, or the posh London address.'

'That's easy for you to say when you never had to go without when you were growing up,' he retorted. 'Your parents had their own farm, their own animals, and chickens. They weren't dirt poor like my parents.'

His parents had been poor, she remembered. The tenement flat they'd lived in, in Dublin, had seemed so dark to her when she'd first visited, but it wasn't the darkness she remembered. It was Connor's mother beaming at her, clearly delighted with her son's choice, and his father enveloping her in a hug even though he could barely walk by then.

'I know my parents were more comfortably off than yours,' she said awkwardly, wishing she could somehow make him understand, 'but there was never any shortage of love in your home.'

'You can't live on love, Brianna,' he said, annoyance tingeing his voice, 'not in the real world.'

She opened her mouth, then closed it again.

'Maybe the truth is I'm just a country girl at heart,' she said with an effort, 'and London was just too big, too impersonal for me. Maybe…maybe if we'd had children it would have made a difference. I don't know, I honestly don't.'

For a long moment he said nothing, and when he did speak his voice was low, bleak.

'We both took the decision to turn off Harry's life-support system, Brianna.'

'I know,' she said unevenly. 'I know we did. I'm not… I don't blame you for that.' She took a deep breath. There was something she had to say to him. Something that had revolved round and round in her mind like a canker for the past two years, and, even if his answer broke her, she still had to ask. 'You never really wanted children, did you?'

He swung round to her, his hair streaming back in the wind, appalled horror plain on his face.

'How can you say that?' he exclaimed. 'How can you even *think* it? Harry was my son, my baby, too. We tried for so many years to have him, and when we lost him… How can you say I didn't want him?'

'Then why, when I was pregnant, did you never seemed as excited as I was?' she pressed. 'I couldn't wait for Harry to be born, and yet you… You never went shopping with me for baby clothes, or helped me choose a cot, or—'

'God dammit, Brianna, I was working flat out, twenty-four seven,' he protested. 'I didn't know whether you would want to go back to work after the baby was born so I wanted to make sure we were financially secure. Just because I didn't go shopping with you, or race around our flat doing high fives all the time, doesn't mean I didn't want him.'

And he was holding something back, she knew he was from the way he wasn't quite meeting her eyes.

'Connor—'

'You seem better now than when I last saw you,' he said.

Better. Was she better? She certainly no longer cried herself to sleep every night, no longer woke up in the dark thinking Harry was somewhere in the house, lost, distressed, needing her, but better now…?

'I don't think you ever get over the death of a child,' she said with difficulty. 'You just somehow get through it, one day at a time. At the beginning, after Harry died, there were days when I wondered if I would even make it to the next day, and days when I honestly didn't care if I didn't. I felt so alone, you see, so very much alone, but now… The pain's still there, the ache and the longing for him is still there, but it's…duller.'

'Why do you keep saying you were alone?' he exclaimed. 'You weren't alone. *I* was there, *I* was with you.'

'But I couldn't talk to you, and you…' She pulled her coat closer to her. It was getting colder, so much colder, but he'd asked her a question, and he deserved an answer. 'You didn't seem to…to care the way I did. When we got home from the hospital, you'd taken everything away. His cot, his clothes, his toys—'

'I was trying to make things easier for you,' he protested.

'I thought…if you saw them…it would only make you more upset.'

'And you thought, if they weren't there, I'd *forget*?' she said incredulously, and he flinched.

'I was trying to help, Brianna, to protect you—'

'What you did was take all the decisions away from me,' she declared. 'I might have wanted Harry's room to stay exactly as it was. I might have wanted to burn every single thing in his room, or pack it all away, or give it to charity, but you didn't give me that choice.'

'I'm sorry, but when we lost Harry—'

'Will you stop saying that?' She flared. 'We didn't lose Harry. He wasn't a…a parcel we inadvertently left behind on a train and never got back. He *died*, Connor.'

His face twisted. 'I know.'

'Then why do you never say it?' she demanded. 'Why do you always say we lost him?'

'Lost…died…' A muscle in his jaw clenched. 'What difference does it make? It means the same thing.'

'No, it doesn't. Connor—'

'Has it all gone, Brianna?' he said, holding out his hand to her hesitantly. 'The love we once shared. Has it all gone?'

She stared back at him silently. She didn't want to hurt him. He looked so suddenly vulnerable, so completely unlike the utterly self-confident Connor she had always known, but he had told her he wanted no lies, no half-truths, only honesty.

'I don't know,' she replied. 'I honestly and truly don't know.'

And she turned and walked away from him, leaving him gazing bleakly after her.

CHAPTER FOUR

'HAVE you seen this?' Connor exclaimed, tossing a copy of the *Penhally Gazette* down onto the coffee table in the staffroom.

Brianna glanced dismissively at the front page, and shook her head.

'I don't read the *Gazette*—haven't ever since they printed that disgusting article about Jess. If Vermin has included some snotty comment about the poor quality of my photograph—'

'Read the article.'

Something about Connor's tone had Brianna putting down her mug of coffee, and picking up the newspaper.

'"Abandoned baby found in St Piran Hospital car park",' she read out loud. '"Sister Flannigan of the neonatal intensive care unit…" blah, blah, blah "…baby has been named Harry…"' She frowned up at Connor. 'OK, so it's not the greatest prose style in the world, but I don't see—'

'Read the last paragraph.'

Obediently, she continued reading.

'"The mother has as yet not come forward,"' she murmured, '"but this newspaper can also exclusively reveal that Sister Flannigan is currently…"' Her eyes flew to Connor's then back to the newspaper, '"is currently living with Connor Monahan, an external auditor brought in by the St Piran Hospital board to determine cost-saving measures which could include ward closures."' Slowly she lowered the newspaper. 'How the hell did he find that out, Connor? How, on God's green earth, was Vermin able to find that out?'

'I was going to ask you the same thing.'

'You think I *want* people to know you're my husband?' she said without thinking, then flushed scarlet when she saw the pain in Connor's eyes. 'I didn't mean that—it came out all wrong—'

'I don't give a damn about him knowing I'm staying at your cottage,' he interrupted angrily. 'To be honest, he wouldn't be much of a reporter if he hadn't done some snooping, and he was bound to notice my car sitting outside your home all night. What I want to know is how he discovered why I'm here, in the hospital?'

'Oh, come on, Connor, it's hardly a state secret,' she protested. 'Rumours about why you were coming to St Piran's started filtering out of Admin over a month ago. The only things we didn't know were who you were, and the actual day of your arrival.'

'Brilliant.' He groaned. 'Just brilliant. My assessment is supposed to be hush-hush. *Nobody* was supposed to know anything about it until I'd made my report—the board were quite specific about that.'

'But it's hardly your fault if St Piran's is a hotbed of gossip,' she replied. 'It's a hospital, Connor. Gossip and rumour go with the territory.'

He sighed, and rubbed his fingers wearily over his face. 'I can only hope the board see it that way.'

'You mean, they could fire you?' She gasped, and he grimaced.

'Breach of confidentiality, going public with something

they wanted to keep private… Let's just say they're not going to be very happy with me.'

'But *you* didn't tell anyone,' she protested. 'It was the gossiping staff in Admin. They're the ones who should be torn to shreds, not you.'

'And you'd care if I was?' he said, unable to hide his surprise, and she rolled her eyes in exasperation.

'Of course I'd care,' she replied. 'I know how much your work means to you.'

He'd far rather she knew just how much *she* meant to him. Far rather he could somehow find the right words, instead of always saying the wrong ones. She'd hardly spoken at all this morning over breakfast, and he hadn't dared to. All he'd been able to think, as he'd stared at her lowered head, was how had they come to this, how had they grown so far apart, that they couldn't even make any kind of conversation any more?

'Connor…?'

She was gazing up at him with concern, and he managed to smile. She'd said things hadn't been right between them even before Harry, and maybe she was right. Maybe he'd somehow lost sight of what she wanted in his determination to achieve what he'd believed they both did, but there had to be a way back for them, a way of reaching her.

'What's done is done,' he said. 'All I can do now is try to achieve some damage limitation.'

And not just in this job, he thought as he followed Brianna back to the ward, and the minute she appeared the entire staff fell awkwardly, and all too guiltily, silent.

'I take it you've all seen this morning's edition of the *Penhally Gazette*?' Brianna said, her back ramrod-stiff, but her cheeks, Connor noticed, were pink. 'So, to satisfy your curiosity, I am not conducting an illicit affair with Mr Monahan. He's my husband.'

Megan threw her an 'I'm so sorry about this' look, Chris's mouth fell open, as did the mouths of the other nurses, but Rita was clearly not going to be quite so easily satisfied.

'But I don't understand,' she said, all innocent confusion, as the nurses around her scattered, clearly not wanting to get involved. 'How can Mr Monahan be your husband when you never said you were married, far less to the man who's auditing this hospital?'

'I fail to see why Sister Flannigan needed to tell anyone anything about her private life,' Connor replied before Brianna could reply. 'And she, of course, understands the need for complete confidentiality regarding the nature of my job.'

'Even so,' Rita said, 'I still think—'

'Oh, I wouldn't,' Connor interjected, his voice soft, and velvet, and deadly. 'I really would seriously recommend you don't. But in the meantime,' he added with a smile that would have had Brianna backing off fast, 'why don't you run away and make sure the rest of the hospital staff knows the latest, stop-press new? I'm sure you must be just itching to spread the word, and it will save Sister Flannigan the trouble of having to post a bulletin on the notice board.'

The ward clerk needed no second bidding, and, when she'd gone, Brianna sucked in a shaky breath.

'Remind me never, ever to cross swords with you,' she murmured, 'but thanks. Again.'

'Any time,' he replied, then caught her gaze. 'And I mean that.'

He did, too, she thought. Connor would have thrown himself in front of a runaway horse to protect her, would have gone fearlessly into battle on her behalf at the merest hint of a threat, but sharing his feelings with her… That was something else entirely.

'Yikes, but that was impressive, Connor.' Megan grinned as she joined them. 'But how in the world did Vermin ever find out you were staying at Brianna's cottage?'

'I'm afraid my car's not exactly forgettable,' Connor replied ruefully, 'plus leaving it outside Brianna's house all night… I guess that was just asking for trouble.'

'I suppose so.' Megan sighed. 'But maybe it's better if everyone knows the two of you are married. Some things… it's not always wise to keep them under wraps. When the truth comes out, as it always does, the repercussions can be worse.'

And she was talking about herself, Brianna realised from the dark shadows she could see in Megan's eyes. Not about Connor and her, but about herself, and Connor knew it, too, judging by his slight frown, and she glanced helplessly across at him and, to her relief, he came to her rescue.

'How are all your little patients this morning?' he asked, and Megan grabbed his question with clear relief.

'Our jaundiced baby seems to be making good progress, as is our congenital hypothyroidism little boy,' she replied. 'Amy Renwick's beautifully stable, and all the other babies are doing very well, though I have to say little Harry's a bit too quiet for my peace of mind.'

'How can a baby be too quiet?' Connor asked, clearly puzzled, as Megan walked over to the little boy's incubator and he and Brianna followed her. 'I would have thought quiet meant content, happy?'

'It can,' Megan agreed. 'And he certainly seems to be responding to the surfactant, but…' She shook her head. 'He just seems a bit lethargic, to me.'

'Just because he isn't constantly moving around in his incubator, as some of our babies do, doesn't mean there's anything wrong with him,' Brianna said swiftly. 'As Connor said, he's probably just a very contented baby.'

Megan nodded, but she didn't look convinced, and a chill of foreboding crept up the back of Connor's neck as he stared down at the baby who was lying, unmoving, in his incubator. As Megan had said, there was quiet, and there was quiet, and he had never once heard this baby cry. Brianna might not think there was anything wrong, but he wondered how much of that was denial on her part because the baby did look like their son. Not strikingly so, but enough to make him feel slightly sick inside.

'My gut feeling is we're missing something,' Megan declared, 'so I want those blood results chased up, more X-rays, a spinal tap, a CT-scan—'

'You think he could be brain-damaged?' Connor gasped, and could have bitten off his tongue when he saw Brianna's face whiten.

'I'm not into guessing games, Connor,' Megan replied firmly, 'and I'm probably simply overreacting, and he's actually one contented little boy, but I want to cover all bases.'

'Right,' he murmured, backing up a step. 'OK, I have notes I want to transfer from my phone to my laptop, so I'll…I'll head off to my office and let you get on with it.'

Megan smiled slightly as Connor strode quickly out of the ward.

'He's getting quite attached to our Harry, isn't he?'

'Who wouldn't when this little one is such a cutesy?' Brianna replied, then took a deep breath. 'The spinal tap… Are you thinking sepsis?'

'Hell, Brianna, I'm not thinking anything,' Megan insisted. 'I just…'

'Have a gut feeling.' Brianna nodded.

She'd had them, too, in the past. A nurse's sixth sense

warning that, despite what their monitors and hi-tech machines indicated, there was something not quite right.

'Do you want me to page Babbling?' she asked, and Megan shook her head.

'Let's wait for those blood results, and while we're waiting we'll do a spinal tap before we pull in our resident Cassandra. And speaking of prophets of doom,' she added dryly, 'I think Rita wants a word with you.'

'Oh, joy,' Brianna muttered with feeling, glancing over her shoulder to see the ward clerk clearly attempting to catch her attention, and Megan laughed.

'Just don't kill her, OK?' she said. 'Removing all that splattered blood from the unit...' She grinned. 'Nightmare.'

But it wasn't Rita who wanted to speak to Brianna outside in the corridor. It was Jess, her face alight with excitement.

'I think I might know who the mother of your abandoned baby might be!' she exclaimed without preamble.

Which was good news, Brianna told herself, as she felt her heart give an uncomfortable, and unexpected, dip. It was tremendous news, the very best of news, and yet she found herself having to struggle to return Jess's smile.

'That's...that's brilliant,' she replied, all too conscious that Connor had come out of the nurse unit manager's office, and was listening intently. 'Who is it?'

'Do you remember me telling you some months ago about the girl I saw who gave me a false name?' Jess replied.

'A false name?' Brianna repeated in confusion, and Jess shook her head at her.

'You *must* remember. She came in the day that poor young car mechanic, Colin Maddern, was killed in a car crash. She told me her name was Marcia Johns, and I thought it sounded odd, and it wasn't until she'd gone I realised why. She'd clearly picked the name from one of the pharmaceutical posters on my wall.'

'I can sort of vaguely remember that.' Brianna frowned. 'But what makes you think she could be Harry's mother?'

The counsellor held up three fingers and counted them off.

'Number one, it was very clear to me she'd been deeply in love with this Colin even though she couldn't have been much older than sixteen. Number two, she gave me a false name, and why would she do that unless she was afraid I might make enquiries and find out who she really was and where she lives?'

'Jess—'

'And number three,' the counsellor continued triumphantly, 'even when I spoke to her I felt she was hiding something, that there was something else she wasn't telling me.'

'Did she look pregnant?' Brianna asked, and for a second Jess looked downcast. Then she brightened.

'She wouldn't have if she was only two, or three, months gone, and this must have been…six…seven months ago.'

'Would you be able to give the police a description of this girl?' Connor asked, to Brianna's acute annoyance, and Jess frowned.

'She was blonde—well, more corn-coloured, really— and her eyes were grey, but the trouble is I only saw her twice. Once when she came to the hospital, and once when I was out with Gio in his car.'

'Nevertheless, I think you should tell the police what you know,' Connor declared, and Brianna bit her lip.

What right did he have to interfere, to put in his

pennyworth? The baby's mother's identity had nothing to do with him.

'Jess, you can certainly go to the police if you want,' she said, 'but let's look at the facts here. You don't know the girl's real name, and you don't even know if she was actually pregnant. All you know for certain is she had blonde hair, and grey eyes, and there must be dozens of girls out there who would fit that description.'

'My own granddaughter, Nicola, for a start,' Rita observed as she came out of her office, clearly having been hovering behind her door, listening to every word, 'and I'm telling you this. If the police start stopping every sixteen-year-old girl in the street and asking if she's recently given birth, there'll be hell to pay from the parents.'

Jess flushed.

'Damn, but I hadn't thought of that. I'm so sorry, folks,' she added. 'It just all seemed to fit, but you're right—I don't have enough information, only guesswork.'

'I still think you should speak to the police,' Connor declared, but the counsellor shook her head.

'If I remember anything else, I will, but right now… For all I know I've just put two and two together and come up with five, and that's not going to help anyone.'

'What will happen to Harry if his mother doesn't come forward?' Brianna asked, and Jess sighed.

'When he's well enough, Social Services will arrange for him to go into care or be fostered, until he can be adopted. Look, I know that sounds awful,' she continued quickly, seeing Brianna's expression, 'but there are some really good foster-parents out there.'

'I suppose so,' Brianna said unhappily, 'but it seems a pretty wretched start in life for a little baby.'

'Brianna…'

She could hear the caution in Connor's voice, the concern, but she didn't turn round—couldn't.

'I wouldn't give up hope yet of his mother coming forward,' Jess observed bracingly. 'It's only been two days since you found him, and there could be dozens of reasons for her not coming back to claim him.'

'Yeah, like her thanking her lucky stars she's got rid of him,' Rita declared, and Jess rolled her eyes at Brianna.

'I have to go,' she said. 'I have wall-to-wall clients today—'

'Which reminds me,' Brianna declared. 'When you've a minute, could you have a word with Naomi Renwick? She's been doing marvellously, managing to keep most of her anxieties pretty much under control since her daughter was born, but I get the feeling things are starting to get on top of her, and...'

'You think she needs someone not directly involved with her daughter's medical care to talk to her?' Jess nodded. 'Not a problem. I can't see her today, but I'll definitely drop by tomorrow.'

'Nice woman,' Connor said as Jess hurried away. 'Seems very caring, as well as capable.'

And if he thought that, then maybe Jess's job would be safe, Brianna realised, letting out a silent whoop of joy.

'Her husband's very nice too,' she replied, just in case Connor was eying up the neurology department for cutbacks. 'Gio Corezzi, the neurosurgeon?'

'I'm sure Mr Corezzi is very nice,' Rita chipped in, before Connor could reply, 'but, when you think about it, what do any of us really know about him?'

'What's there to know?' Brianna said in confusion. 'He's a brilliant surgeon, he's Italian, and he's happily married to Jess.'

'He is *now*,' Rita replied, 'but he wasn't nine months

ago, and don't you think it's odd this baby should be found next to his car?'

Brianna turned slowly to face the ward clerk. 'I'd watch what you were saying, if I was you, Rita.'

'I'm only making an observation—'

'No, you're not,' Brianna interrupted, more angry than she'd been in a long time. 'You're saying that Gio—Gio who loves Jess more than he loves his own life—could have had some…some sort of sordid liaison the minute he arrived in St Piran, and then dumped the woman.'

'I'm only pointing out that it's strange—'

'Have you been talking to Kennie Vernon?' Brianna demanded. 'Because if you have, and I hear this repeated anywhere in the hospital, I'm going to tell Gio what you said, and, believe me, the courts take a very dim—and expensive—view of slander. Understood?'

From Rita's scarlet face it seemed she did, and, as she strode into her office, and slammed the door behind her, Connor shook his head.

'What an absolutely appalling woman. Why on earth does the hospital employ her?'

'Because, despite the fact that she's a nosy, interfering gossip,' Brianna replied, 'she is also, unfortunately, very good at her job.'

'Which is a great pity,' he observed, 'because I would have relished the opportunity of recommending she be given her marching orders.'

'At least she only has two more years to work here before she retires.' Brianna sighed. 'Of course, there's every chance I'll probably have killed her before then, but…'

Connor tilted his head at her. 'You've changed, haven't you?'

'In what way?' she asked, puzzled.

'The Brianna I knew would never have chewed Rita's

head off. She might have wanted to, but she would have been far too afraid of hurting someone's feelings.'

'Yeah, well, maybe I don't care so much about other people's feelings now,' she replied. 'Maybe I care more about what is right.'

He smiled, an odd, almost self-mocking smile.

'You don't need me any more, do you?'

Her eyes flew to his. 'Don't need…?'

'When we first got married, I thought—I sort of expected—that I'd always be…' He shrugged a little awkwardly. 'Your protector, I guess. My role was to be Tarzan—'

'And I was Jane?' she said, and try as she might she couldn't stop the corners of her mouth from lifting. 'Um, Connor, I think maybe you should pick a different comparison because somehow I don't ever see you swinging through the trees wearing only a loincloth.'

'You know what I mean,' he said, his cheeks slightly flushed, 'but look at you now. You have your own home—'

'It's rented.'

'A career you've made all by yourself, a circle of friends, and you didn't need my help to get any of those things. In fact, you probably didn't even need me against Vermin.'

'Oh, yes, I did,' she said with feeling. 'Connor—'

'I'm just thinking, you see,' he said, his face suddenly sad, 'if I'm not your protector, your defender, then there really isn't any place in your life for me now, is there?'

He meant it, she realised. For him, there was only one role that a husband should play in a marriage, and because he believed he was now an irrelevance to her, he was giving her the opportunity to say, 'No, you're right, there is no place for you,' and he would leave, and she'd never see him again.

But was that really and truly what she wanted? She'd

thought it was, when he had first come to St Piran's but, now, staring up at him, seeing his face under the fluorescent lighting, she found herself thinking how very tired he looked, how unexpectedly vulnerable, and how his shirt was ever so slightly crumpled. Which was a stupid thing to think, an inconsequential thing, and she knew it was, but she'd never seen him looking anything but perfectly groomed, and she tentatively put out her hand to him.

'Connor, a man needs to be a whole lot more than simply a protector in a marriage, otherwise we women would only ever marry bodyguards or boxers.'

His lips curved into an uneven smile, and he captured her hand in his.

'Then there's still hope for me—for us?'

She wanted to say, yes, she did so want to say, yes, but there were so many unresolved issues between them, and too many questions still unanswered.

'I can't answer that, not yet. I'm sorry,' she added gently, hearing him sigh, 'but you said you wanted me to be honest, and right now, that's all I can say.'

He nodded. 'I guess…' His shoulders lifted, and he forced a laugh. 'I guess it's better than "Goodbye".'

And before she realised what he was going to do, he'd raised her hand and planted a kiss in the centre of her palm. A kiss so gentle that his lips scarcely brushed her skin, and yet she felt a faint flutter of warmth curl and wrap itself around her frozen heart. A faint flutter that deepened and grew when he held her hand close to his own heart and she could feel it beating.

'Bree…?'

He hadn't called her that for such a long time, not for such a very long time, and tentatively she raised her own hand to touch his cheek, saw him close his eyes, and turn his head so his lips almost touched her fingers, and then he let out a muttered oath when the unit door opened and Josh appeared, looking grimly determined.

'No prizes for guessing who he's come to see,' Connor muttered as he released her hand. 'For a bright man, it's sure taking him a long time to get the message that Megan's not interested.'

'Shush,' Brianna whispered warningly. 'What can we do for you, Josh?'

'I didn't realise you guys were married,' he said, and Brianna rolled her eyes.

'Now, that *was* fast, even for Rita,' she observed dryly, and Josh grinned.

'I want to talk to Megan.'

'Josh, do you really think this is wise?' Brianna said uncertainly. 'She clearly doesn't want to talk to you—'

'But I *have* to talk to her,' the A and E consultant insisted. 'Brianna, please, tell her that.'

'OK, I'll tell her, but don't be surprised if she says she's too busy,' she replied, but, as she turned to go back into the ward, she saw Mr Brooke beckoning imperiously to her from outside his office. 'Oh, damn. Look I'm sorry, Josh, Mr Brooke wants me. Connor, could you find Megan, and tell her Josh really needs to speak to her?'

'I'll try,' he replied.

Which was about as much as anyone could do, Brianna thought as she hurried down the corridor towards Mr Brooke.

'This had better be good, Josh,' Megan declared as she came out of the ward, looking both flustered and irritated. 'Unlike you, who seem to have unlimited free time at your disposal, I am really busy.'

'You're always busy, always avoiding me,' he replied, 'but this is important.'

'It always is, according to you,' she said. 'OK, all right. Spit it out, but make it fast. I have a hundred and one things to do.'

'Rebecca's left me.'

For a second there was no expression at all on Megan's face, then, to Josh's dismay, her face whitened with shock.

'Is this because of me?' she said hoarsely. 'Has she heard rumours about me? Josh, I'll speak to her, tell her that what happened between you and I happened years before she married you, and we didn't even have a proper relationship back then, just…' She bit her lip. 'Just one night of madness that should never have happened.'

'Megan—'

'You haven't told her about Stephen, have you?' she exclaimed, horror tingeing her voice. 'You haven't been insensitive enough to tell her that we had a baby, and he died? Oh, Josh, she must be so hurt—so upset—'

'I haven't told her we had a child. I…' He swallowed convulsively. 'Only you and I know that, and only you and I ever will. Look, Megan, I thought… Rebecca leaving me… I thought…I hoped…you'd be pleased.'

'*Pleased?*' she echoed faintly. 'You thought I'd be *pleased* to have been the cause of someone's marriage ending?'

'I shouldn't have said "pleased"—"pleased" was the wrong thing to say,' he declared desperately, 'and you haven't ended my marriage. Rebecca and I… Our marriage has been slowly dying, bit by bit, for years. It was one of the reasons we moved to St Piran, both of us hoping we might be able to salvage it, but I think we always knew it wasn't salvageable.'

'I'm sorry,' she said, sincerity plain in her face. 'Sorry

for Rebecca, sorry for you. Nobody wants a marriage to fail.'

'I think, perhaps, looking back, that I should never have married her,' he replied. 'That it was a mistake.'

She opened her mouth, then closed it again, and backed up a step, her eyes narrowing.

'A mistake,' she repeated slowly. 'It must be really comforting for Rebecca to know she was a mistake.'

'Megan—'

'But, then, I was a mistake, too, wasn't I, Josh?' Megan continued icily. 'You and I making love when we were students—that was another of your mistakes. Oh, and Stephen. I guess he was *a mistake*, too.'

'Megan, listen to me—'

'You *married* Rebecca, Josh, so presumably you felt something for her at one time?'

He had, he remembered, but the feelings he'd felt for his wife had been nothing like the feelings he'd experienced towards the white-faced, angry woman standing in front of him. With Rebecca he'd felt comfortable, at ease, had thought they wanted the same things from life, while with Megan… His feelings had been so terrifying in their intensity that he'd run from them rather than face them. Run because he'd sensed that Megan embodied everything he'd always feared. Commitment, honesty, family, ties.

'I married Rebecca because I thought…' He let out a long, shuddering breath. 'I thought we wanted the same things, but I don't think we ever really understood one another, whereas you and I…'

'You and I *what*, Josh?' Megan said her voice tight.

'I'm sorry, I'm not explaining this very well—'

'You think you can just take up where you left off, don't you?' she interrupted, disbelief plain in her voice. 'You think that because your wife has walked out on you, I'll be only too ready and willing to leap back into your bed again despite what you did, despite…' Her voice broke slightly. 'Despite you taking everything of any value from me.'

'No, of course I didn't think that,' he protested.

'Then why is it so all-fired important to you that I should know?' she demanded. 'Why do you think it would matter a damn to me whether your wife has left you, or if you're still happily married to her?'

He took a step towards her, and saw her back away still further.

'Look, I'm saying this all wrong,' he faltered. 'It's coming out all wrong.'

'Oh, I think it's coming out just right, Josh,' she retorted. 'Thanks for the update on your private life, but there was no need for you to hurry up here to tell me. I could have waited like everyone else until Rita spread the word.'

And she walked away from him, leaving him gazing in despair after her.

'You want *me* to be the new nurse unit manager?' Brianna gasped as Mr Brooke beamed benignly at her. 'But… why?'

'Because you're not only my most qualified member of staff, you're also the best,' he replied as she gazed at him, open-mouthed. 'And—believe me—those two things don't always necessarily go together.'

'But…'

'I know it's going to mean getting to grips with a whole lot of unfamiliar paperwork, but the job's yours, if you want it. You do want it, don't you?' he added as Brianna stared at him uncertainly.

Nurse Unit Manager. It was her dream job, the job she'd always wanted. Of course she knew it wouldn't be easy. The post carried a huge amount of responsibility, and she'd seen how many hours Diego Ramirez had needed to put in just to keep on top of all the paperwork, but she wanted it, she really did, except… If she accepted the post it would mean there was no possibility of her going back to Connor. He was a city man, with a high-powered city job. He'd never move to Cornwall in a million years, which meant, if she accepted the job, she would be accepting that her marriage was over.

Well, it is, isn't it? her mind whispered, and she took an unsteady breath.

'Mr Brooke, I'm flattered—immensely flattered—you think I can do this—' she began, and Richard Brooke put up his hands quickly.

'I can hear a "but" coming and I don't want to hear a "but". Look, I've put my neck on the line here by telling Admin I want it to be an in-house appointment, so will you at least think about it? I can't give you too long to make up your mind, because we desperately need a replacement for Nurse Ramirez, but—frankly—I can't see why you're hesitating.'

Neither could Brianna as she walked slowly out of Mr Brooke's office. It was what she'd always wanted, to be in charge of the nursing staff in a unit, and if the consultant had only asked her last week she wouldn't have hesitated for an instant, but now… Now she didn't know what to do, and the last person she could talk to it about was Connor.

At least she was able to avoid his far-too-acute gaze for the rest of the day. When she got back to the ward, Megan told her he'd gone to Men's Surgical to interview the staff there and, for a moment, Brianna considered confiding in the paediatric specialist registrar, but one look at Megan was enough to tell her that her friend was struggling with her own private demons. Whatever Josh had so desperately wanted to talk to Megan about, it had obviously upset her greatly, but her closed face did not invite conversation and, for once, Brianna was relieved when her shift was finally over.

'He's still going to be here tomorrow, you know,' one of the night nurses said with a chuckle when Brianna made her customary stop at Harry's incubator to check on him before she left.

'I know,' Brianna replied, 'but I just like to say good-night to him. He doesn't have a mother so...' She shrugged awkwardly. 'Silly of me, I guess.'

The night nurse said nothing, but Brianna knew what the woman was thinking. That she was breaking the cardinal nursing rule of 'Never get too close, never become too involved, with a patient' but she wasn't getting too close. She was simply doing her job, doing the best she could for little Harry, and if a small voice in the back of her head was whispering its own warning, that small voice was just overreacting.

Exactly as Connor was, she thought ruefully when she eventually got home, and found him pacing up and down in front of her cottage.

'I was beginning to think your car had broken down,' he said. 'That I was going to have to come out and rescue you before the storm breaks.'

Actually, he was right about the storm, Brianna realised as she squinted up at the sky. Ominous black clouds were rolling in from the west, the wind was picking up, and small drops of rain were already beginning to fall.

'I thought you might be tired when you got back,' he continued, hovering behind her as she trudged wearily into her cottage, 'so I tossed a coin, and put some chilli in your microwave when I heard your car.' He glanced anxiously at her. 'I hope that's OK?'

'Sounds good,' she said with an effort. 'Have I time to

shower and change? I always think I smell so overpoweringly of disinfectant when I get back from the hospital.'

'Sure.' He nodded. 'You've plenty of time. In fact, take all the time you need. I've already set the table, and put on the fire, so there's nothing for you to do.'

She wished there was as she went upstairs, and showered, and changed into a pair of jeans and a sweater. She wished even more that he would stop being so helpful, so thoughtful, when she didn't want him to be any of those things. It just made everything so much harder.

'You seem a bit preoccupied tonight,' he observed after they'd eaten a largely silent meal. 'Nothing wrong at the hospital, I hope?'

'Everything seemed pretty quiet when I left,' she murmured. 'Megan's going to chase up little Harry's blood tests results. They generally take seventy-two hours, so they're not late, but I know she'll be a lot happier when she sees they're normal.'

And if they're not?

The unspoken words hung between them, and neither of them voiced them.

'What did Mr Brooke want to see you about?' Connor asked as he began to collect their dirty dishes.

'Oh, nothing important,' she said evasively. 'Just boring stuff like paperwork.' He didn't believe her, she knew he didn't, and quickly she went over to the sink, and turned on the tap. 'I'd better get these dishes done. It's getting wilder out there, and we might get a power cut.'

And it was getting wilder, she thought as she stared out of her kitchen window into the darkness. The wind was now buffeting the house, and squally rain was battering against the windows. She loved it when it was like this, so wild and tempestuous. It always made her feel like a small bird in its nest, listening to the elements raging around her, but Connor clearly didn't share her feelings.

'Not very seasonal weather, is it?' he observed with a grimace as he picked up a tea towel. 'March… You think of daffodils, and crocuses, and spring approaching, not howling gales and rain.'

'You can get wild weather at any time of year,' she replied, and he nodded.

'It rained a little on our wedding day, didn't it? Your mother said June would be a lovely month to get married in, and it rained.'

'*Rained?*' she exclaimed. 'Connor, it poured solidly all day, and we had hailstones, and a gale-force wind.'

'Oh, come on,' he argued. 'There might have been the odd shower or two—'

'I don't know whose wedding you're remembering, but it certainly isn't ours.' She chuckled as she added some washing-up liquid to the water in the sink. 'The train at the back of my dress got completely soaked when my father and I had to make a mad dash from the car to the church, we had to have all the wedding photographs taken in the reception hall instead of outside the church because nobody could stand upright, and Ellie Warburton, my flower girl, fell in a puddle, and cried for the duration of the reception.'

'Lord, so she did.' He grinned. 'Why was Ellie one of your flower girls anyway? She didn't seem to know you from a bar of soap.'

'She didn't, but my mother insisted because she's some sort of cousin of mine, twenty zillion times removed, and her family would have been deeply offended if she hadn't been asked.'

'Right,' he said, clearly none the wiser as he began

drying their plates. 'OK, so the weather was bad, but everything else was perfect.'

'You corrected Father Driscoll during the ceremony.'

'I did not!'

'You did too,' she declared. 'When he said, "Do you, Connor, take Brianna Kathleen to be your lawfully wedded wife?" you said, "I, Connor, take Brianna Kathleen O'Donnell to be my lawfully wedded wife." You're not supposed to say the bride's surname.'

'I didn't want there to be any mistake,' he protested. 'I thought there might be dozens of Brianna Kathleens in the world and I wanted to make sure I was marrying the right one—my one.'

'My mother was mortified.' Brianna smiled as she remembered. 'She said she'd never be able to look Father Driscoll in the face again when he told her afterwards that he'd never been corrected in church before.'

'Well, like I said,' Connor declared defensively, 'I wanted to be sure I was marrying my Brianna Kathleen.'

'And then my Uncle Joe sang his party piece at the reception,' Brianna continued with a shudder. 'My father promised faithfully not to let him, but halfway through the evening he said, "Sure, Brianna, a wedding's not a wedding unless Joe sings *Delilah*."'

'Does your Uncle Joe ever remember the right words?' Connor asked, and Brianna shook her head.

'Never.' She laughed.

Laughed with such genuine amusement and happiness that he put down the tea towel and caught her soapy hands in his.

'Do you know what I remember most about our wedding day?' he said softly. 'It was turning round when I heard the wedding march and seeing you coming down the aisle towards me. You looked… Oh, you looked so beautiful it took my breath away, and I thought, Connor, lad, how in the world did you ever get so lucky to win this angel?'

'Flatterer,' she said shakily, trying to pull her hands free without success.

'Gospel truth,' he said huskily. 'All I could think was, Please let her reach my side quickly, before the gods or the fairies snatch her away and keep her all to themselves.'

'Connor, I'm getting soap suds all over the floor,' she protested, completely unnerved by the intensity of his gaze, but he ignored her.

Instead, he reached behind her, and, before she could stop him, he'd unplaited her hair and spread it out over her shoulders.

'Your hair was loose,' he murmured, 'just like it is now, and you had flowers threaded through it. Flowers that matched your bouquet, all the colours of the rainbow they were, but paler, and the scent...'

'Freesias...' she whispered, feeling her heart rate pick up. 'They were freesias.'

'And when I said I would honour and keep you, in sickness and in health, until death us do part, I meant every single word.'

She had meant those words, too, but it hadn't been his death, or hers, that had parted them, it had been Harry's.

'Connor...'

'You never told me you were going,' he said, sliding his hands down her back. She could feel his hands trembling— or perhaps she was. She couldn't be sure. 'How could you do that, Brianna? How could you just disappear, never telling me where you were, whether you were safe?'

'I was wrong,' she said unevenly. 'I see that now, but all I could think was if...if I could just get away from you, from London, from everything that reminded me of Harry, I'd be all right.'

'But why Cornwall—why here?'

'Because…' She closed her eyes, and took a shuddering breath. 'Nobody would know me. Nobody would be able to point their finger and say, "She's the one whose baby died. She's the mother whose baby died," and because they couldn't I thought—not that I would forget—I won't ever forget—that it might be…easier.'

'Bree, I have missed you so much,' he whispered, his voice constricted. 'Missed seeing you, missed hearing your voice, and I have so missed holding you.'

He was holding her now. He'd wrapped his arms around her, and then, gently, oh, so tenderly, he kissed her, and when she sighed against his mouth she heard him groan. A groan that seemed to come from deep down inside him, and it felt so good to be held, so good to be kissed, that she kissed him back, and felt him shudder, but as his kiss became more insistent, and he pulled her even closer to him, she suddenly felt the patent evidence of his arousal, and she flinched. She didn't intend to, didn't mean to, but she flinched, and she knew he felt it because she could see the pain of rejection in his eyes as he drew back from her.

'Connor, I'm sorry,' she said unevenly, 'so sorry, I don't know why I—'

'I understand,' he interrupted bleakly.

How could he, she wondered, when she didn't understand her reaction herself? That she'd wanted to be held by him, she'd wanted his arms around her, but, the moment she'd realised that just holding her wasn't enough for him, something inside her had frozen, something within her had screamed, No.

'It isn't you,' she said. 'It's me.'

'It's all right, *a chuisle mo chroí*,' he said with an effort. 'You've had a long day and you're tired. You should get some sleep. I'll finish clearing up in here,' he continued when she tried to interrupt. 'You get yourself away to your bed.'

'But—'

'Goodnight, Bree.'

He had turned back to the sink, and slowly she walked away from him but, when she reached the kitchen door, she half turned.

A chuisle mo chroí.

Pulse of my heart.

It was what he'd called her on their wedding night, when they'd made love for the very first time, and she wanted to say something, knew she should say something, but no words would come. No words that would explain what she couldn't explain, and, as a tear trickled down her cheek, she slipped away, leaving him gazing out of her kitchen window, his face in shadow.

CHAPTER FIVE

RITA was smiling. It was never a good sign when Rita smiled. Either the ward clerk had discovered a new and particularly juicy piece of gossip, or she was about to dump someone in a very large pile of manure, and, whichever it was, Brianna knew she wasn't up for it today—she really wasn't.

'Something I can help you with, Rita?' she said with an effort as the ward clerk sidled up to her, her face distinctly conspiratorial.

'It's about your husband, Sister Flannigan…'

Don't go there, Rita, Brianna thought. If you value your life, don't ask me why I've been living alone in Cornwall for the last two years while I have a husband in London, because, if you do, you're dog meat.

'What about my husband?' she said coolly.

'Just that it's such very good news that he *is* your husband.' Rita beamed. 'I mean, I think we can now safely say my job is completely secure because he'd never shut down any department you worked in.'

Incredible, Brianna thought as she stared at the ward clerk. The woman was completely incredible, but she wasn't about to let her get away with it.

'I don't think we can say that at all,' she replied. 'In

fact, I can assure you my husband would never allow any personal bias to influence him.'

Rita tapped the side of her nose, and winked.

'Of course you *would* have to say that, wouldn't you, Sister, but enough said, message understood, and I won't say another word.'

Which will be a first, Brianna thought grimly, but as Rita bustled away, her anger swiftly faded.

She had such a headache this morning, such a blinding, thumping headache. She'd scarcely slept last night, had spent every hour tossing and turning, reliving what had happened in her kitchen. At least Connor hadn't appeared in the unit yet, and she wondered if his absence was deliberate. She wouldn't have blamed him. She'd allowed him to kiss her, allowed him to hold her, and then she'd rejected him. Rejected him for no reason she could fathom except, perhaps, her body had been telling her that she no longer wanted him, that there was nothing left of their marriage.

'You OK?'

She half turned to see her staff nurse, Chris, regarding her with concern, and grimaced slightly.

'I have a thudding headache this morning,' she replied. 'And before you ask,' she added, 'I've taken something for it, so I can't take anything else.'

It had been Connor who had pressed the aspirin into her hand, she remembered. He'd taken one look at her face this morning, made her breakfast, pressed the pills into her hand, then suggested she should consider taking the day off, but his solicitude had only made her feel worse.

'I'm afraid I'm going to add to your headache,' Chris declared. 'Vermin's here.'

Brianna swore under her breath.

'If that low-life thinks he can get another interview with me—'

'Actually, he wants to speak to Mr Brooke, though why he thinks our consultant will be able to give him any more information than you did is anyone's guess.'

'Where is he—Vermin, I mean?' Brianna asked.

'I've left him cooling his heels in the corridor.'

'The hospital sewer would have been better,' Brianna replied, then frowned slightly. 'You did tell him Mr Brooke has a clinic later on this morning, after his ward rounds, so he's not going to be able to see him any time soon?'

A look of mock dismay appeared on the staff nurse's face.

'Oops, but would you believe I completely forgot to tell him that?'

'Not for one second.' Brianna laughed. 'But it will do Vermin no harm to kick his heels for a couple of hours.'

'That's what I thought,' Chris declared smugly, then her eyes lit up. 'Your husband's here.'

'Is he?' Brianna said dully, without turning round, and Chris dug her gently in the ribs.

'Talk about dark horses. I don't know how you managed to keep quiet about him. He's quite something, isn't he?'

'You said he was scary,' Brianna reminded her, and the staff nurse's smile widened.

'I still think he is, but in a *very* sexy sort of a way.'

Chris thought her husband was sexy. So, too, she remembered, had the wives and girlfriends she'd sat next to at the dinner parties Connor had taken her to in London. Dinner parties whose sole purpose seemed to be for the businessmen there to boast about the deals they'd struck. Networking, Connor had called it, as she'd sat in silence throughout these meals, feeling completely out of place and uncomfortable. Nobody had ever been interested in her when they'd discovered she was a nurse. Zero networking opportunities, the men had clearly thought, while their wives and girlfriends had eyed Connor up, and tried to flirt with him.

'Couldn't you at least *try* to make conversation?' Connor had said impatiently after one of the dinners. 'The other wives, and girlfriends… They always seem to be able to find something to say, but you just sit there like a little frightened mouse.'

And she'd wanted to say that most of the wives and girlfriends' conversations seemed to involve flirting with him, but she hadn't.

'Your head's still sore, isn't it?' Connor declared as he walked across to her and Chris bustled away.

'It's better now,' she lied, and saw his left eyebrow lift.

'Yeah, right. How's everyone doing?' he continued, glancing at the incubators around them. 'How's the baby who was abandoned?'

'His name is Harry, Connor,' she said irritably. 'He seems quite content.'

Quiet, you mean, Connor thought, and quiet doesn't mean the same as content, you know it doesn't, but you won't accept that.

'Brianna—'

'The little girl with jaundice is progressing well,' she said.

She was deliberately changing the subject, he knew she was, but he knew better now than to push.

'Should the soles of her feet, and the palms of her hands, be quite so yellow?' he asked, and saw Brianna smile.

'They're that colour because she had pretty severe jaundice. Every newborn has elevated bilirubin—it's a by-product of haemoglobin, which is usually eliminated from the body as waste—and it's that excess bilirubin which makes so many babies' skin look yellow. Normally, the baby's liver will start functioning at full speed within a few days, but sometimes they need a little help, which is what we're giving her.'

'And the baby who has congenital hypo…hyper…'

'Congenital hypothyroidism,' she finished for him. 'It occurs when a baby's thyroid gland is absent or under-developed at birth.'

'That sounds serious.'

'It used to be. In the past, a baby could end up with permanent mental retardation, and development delay, but we can now give a synthetic thyroid orally.'

'Fascinating,' he said, meaning it, and she laughed.

'There have been an amazing number of medical advances in recent years, and what is even more marvellous is scientists keep on discovering more and more treatments, more and more cures. Although…' The light in her eyes suddenly dimmed. 'Not for everything.'

He knew what she was thinking, and he didn't want her to be thinking of their son, and this time it was he who changed the subject.

'Little Amy. Mrs Renton's daughter—'

'Mrs Renwick,' Brianna corrected him. 'She's progressing well, too. Naomi isn't doing quite so well but I'm hoping Jess will be able to help her.'

'Maybe we should have seen someone like Jess,' he murmured. 'After Harry…you know…'

'Died,' she prompted. 'Just say it, Connor. Nothing awful is going to happen if you say that word.'

But he didn't.

'Maybe we shouldn't have thought we could go it alone, cope alone,' he continued, his face bleak. 'Maybe if we had accepted the help the hospital offered, things might have been…easier.'

'Maybe,' she murmured, and she looked so suddenly lost that he longed to reach for her, to put his arms around her, but he'd tried that last night and she clearly hadn't wanted his touch.

Was it too late for them? he wondered as he saw her smile past him, and he turned to see Mrs Renwick had arrived. He didn't want to believe it was, but he never seemed able to say the right thing, never seemed able to do the right thing, to give her what she wanted, needed, but that didn't mean he wasn't going to try. It wasn't in him to give in without a fight, and this fight involved the highest stakes he'd ever played for. This was one he simply couldn't lose.

'I'll leave you to it,' he said in a low undertone as Mrs Renwick walked towards them. 'I have notes to copy over to my laptop, and I think Amy's mother looks as though she needs you.'

Naomi did, Brianna thought. There were dark shadows under her eyes, and her face was white, and pinched.

'I think you should go home to bed, Naomi,' she said as Connor slipped away. 'Forgo your visit today.'

'I'm fine,' Mrs Renwick replied. 'I just had a very bad migraine yesterday, the third this week, and they tend to wipe me out.'

Stress, Brianna thought. Mega-, mega-stress.

'Your daughter had an excellent night, and is currently moving all over the place inside her incubator,' Brianna declared with a smile. 'Every time I put her to the top, she manages to make her way to the bottom. In fact, I reckon you've got a future long-distance walker there.'

Naomi didn't even attempt to raise a smile.

'You're very kind, Sister, and I know I must seem like the most negative person in the world to you—'

'Of course you're not.'

'But sometimes it's so hard to keep on being positive. My daughter is the most wonderful, precious, joy to me, but…' Naomi bit her lip. 'I told my husband last night she's going to be our only child. I can't go through this again—I just can't.'

'And statistically you won't have to if you decide to give Amy a little brother or sister,' Brianna said gently. 'Though having had one premature baby does put you at a twenty to forty per cent risk of having another one, look at it another way. It also means there's a sixty to eighty per cent chance you won't.'

Naomi nodded, but Brianna could tell she hadn't convinced her, and she wasn't surprised. Having a premature baby was so emotionally draining for parents. All too often, every day seemed to bring with it a new challenge, a new worry, but if anyone could reassure Naomi it would be Jess.

And the counsellor was as good as her word. She arrived midafternoon, and bore Mrs Renwick off to the parents' room, smoothing over Amy's mother's protestations of not having time by insisting she needed a cup of coffee but hated drinking it alone.

'She's good, isn't she?' Megan observed when Jess and Mrs Renwick had gone. 'I wish we had the time to do what Jess does, but we're so constantly snowed under with all the medical procedures we need to perform on the babies that the emotional needs of the parents far too often get overlooked.'

'She's one of a kind, that's for sure,' Brianna agreed. 'And…' She looked over her shoulder to make sure there was no one near, least of all Rita. 'I *think* her job is safe.

Connor hasn't said so—not in so many words—but he *did* say she was very capable so…'

'It's looking good.' Megan breathed with a sigh of relief. 'He didn't…' She grimaced. 'Look, I know I shouldn't be asking you this, but he hasn't given you any indication of which department he might be recommending for the chop, has he?'

'I'm afraid Connor doesn't talk about his work,' Brianna said ruefully. 'Actually, Connor's not big on talking, full stop.'

'One of the strong, silent types, eh?' Megan smiled, but Brianna didn't.

'You could say that,' she murmured, then cleared her throat. 'I've not seen Josh today.'

'Hopefully he's finally remembered which department he's actually supposed to work in,' Megan replied tersely.

Which pretty well ended that conversation, Brianna thought, but she couldn't leave it there even though she knew she probably should. The specialist paediatric registrar looked as ragged as she felt.

'Megan, I know this is none of my business—'

'His wife's left him, Brianna.'

'Josh's wife?' Brianna said faintly. 'But…'

'Yes, I know,' Megan said, her lips twisting slightly. 'Rita must be really beginning to lose her touch if she hasn't managed to pick up that juicy bombshell yet.'

The specialist registrar's voice was hard, brittle, but if ever a woman was close to tears Megan was.

'I think I saw his wife once at a hospital reception,' Brianna said carefully, 'but I've never met her.'

'She was—is—very beautiful,' Megan said. 'But not happy. I don't…' She took a shallow breath. 'I don't think she was very happy.'

'Was…?' Oh, lord, but this was so very hard to say, but

Brianna knew she had to say it. 'Was that what Josh wanted to talk to you about yesterday?'

Megan nodded.

'Not that it's of the least interest, or consequence to me, of course,' she said. 'I mean, whether he's married or single. It's not like he and I…' Her voice trembled slightly. 'It's not like we mean anything to one another.'

'Oh, Megan—'

'Don't,' the specialist paediatric registrar said quickly. 'Please, don't give me any sympathy, or I'm going to embarrass myself, and you.'

'You could never embarrass me,' Brianna said softly. 'Not ever. Josh's wife leaving him… Do you think…are you hoping…?'

'I don't know what I'm thinking, or hoping,' Megan replied with difficulty. 'I just wish…oh, how I wish…he'd never come to St Piran's, that I'd never had to meet him again.'

Because now I have to think about things I don't want to think about, remember things that might have been better kept buried. That was what Megan was saying, and Brianna understood exactly how she felt.

'Megan, listen to me—'

The specialist paediatric registrar shook her head warningly, and Brianna glanced over her shoulder to see Connor approaching.

'Great timing, Connor.' She sighed as Megan hurried away, and her husband's eyebrows rose.

'I can always go away again,' he offered, and she shook her head.

'Too late, I'm afraid.'

And for more than one thing, she thought with dismay when she saw Mr Brooke sweeping into the ward, all smiles. If Vermin had convinced the consultant that she would be willing to give him another interview she was going to throw a hissy fit. A big one.

'Ah, Sister Flannigan,' Mr Brooke declared. 'The very person I was hoping to see.'

'Mr Brooke, if this is about Vermin—I mean Kennie Vernon,' she began, 'he's had all he's ever going to get out of me.'

'Who's Kennie Vernon?' the consultant said with a frown.

'The reporter who wanted to talk to you. The man who's been hanging about in the corridor for the last couple of hours?' she added helpfully. 'Looks like a very bad eighties rock star, dressed all in black, goatee beard?'

'I haven't seen anyone like that this morning,' Mr Brooke replied in confusion. 'No, this is about you, my dear, and my offer,' he continued, ushering her away from Connor to the side of the ward. 'I really need your decision soon. Time and tide, remember, Sister Flannigan, time and tide.'

'Yes. Absolutely,' she muttered, wishing—oh, wishing so much—that the consultant would simply shut up.

He had such a very carrying voice even when he was trying to talk in an undertone, and though Connor was apparently deep in conversation with Chris he'd always been able to listen to two conversations at once.

'As I told you, I can't wait long,' Mr Brooke continued. 'You know how short-staffed we are, and, if you decide to step up to the plate and accept the nurse unit manager's job, we'll need to advertise for a replacement for your job.'

'I appreciate that,' Brianna said. *Please shut up*, she thought. *Please just shut the hell up.* 'And I'll give you my decision by the beginning of next week.'

'Good. Good.' Mr Brooke beamed, then turned on his heel. 'Ah, Connor. A word with you, if I may? I've had a talk with ENT, and they say you can interview their staff next week if that suits you.'

Brianna didn't wait to hear her husband's reply. She was too busy heading for the ward door. She was due a break, and she intended taking it right now. Not in the canteen—with her luck, she'd probably run into Josh—but the nurses' staffroom sounded good. A coffee, and more aspirin for her head sounded even better.

But her hoped-for peace and quiet didn't last long. Within minutes, Connor had appeared and seemed hell-bent on tearing the staffroom apart.

'Can I assume you've lost something?' she said as he turned his attention to the waste paper bin after riffling through the magazines on the coffee table.

'A memory card.' He frowned. 'I've been transferring my notes on the various departments I've been assessing from my phone to my laptop via a memory card, and I can't find it.'

'That'll teach you to be so damned hi-tech.' She could not help but chuckle. 'Use a clipboard and pen next time like the rest of us ordinary mortals.'

'Oh, very funny,' he said irritably, and she took pity on him.

'What does this memory card look like?'

'About the size of a small matchbox, but wafer thin.'

Brianna stared at the abandoned magazines, the un-washed coffee cups and discarded biscuit packets that lit-tered the nurses' staffroom, and shook her head.

'Yeah, well, good luck with finding something that small in this place.'

'Maybe I left it at your cottage,' he murmured. 'I've already searched the nurse unit manager's office, and it's definitely not in there.'

'Don't you have a back-up memory card?'

He nodded. 'I do, but I'd still like to find the original. It has a lot of sensitive data on it.'

'Should MI5 be worried?' She grinned. 'Maybe we should—'

The rest of what she'd been about to say died in her throat when the staffroom door opened, and Jess appeared, her face shining.

'You look as though you've just won the lottery,' Brianna declared, and Jess's smile widened even further.

'It's something much, *much* better,' the counsellor said excitedly. 'I've remembered something else about the girl who I think could be Harry's mother. It came to me when I was talking to Mrs Renwick.'

'When you were talking to Naomi?' Brianna said, and Jess nodded.

'Naomi was wearing an initial necklace, and I suddenly remembered that the girl I met was wearing one, too. In fact, the second she saw me looking at it, she pushed it down into her blouse.'

'Can you remember what the initial was?' Connor asked when Brianna said nothing.

'M—no, N— Or was it M?' Jess shook her head with frustration. 'It was one or the other, I'm positive.'

'So what you're saying is we should be looking for a teenager, with blonde hair, and grey eyes, who may—or may not—have been pregnant when you saw her, and whose first name could start with the initial N or M?' Brianna declared. 'Jess, apart from the fact that this girl could be a complete red herring, think of all the girls' names that start with those initials. It would be like looking for a needle in a haystack.'

'Not that big a haystack,' Connor observed thoughtfully. 'Knowing it's either N or M would cut out a lot of teenagers in the area.'

'And what use is that?' Brianna said irritably. 'Even if we made a list of all the girls in the area whose Christian names begin with the letter N or M, we can hardly phone them up and say, "Have you been pregnant recently?"'

'Flora,' Jess declared. 'Flora Loveday's the health visitor for Penhally. I could phone her—ask if she's noticed any girl who fits my description. A girl who might suddenly have become rather plump recently.'

'And Flora will give you a complete roasting if you ask her that, you know she will,' Brianna protested. 'She'll cite patient confidentiality, and she'd be right.'

Jess grimaced.

'I know.' She sighed. 'It's just… Oh, this is so frustrating. I feel I'm so close, so very close to finding this girl. All I need is one extra piece of the jigsaw.'

'Jess—'

'I wonder if I could get a list of all the families in the area?' the counsellor continued. 'The electoral roll only gives the names of those old enough to vote—but…'

'And what then?' Brianna said, trying and failing to hide her irritation. 'I don't want to rain on your parade, but maybe you should just give up on this amateur sleuthing, and leave it to the police to track down Harry's mother. Personally, I think she's most likely to be someone from outside the county, rather than a local girl.'

'No, she's local,' Jess declared emphatically, 'and I still think it's the girl I met.'

'Oh, for heaven's sake, why can't you just accept it's not?' Brianna said tartly, and Jess blinked.

'Brianna…' Connor cautioned, and she rounded on him.

'It's true, Connor! This whole scenario of the girl who Jess happened to meet, who may, or may not, have given her a false name, and who may, or may not, be Harry's mother, is crazy, you know it is. I understand that Jess wants to help, but enough is enough!'

'Right,' Jess murmured, beginning to back away, her cheeks darkening. 'I'm sorry—you know—for bothering you like this, and I won't do it again.'

And before either Connor or Brianna could say anything she'd left the staffroom, and Connor shook his head at Brianna.

'That wasn't very kind.'

'Maybe I don't feel kind,' Brianna retorted. 'Maybe I've just heard enough of Jess's half-baked theories to last me a lifetime.'

'And maybe you don't want this baby's mother to come forward at all,' he said, and Brianna got to her feet impatiently.

'Of course I do. I just think—'

She never did complete what she'd been about to say. The emergency alarm sounded, and she was out of the staffroom in a second.

'What's wrong—what's happened?' Connor asked, hurrying after her.

'It's one of the babies,' Brianna replied, frantically washing her hands. 'Something's badly wrong with one of the babies!'

And it was Harry. Harry's monitors which were sounding the alarm, and Megan and Mr Brooke were already at his incubator.

'Pulmonary haemorrhage, Brianna,' Megan murmured, as she hurried round the incubator to insert another IV line. 'Looks like patent ductus arteriosus.'

'What does that mean?' Connor asked, trying not to get in the way, and wishing the monitors would stop making their shrill noise.

'Left heart failure,' Brianna replied tightly, and

Connor closed his eyes, feeling as though someone had punched him.

Heart failure. Their son had died because of an inherited heart defect, which meant it wasn't the same, but it felt like it.

'Why didn't that show up before?' he demanded. 'He's had enough X-rays and scans. Shouldn't it have shown up then?'

'It can sometimes happen to babies who have respiratory distress syndrome,' Megan explained. 'We don't know why, but when it happens it happens fast.'

'I want an echocardiogram, and I want it now,' Mr Brooke ordered.

Chris was gone in a flash, and somewhere in the ward Connor could hear one of the babies crying as though it somehow knew that…

Don't go there, his mind warned. *Don't even think that.*

'Is there anything I can do?' he asked as he saw Brianna flipping switches, changing lines, completely in control, though both her face and lips were white.

'Just keep out of the way,' she replied. 'Are we looking at thoracoscopic surgery?' she continued, glancing across at Mr Brooke.

'There's a strong risk of laryngeal nerve damage if I do that,' he declared as Chris appeared with the echocardiography machine. 'Plus I could end up with a ligation of the pulmonary artery if I make even the tiniest mistake.'

'There's also the mortality rate to consider,' Megan pointed out.

'Which is currently one per cent,' Brianna replied, as she applied some gel to Harry's chest. 'Pretty good odds, I'd say, plus you don't make mistakes, Mr Brooke.'

The consultant shook his head.

'Nice compliment, Sister, but all surgeons can make mistakes, and, with a baby as little as this, we could be also looking at damage to the thoracic duct.'

'Yes, but thoracoscospic surgery is much less risky than a thoracotomy,' Brianna argued, 'and we're running out of time here.'

'Agreed.' He nodded as Chris placed the transducer on Harry's chest. 'OK, let's see what we've got.'

To Connor, the echocardiogram seemed to take an eternity. The pictures on the screen meant nothing to him, but they clearly meant something to Brianna, Megan, Chris and Mr Brooke, because there was a lot of muttering and a lot of pointing.

'What have you decided?' he asked when Chris removed the transducer, and both Megan and Brianna looked at Mr Brooke.

The portly consultant chewed his lip, then nodded.

'Thoracoscospic surgery. Dr Phillips, Sister Flannigan, you'll assist.'

Chris was already pushing Harry's incubator out of the ward, and as Brianna made to follow her Connor put out his hand to stay her.

'He is going to be all right, isn't he?' he said.

'I don't know,' she replied, her bottom lip trembling slightly. 'I honestly don't know. Mr Brooke's a brilliant surgeon. He has lousy people skills, but when it comes to operating, he's the best, but... Look, why don't you go back to my cottage?' she continued. 'I don't know how long the op will take—'

'I'm going nowhere,' he said, but as Brianna turned to leave he added, 'Would it be wrong of me to wish you all luck? I know on the stage it's considered very bad luck to say that, so they say break a leg, but—'

'We'll take your good wishes,' Brianna declared. 'With this one we're going to need all the luck we can get.'

And she was gone, and Connor stood in the centre of the ward, knowing he had never felt quite so alone, while the other nurses bustled about, a kind of normality returned for them.

It had been so different with their own son, he thought as he walked slowly out of the ward and down to the nurses' staffroom. He and Brianna had sat together in the consultant's room, holding one another's hands in a vice-like grip as though that might somehow keep Harry with them, while the consultant had explained very gently, and very kindly, that there was nothing he could do. The damage to Harry's heart was too severe, he'd said, and the kindest thing would be to switch off his life-support system.

The kindest thing.

Connor gritted his teeth. He'd wanted to hit the consultant when he'd said that. Kind shouldn't have meant simply allowing their child to die. Kind should have meant the medical staff doing everything they could, never giving up, not them recommending they switch off the only thing that was keeping their son alive.

With an effort, he pushed open the door of the staffroom and went in. Were there any more depressing places than empty staffrooms and waiting rooms? he wondered as he sat down and let his head fall back against the seat. Brianna had been right when she'd said being able to do something was infinitely preferable to having nothing to do but wait, but wait he would, for as long as it took.

Wearily, Brianna walked down the corridor towards the staffroom. Chris had told her Connor was there, had been there ever since they'd taken Harry to Theatre, and she was grateful, so very grateful, that he'd stayed.

Gently, she opened the door in case he'd fallen asleep, but his head snapped round immediately, and she could see the hesitation in his eyes, the desire to know, and yet the fear of knowing, too.

'He's fine,' she said. 'The op was textbook perfect, and he's back in his incubator, breathing well.'

She saw him exhale, then his eyes scanned her face.

'How are you?'

'Shattered,' she admitted. 'Relieved. Happy.'

'Then, let's go home, Bree,' he said, getting to his feet. 'You're just about out on your feet, and you said yourself he's out of the woods, so let's go home.'

To his surprise, she didn't even attempt to argue, which proved how exhausted she was, and she didn't protest either when he put some food into the microwave when they got home, then pulled out a chair for her.

'I know you probably feel too tired to eat,' he said when the lasagne was ready, 'but you really should try.'

And obediently she picked up a fork. And she did eat, though he very much doubted if she knew what she was eating, but at least she ate.

'You're not still worrying about him, are you?' he said when she finally pushed her plate away, and she shook her head.

'When I was in Theatre,' she murmured, 'all I could think was how fleeting life can be. How, in the blink of an eye, everything can suddenly change, and you never get to do the things you want, or say the things you should, and then it's too late.' She raised her eyes to his. 'Do you remember asking me whether I was sorry I had left, or sorry you'd found me?'

He gazed back at her, clearly confused, obviously wondering why she was saying this now, and then he nodded.

'I remember.'

Say it, Brianna, she told herself. *Tell him everything because you might not ever have this moment again.*

'I was sorry you'd found me because I didn't want you to find me.'

His face twisted. 'I see.'

'No, you don't, because I haven't finished yet,' she said swiftly. 'I left you because I knew I had to get away from everything. From our flat, my memories and, yes, from you because every time I looked at you I saw Harry. Harry dying in my arms, Harry's life slipping away from him, and you...' She took a breath. 'You were slipping away from me, too, and I didn't want to face the fact that not only had my son died, but my marriage was over, so it was better to hide, better not to have to face that truth.'

'But our marriage wasn't over,' he declared, bewilderment plain in his blue eyes. 'Why in the world did you think it was?'

'Connor, even before Harry was born, we might have shared the same flat, but we barely talked, hardly ever saw one another—'

'I was *working*,' he protested. 'You know what working in the city is like. If you rest on your laurels, you don't get considered for the big deals, and I had to keep on working hard if I wanted to stay in the game.'

'But even when you came home, you used to shut yourself away in your study,' she said, 'and I'd wait, and wait, and maybe, if I got lucky, you'd share a few words with me, and I'd go to bed and fall asleep alone, not knowing what you were thinking, or...' Her eyes skittered away from his. 'If you still loved me, or you'd found someone else.'

'You thought I was *cheating* on you?' he exclaimed, plainly dumbfounded. 'Bree, I have *always* loved you, and I always will.'

'Then why did you increasingly shut me out?' she cried.

'And don't tell me you didn't, because you did, you know you did. You hardly ever held me, or kissed me, and...' A faint tinge of colour crept over her cheeks, but she was going to say this come what may. 'We only ever made love if I asked you to.'

He bit his lip savagely, and, at first, she didn't think he was going to answer her, and then he met her gaze, and she saw pain and heartache in his eyes.

'I know we did, and I am sorry, so sorry, but...' He shook his head blindly. 'Oh, hell, but this is so hard for me to say because I don't want to hurt you. You've been hurt so much already.'

'Say it, Connor,' she urged. 'Whatever it is, just say it.'

'I knew...' He took an uneven breath. 'I knew how much you wanted a child—I wanted a son or a daughter, too—but as the years went by, and you didn't become pregnant, I felt...' His eyes tightened. 'You didn't want to make love to me any more—not to me. That all I'd become for you was a sperm donor. Someone you needed to go through the motions with to get yourself pregnant, not someone you wanted to be there for you, not someone you wanted to give you pleasure.'

'You thought that?' she said, horror-stricken by his revelation. 'Oh, Connor, why didn't you tell me, why didn't you say something?'

He clenched his jaw. 'It's hardly the sort of thing you can say to your wife, is it?'

'But it would have explained so much,' she declared. 'I thought you didn't want me any more, that you'd fallen out of love with me, and I was so scared to ask you outright because I thought, If he's found somebody else, I won't be able to bear it.'

'There's never been anyone but you, Bree,' he said simply. 'There never will be.'

'I'm so sorry,' she said with a sob. 'Sorry I made you feel…redundant. I never meant to. I just… I wanted a baby so badly, but my desire for one shouldn't have made you feel you meant less to me than achieving that. Can you ever forgive me?'

To her surprise, he half turned from her, his face pain-racked.

'Don't, Bree, please, don't apologise to me. It only makes me feel worse.'

'Worse?' she echoed. 'What do you have to feel so badly about? I was the one at fault, not you.'

'You've no idea how I wish to God that was true, but it isn't, it isn't,' he said, his voice ragged.

'Connor—'

'You asked me before whether I wanted Harry, and the truth is…' He lowered his head for a second, and, when he looked up again, his eyes were agonised. 'Bree, when you were pregnant, you were so ill all the time. I used to listen to the other men at work, the ones whose wives were pregnant, saying how well their wives looked, how happy and blooming, and every night…' He balled his hands into fists. 'Every night I would go home and find you with your head down the toilet, being sick again. Nothing you ate seemed to stay down, and instead of looking blooming you just seemed to get thinner and thinner.'

'It was a difficult pregnancy,' she said, gently putting her hand on his arm. 'Some just are, and I didn't care about being sick. I just wanted our son.'

'I know you did, but…' He drew in an anguished breath. 'I hated him before he was born, Bree. I knew it was wrong,' he said quickly when she drew back from him, appalled. 'I knew I shouldn't feel that way, but seeing you so ill, knowing he was the one doing it to you... I was frightened. So frightened I was going to lose you, and no baby was worth losing you for, so, yes, you were right, I didn't want him.'

'Not even when he was born?' she said, her eyes dark, her voice barely audible. 'Didn't you want him even then?'

'When he was born...' Pain twisted across his face. 'Oh, Bree, when I saw him I suddenly knew why you hadn't given a damn about being so sick all the time. He was so beautiful, wasn't he, and I thought...' His voice shook. 'I thought, This is my son. This beautiful, tiny, little person is *my son*. And I thought my heart was going to burst with joy, and then...all hell broke loose. The doctors and nurses were running everywhere, and they took him out of your arms, and there were all these tubes and wires, and I thought, Stop it, stop what you're doing, you're hurting him, and you mustn't hurt him.'

'I remember,' she said, her voice suspended.

'And when the doctors said he wouldn't live...' Connor shook his head, and something like a sob broke from him. 'All I could think was, It's my fault. God has listened to me, and decided, OK, if you don't want him, I'll take him away from you.'

'No, Connor, oh, no!' she exclaimed, instinctively reaching for him, but he lurched to his feet, evading her. 'It wasn't like that, you mustn't think like that. No words, or thoughts, of yours could have caused Harry's heart condition. It was an inherited heart defect. A horribly, cruel, inherited defect.'

'I still blame myself,' he said raggedly, screwing his eyes shut. 'Every time I go to bed at night, and close my eyes, I still see him, so small, so fragile, and looking so much like you.'

'I always thought he looked like you,' she said unsteadily, and Connor shook his head.

'You, he was all you, and when he died… Bree, half of me died with him because I'd failed him, I'd failed you.'

'You didn't—you didn't,' she cried, getting to her feet and clasping his hands tightly in hers. 'Connor—'

'All my life I've set myself goals, Bree,' he said hoarsely, 'and I've ticked them off one by one, but the one thing I knew you wanted above everything else was a child, and when they said we should turn off his life support…' A shudder ran through him. 'I wanted to fight with them, to tell them to go to hell, to tell them *I* would save our son if they couldn't, but I couldn't save him, I knew I couldn't, and to feel I had no control, no power to alter anything… that broke me, Bree.'

She stared at him blindly, so wanting to help him, to somehow find the right words to say to help him, because she had never seen him like this before, a man in torment.

'Why didn't you tell me any of this?' she exclaimed. 'Oh, Connor, you should have told me this.'

'You were going through hell, and I…' He bit his lip. 'I didn't want to burden you with how I felt.'

'But we could have shared it,' she protested. 'All I could see was that you didn't seem to care—not like I cared. You wouldn't talk about him—'

'Because I always seemed to say the wrong thing,' he said. 'If I didn't talk about Harry you got so angry, and if I did talk about him you cried, and I couldn't…I couldn't bear to see you cry when there was nothing I could do to make it any better.'

'All I ever needed was for you to let me cry, Connor,' she said, her voice breaking. 'Just for you to let me cry and for you to…to talk about Harry, so I could feel you understood, that you felt the same way I did.'

'I did, Bree. Oh, God, how I did,' he said. 'I wanted him back, too. I wanted to be able to hold him again, and keep him safe, but I couldn't keep him safe, and…' A tear trickled down his cheek, and he pulled his hands out of hers. 'I'm sorry… I have to… I have to…'

He was walking swiftly towards the staircase and she ran after him.

'Connor, wait,' she begged, trying to catch hold of his arm, but he shrugged her off, and began climbing the stairs.

'Leave me be, Bree,' he said over his shoulder, his voice choked. 'I don't…I don't want you to see me like this.'

'Like what?' she cried. 'Showing me you care, showing you feel? Connor, it's not shameful to cry, it's not a sign of weakness.'

He came to a halt at the top of the stairs, his face averted.

'It is,' he said, his voice cracked. 'I should be supporting you, not the other way round.'

'Can't…can't we support one another?' she exclaimed. 'Comfort one another?'

'Bree, enough, please,' he entreated, and she walked round him, and caught his face in her hands.

'Don't, Connor, oh, please…don't shut me out,' she said, 'not this time.'

He screwed his eyes tight shut again, but it didn't help. She could see tears trickling down his cheeks, running into his nose and mouth, and for a moment he stood rigidly still and then suddenly he reached for her, and she caught him and, when he buried his face in her neck, he broke down completely.

Broke down and cried in great shuddering, gasping sobs

that tore at her heart, making her cry, too, but she didn't try to stop his tears, knew how much she'd hated it when he'd tried to stop hers, and knew, too, how much he needed to finally cry.

'I'm sorry, so sorry,' he said eventually, his voice raw, his eyes red-rimmed. 'You shouldn't have had to witness that.'

'Yes, I should,' she insisted, cupping his face with her hand. 'You loved Harry, just as I did.'

'Would…?' She saw him swallow hard. 'Would you stay with me tonight, Bree? I just want to hold you,' he added quickly. 'Nothing else—I just want to hold you, and not… not be alone any more.'

And she nodded, and took him to her bed, and held him close, and eventually they fell asleep, wrapped in one another's arms. And some time in the middle of the night, he woke her, and reached for her, and she knew what he wanted, and this time she wanted it, too. This time she wanted to make love to him, and, as she touched him, and he touched her, they both cried again. Not the racking, heart-rending tears they'd shed in the past, but tears that were healing tears, tears for a past they could not change, that left them clinging to one another, neither of them ever wanting to let go.

CHAPTER SIX

CONNOR smiled slightly as he rolled over onto his back, and heard the small, protesting sigh that Brianna made as she followed him and nestled up again against his side.

It was going to be all right. Everything was finally going to be all right. When he and Brianna had made love last night it had been both a wonderful and also a cathartic experience for them both, and this morning he felt new, reborn, as though the world was yet again full of endless possibilities, instead of the dark and empty place it had been for the last two years.

Today is the first day of the rest of your life.

Who had said that? He couldn't remember, but today was most definitely the start of a new life for both of them and he wasn't going to screw it up this time round. This time he would get it right.

Gently, he put his arm round her, not wanting to wake her, but, when he rested his chin on the top of her head, he heard her yawn.

'What time is it?' she murmured.

He squinted at the bedside clock. 'A little after seven.'

'I have to get up,' she said regretfully. 'Auditors might be able to lie in bed for as long as they like, but nurses don't have that luxury.'

He tightened his grip on her, not wanting to let her go,

and knowing he wanted her all over again as she stretched against him.

'Pity about that,' he said, tracing the length of her spine with his finger and feeling her shiver. 'I was kind of hoping…'

'I'm sure you were,' she said, as she raised her head and looked up at him, her brown eyes dancing, before rolling over onto her back, 'but I need a shower, and some breakfast.'

He propped himself up on his elbow and gazed down at her.

'We could shower together. Very eco, that. Saving water, heating, and think how much faster we'd get clean if we washed each other.'

'Yeah, right.' She chuckled. 'And like I don't know that the state of the planet would be the very last thing on your mind if we got into the shower together. Connor, I don't have time.'

'But I can be real fast when it comes to showering,' he insisted. 'See, what I'd do first would be to put some soap on my hands, and then I'd do this…'

Slowly he smoothed his hands over her shoulders, tracing the length of her collarbone.

'Connor, I really don't—'

'And then,' he interrupted, his voice becoming a little huskier as his palms slid down onto her breasts. 'I'd wash you here. Very carefully, of course,' he continued, hearing her suck in her breath sharply as he began sliding his hands up and down and over each breast, circling and circling them until the nipples peaked, 'because I know how very sensitive your breasts are.'

'Connor, I…I think you should stop now,' she said faintly, and he shook his head at her.

'You see, that's the beauty of us showering together.

You wouldn't have to think,' he murmured. 'And after I'd washed your breasts—because I'm a really thorough sort of a man—I'd cover you with plenty of soap down here,' he continued, sliding his palm down her stomach, slowly, oh, so very slowly, until he cupped her. 'And then,' he added, as he began to stroke and stroke her, easing her thighs further and further apart, 'I'd do this, though of course you'll just have to try to imagine the soap. How very wet it would be, how very warm, how…liquid.'

'I'm…I'm trying not to.' She gasped, biting her lip when his finger slipped inside her and he continued to stroke her, and she felt the heat beginning to build. 'Connor…please… *please stop*!'

'Hey, but it sure does take a lot of effort to get you really clean, doesn't it?' He chuckled as he increased the pressure of his fingers, and she began to writhe beneath him. 'Maybe I'd also need to do this…'

And he bent down and replaced his fingers with his tongue. Gently at first, licking into her so gently, and then his tongue began to probe further, and further inside her, and she put her hands on his head, and arched up against him, as she felt the throbbing begin, the pulsing begin.

'Connor, oh…oh, my…oh, my *God*!'

And suddenly she jerked and convulsed, shaking and trembling, her heartbeat drumming in her ears as the heat went everywhere.

'Good?' he whispered in her ear, and she nodded breathlessly.

'Very good, amazingly good, stupendously good.'

'And there was you thinking it would take me for ever to get you clean if we shared a shower,' he said with a wicked grin.

She stared back at him for a heartbeat, then, before

he knew what she was doing, she had pinned him onto his back.

'My turn now,' she said, her eyes gleaming. 'My turn to play torturer.'

'Really?' he said huskily, exhaling sharply when she began tracing her fingers down his chest.

'Oh, absolutely.' She nodded as she bent her head, and licked one of his nipples, and then the other, and heard him gasp. 'It's only fair, after all. In fact…' she continued, as she slid her hand down his stomach, and he tensed with anticipation. 'In fact…'

'In fact, what?' he whispered as she suddenly sat up.

'Sorry,' she said, her eyes dancing with devilment. 'I'm afraid this is going to have to be put on hold, because I've just noticed the time, and if I don't hurry up and have a proper shower I'm going to be late.'

'*Brianna!*'

'Yes?' she said, her lips curving, as she slipped out of bed and headed for the door.

'I take back what I said about you being an angel,' he protested. 'You're a witch!'

'Probably.' She grinned.

And he laughed. Witch or angel, he honestly didn't care. She was his again, and that was all that mattered.

Except it wasn't, he realised when he grabbed a quick shower after she'd had hers, and hurried down to the kitchen. Normally, the percolator would be on, and the table would be laid, but this morning none of those things had been done. She was standing by the kitchen window instead, gazing out, and, when she heard him come in, the smile that greeted him was tentative in the extreme. Something had clearly happened between the shower and the kitchen, and that something was making her think, and he didn't want her to think, to have any doubts.

'Fruit juice and cereal for breakfast as usual?' he said brightly.

'Fine,' she replied, retrieving two bowls from the cupboard and putting them on the table.

'Coffee or tea? It will have to be instant if you want coffee,' he added. 'It will take too long if we wait for the percolator.'

'Instant coffee,' she murmured. 'And plenty of it. I find I need lots of caffeine in the morning nowadays.'

'Me, too, or I'm hell to live with.' He grinned. 'Or hellier than I would be.' He frowned. 'Is there such a word as hellier?'

'I expect so,' she said. 'Or if there isn't, there should be.'

Something was most definitely wrong, he thought as he switched on the kettle, then took some orange juice out of the fridge and filled two glasses. Everything had been perfect, just perfect, and now she looked nervous, unsure, as though there was something she wanted to say but wasn't quite sure how to phrase it.

The job, he suddenly realised. It would be that damn job Brooke had offered her. He'd overheard the consultant asking her about it, and she clearly wanted to take it, but she'd realised he wouldn't want to move here, and she was right. Penhally and St Piran were probably very nice for holidaymakers who weren't big on excitement, but what sort of work would he get here? Hell, he'd be reduced to making spreadsheets, and advising the local butcher and baker on their tax returns. Well, it wasn't a problem. There must be dozens of nurse unit managers' jobs in London, and he'd help her scour the nursing magazines for them, and then she could have what she wanted, and he could, too.

'Something wrong?' he said, deliberately giving her an opening, but she shook her head.

'No, no problem,' she replied with a smile he didn't buy for a second.

OK, he thought. Give her time, give her space, don't crowd her, she'll mention the job when she's ready.

'Cream or milk on your cereal?' he asked. 'Actually, scrub the cream,' he added with a frown as he noticed the use-by date. 'You know, you really will have to go shopping.'

'I'll do it before I come home tonight,' she murmured, then he saw her take a deep breath.

Here it comes, he thought. Here comes the 'Mr Brooke has offered me the job I've always wanted, and I don't know what to do about it', so say the right thing this time, Connor, or you're toast.

'I was just thinking about Harry,' she said, taking him completely by surprise. 'The baby I found, not our son,' she added quickly, 'and I was wondering…if his mother doesn't ever come forward…how would you feel…?' She rearranged the salt and pepper cruet on the kitchen table. 'How would you feel about us adopting him?'

Oh, *hell*. He'd known she was getting far too close to this child, much too involved, but he'd never imagined anything like this, hadn't for one second seen this coming.

'Bree—'

'If his mother never claims him,' she said quickly, 'he'll be sent to a foster-home, and though I'm sure they're wonderful places—nothing like the orphanages of the past— they're not like a real home, are they? Connor, we could give him a home, be his parents,' she continued, eagerness plain in her eyes. 'I know he wouldn't be ours in the sense of us being his real mother and father, but we could give him so much.'

'I understand that,' he began carefully, 'but, sweetheart, we're both still young, and though I know it took us a long time to conceive Harry, that doesn't mean we couldn't try for a child of our own again.'

'*No!*' she said vehemently. 'The heart defect Harry was born with, it's an inherited condition, so it could happen again, and to wait for nine months, feeling him—or her—growing inside me—always wondering, always fearing, never knowing... I can't do that, I *can't*.'

'But—'

'The little Harry in the hospital...he *needs* me, Connor, and we have so much love we could give him.'

Slowly he walked over to her, and put his hands on her shoulders, forcing her to look up at him.

'I know we do, but, Brianna, are you sure you want this child for the right reasons?'

She shook her head impatiently.

'What better reasons could there be than me wanting to give him a home, parents, love?'

'You could do that for our own child—'

'I've explained to you why I won't risk that,' she declared. 'Weren't you listening—didn't you hear what I said?'

He *had* heard, he thought. Much more than she probably wanted him to hear.

'Bree, what you're saying is, you want a baby, but you want a no-risk baby,' he said gently. 'You want the baby in the hospital because, though he has health problems, they're health problems that can be cured, and you'll be able to take him home. You're scared, Bree,' he continued as she tried to interrupt. 'You're scared of the unknown, of what might happen if we try for another child—and I can understand that, I feel the same way—but that isn't the right reason to adopt this child.'

'I want him because I can give him what he doesn't

have,' she protested, shrugging herself free from his hands. 'A mother, a father, a home. Why is that so very wrong?'

'It isn't, if it was the whole truth, but it isn't, you know it isn't. Bree, after Harry died, I read up on heart defects. They can be detected now by antenatal screening at eighteen weeks—'

'And then what?' she interrupted. 'If the scan discovered there was something wrong, do you honestly think I would opt for an abortion? I'd have to carry on with the pregnancy, knowing…' She took a ragged breath. 'Knowing that the baby inside me was going to die, just like Harry died, and I don't think I'd be able to survive that.'

He wanted to argue with her. He wanted to tell her that perhaps it wouldn't happen, that maybe the odds would fall on their side this time, but she looked so stricken, and the Harry in the hospital did need a home. Would it be so very wrong to agree to what she wanted even though he knew, instinctively, that it was for all the wrong reasons?

'Connor?'

She was waiting anxiously for his reply, and he sighed.

'Even if I agree to this, it's only been four days since you found him. His mother could still come forward.'

'A normal mother wouldn't have left her child for four hours, far less four days,' she argued back. 'And much as I don't want to agree with Rita, maybe she's right, maybe Harry's mother doesn't want him, which gives us all the more reason to give him a home, where he'd be wanted.'

'And then there's the actual adoption process,' he continued. 'There are couples who have been on waiting lists for years, and just because he's in your ward doesn't mean you can jump the queue.'

'I know that—I understand that,' she insisted, 'but we could try. Will you at least agree that we could try?'

Her eyes were large, pleading, and he wished he could

think of something to say that would dissuade her. He didn't want her to be hurt again, he so desperately didn't want her to be hurt, but he knew how high the odds were against any adoption agency fast-tracking them to the top of their list, and those odds were too high.

'Connor. Please,' she continued softly, and he sighed, then nodded reluctantly.

'If the baby's mother doesn't come forward, we'll see if adopting him is possible,' he said, and saw her face light up with a smile that tore at his heart.

'Thank you,' she said fervently. 'You won't regret it, I know you won't.'

He hoped to heaven he wouldn't, as he watched her hurry across the kitchen to take the cereal packet out of the cupboard, her step light, her lips still curved into a happy smile. He could only hope to heaven that everything would turn out all right.

'You're looking very happy this morning, Sister,' Naomi Renwick declared.

'I feel happy.' Brianna smiled. 'It's a lovely spring morning, all of the babies had an excellent night, including your daughter, so what more could I wish for?'

'My wish would be to take my daughter home,' Naomi replied. 'I know, I know,' she continued as Brianna opened her mouth to interrupt, 'she's doing really well, and in a couple of weeks you're going to try feeding her orally, but...'

'You want to take her home now,' Brianna finished for her, and when Mrs Renwick nodded, she put her arm round her. 'It *will* happen, honestly it will. Good grief, even Mr Brooke is happy with her, and you won't often hear me putting the words "Mr Brooke" and "happy" in the same sentence.'

Naomi chuckled. 'That's what Mrs Corezzi said yesterday. She's very nice, isn't she?'

'She's one of the best.'

'And so are you, Sister Flannigan,' Mrs Renwick declared, and, before Brianna realised what she was about to do, Naomi had leant forward and kissed her cheek. 'In fact, if there was an award for nurse of the year, you'd get my vote.'

'And now you've got Sister Flannigan completely speechless.' Megan laughed as she joined them. 'And that takes some doing, I'm telling you.'

Naomi laughed, and Brianna laughed, too, but her cheeks were burning when she accompanied Megan across the ward.

'That was very nice of her to say,' she murmured. 'Not that I am—or could be—nurse of the year, but—'

'Brianna, you're damn good at your job so no more of this false modesty,' Megan insisted. 'And talking about jobs,' she continued, lowering her voice, 'a little bird in the shape of our portly consultant tells me you're going to be our new nurse unit manager?'

'I haven't accepted the job yet, Megan,' Brianna replied quickly. 'I'd like to, but it's…complicated.'

'One of the complications wouldn't happen to be a certain man who has a very definite spring in his step this morning, would it?' Megan said, her eyes twinkling, and Brianna smiled.

'Connor, and I… We had a long talk last night—'

'I'd say you did a lot more than talk, judging by how you both look today,' Megan said shrewdly, and, when Brianna crimsoned, she chuckled. 'Knew it. So, what's the problem?'

'I do love him, Megan,' Brianna replied. 'I loved him when I married him, and the love's still there. A bit bruised, a little bit battered, perhaps, but it's still there, and this time I think we could make our marriage work, make it a partnership of equals, but…'

'Not here in St Piran.'

It was a statement, not a question, and Brianna bit her lip.

'What would he do here, Megan? His whole career is centred around London. Coming to hospitals like St Piran's… It's a one-off commission, not a permanent job.'

'He could change his life, his career,' the paediatric specialist registrar pointed out. 'People downsize all the time, throw up their high-powered jobs and move to the country to keep chickens or pigs.'

Brianna let out a giggle. 'Can you honestly see Connor keeping chickens or pigs?'

'Well, no,' Megan conceded, 'but I'm sure there's lots of other things he could do if he put his mind to it.'

'How can I ask him to do that?' Brianna protested. 'He's happy where he is.'

'So, in this partnership of equals,' Megan said slowly, 'you're going to be the one who has to give up everything, and return to London?'

Return to London. Just the thought made Brianna's heart plummet. Return to their modern flat, the anonymous streets, to feeling as though her life was on hold again.

Except it wouldn't be like that, she thought as her eyes drifted past Megan to little Harry's incubator. If everything went well, she would have Harry, she would have a child, and that would make everything different. It would.

'It will work this time,' she said firmly. 'I'll make it work.'

'If you say so,' Megan replied. 'Just…'

'Just what?' Brianna asked, seeing her friend's face grow suddenly serious.

'Don't tell Mr Brooke you don't want the job, at least not yet. Connor will be here for another four or five weeks, so take that time to make sure you've both resolved everything between you.'

'I will.' Brianna smiled. 'But you worry too much.'

'Probably,' Megan admitted, 'but just be careful, OK?'

There was nothing to be careful about, Brianna thought as she walked over to little Harry's incubator, and smiled down at him. Everything was going to be fine. She just knew it, could feel it. Harry had come through the operation with flying colours, and already she could see he was brighter, more alert, and Connor had just been trying to protect her when he'd talked about the difficulties of adoption. The authorities were bound to see they were an ideal couple. They were both still young, were comfortably off, had been married for ten years, and she'd give up work, be a stay-at-home mum, so Harry would never have to come home from school to an empty house. And there were so many parks in London, it would almost be like being in the country. And her parents would love him, she knew they would, and—

'Brianna.'

'Are you trying to give me a seizure?' she protested, whirling round to see Connor standing behind her. 'Please don't creep up on me like that, not when I'm miles away.'

'I saw that.'

Something was wrong, she realised. His face was carefully blank, his eyes even more so, and, when she smiled encouragingly up at him, he didn't smile back.

'Hey, whatever it is can't be that bad,' she declared, and saw him flinch.

'There's someone outside you need to see,' he said.

Even his voice sounded strange, as though it was being forced out of him.

'Look, if it's Vermin again,' she began, 'you can tell him—'

'It's not Vermin. It's…' He shook his head. 'I think you should come.'

'Connor, you know I don't like surprises,' she protested. 'Can't you just tell me who it is?'

He didn't answer. He simply walked over to the ward door and opened it, and she sighed.

'This is crazy,' she grumbled. 'I'm really busy right now, so I'm warning you, whoever it is had better want me for a very good reason.'

He still didn't say anything and, when she first went out into the corridor, she was none the wiser. Rita was standing there with a face like stone. No big surprise there, she thought wryly. Jess was beaming broadly at her, but, then, Jess always had a sunny expression, and to Jess's left stood a large, jolly-looking woman in her early forties whom Brianna didn't recognise at all.

Blankly, Brianna glanced back at Connor. Was this a deputation of some sort, a fundraising committee? Puzzled, she shifted her gaze back to the three women, and then she saw her. Standing awkwardly behind the jolly-looking woman, looking, oh, so shy and nervous, was a young girl. A young girl who couldn't have been any more than sixteen. A young girl with corn-coloured hair and large grey eyes, and Brianna dug her fingernails into the palms of her hands until they hurt.

'My name's Marina Hallet,' the jolly-looking lady declared, 'and this is my daughter, Nicola. She's the one who left the baby in the car park. She's Colin's mother.'

'Colin?' Brianna repeated, through lips grown suddenly dry.

'That's his name,' the teenager said softly. 'What I called him—after his father.'

'And we know one another, don't we, *Marcia*?' Jess smiled, and Nicola Hallet looked shamefaced.

'I'm sorry about lying to you that day in the hospital, Miss Carmichael—'

'Her name is Mrs Corezzi now, Nicola,' Rita declared irritably. 'Can't you at least try to get something right for once in your life?'

Nicola looked crushed, and Jess leant towards the girl, a gentle smile on her face.

'Nicola, please call me Jess. All my friends do,' she added, and Brianna heard Rita give a very deliberate sniff.

A sniff that everyone completely ignored.

'I should have told you my real name,' the teenager continued awkwardly. 'I should have said my name was Nicola Hallet, but…'

So Jess had been right, Brianna thought dully. The initial necklace that the girl she'd seen wearing *had* been either an N or an M. It was an N.

'Look, why don't we all go into the staffroom?' Jess suggested. 'It will be a lot more comfortable than standing out here in the corridor.'

'I'd really like to see my grandson,' Mrs Hallet said quickly, and Brianna saw Rita wince.

'And you will,' Jess declared, 'but I'm sure Sister Flannigan must have lots of questions for you.'

'Yes, of course,' Brianna said automatically.

But she didn't want to ask any questions, she didn't want to know anything at all about the teenager, or her family.

She just wanted them to go away, and give her back her dream.

'Aren't you coming in with us?' she said as the four women trooped into the staffroom, and Connor didn't move at all.

'I can't,' he said softly, 'you know I can't. Patient confidentiality, remember?'

He was right, she knew he was, but she suddenly felt so very alone, and he must have sensed it because he clasped her hands tightly.

'I'll be right out here,' he said. 'I won't go anywhere. I'll stay right out here, and wait for you in the corridor.'

Which was where she wanted to be, she thought as she stiffened her back and walked into the staffroom in time to hear Mrs Hallet tell Jess her family owned a fruit-growing farm near Penhally.

What difference did it make what kind of farm the Hallets owned? It wasn't important, it didn't matter; and before she could stop herself she rounded on Nicola.

'Why did you leave your son—abandon him?' she demanded.

Her words were harsh, she knew they were as she saw the teenager flush and heard Jess suck in her breath, but she didn't care. She wanted answers. Little Harry deserved them.

'The silly girl was frightened to tell us she was expecting a baby,' Mrs Hallet declared before her daughter could answer. 'We didn't even know she was going out with Colin Maddern from the garage, far less that she was pregnant. If only she'd told us. When I think of all those months when she must have been so frightened...' Mrs Hallet shook her head. 'I don't know how she coped, I really don't.'

'And you didn't realise—didn't notice your own daughter was pregnant?' Brianna exclaimed, not pretending to hide her disbelief even though Jess was staring at her with clear dismay.

'I know I should have done,' Mrs Hallet admitted, 'but what with the work on the farm, and my family of seven… You see, there's always something happening, some crisis, and Nicola… She's always been the quiet one, the one with her head stuck in a book, and…' She smiled apologetically at her daughter. 'She's always been a little on the plump side so I didn't notice any change in her.'

'I wore lots of baggy clothes,' Nicola murmured, 'and like Mum said, there's always so much going on in our house no one noticed I was getting bigger.'

And she looked so young, so very young, Brianna thought, feeling a hard lump in her throat that no amount of swallowing seemed to move. 'How old are you, Nicola?' she asked.

'Sixteen. Sixteen years and four months to be exact,' the girl added hurriedly.

As though those four months made any damn difference, Brianna thought. Nicola was still a mother, while she… She was never going to be one.

'Why did you leave him in the car park?' she exclaimed. 'Nicola, he could have *died* there!'

The teenager's eyes filled with tears.

'I was bringing him to the hospital because I knew there was something wrong with him,' she replied. 'When I tried to feed him he didn't seem to know what to do, and his breathing wasn't right, but the first person I saw was Grandma, and I knew she'd have a go at Mum, say it was all her fault that I'd got pregnant at fifteen. But it wasn't Mum's fault. Colin and I… We never intended to make love—we were going to wait—but…'

'These things just happen,' Jess said, shooting Brianna

a puzzled glance, and Nicola nodded and wiped her nose with the back of her hand.

'Colin…he said we'd get married if I found out I was pregnant, and I know we would have, because he loved me, and I loved him, but then…' The tears in the teenager's eyes began to spill over. 'He was killed, and he never knew… He never knew he had a son.'

And I think I knew him, Brianna thought dully as Jess leant forward and pressed a handkerchief into the teenager's hand, and she remembered the day she'd had trouble with her car months ago, and she'd stopped at the garage in St Piran, and the young mechanic there had mended it for her.

'Your Colin… He had black hair, and a lovely smile, didn't he?' she said, trying to keep her voice even but knowing she was failing miserably.

'You knew him?' Nicola said eagerly.

'I met him once,' Brianna replied. 'And I remember his smile.'

And how I'd thought that my Harry might have looked just like the young mechanic, if he'd lived and grown up.

'Why didn't you come back later, after your grandmother had gone?' Jess asked, and Nicola bit her lip.

'I meant to—I intended to,' she said, 'but Colin's breathing seemed to be getting worse, and then I saw you. I remembered how kind you were before, and I know I should have told you I was pregnant, but I was scared you'd tell Grandma, and she'd make me get an abortion, and I didn't want to have an abortion.'

'No one would have made you have an abortion,' Nicola's mother declared, shooting Rita a look that defied her to argue. 'You loved this boy, and he loved you, and your father and I would have helped.'

'But why didn't you just give the baby to Jess?' Brianna

protested. 'Why leave it where it might not be found for hours?'

'I guess I panicked,' Nicola replied. 'I recognised the car—I'd seen Mrs Corezzi—Jess—out in it, and I thought it was hers, that she was leaving the hospital so she'd be sure to find my son. I waited,' she added quickly. 'I didn't just go. I waited until you picked him up, so I knew he was safe.'

'And the first we knew of any of this was when she broke down in tears over that photograph in the paper,' Mrs Hallet said. 'That was when the whole story came out.'

'Can I see him?' Nicola asked. 'Can I see my son?'

'I'd like to see him, too,' Mrs Hallet declared, 'and I'm sure his great-grandmother would just love to see the newest addition to our family, wouldn't you, Rita?'

The ward clerk looked as though she would have preferred to have been force-fed poison, but she managed a tight-lipped nod.

'Of course you can see him,' Jess declared, 'but I have to warn you that you might find the sight of him a bit upsetting. He's been very ill, you see,' she added as Nicola looked from her to Brianna in panic. 'He had to have an operation yesterday, and though he's come through that well, he has a lot of tubes and wires attached to him to help him breathe.'

'You mean, he might...he could...die?' Nicola said, fresh tears welling in her eyes.

'No, he won't die,' Brianna said with difficulty. 'The tubes and wires are only temporary, a precaution.'

'And the important thing to remember is, under all the tubes and wires, he's still your son,' Jess said gently. 'He's still your baby.'

Your baby.

Not my baby, Brianna thought as Jess led the way out

of the staffroom, and she followed slowly. He was Nicola Hallet's baby, and she was happy about that—of course she was—because a baby should always be with its mother. It was the natural order of things, it was what was right.

'Are you OK?' Connor said the moment he saw her, his eyes worried, his face drawn.

'Of course I am,' she replied. 'Why wouldn't I be?'

'Brianna—'

She swept past him into the ward, her head held high, but, as she stood to one side of the incubator, and saw Mrs Hallet beam with clear pleasure at her grandson, and Nicola gaze down at him with such love in her eyes, she felt her heart twist inside her. Connor's eyes were fixed on her, she knew they were, but she couldn't meet his gaze, knew she would see sympathy there, and she didn't want to see sympathy, but when the baby stretched up one of his tiny hands towards his mother's face, she couldn't bear it. She just couldn't bear to be there, witnessing this reunion, and quietly she slipped out of the ward, needing to get away, to go anywhere, just so long as it was away.

'Brianna, wait!'

Connor had come after her, and she didn't want to see him, or hear his unease.

'You'll have to excuse me,' she said, turning her back on him, fast. 'I have things to do, paperwork—forms—to fill in...'

Quickly, she began to walk away from him, but he caught her by the elbow and steered her deliberately into the nurse unit manager's office.

'Brianna, sweetheart, you don't have to be brave,' he said, and she could see the anxiety in his eyes for her. 'I know how hard this must be for you.'

'It's not hard at all,' she said brightly. 'I'm fine, perfectly fine. It's great that Harry—Colin's—mother has come forward for him. Absolutely great.'

'She seems a very sweet girl,' he said carefully.

'And I'm sure she'll look after him perfectly well even though she's just sixteen,' she declared, picking up a piece of paper from his desk, then putting it down again, 'and it's not little Harry...' She bit her lip. '*Colin*'s fault he'll have the great-grandmother from hell.'

'I think we can be sure Nicola's mother will tell Rita to back off in no uncertain terms.'

She nodded. 'Yes, of course she will, but...' She picked up the sheet of paper again. 'Connor, how can we be sure this girl is his mother? I mean, what proof do we have?'

'Jess recognised her as the girl who came in that day.'

'But that doesn't prove anything, does it?' she argued back. 'Just because she's the girl Jess saw doesn't mean—'

'Brianna, she's his mother, you know she is,' he interrupted gently, 'and, though she's very young, I think she has a sensible head on her shoulders, and her mother and father will help her, make sure she does right by the little boy.'

'Yes, of course they will,' she murmured. 'And Mrs Hallet looked nice. Don't you think she looked nice?' she added, all too aware she was talking too much, but if she stopped...if she stopped... 'And the Hallets have a farm, so Colin will have all those wonderful places to play in, just as I did when I was a child, and I'll see him occasionally, won't I—around and about in Penhally. Not often, of course, but I might see him sometimes—'

'Oh, Bree—'

'And it won't matter that he won't remember me,' she said on a sob, 'because that's as it should be. He'll have his real mother, and lots of aunts and uncles, and probably grandparents—'

'Bree, I'm so sorry,' Connor said, his heart breaking for her, 'so very, very sorry. I know you wanted him, had grown to care for him.'

'But I'm not his mother, am I?' she said, as tears began to roll down her cheeks. 'And a baby...a baby should always be with his mother. Except he did look so much...so very much like Harry, and now...and now...'

And Connor reached for her, and she stepped into his arms, and he held her tight, and didn't tell her not to cry, knew better now, and thanked God that the tears she wept into his shoulder weren't like the tears she'd shed for their own Harry. That these were tears of regret, tears for what could never be, what he suspected she'd always known, deep down, could never be, and yet had still hoped.

'I'm OK now,' she hiccupped when her tears were finally spent.

'You're sure?' he said anxiously, drying her face with his fingertips, scanning her eyes with concern.

'Yes,' she said, beginning to nod, then shook her head. 'No, I'm not, but I will be.'

'Honestly?' he said, and she manufactured a smile.

'Honestly.'

'I think we should go home,' he said, and she closed her eyes.

'I can't—I have another two hours of my shift to work.'

'I'll square it with Megan—she'll understand.'

Going home sounded good. Getting away from the unit for even a little while seemed even better.

'OK. All right,' she said.

Connor made for the door, then stopped. 'You will still be here when I get back, won't you?'

'I'm not going anywhere,' she said with a trembling smile. 'Not without you.'

And he smiled. A wide, comforting smile that warmed her bruised and battered heart.

'Give me two minutes,' he said. 'I won't be any longer.'

She hoped he wouldn't be. She didn't want Rita to suddenly appear. The ward clerk might have been a thorn in her side ever since she'd come to St Piran, but she could not find it in her to gloat over Rita's clear discomfiture, though she knew many of the hospital staff undoubtedly would. All she wanted was to go home, to have some peace and quiet to come to terms with Nicola's appearance, but peace turned out to be in short supply when Connor returned and they walked together down the stairs towards the exit.

The nearer they got to the ground floor, the more Brianna became aware of the sound of angry voices. Voices that seemed to be raised in unison, in something that sounded almost like a chant, and when she and Connor reached the entrance hall to the hospital she stopped dead.

The forecourt in front of the hospital was a seething mass of people. People of all ages and sexes who were carrying placards with the letters 'SOB' painted on them.

'What in the world…?' she began, as Connor let out a muttered oath. 'It looks like some kind of demonstration, but what on earth are people demonstrating about, and what does SOB mean?'

'Brianna, come back into the hospital,' Connor said quickly. 'I need to talk to you. My report…it's nowhere near completed yet. I still have lots of departments to assess, and what I've written is simply an initial recommendation, based on my first impressions, not a definitive view.'

'But, how would anyone know what you'd written?' she said in confusion. 'Not even the secretaries in Admin are good enough to read your mind.'

'My notes were on that memory card—the one I lost

or…' Connor came to a halt and frowned. Kennie Vernon was amongst the demonstrators, notebook in hand, and he smiled when he saw Connor, a smile that was triumphant, and Connor swore, long and low, and fluently. 'He must have taken it. It was in the staffroom with my laptop yesterday when he came in to see Brooke. That low-life reporter must have taken it.'

'But what did your notes say?' Brianna demanded, still confused. 'What do all these banners mean?'

'Bree, I'm sorry, those notes were private, no one was supposed to see them yet, and they're only my thoughts, suggestions…'

His voice trailed away into silence, and as she stared at him blankly the penny dropped, and her blankness gave way to anger. A seething, furious anger.

'SOB,' she said. 'It stands for Save Our Babies, doesn't it? You've recommended to the board that they shut down the neonatal intensive care unit.'

'Brianna, it's not definite yet—'

'But you've recommended it,' she repeated. 'You looked at our unit, and you had the…the callousness…the insensitivity…to actually say it wasn't doing a good job!'

'It's not a question of whether it's doing a good job or not,' he said defensively. 'The work that's done in the unit is second to none—I would never disagree with that—but I have to go by the statistics—figures. The unit in Plymouth can cater for double the amount of babies—'

'Cater?' she exclaimed. '*Cater?* Connor, we're not some sort of fast-food restaurant, we're a specialist nursing centre!'

'Brianna—'

'And if you shut us down it's not simply a case of saying, well, all the babies can go to Plymouth. What about the winter, when the roads are icy, or blocked with snow? What about the height of summer when the road is packed with slow-moving caravans and sightseeing tourists? That thirty-mile journey could take an hour—more!'

'If it's a real emergency you have a helicopter service—'

'Which could be out on another call when we need it, or grounded by ice or gale-force winds.'

'Brianna—'

'It's always been figures and numbers, for you, hasn't it?' she said furiously. 'Forget about what people—real people—want or need. Connor, can't you see that not everything can be neatly tied up in a balance sheet?'

'But it makes good medical as well as economic sense,' he protested. 'Can't you at least see that?'

It also meant something else, she realised. Something that was altogether much, much closer to home.

'There'll also be no nurse unit manager's job for me either, will there, if you shut us down?' she said icily. 'Is that why you're doing this, because you think if I don't have a job I'll come back to you?'

'Of course that isn't what I thought!' he exclaimed, anger darkening his face. 'Brianna, listen to me—'

'And to think I told Rita you'd never let personal bias influence your work,' she continued, fury plain in her voice. 'You took one look at Penhally, and St Piran, and thought dead-end places. You thought no way would I ever want to live here, so let's make sure Brianna can't either, and then she'll meekly come back with me to London.'

'That never occurred to me for a second,' he flared.

'Just like it didn't occur to you last night to tell me what you were planning to do with my unit,' she retorted. 'You let me think you'd changed, Connor. You made me think you cared—'

'I did—I do—'

'Then how can you even *think* of shutting down an

NICU?' she cried. 'It's where Harry spent his few hours of life, where all these babies I look after get a chance to live. OK, so we couldn't save Harry, but just because we couldn't it doesn't mean you should deny all these other babies that chance.'

'Brianna—'

'I want you out of my house when I get home tonight,' she said, her voice shaking with anger. 'I want you, and your posh designer suits, and your expensive shirts and shoes, and your damn, all-singing-all-dancing phone out of my house by the time I get home, and if they're not I'll dump the whole lot in my garden.'

'Can't we at least sit down and talk about this like sensible human beings?' he exclaimed. 'If you would just let me explain—'

'There's no need to,' she interrupted, 'because I already know what you are. You're a bastard, Connor. A complete and utter bastard.'

And she walked away from him, pushing her way through the demonstrators who had now spilled out of the forecourt and into the hospital foyer, only to discover her way barred by Kennie Vernon. Normally she would have walked straight past him, but this time she didn't. This time she stopped and, sensing a scoop, he pulled out his pen.

'Do you have a comment for me, Sister Flannigan, for our readers?'

Brianna glanced over her shoulder. Someone in the crowd had clearly recognised Connor because he had been surrounded by demonstrators, and was being heckled mercilessly.

'Yes, I have a comment to make,' she said, completely uncaring of what Admin might say when they saw her words on the front page of tomorrow's paper. 'I think even the idea of shutting down our NICU is an appalling one.

We have an excellent unit here. A unit that serves the needs of the local community, and I am fully behind this protest, and I wish the organisers well.'

And she made for the stairs, looking over her shoulder only once, when a great cheer went up. Someone had thrown an egg at Connor. An egg which had landed smack-bang on the front of his smart city suit. And her one thought as she headed back to the unit was she wished she'd had an egg because she would have thrown it, too.

CHAPTER SEVEN

'WE NEVER thought this day would come, Sister Flannigan.' Naomi Renwick beamed. 'To be finally taking Amy home...'

'And I've taken a photograph of her—for your graduation board,' Naomi's husband declared. 'So other mothers and fathers can see there truly can be light at the end of the tunnel.'

'It's a lovely picture,' Brianna said as she took the photograph Mr Renwick was holding out to her. 'Thank you very much.'

'We were hoping we might see Mr Monahan before we go,' Naomi said. 'He's been so supportive over this last month, always stopping by for a chat whenever my husband and I have visited Amy in the evening.'

'He has—he did?' Brianna said faintly. 'I...I didn't know that.'

'He's a nice bloke,' Mr Renwick observed, 'and he seemed quite taken with our Amy. As I said to him, you're clearly getting broody, Connor, so maybe you and Sister Flannigan should be thinking about having kids of your own soon.'

'And...and what did he say to that?' Brianna asked through a throat so tight it hurt.

'He just smiled,' Naomi replied. 'Look, I know he got

a lot of very bad press after his notes were published in
the *Gazette*,' Amy's mother continued quickly as Brianna
took a shaky breath, 'but we can honestly say your husband
never had anything but praise for the unit when he was
talking to us.'

Connor hadn't simply got bad press, Brianna remembered. The board had been forced to issue a statement
declaring no decision had been made about any cuts to
services, but nobody in the hospital had believed that.
Everyone simply thought that if NICU couldn't be closed
because of the public outcry, it only meant some other
department would be shut down instead.

'Connor did say he would definitely see us and Amy
before we left,' Mr Renwick said, 'and I told him we'd be
collecting her at four o'clock, so maybe we could give him
another few minutes?'

The couple didn't have to. The ward door had opened,
and Connor appeared.

'You made it, Connor.' Mr Renwick beamed. 'We
thought you might have forgotten, or been too busy.'

'I'd never be too busy for such a momentous occasion,
and I most certainly wouldn't forget,' he replied.

And his gaze was fixed firmly on the Renwicks, Brianna
noticed, but what had she expected? He'd tried to talk to her
over the past five weeks, had left innumerable messages on
her answering-machine, had once even come to her cottage,
and she'd refused to open the door. She'd been so angry, so
very angry. A part of her still was, and yet, as she gazed
up at him, all she could think was this was his last day in
the hospital. Tomorrow he would leave St Piran, and, when
he left, their marriage would be finally, and irrevocably,
be over.

'Sister Flannigan, can we take a photograph of you
and Connor together?' Mr Renwick asked. 'It would be

something to show Amy when she grows up. A picture of the husband-and-wife team who helped her parents so much.'

'I really think it should just be a photograph of Sister Flannigan,' Connor said quickly, but Naomi shook her head.

'I want the two of you together,' she said.

Which was fine in theory, Brianna thought, but not so fine in practice. Naomi clearly wanted a 'happy couple' photograph, and neither of them fitted that bill any more.

'Connor, can't you at least put your arm around her?' Naomi protested. 'You're standing there looking like she's a complete stranger, and Sister Flannigan, a smile would be nice. I don't want Amy looking at this photograph in years to come and saying, "Yikes, they look grim", and I'm sure you don't want a picture of yourselves looking like a pair of stuffed dummies.'

And Connor dutifully put his arm around her, and Brianna forced herself to smile, and tried very hard not to cry.

All the dreams she'd had ten years ago on their wedding day. All the plans she'd made, the hopes she'd had, and now the last photograph of them together would be of her wearing a manufactured smile, and him not even attempting to smile at all.

Tell him you don't want him to go, her heart whispered. Tell him you want him to stay here, to try to make your marriage work.

But she couldn't. Connor and Cornwall were as compatible as cheese and gravy, and she couldn't go back to London with him. She knew she would just shrivel up and die in the city so, when the Renwicks carried their daughter out of the ward, she kept her gaze firmly fixed on them, and only let out the breath she knew she'd been holding when she heard the ward door shut.

'Colin's had three full bottles today,' Nicola Hallet said proudly as Brianna slowly walked past her. 'Dr Phillips said if he keeps on progressing like this she'll be recommending he's moved out of NICU and into Special Care, and after that...' Nicola beamed. 'Home. I'll finally be able to take him home.'

'That's terrific news, Nicola,' Brianna said, meaning it.

Young though the teenager might be, Nicola was proving to be an excellent, and completely devoted, mother, coming in every day to feed and bathe her son, and to talk and play with him.

'Your husband said he wants me to keep in touch with him, to let him know how Colin is, when he goes back to London,' Nicola continued, gazing fondly down at her son. 'Wasn't that kind of him?'

'Very kind,' Brianna said unevenly. 'When...when did he say all this?'

'On one of his visits to the unit,' Nicola replied. 'He's been coming here a lot in the evening.'

Who else had Connor been talking to? Brianna wondered, taking a shaky breath. First the Renwicks, and now Nicola, but *why*? What had drawn him back here, apparently night after night?

'Nicola—'

'How's my favourite boy in all the world?' Jess asked with a smile as she joined them.

'Dr Phillips said she's thinking of moving Colin to Special Care next week,' Nicola answered.

'That's wonderful news,' the counsellor declared, then glanced across at Brianna. 'Have you a moment?'

'Something wrong?' Brianna asked as she followed Jess across the ward, and the counsellor shook her head.

'I passed Connor in the corridor on my way in, and he said he'd like a word with you, if you've time.'

He wanted to say goodbye, Brianna realised, and she didn't want to say goodbye, didn't think her heart could take that.

'I'm afraid I'm rather busy at the moment,' she lied, and Jess sighed.

'Brianna, talk to him,' she said softly. 'What harm can it do just to talk to him?'

'Jess, what is there left for us to say that we haven't already said?' Brianna said sadly. 'I think a clean break, with no goodbyes, is best.'

'And you truly believe that?' Jess said with eyes that saw too much.

'Jess, just leave it, OK?'

'But, Brianna—'

She didn't give the counsellor time to finish. Instead, she walked over to one of the monitors, and swallowed hard. If talking to Connor would have changed anything, she would have done it in a minute, but it wouldn't change anything, she knew it wouldn't.

Determinedly, she picked up the pile of files stacked on the nurses' work station. She should have tackled them days ago, but she'd been so tired recently. Tired and uncharacteristically weepy, and she bit her lip. Maybe she should never have accepted the nurse unit manager's job. Maybe she just wasn't up to it, and she ought to simply tell Mr Brooke so.

'Brianna?'

She glanced over her shoulder to see Megan standing behind her.

'I've just passed Connor in the corridor,' the paediatric specialist registrar declared, 'and he said he'd like—'

'A word with me,' Brianna finished for her. 'Yes, I know.'

'I can hold the fort for you here, if you want. It would be no trouble.'

'Look, what is this?' Brianna exclaimed, taking refuge in anger. 'If it's not you, it's Jess, trying to push me out the door to talk to him.'

'I just thought that, as this is his last day…'

'I know what you thought,' Brianna said tightly, 'and, trust me, it isn't going to happen.'

'Brianna, don't you think you should at least let him say what he wants to say?' Megan said, her eyes concerned. 'You can tear him to shreds afterwards if you want, but, when he's been the one continually holding out the olive branch, couldn't you at least meet him halfway and hear him out?'

'Yeah, right. Like you do with Josh, you mean?' Brianna snapped. 'I can't say I've seen any signs of that.'

Megan flushed scarlet, opened her mouth, then closed it again tightly.

'OK, if that's how you feel,' she said, 'but I'm not going out there to tell him you won't see him. You can do that yourself, or you can leave him standing in the corridor waiting for hours in the hope you might change your mind. Your choice.'

'Megan—'

The paediatric specialist registrar had walked away, and Brianna started after her, then stopped. What in the world was happening to her? Megan and Jess both meant well, she knew they did, and yet she'd chewed their heads off. Chewed the heads off the two women she'd always thought of as friends, and she wanted to burst into tears again, and she really had to stop wanting to burst into tears.

Go and see him, a little voice whispered at the back of her mind. *You want to, you know you do, so go and see him*.

I can't, her heart cried. I can't. I don't want to say goodbye.

It will be the last time you ever see him, the little voice whispered. *The last time you'll ever see his face.* And before she was even aware she was moving, she was out in the corridor and he was there, waiting for her.

'Thanks for agreeing to see me,' he said.

Lord, but he looked so nervous, so awkward and uncomfortable, totally unlike her normally super-confident husband.

'Megan and Jess, seemed to think it was important,' she replied, only to realise, too late, just how awful her words sounded, as though her friends might care about him but she did not. 'I mean—'

'I thought you should know what's in my report to the board before it becomes common knowledge tomorrow,' he interrupted.

'You don't have to tell me the details,' she said quickly. 'I don't need to know before anyone else does.'

'Yes, you do,' he insisted. 'I've recommended no departments, or wards, should be shut.'

She blinked. 'None?'

'I've had a lot of time to think over this past month,' he declared with a rueful half-smile, 'and I've realised you were right. Not everything can be measured on a balance sheet.'

'But, if you don't suggest any cuts, won't the board simply bring in someone else to audit us?' she protested.

'They need to save money, and won't they reason that if you can't find a solution then maybe somebody else might?'

'I've shown them how they can save money,' he replied. 'I've recommended cancelling the new, all-singing, all-dancing computer system they've ordered. Their old computer system—with some modifications—is more than up to the task.'

'Right.' She nodded.

He backed up a step. 'Well…that's all I wanted to tell you, so…'

He was going and, as she stared up at him, saw how careworn he looked, how very weary, she knew she still loved him. Despite everything he'd done, despite everything that had happened, she still loved him, and surely there had to be some way back for them, some way they could still be together?

'Connor…'

He stopped, and something that looked almost like hope stirred in his deep blue eyes. 'Yes?'

'I just wanted to say—you know—thank you,' she said awkwardly. 'On behalf of the parents, and the babies, I mean,' she added.

'That's OK,' he muttered.

Oh, Lord, but why had she said that? She'd always been the one who'd accused him of not talking, of not saying what he was really thinking, and now she couldn't seem to find the right words.

'You'll be going back to London tomorrow?' she said desperately.

'Not immediately,' he replied. 'I thought I might stay on here for a little while, have a holiday.'

Despite herself, her lips curved.

'You're not going to find much to do in Penhally in

April,' she observed, and saw an answering, hesitant, smile appear on his lips.

'Maybe I'll take up beachcombing,' he said. 'How's the new job going?'

'Tiring,' she admitted. 'I hadn't realised before just how much paperwork was involved.'

'You look tired,' he observed. 'Just don't overdo it, OK? I've had to learn the hard way that there's more to life than work.'

He's given you an opening, she thought, so use it. Use it now, but she didn't get a chance to.

'How's Rita?' he continued, and, when she rolled her eyes, he laughed. 'That good, eh?'

'She was pretty subdued for about a week, but she bounced right back again pretty quickly. As she said to me, "Sister Flannigan, the Bible does say that charity begins at home, so I'd hardly be a good Christian if I didn't find it in me to forgive my own granddaughter's transgressions."'

'She actually said that?' Connor gasped, and Brianna nodded.

'Yup, she did. I'm afraid nothing keeps our Rita down for long.'

'You know, in a weird way, I think I'm going to miss her,' he observed. 'Of course, it's going to be in a *very* weird way.'

Brianna laughed and, as he half turned, clearly thinking their conversation was over, she took a step forward.

'The Renwicks told me you've been visiting the unit in the evening,' she said. 'Nicola said you've been talking to her, too.'

'They're a nice couple, and she's a sweet kid, so...' His shoulders lifted awkwardly.

'But why, Connor?' she asked. 'Your assessment of

NICU was over weeks ago, so why did you keep coming back here?'

To her surprise, a deep tide of colour crept over her husband's cheeks.

'It's stupid—silly,' he muttered. 'Not worth talking about.'

'Tell me,' she pressed.

'You'll think I'm crazy.'

'Just tell me,' she protested, and saw him take a deep breath.

'Because it's where you work, and being in the unit... Sometimes I caught a hint of the soap you use, and it made me feel...close to you again, as though I was still a part of your life.'

Tears welled in her eyes. 'Oh, Connor—'

'Told you it was stupid, didn't I?' he said awkwardly, and she shook her head.

'No,' she replied with difficulty. 'I don't think it's stupid at all.'

'I'd better go,' he said again. 'I've taken up more than enough of your time.'

She put out her hand quickly.

'This holiday you're taking,' she said hesitantly. 'It seems like such a waste of money for you to stay in a hotel. You...you could move back into my cottage tomorrow, if you want. I mean, it would give us more time to talk,' she continued, feeling her cheeks beginning to darken as he stared at her, his face expressionless. 'And I...I would very much like for us to talk some more, if...if you'd like to, that is?'

A smile curved the corners of his mouth. A smile that grew, and grew.

'I would like that very much indeed,' he said, and she smiled in return, a suddenly shy, self-conscious smile.

'I'd better get back to work,' she said, 'otherwise they'll be sending out a search party for me.'

He nodded, and she turned, but she must have turned too fast because a wave of giddiness swept over her, and if Connor hadn't caught her she would have fallen.

'Are you OK?' he said anxiously.

'Rush of blood to the head, that's all,' she said, wishing the walls in the corridor would stop moving.

'You're sure?' he pressed. 'Hell, Brianna, you're chalk-white.'

'I'm fine—just fine,' she said shakily, taking several deep breaths. 'I shouldn't have skipped breakfast this morning, but I felt a bit queasy.'

'You'll have breakfast every morning when I move back in, and no arguments,' he said firmly, and she laughed.

'Going to be the flatmate from hell, are you?' she said, and he smiled but she could see his eyes were still concerned.

'When it comes to your health, you bet I am,' he declared.

She still felt slightly sick, and giddy, she realised as she walked away from him back into the ward, and it was weird. She didn't get sick—never had done. It had always been Connor who contracted every cold or infection going. She'd used to laugh, and tell him he could be the one-stop shop for medical students practising their skills, and he hadn't appreciated the joke. The only time she'd ever felt sick...

She came to a halt in the middle of the ward, her heart suddenly racing. The only time she'd ever felt sick had been when she'd been expecting Harry. The only time her emotions had been all over the place, as they were right now, had been when she'd been pregnant with Harry.

'No,' she whispered, as she desperately tried to count

back to the night when she and Connor had made love. 'I can't be. I can't.'

But she could.

Keep calm, she told herself, don't panic, keep calm. You could simply be late. You've only missed one period, and stress can do that. It took seven years for you to conceive Harry so the odds on you conceiving in one night are minuscule.

But not impossible.

'Chris, I just need to slip out for a moment,' she said, hoping her voice didn't sound nearly as strained as she thought it did.

It couldn't have done because the staff nurse simply nodded vaguely, and quickly Brianna left the unit and headed for Gynae.

No matter how long she stared at the thin blue lines they didn't go away. She'd sneaked three pregnancy kits out of Gynae, had been determined to leave nothing to chance, and each and every one of the kits said the same thing. She was pregnant.

'Brianna, are you in there?' Megan called, from outside the staffroom toilet.

'Yes…I'm here,' she managed to say.

'A and E have phoned. Four-month-old on its way to us. Mother seriously injured in a car crash, baby looks to have nothing more than minor lesions but they want us to check him out.'

And I don't want to do this, Brianna thought, squeezing her eyes shut. I can't deal with this, not right now, but she knew she must.

'I'll be out in a minute,' she said, and, when she heard Megan's footsteps fading away, she stared at the pregnancy kits on the floor in front of her.

One pregnancy test could get it wrong, but it was impossible for three to give the wrong result. A baby was growing inside her, and no amount of staring at the kits would alter that. No amount of willing the results to be different would change them, and stiffly she got to her feet, and even more stiffly walked out of the toilet, down the corridor, and into the ward.

The heat enveloped her instantly, but it didn't comfort her as it normally did. All she could see were the IV lines, tubes and incubators. All she could hear was the rasping sound of the ventilators, the constant bleep of the monitors, and in seven months' time, if she didn't go full term, as she hadn't before, she'd be back in here, not as a nurse but as a mother. A mother whose child's life would be attached to all those tubes and wires. A mother whose child would be clinging to life. A sob broke from her.

'Brianna, what's wrong?'

Megan was standing in front of her, her eyes full of concern, and Brianna shook her head.

'I have to get out of here.'

'But—'

'I can't bear this, I can't!' Brianna exclaimed, all too aware that Chris was gazing at her open-mouthed, Mr Brooke looked stunned, and Josh...

He was there, too, and he was walking towards her, worry and confusion written all over his face, and she turned and ran. Out of the ward, out of the unit, not knowing know where she was going, not even caring, just so long as she got away.

'Brianna, wait up a moment!'

She didn't want to wait as she heard Megan running after her. She was going to have wait for the next eight months, endure eight whole months of fear, and she pressed her fist against her mouth hard as another sob came from her.

'Brianna, what's happened? What's wrong?'

Megan had caught up with her, was trying to steer her into the on-call room, and she tried to pull herself free, but the paediatric specialist registrar was a lot stronger than she looked.

'Megan, let me go,' she said, her voice raw. 'Please, just let me go.'

'No way,' her friend replied. 'You're clearly very upset. Shall I get Connor? I can phone him—'

'No—no—don't get him!' Brianna begged. 'Please, don't get him!'

'Then tell me what's wrong, what's happened, because I swear I'll phone him if you don't,' Megan replied, her eyes dark with anxiety.

Slowly, Brianna went into the on-call room, and sat down heavily on the bed.

'I… Oh, God, Megan. I'm pregnant.'

The specialist paediatric registrar stared at her silently for a heartbeat, then sat down beside her.

'And I take it this is not good news?' she said gently.

'It's the worst news,' Brianna cried. 'The very worst news in the world!'

Megan's eyes darkened with an expression Brianna didn't understand, then she cleared her throat.

'The baby…is it Connor's?' she asked hesitantly, and when Brianna nodded she sighed. 'Look, I know you're not exactly on speaking terms with him at the moment, but you told me just a few weeks ago that you loved him, and maybe you can resolve whatever's driven you apart, and even if you can't, lots of women are single mothers—'

'I know,' Brianna interrupted. 'I know all that, but it isn't that simple, Megan, I wish to God it was. Three years ago Connor and I…we had a child. We'd been trying for a baby for seven years, and when I discovered I was pregnant it was…' She took an uneven breath. 'It was like having all of my birthdays and Christmases in one go.'

'What happened?' Megan asked, her eyes fixed on her.

'I must have had one of the worst pregnancies ever,' Brianna replied. 'I was sick the whole time, but I didn't care. I used to talk to him, Megan. All the time I'd talk to the baby, tell him what I was doing, what I could see, and tell him how…' Tears spilled over her cheeks, and she didn't rub them away. 'How he was going to be the most loved baby in the whole world, and when he was born… Connor—he says he looked like me, but he didn't. He looked like him, and he died, Megan. He only lived for twelve hours, and then my beautiful, precious son died.'

'Oh, Brianna, I am so sorry,' Megan declared, her own eyes filling, 'and discovering you're pregnant again… You must be scared to death, but just because your son died doesn't mean every other baby you have will die, too.'

'He had an inherited heart condition, Megan, and you know what that means. It means there's a very strong likelihood it will happen again.'

'Brianna, listen to me—'

'Why?' Brianna hurled at her. 'What's the point? You don't understand—you can't. You've never given birth to a child and been forced to watch him die. You've never watched your baby slowly slip away from you, knowing there was nothing you could to stop it.'

'I have.'

Brianna's eyes flew to her friend's, and she saw such an unutterable pain there that for a moment she forgot her own despair.

'You had a baby?' she whispered.

'A son, like you,' Megan replied, her voice low, but there was no mistaking the heartache in it. 'He was born eight years ago when I was a student doctor. His father was a doctor, too, working in the same hospital as me, and he was so handsome, Brianna. Handsome, and charming, and such fun, and I…' She closed her eyes. 'Even though he never seemed to notice me, I guess I was a little in love with him right from the first moment I saw him.'

'You're…you're talking about Josh, aren't you?' Brianna said hesitantly, and Megan nodded.

'I always thought I was too quiet for him, too studious, and then…' She took a breath. 'I went to a party, and he was there, and suddenly he seemed very interested in me, and…' A tear ran down the paediatric specialist registrar's cheek, and she brushed it away. 'It wasn't a one-night stand, Brianna, not for me. I thought it was the start of something special, but…'

'He walked away when he discovered you were pregnant?' Brianna said tentatively, and Megan laughed.

A harsh, bitter laugh that made Brianna wince.

'I didn't even get the chance to tell him I was pregnant. We were supposed to meet up the next day, and he stood me up, and when I saw him a few days later, he blanked me. He just walked straight past me as though he'd never met me, far less made love to me.'

'Oh, Megan—'

'When I discovered I was pregnant, my career was just taking off, and I thought, I can't give this baby a home. I can't give him the attention he deserves, so I was going to have an abortion until I saw the scan. When I saw this tiny figure inside me…' She shook her head. 'This tiny, oh, so perfect little human being inside me…'

'You couldn't go through with it.'

'He was my baby, Brianna, my little boy, and even if his father didn't want him, I did, and then…' Megan took a deep breath, and Brianna could see her friend's lips were trembling. 'I collapsed in the street when I was twenty-three weeks pregnant. Placental abruption, that's what the doctor in A and E said, and I was bleeding out, and I could hear someone shouting, "She has to be saved. The baby can't be saved, but we can save her", and I didn't want them to save me. I...' A sob escaped her. 'I just wanted to die, to be with my son, but they didn't let me die. They performed a complete hysterectomy, which means I can't ever have any more children.'

'Oh, Megan,' Brianna cried. 'I am sorry...so, so sorry.'

'I have relived that day so many times, Brianna,' Megan said, her voice shaking. 'Wondered so often if maybe Stephen knew I'd considered having an abortion, and, because he thought I didn't want him, he decided I was better off without him, but I wasn't. I wasn't.'

'But, having been through all that, having suffered the death of a child, can't you see why I can't face this again?' Brianna insisted. 'Can't you understand that I can't carry a child, grow to love it, and then have that baby die, too?'

'Brianna, statistically, the odds that everything might be all right—'

'*Might* be—*could* be. Megan I don't want *might*,' Brianna protested. 'I don't want *could*. I want you to tell me this baby will live!'

'I can't promise you that—no one can,' Megan replied. 'Brianna—'

She'd already got jerkily to her feet.

'I want to go home, Megan. I just want to get away from here, and go home.'

'But, Brianna...'

Her friend was already heading out of the on-call room, and for a moment Megan stared indecisively after her, then pulled her mobile phone from her pocket and dialled quickly.

'Pick up your phone, Connor,' she muttered. 'This is important, so pick up your damn phone!'

But he didn't. She'd reached his voice mail, and the last thing she wanted was his voice mail, but she left a message anyway, and then she left the on-call room only to stop dead. Josh was standing outside in the corridor, and his face told her everything.

'You heard,' she said flatly, and, when he nodded she shrugged, though her eyes were dark with shadows. 'There's no need to look quite so shocked. It's not as though you didn't already know about Stephen, and my hysterectomy.'

'Megan—'

She didn't let him finish. She simply walked back into the duty room and slammed the door, but he came in after her.

'Megan, if I could have saved Stephen, I would,' Josh said hoarsely. 'But he was too little, too premature, you know he was, and if we hadn't carried out the hysterectomy, you would have *died*, and I couldn't have borne that. Losing you as well as my son—'

'Are you asking me to believe you *cared*?' she demanded, her voice hard. 'If you are, then it's too little, too late.'

'Megan, listen to me,' he begged, his face white. 'You cannot possibly hate me more than I hate myself right now. When I held Stephen in my hands for those few brief moments, when I saw he wasn't breathing, knew he would never breathe—'

'Don't, Josh,' she protested, her face stricken, 'please *don't*—'

'And they rushed you to Theatre, and you were losing so much blood—'

'If you cared that much then why did you walk away from me?' she cried, her voice cracking. 'I thought we'd meant something to one another that night, and yet you didn't even turn up the next day as we'd arranged.'

'I was scared, Megan. My father…' He shook his head. 'He hurt my mother time and time again with his affairs, and yet she kept on taking him back, and taking him back, and I thought, if that's love, I want none of it. If that's what giving your heart means, I can't do that, so all my life I've refused to allow myself to get too close to anyone for fear I'd hurt them, or they'd hurt me.'

'And yet you married Rebecca,' she pointed out, and he bit his lip.

'I should never have done that—I see that now—but I married her because I was lonely. I married her because I was unhappy, and I married her because…' He sucked in an uneven breath. 'She wanted so little from me. I'm ashamed to admit that—I should never have married her when all I felt for her was a liking—but I thought she was happy. I told myself she was, but she wasn't.'

'Josh—'

'Megan, I have ruined three lives,' he said desolately. 'Yours, my wife's, my own, and though I deserve everything I've got—my wife walking out on me, you hating me—neither you nor Rebecca deserve the pain I've inflicted on you both.'

'I don't hate you,' Megan said, her voice trembling. 'I may have once, a long time ago. I may even have wished you'd never come back into my life, but I don't hate you. I don't think I ever could.'

'I know I can never make it up to you,' he said. 'I know I can never expect you to forgive me, or to care for me the way I care for you—'

'You care for me?' she interrupted, and he smiled, a lopsided, crooked smile.

'I realise now, though it's too late, that I always have, and I just want to say I'm sorry. I know that's a pathetic thing to say,' he continued, as a tear trickled down Megan's cheek, 'a completely inadequate thing to say, and I wish there were bigger words, better words I could use to convince you I truly am sorry for all the pain and heartache I've caused you, but there aren't.'

'I don't need bigger or better words,' she said on a sob. 'Those words are enough.'

'Are you saying…?' His eyes met hers, and he swallowed hard. 'Are you saying that maybe…maybe you could learn to care for me again?'

'Josh, I always have,' she said simply, 'and, God help me, I think I always will.'

And when he hesitantly held out his arms to her she walked straight into them, and when he kissed her it was as though the last eight years had never been. As though all the heartache and pain they'd both endured had never happened. And he'd said he'd cared for her. OK, so he hadn't said the 'L' word, but she knew he meant the 'L' word, he truly did, and the shiver she felt when she heard the lonely wail of an approaching ambulance, a wail that sounded so like a lost soul crying for the happiness it could never have, meant nothing. It didn't, she told herself, so when he deepened his kiss, held her even closer, moulded his body to hers, and she felt herself melting, and dissolving in his heat, she didn't stop him when he stretched behind him, and turned the lock on the on-duty call-room door.

* * *

Brianna's house was in complete darkness when Connor reached it, and if it hadn't been for her car parked outside he would have thought she wasn't home.

'Brianna needs you,' Megan had said, sounding frantic on his voice mail. 'She's gone home, and she really needs you, Connor.'

He'd driven like a maniac along the narrow Cornish roads, broken the speed limit the whole way, and now...

Hesitantly, he tried the front door, and it opened immediately. Was that good, or bad? He didn't know, and even more hesitantly he walked down the hall to the sitting room. The room was in darkness, just like the rest of the house, but moonlight was streaming through the window and he could just about make Brianna out, sitting motionless and hunched on the sofa.

'You know, you really should lock your front door,' he said, switching on one of the table lamps. 'I could have been anyone. A burglar, a serial killer, a door-to-door salesman trying to sell you a hundred and one things you never ever wanted.'

She didn't so much as turn her head, and he shivered. The room was freezing, and quickly he switched on the gas fire, and watched the fake flames spring to life, before turning back to her.

Had she moved at all? He didn't think she had.

'I expect I'm the last person in the world you want to see,' he said, walking over to the sofa and sitting down beside her, hoping to at least provoke a response, but he didn't. 'Megan rang me. She was worried about you.'

Still she didn't move, and tentatively he reached out, and took her hand in his. Lord, but her fingers felt like ice, and the shiver he'd felt earlier became more pronounced.

'Has something happened at the hospital?' he asked, wishing she would look at him, say something, anything.

'Has someone upset you, or is it one of the babies? Has one of the babies become very ill?'

Still she said nothing, and he gripped her hand tighter.

'Bree, for God's sake, say something, because you're scaring the hell out of me,' he said, and she was. 'Are you ill? You had that giddy spell earlier—is it something to do with that, and there's something wrong with you? Look, whatever it is, we can deal with it. I'm not going to walk away, I'm not going to leave you—'

'I'm pregnant.'

Her voice was so low, he wasn't sure he'd heard her correctly, and he half shook his head.

'I'm sorry, but did you just say…?'

'I'm pregnant, Connor,' she said dully. 'The night little Colin Hallet had his op, when we made love, I must have conceived a baby then.'

'But that's…' His face lit up. 'Oh, Bree, that's wonderful news, the very best of news.'

Her head snapped round to his.

'*Wonderful* news—*the very best* of news?' she cried. 'I don't want to be pregnant, Connor. Can't you understand, *I don't want to be pregnant*!'

'Bree, I know this is a shock, something you never planned,' he declared, putting his hands on her shoulders, 'but you're going to have a baby—*a baby*—and it's what you always wanted, and if…' His face twisted slightly. 'If you don't want me in your life to share this with you, I'll understand. All I'll ask of you is that you let me sometimes be there, for the child.'

'What if it dies?' she exclaimed, getting jerkily to her feet, her face white, her eyes desperate. 'What if this baby dies, too, Connor? Before—because of my job—I knew things could sometimes go wrong, but I only knew it in an abstract way, something that happened to other people, not to me, but it *has* happened to me, and it could happen again—we both know it could. Even if I do all the right things, even if I never take any risks, just like I didn't with Harry, it could happen again. This baby could have the same inherited heart defect, and it could die!'

'It might not,' he said, reaching for her only to see her evade him, 'and if it does we'll face it together.'

'That's easy for you to say,' she said, a tear running down her cheek, and she dashed it away. 'You won't be able to feel him, or her, moving inside you. You won't lie awake at night, thinking he hasn't moved in a little while, and does that mean he's not alive any more. You were right about Nicola's baby. I wanted him because he had no one. I wanted him because he looked so like our Harry, but I also wanted him because…' Another tear trickled down her cheek and she let it fall. 'He was *whole*, Connor, he was going to live, and to have to wait to find out if this baby…'

'So, you're going to have an abortion?' he said, watching her face. 'You're going to abort this baby, not even give it a chance to live, is that it?'

She stared at him, her mouth working soundlessly for a moment, then before he knew what was happening she was standing in front of him, pounding his chest with her fists.

'How can you say that?' she cried, hitting him with every word she spoke. 'How can you even think I'd kill my child? Of course I would never kill my child, never, *never*!'

'I know,' he said, quickly catching her wrists with his hands. 'Brianna, I *know* you wouldn't, and that's why the only thing you can do is to go on with this, and we can face it together, we can do it together, if…' He searched her face. 'You want me in your life, that is? I know I've made mistakes,' he continued as she tried to interrupt. 'I know I've got things wrong, but I have never ever stopped loving you.'

'And I haven't ever stopped loving you,' she said brokenly. 'I think…maybe…we just sort of lost one another somehow along the way, but I am so scared, Connor, so scared. If this baby dies, too…'

'I'm scared, too,' he admitted, taking her into his arms, and holding her tight. 'In the past, I always thought I had control over my life, my future, but now I know that was nothing but an illusion, that none of us have any control, that all we can do is hold onto one another through the good times, and the bad, and pray and hope.'

'I want certainty, not hope,' she sobbed into his chest. 'I want to know for sure, not have to pray.'

He tilted her head back so she had to look at him.

'I know, and I think that's what we all want, but life isn't like that. For such a very long time I thought, Why my son, why did this have to happen to my son? But now I know there is no answer to that. When Harry died—'

'You said the word,' she interrupted. 'Do you realise that's the first time you've ever said the word?'

'I couldn't say it before, because saying it…' Connor swallowed hard. 'It made it so final, so irrevocable. It meant I had to accept he was never, ever coming back.'

'And he isn't, is he?' she said, and Connor shook his head, a muscle in his jaw quivering.

'No, but do you remember when they took him off the life-support machine, and you were holding him in your arms, and I had one of his tiny hands in mine…? Do you remember him opening his eyes, and looking at us before he died?'

She nodded with difficulty. 'I remember.'

'I think now he was saying, "I love you both, and I know

you love me, but I have to go now. I can't stay with you any longer."'

'Oh, Connor...'

'Brianna, there was a time when I thought I couldn't face going on without him,' he said shakily, as tears spilled down her cheeks. 'I couldn't see any future without him, but he's gone on without us, and we have to go on without him. We won't ever forget him—we can't, not ever—and he will always have a treasured place in our hearts, but we have to look forward and not back.'

'I can't go back to London with you,' she said quickly. 'I know you love the city, but I love it here.'

'We're staying here. We might need to look for a bigger house once the baby comes, unless your landlord will let us build an extension, but we're staying in Penhally.'

'But you'll be so miserable,' she protested, 'and where would you work?'

'I would never be miserable with you beside me,' he said, willing her to believe him, 'and I've already got a job in St Piran.'

'You've got a job?' she said, and he smiled.

'The hospital board want me to be their financial advisor.'

'And you were offered this job, and accepted it, and never told me?' she said in confusion.

'I knew you didn't want to see me, to talk to me,' he said, his voice low, 'but I hoped, if I stayed here...' He lifted his shoulders awkwardly. 'Maybe in time you might grow to love me again.'

'I do, I always have, but...' She tried to stop her lips from trembling, but she couldn't. 'Will the baby be all right this time, Connor?'

He cupped her face in his hands, his blue eyes holding hers.

'I don't know, but whatever happens we're in this together. No matter what the future brings, we will *always* face it together.'

EPILOGUE

'AND how is my gorgeous wife this morning?'

'Your gorgeous wife feels like a barrage balloon that is about to burst.' Brianna sighed as she eased herself out of her seat.

'Back still sore?' Connor said sympathetically, coming up behind her and rubbing it gently.

'It must be the way I was sleeping—or rather not sleeping—last night,' she replied ruefully. 'I just couldn't get comfortable.'

'I'm not surprised.' Connor grinned, sliding his hands round to caress her swollen stomach. 'With two little munchkins in there, and only two weeks left until your due date, they're probably finding it a bit crowded.'

Brianna grimaced. 'Judging by how much they're kicking, that could be true.'

'Maybe they're both boys?' Connor exclaimed. 'Destined to be future world-class football players.'

Brianna closed her eyes. 'I just want them both to be all right.'

His arms tightened round her. 'They will be. Trust me.'

It wasn't a question of trust, she thought as she let her head fall back against his chest. It was a question now of luck, of the odds being stacked not once, but twice in their favour, and she didn't even want to think about what the chances of that happening might be.

'Stop worrying,' Connor said softly, clearly reading her mind, and she tried to smile, but it was hard.

She'd had a scan at twelve weeks, which had revealed she was expecting twins, but she'd refused to go for any more tests. She was more than happy to let the GP in Penhally regularly check her blood pressure, and to keep making sure there were still two little heartbeats, but she'd point blank refused to have any other kind of test, and Connor had backed her all the way.

'We'll deal with whatever happens when we have to,' he had told the GP, and, though the doctor hadn't been happy, he'd said no more.

'I was just thinking,' Connor continued hesitantly. 'Given that we're shortly going to be having two little babies in our home, are you quite sure you don't want the baby shower Jess and Megan want to throw for you?'

'Tell them I'm really touched, but no,' Brianna replied. 'I know everyone thinks I'm stupid, but…'

'You don't want to tempt fate,' Connor finished for her. 'Understood, though you do realise our children's first beds are going to be a couple of drawers because you won't even let me buy cots?'

'Connor—'

'And I'm sure they'll love the drawers,' he said, planting a kiss on the top of her head, then releasing her. 'I won't be late home tonight. I want to get the last of the onions, and carrots out of the ground before winter really sets in.'

She shook her head, and laughed. 'You and your vegetables. You'll be wanting us to buy chickens next.'

'Been reading my mind, have you?' He grinned, and she laughed again.

He'd taken to country living with an enthusiasm that

had amazed her. Never would she have thought her city-loving husband would have spent all of his spare time in the garden, creating a vegetable patch, but he had.

'No regrets?' she said. 'About living so far away from everything here in Cornwall?'

'Not a one. Everything I want is here.' He cupped her cheek, his blue eyes soft. 'I was just too blind and stupid to see it before.'

'And you're going to be late,' she said, catching sight of the kitchen clock. 'Give my best to the troops on the front line.'

'I will.' He nodded. 'You have my number in case you need me?'

She rolled her eyes.

'Connor, your number is the same number it was eight months ago, so get out of here.'

He turned to go, then came back, and took her in his arms. 'Have I told you this morning that I love you?'

'Twice.' She chuckled, as he kissed her. 'Though how you can love me when I look like a blob...'

'You have never looked more beautiful,' he said huskily, and her eyes filled.

'Lord, being pregnant isn't half playing havoc with my emotions,' she said tremulously. 'Now, will you *please* get out of here before I have to call the board and tell them their financial adviser is a fruitcake?'

'They already know that,' he replied, bending his head, clearly intent on kissing her again, and she fended him off.

'*Go!*'

She could hear him laughing as he went down the drive, and, when he drove away, she smiled as she absently rubbed her back. She hadn't ever been this happy, not even back in Killarney, and her pregnancy had been so much easier this time. She'd actually felt well instead of wretched, and all she needed now was…

'No,' she told the kettle as she made herself a cup of coffee. 'No thinking about what's going to happen in two weeks' time. Connor said it was forbidden.'

Which didn't mean she didn't constantly think about it, she realised as she drank her coffee. The nearer her due date loomed, the more frightened she was becoming.

'I'd much rather the two of you just stayed in there,' she told her bump. 'Where you're safe.'

One of the inhabitants of the bump kicked, and she winced slightly.

'I know, I know,' she said. 'You're eager to see the world, but stay where you are. You've only two more weeks to wait, and I have this laundry to do. Ninety-nine per cent of which,' she continued wryly as she bent to pick up the wash basket, 'appears to consist of your father's shirts, but I promise you I'll wean him out of his city suits one day.'

But not right now, she thought as a pain suddenly shot through her, and as she doubled up she felt something wet and warm trickle down her legs.

No! her mind exclaimed as she stared down and saw a bloody show among the liquid on the floor. Not now. She couldn't be going into labour now. It was too soon, too soon, and she took a deep breath and clutched the kitchen table tight, but the pain in her back was getting worse, a lot worse, and frantically she scrabbled for her mobile and dialled Connor's number.

He answered almost immediately, and she could hear the sound of traffic in the background which meant he had approached the town of St Piran.

'Connor Monahan here,' he declared cheerfully. 'World-renowned but also very modest financial advisor to St Piran Hospital, grower of the best onions in Cornwall, and lucky enough to be married to the most beautiful woman in the entire world, and, yes, I am remembering you want me to pick up some milk before I come home tonight.'

'Connor…' She struggled to keep her voice calm, but it didn't work. 'Connor, my waters have broken.'

For a second there was complete silence down the phone, then she heard him exhale, and the sound of his car accelerating.

'I'm on my way back. Stay where you are. Don't move.'

She wasn't going to, she thought as the phone went dead. She was going to stay right where she was and pray. Pray like she'd never prayed before.

'You're doing really, really well, Brianna,' the midwife declared encouragingly. 'Just a few more pushes and your first baby should be here.'

'Are…are the heart rates still OK?' Brianna gasped, trying to squint round at the monitor. 'No sign of any distress, abnormality?'

'Can you just concentrate on what you're supposed to be doing?' The midwife laughed. 'Honestly, you nurses and doctors make the worst possible mums-to-be. You know too much, that's the trouble. And, no, there's absolutely no sign whatsoever of either of your babies having difficulty,' she continued as Brianna made to interrupt. 'OK, another contraction's coming so work with it,' she added as Brianna let out a groan, and bore down hard.

'Is she OK?' Connor asked, his face chalk-white. 'My wife… Is she OK?'

'She's doing beautifully.'

'But it's been twelve hours,' Connor protested, wiping his forehead with one hand while holding onto Brianna's hand with the other. 'She's been in labour for twelve hours. Maybe you should be thinking of a Caesarean, or—'

'Shut…up…Connor,' Brianna said through her teeth.
'I…don't…want…a…oh…oh, my Lord…here comes another one.'

'Push, push,' the midwife ordered. 'The head's already
out. We just need one more push, just one more, and…
Oh, beautiful—just beautiful.' She beamed. 'You have a
daughter, Brianna, a lovely daughter.'

'Is she all right?' Brianna asked, trying to lever herself
upright, only to have to lie down again fast as another
contraction rippled through her. 'Is she all right?'

'She's beautiful, Bree,' Connor said, his voice choked,
his eyes shimmering. 'Just beautiful.'

'But is she all right?' Brianna insisted.

'She's fine, just fine,' the midwife said reassuringly.
'You have a lovely, healthy, perfect baby. Now, keep on
working with the contractions, keep working with them. I
know you're very tired, but half the hospital staff seem to
be outside in the corridor, desperately waiting for news,
and we don't want to keep them waiting too much longer,
do we?'

Brianna gripped Connor's hand again tightly, and heard
him suck in his breath. He was going to be lucky to survive
this without having any broken fingers, she thought, but
the chuckle which would have broken from her was cut off
as yet another contraction swept over her.

'Number two is on its way,' the midwife announced.
'Breathe with the pain, Brianna, go with it—don't fight
it.'

'I'm…not…fighting…it,' Brianna protested, her face
scarlet, her forehead beaded with sweat. 'I'm really not.
I'm just…oh…oh, my…this is…'

'Hard,' Connor finished for her. 'I know it is, but you
can do it, Bree. I can see the head crowning. You can do
this. I know you can.'

And Brianna took a deep breath, and, with a harsh, guttural cry, pushed for all she was worth, and heard the midwife give an ecstatic whoop.

'She's here, Brianna. You have another little girl, and how you're ever going to tell your daughters apart... My heavens, they're like two peas in a pod, and the spitting image of their father.'

'Is she all right?' Brianna demanded. 'Is she...is she all right, too?'

'Absolutely,' the midwife announced.

For Brianna, all she wanted was to make sure her daughters were all right, to see for herself that they really and truly were all right, and when the midwife finally placed one of the babies in her arms she glanced quickly across at Connor and saw he was crying.

Crying and smiling at the same time, as he held their other daughter in his arms. A baby who was just as pink and healthy-looking as the one Brianna was holding. A baby who was breathing normally, and not erratically. A baby whose little face was screwed up in protest. Brianna let out a hiccupping laugh. A laugh that was pure relief and joy.

'Can I let the crowd outside in the corridor know the good news?' the midwife asked. 'The way they've been staked out all day, refusing to budge, you'd think these two babies were theirs. And, of course, they'll want to come in and see them, but...' She looked from Brianna to Connor, and smiled. 'Not yet, I think. The next few minutes are just for you. All four of you.'

And quickly the midwife bustled out the door, and Connor carefully placed the baby he was holding into Brianna's other arm, then sat down on the bed beside her.

'Oh, Bree, just look at them,' he said huskily. 'They are

just so…so…*beautiful*. And she's wrong—the midwife's wrong—they both look like you.'

'And Harry—they look like Harry, too, don't they?' Brianna said with an unsteady smile. 'I never thought this day would ever come, Connor. I never thought I would ever be able to think of Harry and smile. Every time I thought about him, I'd feel as though my heart was being ripped to pieces, but now… I just wish he could have been here, to see his little sisters, but I'm so grateful we had him even for that very short time.'

'I know,' he said softly. 'I feel the same way.' And then he laughed as an eruption of applause broke out in the corridor outside. 'Sounds like the midwife's just told everyone the good news.'

'We'll have to let them in soon, but do you realise we haven't even chosen names for our daughters?' Brianna declared. 'I didn't want to even think about names in case… you know…'

'Rhianna,' Connor said. 'I'd like to call one of them Rhianna, after your mother, if that's OK?'

'I'd like that, and I know she will.' Brianna nodded. 'And Aisling. Can we call our other daughter Aisling after your mother?''

'Are you sure?' Connor said unsteadily. 'It's a pretty old-fashioned sort of a name—'

'It's a beautiful name,' Brianna interrupted, planting a kiss on the top of each of her daughters' heads. 'Aisling and Rhianna. Our children.'

Connor delved into his pocket, and pulled out his wallet. For a second he stared down at it, then he carefully extracted a photograph and propped it up on the cabinet beside her.

'Aisling and Rhianna and Harry,' he said huskily. 'Our three beloved children.'

Tears welled in Brianna's eyes as she looked at the photograph.

'I didn't know you had that. You never said—never told me.'

'I took the photograph just after Harry was born, never thinking that…' He shook his head. 'And I couldn't throw it away, though even though looking at it always gave me pain, because it would have felt like I was throwing him away. I would have shown it to you, but…I thought…'

'I know.' She smiled tremulously. 'I know what you thought.'

From outside the labour ward they could hear the sound of raised voices, and Connor sighed.

'Sounds like they're getting restless out there,' he observed. 'Are you ready to let them in to see the new additions to the Monahan family?'

Brianna gazed down at her two daughters, then up at him.

'With you at my side, I'll always be ready for anything.'

And after Connor bent his head and kissed her, then slid off the bed to open the labour-ward door, Brianna glanced at the photograph on the bedside table and smiled.

'I love you, Harry,' she whispered. 'And I always will.'

ST PIRAN'S: PRINCE ON THE CHILDREN'S WARD

SARAH MORGAN

CHAPTER ONE

TASHA rehearsed her speech as she walked through the busy emergency department towards the on-call room. Inside she was panicking, but she was determined not to let that show.

Hello, dear darling brother, I know you're not expecting me, but I thought I'd just drop in and see how you're doing. No, she couldn't say that. He'd know instantly that something was wrong.

You're looking gorgeous today. No, way too creepy, and anyway they usually exchanged insults so he'd definitely know something was up.

Josh, of all my brothers, you've always been my favourite. No. She didn't have favourites.

You're the best doctor in the world and I've always admired you. That one just might work. Her brother certainly was an excellent doctor. He'd been her inspiration. And her rock. When their father had walked out, leaving his four children and his fragile, exhausted wife, it had been Josh, the eldest, who had taken charge. Wild, handsome Josh, whose own marriage was now in a terrible state.

But at least he'd had the courage to get married, Tasha thought gloomily. She couldn't ever imagine herself doing anything that brave.

Was it because of their parents, she wondered, that all the O'Haras were so bad at relationships?

Since her last relationship disaster, she'd given up and concentrated on her career. A career couldn't break your heart—or so she'd thought until a few weeks ago.

Now she knew differently.

Terror gripped her

She'd messed everything up.

Hating the feeling of vulnerability, Tasha stopped outside the door. Fiercely independent, it stuck in her throat that she needed to ask her brother for help, but she swallowed her pride and knocked. She needed someone else's perspective on what had happened and the one person whose judgement she trusted was her older brother.

Seconds later the door was jerked open and Josh stood there, buttoning up his shirt. His hair was dishevelled and he was badly in need of a shave. Clearly he'd had a night with no sleep but what really caught her attention was the stupid grin on his face. A grin that faded the instant he saw her.

'*Tasha?*' Astonishment was replaced by shock and he cast a fleeting glance over his shoulder before pushing her back into the corridor and closing the door firmly behind him. 'What are you doing here?'

'What sort of greeting is that?' Badly in need of a hug, Tasha heard her voice thicken and the bruises of the last month ached and throbbed inside her. 'I'm your little sister. You're supposed to be pleased to see me.'

'I am, of course, but—Tash, it's seven-thirty in the morning.' Josh let out a breath and rubbed his hand over his face to wake himself up. His free hand. The one that wasn't holding the doorhandle tightly. 'I wasn't expecting— You took me by surprise, that's all. How did you know where I was?'

'I asked one of the nurses. Someone said they thought you were in the on-call room. What's wrong with you? You look ruffled.' It was the first time she'd seen her cool, confident brother anything other than immaculate. Tasha looked from him to the door that he was holding tightly shut. 'Did I wake you?'

'No. I— Yes, but it doesn't matter.'

'Busy night?'

'Sort of.' His gaze darted to the corridor and back to her. 'What are you *doing* here, Tasha?'

Because she was watching his face, she saw the fevered expression in her brother's eyes and the way the flush spread across his cheekbones. The signs pointed to one thing…

He had a woman in the room.

But why be so secretive about the whole thing? His marriage to Rebecca was over—there was no reason why he shouldn't have a relationship. Surely he wasn't embarrassed about her knowing he had a sex life? It was no secret that women found her brother irresistible.

Still, it was a relief to find an explanation for his weird behaviour and she was about to tease him unmercifully when she remembered that she couldn't afford to antagonise him.

Instead, she gave him a playful punch on the arm. 'I thought I'd just drop in and see you.'

'Before breakfast?'

'I'm an early riser.'

'You mean you're in trouble.' His dry tone reminded her that her brother knew her too well.

Tasha thought about everything that had happened over the last month. *Had she done the wrong thing?* 'Not trouble exactly,' she hedged. 'I just thought it was a long time since we'd had a good chat. Is there somewhere we can talk?' She glanced at the on-call room but he jerked his head towards the corridor.

'My office. Let's go.'

Feeling like a schoolgirl on detention, Tasha slunk after him through the department, aware of the curious stares of the staff. The main area was packed with patients, including a young girl lying on a trolley, holding her mother's hand. Noticing that the child was struggling to breathe, Tasha moved instinctively towards her just as a doctor swept up in a white coat. With a murmur of apology, Tasha moved to one side, reminding herself that this wasn't her patient. Or even her hospital. She didn't work here, did she?

She didn't work anywhere.

Her stomach lurched. Had she been impulsive and hasty? *Stupid?*

It was all very well having principles, but was there a point where you should just swallow them?

Trapped by sudden panic, she paused. The conversation drifted towards her. 'Her hay fever has suddenly made her asthma worse,' the mother was telling the young doctor. 'Her breathing has been terrible and her eyes and face are all puffy.'

Tasha gave the child a sympathetic smile, wishing she was the one taking the history and searching for the problem. The fact that her hands ached to reach for a stethoscope simply renewed her feeling that she might have done the wrong thing.

Medicine, she thought. She loved medicine. It was part of her. Not working in a hospital made her feel like a plant dragged up by its roots and thrown aside. Without her little patients to care for, she was wilting.

Biting her tongue to stop herself intervening, she followed her brother down the corridor but something about the child nagged at her brain. Puffy eyes. Hay fever? Frustrated with herself for not being able to switch off, she quickened her pace. It wasn't her business. This wasn't even her department. And anyway, what did she know? She was feeling so battered and bruised by the events of the past few weeks she didn't trust herself to pass opinion on anything, not even the adverse effects of a high pollen count. Feeling really dejected, she followed her brother into his office.

It was stacked with books and medical journals. In one corner was a desk with a computer and an overflowing tray of paper. Tasha noticed that the photograph of Rebecca had gone and she felt a stab of guilt that she hadn't asked how he was. Was she was turning into one of those awful people who only thought about themselves? 'How are you doing? How are things with Rebecca?'

'Cordial. Our separation is probably the first thing we've ever agreed on. It's all in the hands of the lawyers. Sit down.' Josh shifted a pile of medical journals from the chair to the floor but Tasha didn't feel like sitting down. She was filled with restless energy. The stability of her brother's life contrasted heavily with the instability of her own. She'd been sailing along nicely through life and now she'd capsized her boat and she had no idea where the tide was going to take her.

The lump in her throat came from nowhere and she swallowed hard.

Damn.

Not now.

As the only girl in a family of four older brothers, she'd learned that if you cried, you never heard the last of it.

Fighting the emotion, she walked to the window and opened it. 'I love Cornwall.' She closed her eyes and breathed deeply. 'I've lived in so many places since I became a doctor and yet this is still home. I can smell the sea. I can't wait to pick up my surfboard. I've been trapped in a city for too long.' The plaintive shriek of a seagull made her open her eyes and for a moment the memories threatened to choke her.

Home.

'So, what brings you banging on my door at this unearthly hour—what have you done?' Josh sounded distracted. 'Please tell me you haven't killed a patient.'

'No!' Outrage was sharp and hot, slicing through the last of her composure. 'Far from it. I *saved* a patient. Two patients, actually.' Tasha clenched her fists, horrified to realise just how badly she needed someone else to tell her she'd done the right thing. *That she hadn't blown her career on a childish whim.* 'I had an incident—sort of. You know when you just have a feeling about a patient? Perhaps you haven't actually had test results back from the lab, but sometimes you don't need tests to tell you what you already know. Well, I had one of my feelings—a really strong feeling. I know it wasn't exactly the way to go about things, but—'

'Tasha, I'm too tired to wade through hours of female waffle. Just tell me what you've done. Facts.'

'I'm not waffling. Medicine isn't always black and white. You should know that.' Tasha's voice was fierce as she told him about the twins, the decisions she'd made and the drug she'd used.

Josh listened and questioned her. 'You didn't wait for the results of the blood cultures? And if it wasn't on the hospital-approved formulary—'

'They had it in stock for a different indication. You remember I went to the conference of the American Academy of Pediatrics last year? I told you about it when we met for supper that night. The data is *so* strong, Josh. We should be using it in Britain, but it's all money, money, money—'

'Welcome to the reality of health-care provision.'

'The drug is at least fifty per cent more effective than the one I was supposed to use.'

'And three hundred per cent more expensive.'

'Because it's good,' Tasha snapped, 'and research of that quality comes at a price.'

'Don't lecture me on the economics of drug development.'

'Then don't lecture me on wanting to do the best for my patients. Those babies would have died, Josh! If I'd waited for the results or used a different drug, they would have died.' In her head she saw their tiny bodies as they lay with the life draining out of them. She heard their mother's heartbreaking sobs and saw the father, white faced and stoical, trying to be a rock while his world fell apart. And she saw herself, facing the most difficult decision of her professional life. 'They lived.' She felt wrung out. Exhausted. But telling her brother had somehow made everything clearer. Whatever happened to her, whatever the future held, it had been worth the price. She didn't need anyone else to tell her that.

'The drug worked?'

'Like magic.' The scientist in her woke up and excitement fizzed through her veins. 'It could transform the management of neonatal sepsis.'

'Have you written it up for one of the journals?'

'I'm going to. I just need to find the time.' And now she had time, she thought gloomily. Oodles of it.

'But the hospital authorities didn't approve and now you're in trouble?'

'I didn't exactly follow protocol, that's true, but I'd do the same thing again in the same circumstances. Unfortunately, my boss didn't agree.' Tasha turned her head and stared out of the window. 'Which is why I resigned.' Saying the word made her heart plummet. It sounded so—final.

'You did what?' Josh sounded appalled. 'Please tell me you're kidding.'

'No. I resigned on principle.' The anger rose, as fresh and raw as it had been on that morning when she'd faced her boss after two nights without sleep. 'I said to him, *What sort of department are you running when your budget comes before a baby's life?*'

'And no doubt you went on to tell him what sort of department he was running. Tactful, Tasha.' Josh rubbed his hand over his jaw. 'So you questioned his professional judgement and dented his ego.'

'A man of his position shouldn't need to have his ego protected. He shouldn't be that pathetic.'

'Did you tell him that as well?'

'I told him the truth.'

Josh winced. 'So…I'm assuming, given that he was the sort of guy to protect his ego, that he didn't take it well?'

'He's the sort of person who would stand and watch someone drown if health and safety hadn't approved a procedure for saving them. He said the manufacturer did not present a sufficiently robust economic analysis.' Tasha felt the emotion rush down on her and forced herself to breathe. 'So then I asked him if he was going to be the one who told the parents they'd lost both their babies because some idiot in a suit sitting behind his desk had crunched the numbers and didn't think their children's lives were worth the money.'

Josh closed his eyes briefly. 'Tasha—'

'Sorry.' The lump in her throat was back and this time it wasn't going anywhere. 'I *know* I should have been unemotional about the whole thing but I just can't be. Honestly, I'm steaming mad.'

'You don't say? Are you about to cry on me?'

'No, absolutely not.'

'The only time I've ever seen you cry was when Cheapskate died.'

They shared a look. Cheapskate had been the dog their mother had bought after their father had walked out. Tasha remembered hugging his warm body and feeling his tail thumping against her leg. She remembered thinking, *Don't ever leave me,* and then being devastated when he'd done just that.

'He was a great dog.'

'He was a lunatic.' But Josh's eyes were gentle. 'Tell me about those babies you saved. Are they still doing well?'

'Discharged home. You should have seen it, Josh. You know what it's like, trying to calculate these paediatric doses—they never have trial data in the right age of child, but this…' She smiled, the doctor in her triumphant. 'It's why I trained. To push boundaries. To save a life.'

'And you saved two.'

'And lost my job.'

'You shouldn't have resigned.'

It was a question she'd asked herself over and over again. 'I couldn't work with the man a moment longer. He was the sort who thought women should be nurses, not doctors.

Basically he's a—a—' She bit off the word and Josh gave a faint smile.

'I get the picture. Has it occurred to you that you might be too idealistic, Tasha?'

'No. Not too idealistic.' The conviction came from deep inside her. 'Isn't that why we're doctors? So that we can push things forward? If we all did what doctors have always done and no more, we wouldn't have progress.'

'There are systems—'

'And what if those systems are wrong? I can't work for someone like that. Sooner or later I would have had to inject him with something seriously toxic…' Tasha gave a cheeky smile '…but first I would, of course, have made sure it was approved by the formulary committee.'

'You're incorrigible.'

'No, I'm a doctor. I can accept that there are some patients I can't help. What I *can't* accept is that there are some patients I'm not allowed to help because someone has decided the treatment is too expensive! I mean, who decides what's important?' Tasha paced across his office, her head swirling with the same arguments that had tormented her for weeks. 'I told him that if the chief executive took a pay cut we'd be able to easily fund this drug for the few babies likely to need it.'

'I'm beginning to see why you felt the need to resign.'

'Well, what would you have done?'

'I have no idea.' Her brother spread his hands. 'It's impossible to say if you're not in that situation. Why didn't you wait for the blood cultures? Or use the first-line choice?'

'Because the twins were getting sicker by the minute and I felt that time was crucial. If we'd waited for that one drug, only for it to fail… My instincts were shrieking at me, Josh. And even while I was running tests, my consultant was telling me it wasn't sepsis and that the twins were suffering from something non-specific caused by the stress of delivery.' And she'd spun it around in her head, over and over again, looking for answers. 'Sometimes you see a patient and you're going through the usual and it all seems fine, except you know it isn't fine because something in here...' she tapped her head '...something in here is sending you warnings loud and clear.'

'You can't practise medicine based on emotion.'

'I'm not talking about emotion. I'm talking about instinct. I tell you, Josh, I *know* when a child isn't well. Don't ask me how.' She held up her hand to silence him. 'I just know. And I was right with the twins. But apparently that didn't matter to Mr Tick-All-The-Boxes Consultant. He has to play things by the book and if the book is wrong, tough. Which is a lame way to practise medicine.'

'And no doubt you told him that, too?'

'Of course. By the time he'd had all his evidence, he would have had two dead bodies. And he was angry with me because I saved their lives. He could have had a lawsuit on his hands, but did he thank me?' The injustice of it was like a sharp knife in her side, digging, twisting. 'Haven't you ever used instinct when you treat a patient?'

'If by instinct you mean clinical judgement, then, yes, of course, but, Tasha—'

'Wait a minute.' Tasha interrupted him, her brain working and her eyes wide. 'That little girl—'

'What little girl?'

'The one waiting to be seen in the main area. I heard the mother say that hay fever was making her asthma worse, but her eyelids were swollen and her face was puffy. I thought at the time that something wasn't right—just didn't seem like allergy to me—and—'

'That little girl is not your patient, Tasha.'

'She was wheezing.'

'As she would if she had asthma.'

'As she would if she had left-sided venous congestion. I knew there was something about her that bothered me.' Tasha picked up his phone and thrust it at him. 'Call the doctor in charge of her, Josh. Tell her to do the tests. Maybe she will anyway, but maybe she won't. In my opinion, that child has an underlying heart condition. Undiagnosed congenital anomaly? She needs an ECG and an echo.'

'Tasha—'

'Just do it, Josh. Please. If I'm wrong, I'll give up and get a job in a garden centre.'

With a sigh, Josh picked up his phone and called the doctor responsible for seeing the child.

While he talked, Tasha stood staring out of the window, wishing she didn't always get so upset about everything. Why couldn't she be emotionally detached, like so many of her colleagues? Why couldn't she just switch off and do the job?

'She's going to do a full examination, although she thinks it's asthma and allergy combined. We'll see. And now you need to relax.' Josh's voice was soft. 'You're in a state, Tasha.'

'I'm fine.' It was a lie. She'd desperately wanted a hug but was afraid that if someone touched her she'd start crying and never stop. 'But I do find myself with a lot of free time on my hands. I thought…' She hesitated, *hating* having to crawl to her brother. 'You're important. Can you pull a few strings here? Get me a job? The paediatric department has a good reputation.'

'Tasha—'

'Paediatrics is my life. My career. I'm good, Josh. I'm good at what I do.'

'I'm not debating that, but—'

'Yes, you are. You're worrying I'll mess things up for you here.'

'That isn't true.' Josh stood up and walked over to her. 'Calm down, will you? You're totally stressed out. Maybe what you need is a break from hospitals for a while.'

'What I need is a *job*. I love working with kids. I love being a doctor. And then there's the practical side. I was living in a hospital flat so now I'm homeless as well as jobless.'

Tasha felt as though she had an enormous mountain to climb. 'Resigning seemed like the only option at the time. Now I realise why more people don't resign on principle. It's too expensive.'

'I can't pull strings to get you a job at the hospital, Tasha. Not at the moment. We've spent a fortune opening a new paediatric burns unit. There's a head-count freeze.'

'Oh.' Her stomach swooped and fell as another door slammed shut in her face. 'No worries. I'll sort something out.' She tried to subdue the niggling worry that her last consultant wouldn't give her a decent reference. 'Sorry, I shouldn't have asked you. I shouldn't have just shown up here.' *The list of things she shouldn't have done was growing.*

'I'm glad you did. It's been too long since I saw you. All you've done for the past three years is work. Since things ended with Hugo, in fact.'

Hugo? Shrinking, Tasha wondered why her brother had chosen that particular moment to bring up her disastrous love life. Could the day get any worse? 'I love my work.' *Why was he looking at her like that?* 'What's wrong with loving my work?'

'No need to get defensive. Maybe it's time to take a break. Rediscover a social life.'

'Social life? What's that?'

'It's part of work-life balance. You were going to get married once.'

The reminder scraped like sandpaper over sensitive skin. 'A moment of madness.' Tasha spoke through her teeth. 'Do you mind if we don't talk about it? Just thinking about Hugo makes me want to put my fist through something and at the moment I can't afford to pay for the damage. Anyway, you're a fine one to talk. You're a total workaholic.' *But he'd spent the night with a woman.*

Tasha wondered if he'd confide in her, but Josh was flicking through some papers on his desk.

'How flexible are you?'

'I can touch my toes and do a back flip.' Her joke earned her an ironic glance.

'The job,' he drawled. 'How would you feel about a break from paediatrics?'

'I love paediatrics, but...' But she was desperate. She needed something. Not just for the money but to stop herself thinking and going slowly mad. She needed to be active. 'What do you have in mind?'

'I happen to know a man in desperate need of twenty-four-hour nursing care for the next month or so. He's asked me to sort something out for him.'

Tasha instinctively recoiled. 'You want me to give bed baths to some dirty old man who's going to pinch my bottom?' She frowned at the laughter in her brother's eyes. 'What's so funny about that? You have a sick sense of humour.'

'What if I tell you the guy in question happens to be seriously rich.'

'Who cares?' Tasha thrust her hands into the back pockets of her jeans, wondering what Josh was finding so funny. Her brother was clearly enjoying a joke at her expense and she felt a flash of irritation that he could laugh when she was in such a mess. 'What's the relevance of his financial status? You think I'll nurse him, he'll fall in love and marry me, then I'll kill him off and inherit his millions? When you suggested a job change, I didn't realise you were talking about a sugar daddy.'

'He's too young to be your sugar daddy.'

'And I'm not interested in marriage. I'm a cold-hearted career-woman, remember? I'm dedicating my life to my patients. So far my longest and most successful relationship has been with my stethoscope.'

'This guy isn't interested in marriage either, so you'll make a good pair. Strictly speaking, he should be in hospital for at least another week but he's creating hell so they're happy to discharge him providing he arranges professional help. He needs someone medical to deliver quality care at home and he's willing to pay premium rates.' He named a figure that made Tasha's jaw drop.

'He obviously has more money than sense. What's the catch?'

'The catch is that he's an athletic, super-fit guy who isn't used to being stuck in bed. As a result his temper is somewhat volatile and he's terrifying everyone who comes within a metre of him. But I'm sure you'll cope with that. I'm guessing it will take you about—oh—five minutes before you point out his shortcomings.'

'As jobs go it doesn't sound appealing...' But it was a job. And it was just for a couple of weeks. 'I suppose it would give me something to do while I look for a more progressive paediatric department. A place where the patient takes priority over paperwork and protocol.' Tasha frowned as she weighed up the pros and cons. 'So basically I have to help Mr Grumpy Guy with his physio, say *There, there* when he's cranky, feed him antibiotics and check he's not weight bearing. Anything else I need to know? Like his name?'

Josh smiled. 'His name, little sister, is Alessandro Cavalieri.'

Tasha felt the strength drain from her legs. Her heart pounded with a rhythm that would have concerned her had she not been too busy staring at her brother. 'Alessandro? *The* Alessandro?'

'The very same. His Royal Highness.'

She hadn't thought it was possible for the whole body to blush. Suddenly she was a teenager again and sobbing her heart out. 'The answer is no.' The words stumbled out of her mouth, disjointed, shaky. 'No! And don't look at me like that.'

'I thought you'd jump at the chance. You were crazy about him. He was all you ever talked about—Alessandro, Alessandro, Alessandro.' Josh mimicked her tone and Tasha felt the flush of mortification spread from her neck to her ears.

'I was seventeen,' she snapped. 'It may have escaped your notice but I've grown up since then.' But not enough. Not enough to be cool and detached. Not Alessandro. *No, no, no.* The humiliation crawled over her skin.

'I know you've grown up. That's why I'm offering you the job. If you still felt the same way you felt about him back then, you wouldn't be safe.' Josh's eyes teased her. 'Oh, boy, were you dangerous. Teenage hormones on legs. You threw yourself at him. Being royalty, he travelled everywhere with an armed guard but the person he really needed protection from was you. Every time he turned round, there you were in another minuscule bikini. I seem to remember he told you to come back when you'd grown a chest.'

Tasha relived humiliation and discovered it was no better the second time around. Dying inside, she folded her arms and gave her brother a mocking smile. 'Laugh it up, why don't you?'

'My little sister and the prince. You used to scribble his name all over your school books. I particularly liked the *Princess Tasha* you carved on the apple tree in the garden, although the heart was a weird shape.' Josh was clearly enjoying himself hugely and Tasha tapped her foot on the floor, irritated on the outside and squirming on the inside as she remembered those horrible, hideous months.

She'd been a little girl with very big dreams. And when those dreams had burst… 'Have you quite finished?'

'For now. Good job you were a late developer or he might have taken you up on your offer. Alessandro has always had a wicked reputation with women.'

And her brother clearly had no idea just how well deserved that reputation was, Tasha thought desperately, trying to block out images she just couldn't face.

Josh was still smiling. 'Anyway, he's been nagging me to find him someone to nurse him but it's been a nightmare because of the security clearance. And I have to be careful who I give him because if they're pretty he'll seduce them.

It's unbelievably complicated. You have no idea how much red tape we're trying to cut through. If we wait for the palace to approve someone, the guy will be in hospital for at least six months and that can't happen because the press are disrupting the place.'

'Why is security a problem?'

'He's the crown prince. Don't you watch the news? His older brother was killed in an accident. All very tragic.' Josh rummaged through the papers on his desk and pulled out a newspaper. 'Here. Your teenage crush is now officially Europe's most eligible bachelor.'

Tasha snatched the newspaper from him. Her head was filled with unsettling images of Alessandro playing in the garden with her brothers. *Alessandro stripped to the waist, a sheen of sweat on his bronzed chest as he kicked a ball into the goal with lethal accuracy.* 'I read about his brother. It was completely awful.' She tried to imagine bad boy Alessandro as Crown Prince. Nothing about the way he'd treated her had been princely. 'He was the black sheep of the family.'

'Alessandro always had a difficult relationship with his parents but he was close to his brother. It's been hard for him. And he's now heir to a throne he doesn't really want. He prefers his freedom.'

Freedom to break hearts all over the world. 'I can't imagine Alessandro in a position of responsibility.' And that was the attraction. Restless, edgy, a danger-seeker. The devil in him had drawn her.

'He wasn't given any choice. It's a matter of succession. He's the heir, whether he likes it or not. So what do you think? I'd say it's the perfect job for you.' Josh was looking pleased with himself. 'You idolised him.'

'I did not idolise him. And the last thing I want to do is act as nurse to Alessandro Cavalieri,' she snapped. 'He's arrogant, full of himself…' *Super-bright, scorching hot and sexy as hell.*

He'd—and she'd—

Oh, God.

Feeling the blood rush into her cheeks, Tasha turned to look out of the window. She couldn't face him.

Sexual awareness shot through her, as unexpected as it was unwelcome. The man wasn't even in the room, she thought angrily, so why did she feel hot all over?

It was just her memory playing tricks.

What you found sexy at seventeen just made you angry at twenty-eight.

This was the man who had destroyed her dreams. He could have treated her kindly and let her down gently, but instead he'd been brutal. Cruel.

She should thank him, Tasha thought numbly. He'd screwed up her confidence and her relationships with men, but he'd done wonders for her career. When she'd finally emerged from under the rubble of her fantasies she'd given up on relationships and focused on her studies. Instead of parties, she'd spent her evenings with books. And her family hadn't questioned it. Her brothers had just been relieved that wild Tasha had finally settled down to study. They had no idea what had happened that night.

Thank goodness.

Josh would have killed him.

Her brother was idly flicking through correspondence, apparently unaware of her trauma. 'He was pretty arrogant, I suppose…' Josh signed a letter. 'But that was hardly surprising. When we were at university, women couldn't leave him alone.'

Tasha stood stiff as a board. 'Really?'

'You were crazy about him.' Josh dropped the letter in his in tray. 'Are you embarrassed to face him again?'

'No! Of course not! I just—have better things to do with my time, that's all. I'm a paediatrician. I need a job in paediatrics. I need to think of my CV.'

'Because it's just that it occurred to me that you did flirt with him a lot.'

I want it to be you, Alessandro. I want you to be the first.

Tasha felt as though she'd been plunged head first into a furnace. 'I was a teenage girl. I flirted with everyone.' Why was she reacting like this when it had happened almost ten years ago? *Get over it, Tasha.*

But humiliation wasn't so easily forgotten. Neither was Alessandro, which was crazy because she probably wouldn't even find him attractive any more. It had just been the whole prince thing and her impressionable, romantic teenage brain.

She knew better now.

Tasha leaned against the wall, forcing herself to breathe slowly. *Unfinished business*, she thought. He'd walked away and left her wounded. She'd never had the opportunity to defend herself, to tell him how much he'd hurt her.

Anger flashed through her, sharp and bright.

There was no way she could nurse him through a broken ankle. She was more likely to break the other one for him.

Tasha opened her mouth to turn her brother down and then a thought flitted into her brain. Shocked, she shook her head. *No. She couldn't do that.* It would be juvenile. Shallow. It would be…

Fun?

Satisfying?

It would teach him a lesson.

'This nursing job…' Her lips moved and she heard herself speaking. 'Does it involve moving in with him?'

'Yes, of course. He needs someone there day and night for a month or so. Maybe a bit longer.'

Day and night.

That was plenty of time to drive a man out of his mind. *To make him sorry.*

She'd show him that he no longer had any effect on her and at the same time she'd finally purge him from her mind. The spectacular man in her head was the product of a teenage fantasy. Living with the reality would cure her of that once and for all. And it would give her a chance to restore her dignity.

Josh put his pen down slowly. 'You're thinking about it? A moment ago you were telling me he was arrogant and full of himself.'

'He was young. He's probably changed.' She didn't believe it for a minute. A man like Alessandro would never change. Looks, wealth and influence were welded together. 'It would be great to see him again. I'd like to help him.' Tasha tapped her foot on the floor as she considered the various forms that 'help' could take.

'You're sure you won't find it awkward? You were crazy about him.'

'Awkward? Gosh, no.' She told herself that whatever awkwardness she was going to feel would be eclipsed by his. And she'd be so dignified and mature about the whole thing, that would make him feel even worse. The plan grew in her head. 'I have to warn you, I'm not much of a nurse, Josh. I'm good with kids but moaning adults with man-flu drive me up the wall. I just want to tell them to pull themselves together.'

'It isn't man-flu. His ankle shattered and so far he's been back to Theatre four times. On top of that he has a couple of broken ribs and countless bruises.'

'So you're saying he's pretty much helpless?'

Better and better...

'Completely helpless. That's why it's important that we find the right person. He doesn't want to find himself trapped with someone who doesn't understand him.'

'Right. Well, that's good because I do understand him.' *She understood him perfectly.* He was a rich, handsome playboy who treated women like flashy accessories. His idea of permanency was two dates.

'It's important that whoever looks after him knows what he needs.'

Tasha looked sympathetic. 'I know *exactly* what he needs.'

A wake-up call. A lesson in how to treat women properly. He was used to fawning women treating him with deference. And she needed to finally prove to herself that Alessandro Cavalieri was well and truly in her past. 'I'm very good at persuading patients to take their medicine, so I think I'm just the woman for the job.'

'I'm sure you are. You have good instincts and you're not scared of him. The staff here are intimidated by his status and afraid to tell him what he needs to do. He's walking all over them.'

'That can't be good for his broken ankle,' Tasha said lightly. 'Don't worry. I won't let him walk over me.' *Not this time.* This time she was going to be the one doing the walking.

She looked down at her trainers and wished she was wearing heels.

Josh was watching her. 'You're not going to fall for him again, are you?'

Tasha's laugh was genuine. 'Absolutely no chance of that.' She wasn't that stupid, was she? 'The only thing on my mind is my next job.'

'OK. Good—so you'll do it? Nag him about his physio and make sure he doesn't sneak women into his bed when he's supposed to be resting? Take care of him? That's great. Why don't you pop and see him right now? He's in a private room. I can give you directions.'

Right now?

Tasha's smile faltered. Her heart trebled its rhythm. No, not right now. She'd just lost her job. Well, not exactly *lost* it as such—she'd thrown it away. The last thing she needed was to heap on the humiliation. Facing Alessandro took serious preparation. She needed to get her head together. She needed to look her best.

Aware that Josh was looking at her, Tasha breathed slowly and tried to slow her pulse rate. If she said no, her brother would ask questions. And the longer she waited, the more the anticipation would eat into her. And the advantage of doing it right away was that Alessandro wasn't forewarned. He wasn't expecting to see her.

Tasha strolled to the mirror in the corner of the office and stared at her reflection. Green eyes stared back at her. Green eyes that showed lack of sleep and stress. Doctor's eyes.

Apart from the shadows and the obvious exhaustion, she didn't look that bad, did she?

Mouth too big, she thought. Freckles. Dark hair that twisted and curled over her shoulders. All wrong. As a teenager, she'd been horribly conscious of her gypsy looks. She'd envied the girls with sleek blonde hair and china-blue eyes.

Insecurity crawled through her belly and she glared at her reflection, refusing to allow herself to think like that. At least she had a brain, which was more than could be said for most of Alessandro's women.

But there was no doubt that there was work to be done before she faced her past. Alessandro Cavalieri spent his time with the most beautiful women in the world. Facing him with confidence required more than an emergency repair job, but it would have to do.

With a sense of purpose, Tasha pulled her make-up case out of her bag.

'Poor Alessandro.' She darkened her lashes and added blusher to her cheeks. Not much. Just enough to help the 'natural' look. 'He must be going crazy, stuck in bed. You're right. What he needs is personal attention.'

And she was going to give him personal attention.

By the time she'd finished with him, a shattered ankle was going to be the least of his worries.

She was going to make him writhe with guilt for crushing her dreams so brutally. It was time he realised that women had feelings.

Josh was watching her in bemusement. 'Why are you putting on make-up?'

'Because I care how I look and because I want to look

professional.' Staring into her bag, she selected a subtle gloss lipstick. 'Last time we met, I was a teenager. That's how he's going to remember me. I need to look like an adult—like someone capable of taking care of him.'

'You look very happy all of a sudden for someone who has just lost their job. A few moments ago I thought you were going to cry.'

'Me? Cry? Don't be ridiculous. Don't worry, Josh. I'll take good care of your friend.' Tasha tugged at the clip and her hair tumbled long and loose around her shoulders. Smiling to herself, she gave her head a shake. 'I'll take *extremely* good care of him.'

Alessandro Cavalieri had taken her fragile teenage heart and ground it under his feet.

Payback time, she thought as she added the high-shine gloss to her lips.

It was going to be her pleasure to give him exactly what he deserved.

And maybe, just maybe, once he'd given her a big, fat grovelling apology, she'd be able to put the whole episode behind her.

CHAPTER TWO

'YOUR Highness, you *can't* use your phone in the hospital.'

Alessandro turned frustrated dark eyes onto the nervous nurse, his temper reaching combustion point. 'Then get me out of hospital,' he said silkily, and watched as she bit her lip nervously.

'I'm really sorry but I don't have the authority to do that. You have an infection, Your Highness, and—'

'Stop calling me Your Highness.' The snap of the words was accompanied by a rush of guilt. *She was just a kid.* It wasn't her fault that he wanted the rank and title about as much as he wanted a badly smashed ankle and bruised ribs. 'I apologise,' he growled. 'Being stuck in here hasn't done much for my mood. I'm used to being active.' And lying in bed gave him too much time to think about things he spent his life trying to forget.

The darkness licked at the edges of his mind threatening to engulf him. With a huge effort of will, he pushed it back.

Not now.

The nurse stood rigid, clearly overawed by her royal patient. 'The Chief Executive of the hospital called while you were with the consultant and asked me to tell you that he's increased security so that there's no repeat of yesterday's fiasco—he apologised profusely, Your Highness. We have no idea how that journalist managed to climb up the drainpipe to your room.' She all but curtseyed but this time Alessandro kept his temper on a tight leash. It was obvious that she wasn't going to be able to behave naturally with him, and he'd encountered that all too often in his life to be surprised. No one behaved naturally with him. Everyone had an agenda.

'I'm used to journalists climbing drainpipes and crawling through the windows. It's a fact of life.' He reached for a glass of water, gritting his teeth against the agonising pain that shot through his body.

'Let me help you, sir.'

'I can manage.' Alessandro growled the words just as his shaking hand deposited most of the water over his chest. He switched to Italian, his native tongue, and swore long and fluently while the flustered nurse quietly removed the glass from his white fingers, refilled it and handed it to him.

She stared at his T-shirt, now clinging to his chest. 'Do you want me to—?'

'No. I'm fine.'

Dragging her eyes away from his muscles, the girl swallowed. 'Your senior adviser called, sir. He wanted you to call him urgently.'

Alessandro leaned his head back against the pillow and suppressed the urge to laugh out loud. That was the one good thing about this mess—his advisers were climbing the walls. The wicked side of him revelled in the chaos his accident had caused. 'I can't call him,' he drawled. 'You've just told me I'm not allowed to use my phone.'

'There's a phone by your bed, sir—Your Highness.'

For God's sake— 'You can call me Alessandro. And I think we've both just established that I can't reach anything that's by my bed.'

'There were a few other calls, Your Highness.' She gave him a nervous glance. 'Five journalists and four—er—women. None of them left their names. And Her Highness Princess Eleanor called when you were in the bathroom. She said not to bother calling her back but she left you a message.'

'Which was?'

'She saw on the news that the hospital is besieged by journalists and she asked that you be discreet about what you say to them.'

Alessandro gave a humourless smile.

The dull ache inside him turned into a dark black hole that threatened to suck him down.

So his mother had finally called.

Not when his accident had been announced as a newsflash and no one had known his condition. Not out of concern when he'd been rushed into Theatre for emergency surgery. Not to ask how he was or send love. No, his mother had called because she was worried about his image. Or rather she was worried about *her* image.

You have to think about how you present yourself, Alessandro. It affects all of us.

Wiping the cold, disapproving tone from his head, Alessandro sought distraction. The nurse was pretty, he realised, and he hadn't even noticed. Which said a great deal about his current state of mind. He had a wicked impulse to drag her to the window and kiss her senseless in front of the crowd of hopeful photographers.

But that wouldn't be fair on the girl.

Or on Miranda.

Thinking of Miranda was enough to kill his mood.

He was going to have to make a decision. They couldn't go on like this any longer. It wasn't fair on either of them.

'I don't suppose I can bribe you to smuggle me out of here?' He tried to look as non-threatening as possible. 'I own a home up the coast. Incredible views from the master bedroom.'

The nurse flushed scarlet and her eyes met his. He saw the excitement there and the way her lips parted as she caught her breath. Unfortunately he could also read her mind, which was busy spinning dreams ending with 'nurse marries Prince'.

Thinking of his parents' dutiful, entirely loveless marriage, he felt suddenly cold.

He had no idea why marriage was the ultimate goal for so many people. To him it seemed like the road to hell. He'd rather be trampled by a whole herd of horses than commit to one woman for the rest of his life. Especially a woman whose only interest in him was the fact he had royal blood.

'You understand that this is a purely indecent proposal.' He shifted his leg, but it did nothing to ease the pain. 'My house has amazing sea views from every room and a hot tub on the deck. You can scrub my back and give me a private physio session.'

'This is Cornwall.' A crisp female voice came from the doorway. 'If she uses the hot tub in April, she'll catch pneumonia. Hello, Alessandro. You look as though you're in a filthy mood. Hope I'm not supposed to bow or curtsey.'

It was a voice he hadn't heard for more than a decade, but the recognition was immediate and powerful. His body tightened in a reaction so basic, so elemental that he was relieved that he was confined to bed, with all the privacy that afforded. Temptation, he thought, wasn't something a man easily forgot. And Natasha O'Hara had been temptation on legs. A girl, desperate to become a woman. At seventeen, she'd tried everything to get him to notice her.

And he'd noticed.

Oh, yes, he'd noticed.

Remembering, Alessandro felt his muscles tighten. Sweat dampened his brow. He wasn't sure whether the pain in his chest was due to fractured ribs or guilt.

He'd treated her badly.

She strolled into the room with a confidence that told him the awkward teenager was long gone. There was no sign of the stiff formality that everyone else displayed around him. She didn't blush, call him 'Your Highness', or look as though she was about to bow and scrape at his feet. Her gaze was direct and challenging and he would have laughed with relief if it hadn't been for the uncomfortable feeling deep inside him. Tasha had always shown guts and intelligence. If someone had told her to bow or curtsey, her response would have been to ask why. One of the reasons he'd loved spending time with her was because she'd treated him as a normal human being.

And in return he'd broken her heart.

He shifted uncomfortably in the bed, but the guilt stayed with him.

Was she the sort of woman who bore grudges? Not for a moment did he think she would have forgotten that summer any more than he had.

'Are you going to pretend you don't recognise me?' Her tone was light and friendly and if she was bearing a grudge there was no sign of it.

Alessandro relaxed slightly. Maybe the guilt was misplaced. She'd been very young, he reasoned. He'd probably barely featured on her adolescent landscape. Everything healed quickly in childhood—broken bones and broken hearts.

Still watching him, she paused beside the bed. Her top was a vivid scarlet and she wore it tucked into skinny jeans, her dark hair tumbling down her back in snaky black curls. She looked like a cross between a gypsy and a flamenco dancer and Alessandro felt his mouth dry and his body harden in an all-male reaction.

The wild child had grown up.

'You've spilt water on your T-shirt.' She eyed his damp chest and he felt something stir inside him.

'It isn't easy manoeuvring with a broken ankle and two broken ribs.'

'Poor Alessandro.' Her voice poured over him like honey, soft and sympathetic. 'So that's why you're so cranky. It must be awful to feel so helpless.'

Pain gnawed at his temper, fraying his control. He'd kept his mind off the pain by thinking of ways to get himself out of the hospital, but her presence disturbed his focus. And the way she was looking at him felt wrong. He would have expected her to be angry with him or, if not angry, then at least a little shy? Or maybe embarrassed. After all, he'd— Alessandro moved awkwardly and pain rocketed through him. 'What are you doing here?' He ruthlessly ignored the pain. 'Josh mentioned that you worked at a hospital miles away.'

'Not any more. I'm…' she paused and then smiled '…in between jobs.'

Their eyes met and held and Alessandro wondered what the hell he'd done to deserve this extra punishment. 'You're looking good, Natasha.' *Too good,* he thought, noticing in that single reluctant glance that her body had fulfilled its teenage promise. As a girl, she'd been teenage temptation. As a woman, Natasha O'Hara was a vision of glorious curves that made a man think of nothing but wild sex. And thinking of wild sex made him ache in the only place that wasn't already aching, so he looked away from those smooth arms, tried to block out the image of those slender limbs and told himself that the last glossy mouth he'd kissed had led to nothing but trouble.

'Thanks, Nurse…er…' She squinted at the name badge. 'Carpenter. You've taken enough abuse from this patient for one day. I'll take it from here.'

Nurse Carpenter's face fell. 'But I've just come on duty and His Highness needs—'

'I know exactly what His Highness needs.' The words were a polite but firm dismissal and Alessandro tried to remember whether she'd had that air of command as a teenager. No, definitely not. She'd been full of wide-eyed, barely repressed excitement and optimism. 'Hopeless romantic' hadn't begun to describe her.

The nurse gave Alessandro a final wistful look and melted away.

Tasha closed the door firmly, leaving the two of them

enclosed in the private room. 'Yes, Your Highness, no, Your Highness—it must drive you crazy. Or do you like your women servile?'

She was such a contrast to all the other people he'd come into contact with since he'd crashed into the mud on the polo field that Alessandro found himself laughing for the first time in weeks. 'Definitely not servile.'

'Good, because if I have to call you Your Highness every two minutes, this is never going to work.'

Alessandro watched as she strolled across the room. Something about the way she was looking at him made him uneasy. Or maybe it was just the guilt, he thought. It was definitely there, shimmering underneath the surface. 'What are you talking about?'

'You have to stop eating the nurses for breakfast, Alessandro. They're all terrified of you.'

'I'm a pussy cat.'

Her mouth flickered. 'Right.'

'Maybe I'm a little cranky, but I'm not good at lying in bed, doing nothing.'

'Then you'd better get used to it.' Her gaze was frank and direct. 'I looked at your X-rays. You won't be walking on that ankle for a while. You've made a mess of your bones.'

'Not me. The horse.' But it had been his fault and the knowledge gnawed at him. He'd been distracted. To take his mind off that, he studied her closely. *Was she taller or was it the way she held herself?* There was a confidence about her that hadn't been there a decade before. A knowledge of herself as a woman. It showed itself in the way her hips swayed when she walked and the hint of cleavage revealed by the neck of her casual top. Trapped and immobile, unaccustomed to feeling helpless in any situation, Alessandro set his teeth and tried to think cold thoughts. 'What are you doing here, Tasha?' He hadn't seen her since that night—the night when he'd left her sobbing, her make-up streaked over her beautiful face.

He pushed the memory aside, trying to lose it in the darkness of everything else he was trying to forget.

'Rumour is you're looking for a nurse so you can escape from this place.'

'In this case rumour is correct.' But he was starting to wonder whether being trapped at home with a star-struck nurse who called him Your Highness every two minutes might not be just as irritating as being in hospital.

'I can't imagine who would want the job. As temperaments go, yours is pretty volatile.'

'Once I'm out of here my temper will be just fine. Josh promised to find me a nurse by the end of the day. Do you know if he's had any luck?'

'Depends on your definition of luck.' She picked up the phone that he'd slung on the bedcover. 'You shouldn't be using this in the hospital. It's breaking the rules.'

'So I've been told. Trouble is, I've never been much good with rules.'

Her beautiful mouth flickered into a tiny smile of mutual understanding. 'That's one thing we have in common, then. But while you're in here, you have to behave.'

'Discharge me and I'll behave. So—has he found me a nurse?'

'Not a nurse, exactly.'

'What's that supposed to mean? I have to have someone who knows what they're talking about. And preferably someone who doesn't call me Your Highness at the end of every sentence.' He needed to get out of here before lying here trapped with his own thoughts drove him crazy. He needed distraction.

Tasha lifted her head. Her gaze connected with his. '*I* know what I'm talking about. And I have no intention of calling you Your Highness.'

'You?' Alessandro felt shock thud through his gut. 'You're a children's doctor.' She was also someone he'd carefully avoided for over a decade.

'I'm a doctor. My speciality just happens to be children. But I have all the skills necessary to assist your rehabilitation. I can nag you to do your exercises, throw away the junk food and make sure you take lots of healing early nights—' humour lightened her voice '—on your own. I've never been anyone's nurse before but I'm a quick study.'

His mouth felt dry but he was in too much pain to try and reach for his glass again. 'You're offering to nurse me?'

'We're old friends, Alessandro. It's the least I can do.' Her smile was warm and genuine, so why did he feel so uneasy?

Something didn't feel right.

He decided that this was one of those occasions that merited the direct approach. 'You and I, we didn't exactly part on good terms.'

'No. You were a complete bastard,' she said frankly, 'but that was a long time ago. I was at an impressionable age. Do you honestly think I'm still bothered about something that happened almost ten years ago? That would be ridiculous, don't you think?'

Would it?

He looked at her for a long moment, his eyes searching out the true sentiment behind the lightly spoken words. 'Tasha—'

She leaned towards him, mockery in her gaze. 'I was seventeen years old. I had no taste, and I was overwhelmed by the fact that you were a prince. And now we've got that out of the way, can we just forget it? No girl should be made to feel embarrassed about the foolish crushes she had as a teenager. So what do you say, Alessandro? Am I hired?'

Josh opened the front door of his house, his mood swerving between elation and guilt.

He tried to push the guilt back where it belonged.

His marriage to Rebecca was over. She was the one who had called time on their relationship and moved out. They'd wanted different things. Right through their relationship, they'd wanted different things.

As he hung up his jacket Megan's fragrance engulfed him, wrapping him in memories.

Maybe he'd moved on a bit quickly, but he was human, and when it came to Megan…

Just thinking about her lifted his mood, and he closed the front door, relieved that Tasha had refused his invitation to come home with him. He needed time to think, but already his mind was racing ahead, thinking of the future. He wanted Megan here, with him, all the time. He wanted to laugh with her over a meal, he wanted to sleep with her and wake up with her. They were adults, weren't they? He was past the age of wanting to creep around like a teenager. Snatched moments in the on-call room would never be enough for him. He knew what he wanted now.

He wanted Megan. In his life. For ever.

Energised by a certainty he'd never felt before, Josh checked his phone, hoping to find a message from her, but there was nothing and he was surprised by the strength of the disappointment that thudded through him.

Had she gone back to sleep after he'd received the call that his sister was in the department? He imagined her still lying there, in sheets tangled from the heat of their loving, dreaming about what they'd shared.

Was she planning even as he was planning?

Pondering that question, he threw his keys on the table, feeling lighter than he had in months. Smiling slightly, he retrieved the post from the floor and strolled into the kitchen, lured by the promise of strong coffee.

'Hello, Josh.' Rebecca sat there, her beautiful face pale, her eyes sharp with accusation.

Reality slapped his dreams in the face.

Josh felt the lightness evaporate and a sick dread that he couldn't identify settled around him like a dark cloak. 'What are you doing here?'

'I'm your wife, Josh.' Her tone was brittle. 'This is still my home.'

Guilt churned inside him. It was hard to remember they'd ever been close. Hard to remember that once they'd chosen each other.

'Where were you last night?'

He bit back the urge to tell her to mind her own business. 'At the hospital. It's where I work.'

'But you weren't working, were you? And don't bother lying to me because I phoned the hospital to ask where you were.' She gave a thin smile. 'Consultant's wife's privileges. No one knew where you were, but they did know you weren't on duty.'

Josh felt as though the walls of the house were closing in on him. Moments ago his future had seemed so clear. Now all he saw was murky black. 'Rebecca—'

'Am I supposed to be grateful that you didn't have sex with her in our bed?' Her fury snapped chunks out of the fragile remains of their relationship. 'Who is she, Josh? And don't bother denying there's someone else because I can see it in your eyes.'

It wasn't just in his eyes. It was in his heart. It was all through him and it gave him strength to do the right thing. *To fight.*

Josh straightened his shoulders. 'There is someone. You and I—our relationship is over, Rebecca. We've agreed that, and—'

'I'm pregnant.'

The silence in the room was absolute. It was as if the words had stopped time but he knew it wasn't the case because the hands of the kitchen clock were still moving.

Pregnant. A baby.

Josh felt strangely detached. The words floated through his numb brain but didn't settle. Pregnant. It was as if he was outside himself, looking in. And then reality punched him in the gut. Denial burst to the surface, driven by a desperate need to hold onto the dream. 'No.' The word was dragged from deep inside him. 'You can't be. That isn't possible.'

'Why? Because it isn't convenient for you? Because it isn't what you want?' Her voice rose. 'I've got news for you, Josh. Babies don't always come along at the most convenient moment in your life.'

He knew that. Just hours ago Megan had finally confirmed that the baby she'd lost so traumatically eight years earlier had been his—a cruel epilogue to the night both of them had spent in hell. His decision to save Megan's life all those years before had cost her a child. Their child. The knowledge intensified a guilt and pain that had never left him.

When he and Rebecca had split, his first thought had been, *Thank goodness we didn't have kids.*

And now…

'You know I don't want children.'

Rebecca's laugh was devoid of humour. 'Maybe you should have thought about that before you had sex with me.' There was a coarseness to her declaration that made him feel like scrubbing his skin.

'That was a mistake.' Josh stood still, the ache in his heart more painful than anything physical that she could inflict on him. Now, with some distance, he couldn't imagine why they'd had sex again. What had driven him back into her bed? His brain tried to drag out details from that night but all he remembered was her, urging him on… 'Did you do it on purpose?' Blind with pain, he shot the words at her, wanting the truth even though he knew it wouldn't change the facts. The colour in her cheeks answered his question and he swallowed down the bitter taste of contempt. 'You chose to bring a child into a dead, loveless marriage?'

'You chose to have sex with me,' she said acidly. 'So it's not completely dead, is it? Or maybe you've conveniently forgotten that night.'

No, he hadn't forgotten. The memory sat in his gut, the regret hard and undigested. Of all the mistakes he'd made in

his life, that was the biggest. If he could rewind the clock…
'You were taking the Pill.'

'I'm pregnant, Josh. Nothing either of us does or says is
going to change that. So before you get too deeply embedded
in this exciting new relationship of yours, we need to think
what we're going to do. You're going to be a father.'

CHAPTER THREE

As IDEAS went, this had been one of her worst.

Tense and on edge, Tasha paced around Alessandro's stunning, contemporary clifftop home, wishing she'd never agreed to the plan. But refusing would have invited awkward questions from Josh. And anyway, she hadn't thought for a moment that she'd feel anything for Alessandro except mild contempt.

She'd planned to wash the boy out of her hair—she'd forgotten that the boy was now a man. A man who oozed sex appeal and natural authority even when badly injured. From the moment she'd walked into his private room and seen him watching the nurse through those slanting, slightly mocking eyes she'd known she was in trouble.

The nerves jumped in her stomach and she realised how long it had been since she'd been around a man who had that effect on her. The few relationships she had, she was careful to keep light and casual. She preferred it that way.

Her usual confidence deserting her, Tasha kept her back to him and focused her attention on the house. The place was incredible. Built on one level, floor-to-ceiling glass wrapped itself around the house, giving uninterrupted views over the beach from every angle of the living room. Deep soft sofas in ocean colours grouped around a large blue-and-white-striped rug and there were touches of the sea everywhere. Elegant pieces of driftwood. An old anchor. And then there were the paintings and the books.

Tasha glanced in envy at the bookshelves and wished she had a free month to read her way through the collection while lying on one of those squashy sofas and occasionally looking at the view. Somehow the place managed to be stylish and contemporary while maintaining a cosy, intimate feel.

'How on earth did you find this place?'

'I knew where I wanted to live. When this house came up, someone tipped me off.'

Knowing how much property cost in this part of the world, Tasha gave a wry smile. 'I dread to think how much you paid.'

'The real problem was planning permission. The original house was structurally unsound and we had to persuade them that this would enhance the landscape.'

Tasha glanced up at the double height living room, awash with light. 'Your architect was clever.'

The view alone would have fetched millions. Outside, a wide deck curved around the house, a glass balustrade offering some protection while ensuring that not a single element of the outdoors was lost. The home shrieked style and sophistication. And then there were the gadgets…

It was a contemporary palace, she thought, *fit for a playboy prince.*

The evidence of wealth was everywhere and the high-tech security meant there was no forgetting the identity of her patient. From the moment the electronic gates had opened onto the long winding drive that led up to the clifftop house, she'd been aware of the security cameras. And then there was the team of highly trained security staff who worked shifts protecting the prince.

Tasha risked a glance at him and thought to herself that he didn't look like a man who needed anyone's protection. From the dark stubble on his jaw to the dangerous gleam of his eyes, he was more pirate than prince.

It occurred to her that she'd only ever met him in her world. Never in his. She'd never thought of him like this, with protection officers on twenty-four-hour rotation.

At seventeen she'd been in awe of the fact that he was actually a prince, but she'd never thought about what that really meant. To her, the word 'prince' made her think of fairy-tales. Of chivalry, bravery and honour. To a little girl whose father had walked out, those qualities had seemed like riches. She still remembered her reaction when Josh had told her his university friend was coming to stay. Her mouth had dropped open and she'd said those words that afterwards she'd regretted for years. *'A real, live prince?'* From that moment onwards she'd been doomed to a lifetime of teasing by her older brothers, but at the time she hadn't even cared. Meeting a prince had been the ultimate romantic experience for a teenager just discovering boys. Her brain had taken up permanent residence in dreamland. Right from the day he'd stepped out of his armoured car, the sun gleaming off his glossy dark hair, she'd carried on dreaming. At twenty, Alessandro Cavalieri had been insanely handsome, but what had really drawn her had been his charm. Used to being on the receiving end of nothing but verbal abuse from her brothers and their friends, his charisma had been fascinating and compelling. Instead of treating her as a tomboy, he'd treated her as a woman. She'd never stood a chance.

She'd dreamed her way through countless lessons, concocting scenarios where Alessandro ignored all the beautiful girls who threw themselves at him because he couldn't look at anyone but her. The reality had been so far removed from the fantasy that the inevitable crash between the two had been catastrophic.

Reminding herself of that fact settled the nerves in her stomach. True, he was even more spectacular to look at now, but she was no longer a dreamy, romantic teenager. Neither was she interested in a relationship with a man whose only commitment was to his own ego. She was past the age when a handsome face was the only thing she noticed.

Relieved to have rationalised the situation, Tasha started to relax. 'The view of the beach is good. The surfing here is some of the best in Cornwall and it's never busy because of the rocks. You have to know what you're doing.'

'Josh told me you all used to spend hours surfing here when you were kids.'

'It used to drive our mother out of her mind with worry.' She rested her head against the glass. 'It's been so long since I surfed.'

'That surprises me. I can't imagine you working in a city.'

'That's where the job was.' *Was.* Tasha felt a ripple of panic but masked it quickly. 'Anyway, it feels good to be home. Familiar.'

'There's a private path from the terrace that leads straight down onto the beach. It's the reason I bought this property. You can surf from the front door. Did you bring your wet-suit?'

'Of course.' Tasha thought about the suitcases in her car. She was like a snail, she thought, carrying her world around on her back. And what was she doing, talking surfing with him? The point of this wasn't to be intimate or cosy. Deciding that it was never too soon to start inflicting a little extra pain, she gave a sympathetic smile. 'Shame you can't join me.'

'Thanks for the reminder.' The irritation in Alessandro's voice confirmed that her arrow had found its target.

'At least I'll be able to get out there and surf, and I'll give you a report,' Tasha said kindly, feeling a flash of satisfaction as she saw his jaw tighten. *Oh, boy, are you going to suffer.* She was about to twist the knife again when he shifted position and she saw pain flicker in his eyes. His naturally olive skin was several shades paler than usual and she could see the strain in his face. The physician in her at war with the woman, Tasha strolled over to him. 'Moving you from the hospital to here must have been a painful experience.'

'It was fine.'

He hadn't uttered a word of complaint but she knew that he must have been in agonising pain. 'I'll try and help you find a comfortable position.'

'I'm perfectly comfortable. And I don't need your help.'

'That's why you're paying me, remember? To help you. You need a nurse to look after you.'

'I needed a nurse because they wouldn't discharge me from hospital without one. Not for any other reason.' Jaw clenched, Alessandro manoeuvred himself onto the sofa, the pain involved leaving him white-faced. The muscles of his shoulders bunched as he took his weight on the crutches. 'I don't need to be looked after.'

Tasha found herself looking at those muscles. Pumped up. Sleek and hard. She frowned. *So what?* It took more than muscles to make a real man. 'So if you don't need to be looked after, what am I expected to do? File my nails?'

'You can do whatever you like. Read a book. Watch TV. Surf—although if that's how you spend your day, I'd rather you didn't tell me about it.' He dropped the crutches onto the floor with a clatter that said as much about his mood as the black frown on his face. 'Do whatever you like. Consider it an all-expenses-paid holiday.'

But she wouldn't choose to take a holiday with him, would she?

Ten years had done nothing but add to his physical attractions, she thought irritably. It was all very well reminding herself that looks didn't count, but everything about him was unapologetically masculine and being alone with him made her feel jittery. Which was ridiculous, she told herself, given that he could barely walk. He was hardly going to leap on her, was he? Anyway, he'd made it clear years before that he didn't find her attractive.

Reminded of the 'flat-chested' comment by her brother,

it was all she could do to stop herself thrusting her chest forward. 'Now that I'm here, you might as well at least let me fetch you a drink.'

'Thanks. A drink would be good.' The tension in his voice reflected the pain he was fighting. 'Whisky is in the cupboard in the kitchen and you'll find glasses on the top shelf. Join me. We'll have drinks on the terrace if I can get myself there.'

Drinks on the terrace?

Tasha felt a flash of alarm. No way. Lounging on the deck, watching the sun go down over golden sand was far too intimate a scenario. That wasn't what she had in mind at all. This was about inflicting pain, not taking pleasure. Not that she thought she was in any danger of falling for him again, but as a scientist reviewing the evidence she had to concede that it had happened before.

'A drink sounds like a good idea, but forget the terrace. You only just sat down, and if you keep moving you'll just make the pain worse.' Whisky, she thought, laced with arsenic or something equally poisonous. Or maybe just whisky along with the powerful painkiller and antibiotics he'd been prescribed. It would knock him unconscious and then she wouldn't need to worry about falling for his dangerous charm.

Not that he seemed charming right now. Pain had made him irritable and moody and he leaned his head back against the sofa, jaw clenched, eyes closed. 'I'll have it straight. No water. No ice.'

In other words, nothing to dilute the effects of the alcohol.

Tasha walked into the kitchen, knowing that every movement she made was being followed by those fierce black eyes. She remembered him telling her that his ancestors had been warriors, descendents of the Romans who had once colonised the Mediterranean island of San Savarre that was his home. It was all too easy to imagine Alessandro Cavalieri in warrior mode.

Irritated with herself, shrugging off those thoughts, she opened cupboards until she found whisky. Closing her hand around the bottle, she hesitated. It would be really bad for him to drink with the tablets, but Alessandro didn't seem to care. Clearly he was seeking oblivion. He'd drink whisky and to hell with the consequences. In fact, he'd probably enjoy the experience of alcohol and painkillers. Tasha put the bottle back. She wasn't here to do what he wanted. She wasn't here to make his life comfortable. It was already comfortable enough.

She glanced around her. The kitchen was like something from an upmarket show home. Light poured through a glass atrium and reflected off shiny black granite work surfaces. It was smooth and streamlined, designed for practicality as well as show.

'I could almost want to cook in a place like this,' Tasha muttered, yanking open the door of the tall American fridge and staring at the contents. 'Nothing but champagne and beer—typical man. What about food?' Exploring the lower shelves, she found some mouldy cheese and a dead lettuce, which she removed and dropped in the bin. 'Good job I went to the supermarket.'

While the ambulance crew had been preparing Alessandro for the transfer home, she'd taken herself into St Piran on a shopping trip for provisions. She'd spent several hours carefully selecting items to help her with her plan, thinking carefully about what would help her cause. Abandoning the idea of using anything from his fridge, she reached for her bag of supplies and pulled out a packet of herbal tea.

Perfect.

She'd yet to meet a man who enjoyed herbal tea.

Humming happily, Tasha boiled water and found two mugs.

Carrying the tea back to the living area, she put the tray down on the low glass table and waited expectantly.

The wait was worth it. His reaction was everything she'd hoped for.

Alessandro stared in disbelief at the pale yellow liquid steaming in the mugs. 'What the hell is that?'

'Herbal tea,' Tasha said earnestly. She groped around for something convincing to say about it. 'It will be good for you. It boosts the immune system and works as a—as a—as an internal cleanser.' As a highly trained clinician, she couldn't believe she was spouting such unscientific nonsense and she braced herself for Alessandro to burst out laughing and demand she show him the data to support her claims, but he didn't. Instead he glowered at her, his eyes narrowing to two dangerous slits.

'Is this a joke? This is your idea of taking care of me?'

'Absolutely. I'm doing what's good for you.'

'Whisky would be good for me.'

Tasha made an attempt at a timid smile. Given that she'd never done 'timid' before in her life, she was reasonably pleased with the result. 'Don't be angry,' she coaxed. 'I remembered afterwards that the whisky won't go well with painkillers and antibiotics so I went for tea instead. I'm supposed to be looking after your health, remember? That's why I'm here. Try it. It's delicious. Caffeine-free and *so* healthy.'

His gaze slid from her eyes to the contents of the mug. 'It looks like something that's come straight from the drains.'

'Really? I find it delicious.' To prove her point, Tasha took an enormous gulp of hers and just about managed not to spit it out. *Utterly vile.* 'Mmm. Are you sure I can't tempt you?'

'Is that a serious question?' The dangerous gleam in his eyes was a reminder to Tasha not to underestimate him. He wasn't tame. And he wasn't a pussy cat. He was a man who was used to controlling everyone and everything around him.

And it was clear to her now that he really didn't want

anyone there. He'd only agreed to it to facilitate his early discharge.

She gave a faint smile. That was good, wasn't it? She didn't want him to want her here. That was the whole point. She was here to make his life difficult and uncomfortable while proving to herself that his charm had just been the creation of her hormonal teenage brain. So far she was doing well.

Apart from that initial jolt she'd felt when she'd first seen him lounging in the hospital bed, she had herself well under control.

She ignored the tiny voice inside herself that warned her she was playing with fire—that however dangerous he'd been as a boy, the threat was magnified now he was a man.

Handing him a glass of water, she kept up the sympathy. 'Take your antibiotics and painkillers now and then you can have another lot before you go to bed.' Unable to switch off the doctor inside her, she frowned at his leg. 'You should keep that elevated. Wait a minute…' She grabbed three cushions from one of the sofas and carefully repositioned his leg. Although she was gentle, she knew the pain had to be agonising, but Alessandro didn't murmur and she felt a flash of grudging respect. At least he wasn't a wimp or a whiner. 'How does that feel?'

'As if a horse trampled on it?' His dry humour bought a smile to her lips but she killed it instantly, unsettled by the ease with which the smile had come. She didn't want to find him amusing any more than she wanted to find him attractive. And then her eyes met his and the desire to smile faded instantly.

Sexual tension punched through her, stealing her breath and clouding her mind. The power of it shook her.

'Take your tablets,' she croaked. She wanted to look away but there was something about those sexy dark eyes that wouldn't allow it.

How long they would have stayed like that she didn't know because the phone suddenly buzzed, breaking the spell.

'Leave it,' he said roughly, but Tasha was relieved and grateful for anything that gave her an excuse to turn her back on him. She felt dizzy. Light-headed—as if she were floating.

'It could be someone important.' Her hand shook slightly as she picked up the phone. *Note to self,* she thought. *Don't look at the guy unless you have to.* 'Hello?'

A woman's voice came down the phone, smooth and sultry.

The dizziness faded in an instant and Tasha thrust the phone at him, plummeting back to earth with a bump. 'It's for you. Someone called Analisa. She doesn't sound too happy.' *And that made two of them.* Clearing the tray, Tasha stomped back into the kitchen.

What the hell was she playing at? Staring at a guy like some sort of dreamy teenager!

Scowling, she tipped the herbal tea down the sink.

If she'd needed reminding what Alessandro was like, it was that phone call.

She didn't understand the language, but it was obvious that Alessandro wasn't spending time placating the woman. Judging from his bored tone, it wasn't going to bother him if Analisa or whatever her name was didn't phone back.

And that, Tasha thought angrily, summed up Alessandro Cavalieri. He didn't care how many women he hurt. Flirt today, dump tomorrow.

She took her time in the kitchen and by the time she strolled back into the living room, Alessandro was no longer on the phone. 'Did you take those tablets?'

'Yes. They would have gone down more easily with whisky.'

'You're going to need a clear head to handle all those women who keep calling you.'

'Are you jealous?'

'Oh, please!' Tasha moved the crutches out of the way before he tripped and did more damage. 'Don't flatter yourself. Fortunately for both of us, I've grown out of the girl-meets-prince fantasy.'

'Good, because girl-meets-prince has never done anything for me. It's all fake.' His tone was irascible and suddenly she wished she'd stayed in the kitchen.

The house was huge, and yet suddenly it seemed small. It was all too intimate, too—*terrifying?*

'You're very bad-tempered. That's probably because you're hungry. If you're sure I can't tempt you with some of my lovely, delicious tea, I'll go and make us some supper instead.'

'You'd better phone for a take-away because there isn't anything in the fridge.'

'Actually, there was, but most of it looked ready for a post mortem so I threw it away. The only thing within use-by date in your fridge is the champagne, and last time I looked that wasn't listed as one of the five major food groups.' Ignoring the empty space on the sofa next to him, she sprawled in one of the chairs, curling her legs underneath her. 'I gather you don't cook.'

'I have a chef, but while I've been in hospital I gave him time off.'

A chef? 'Yes, well, next time tell him to clean the dead bodies out of the fridge before he leaves. Lucky for you I had the foresight to pick up some food on the way so we're not going to starve.'

'I don't expect you to cook. That isn't why you're here.' His face was paper white and she could see that the slightest movement caused him agony. 'Anyway, I'm not hungry.'

'If you don't eat, you won't recover. Why do you have a chef?'

'I'm a useless cook. And I'm usually too busy to cook. I eat out a lot.'

With women like the sultry Analisa. 'Well, that's not a problem. It will be my pleasure to make you delicious treats.' Generally she hated cooking, but Tasha decided not to share that with him. She'd already decided what she was cooking him for dinner. 'In fact, why don't I get started? You ought to have an early night.'

'I'm not big on early nights.' Those dark eyes found hers. 'Unless there's a reason.'

'A broken ankle and bruised ribs are a reason.' Rejecting the chemistry, Tasha uncurled her legs and stood up. 'The body heals better when it's rested.'

'So you're good in the kitchen?'

'I'm good in every room, Alessandro.' Leaving him to dwell on that comment, Tasha walked back to the kitchen and closed the door firmly behind her.

The irony didn't escape her. Normally she avoided the kitchen. Here, it felt like a refuge from Alessandro.

Trying not to think about him, she emptied her bags over the shiny black work surface and picked up a small bag of extra-hot chillies.

Stir-fry, she thought, *with a kick*.

She couldn't kick him herself, but this should do the job for her.

But as she chopped and sliced she discovered that it was impossible not to think about him. And thinking made her wonder about the dark clouds she saw in his eyes. She'd been a doctor long enough to recognise when someone was suffering. And she didn't think the dark emotions swirling around him had anything to do with the accident.

Might have caused the accident, though, she mused, slicing onion with surgical precision.

Minutes later she had noodles cooking in boiling water and she was stir-frying a generous quantity of garlic, red chilli and ginger. Making a guess at the timing, Tasha gamely tipped in vegetables and juicy prawns and finally added the noodles.

As it sizzled, she turned to the other pan and stirred the contents. It looked identical except for one ingredient—it lacked the copious amounts of red chilli.

Just don't mix them up, she reminded herself as she plated the meal, adding a touch of garnish to make the dish extra appetising.

Pleased with the result, she walked through to the light, airy living room. The sun had dipped below the horizon and the evening was cool. Alessandro lay sprawled on the low sofa where she'd left him, staring with brooding concentration at the waves crashing onto the shore.

'The first time I surfed here I was twenty. Josh brought me.'

And she'd followed them. Egged on by her best friend from school, they'd hidden, giggling, behind the rocks, watching as her brother and his sexy friend stripped down to board shorts.

Tasha put the plates down on the table with a clatter. 'I would have thought a playboy with a private jet and your surfing skills would have chosen North Beach, Hawaii, or Jeffreys Bay in South Africa.'

'I love Cornwall. Staying with your family was one of the happiest times of my life.'

The words pushed her control off centre and Tasha felt her stomach lurch. It had been the happiest time of her life, too. Which had made the abrupt ending even harder. 'Our home wasn't exactly big—it must have felt like a shoebox to you after palace life.'

'It felt like a proper home. And I envied the way you could all just get on with your lives without having to think about crowds and security.'

As a teenager she'd thought it was impossibly glamorous having security guards, but now she could see that it might be an inconvenience, especially for an active, athletic guy like Alessandro.

'I guess Cornwall is a pretty low-profile place.'

'It's not bad. Fortunately this house isn't too accessible. How often do you surf?'

'Me?' Tasha handed him cutlery. 'Not as often as I'd like

to because I generally work long hours. Normally, that's the way I like it. I'm a career girl. But now that I'm looking after you…' she shrugged '…I intend to make up for lost time.'

'So if you're a career girl, how come you're not working right now?'

Unwittingly he'd tapped into her deepest fears. That she might not be able to find another job. *That her altercation with her last boss might have blown her reputation to smithereens.*

Tasha opened her mouth and closed it again, unsettled by the sudden desire to confide. She stifled it, knowing that confiding was the first step towards intimacy. And she didn't want intimacy with this man. 'I'm in between jobs. I've cooked a stir-fry. I hope that's all right with you.'

'Looks delicious.' He picked up a fork. 'I can imagine you as a children's doctor.'

'I'll take that as a compliment. Do you want to try and eat at the table?'

'No, this is fine. You're right that moving around hurts. I think the journey to the bedroom will be enough of a challenge for one evening.'

As he shifted position, her eyes were drawn to his body.

No man had a right to be so good looking, Tasha thought as she registered the strength in those wide shoulders. It should have been enough that he was a prince. And rich. Looking like a sex god as well was just too many gifts for one person.

She might have been irritated if it hadn't been for the fact he was about to eat her food. And that was going to be a real test of manhood.

Hiding a smile, Tasha turned her attention back to her own plate. 'I love your kitchen. The design is fantastic. A whole different experience for me. Dinner for me is usually a cardboard sandwich from the hospital cafeteria at three in the morning.'

'It didn't look anything like this when I bought it. The

rooms were small and the whole place was pretty dark. I worked with an excellent architect and we knocked down almost every wall, put in the skylights…' He glanced up at the roof of the double-height sitting room. 'We decided it was worth gutting the place because it had such potential. We opened it up, let the light flow in. This is delicious, by the way. You're a good cook.'

Delicious? *He thought it was delicious?*

Tasha stared at him in disbelief. 'You like it?'

'After two weeks of hospital food?' He twisted noodles around his fork with skill and precision. 'This is heaven.'

He had to be kidding. It had to be a double bluff. Unless…

Tasha stared down at her own plate. Had she mixed them up?

Cautiously, she took a mouthful, waiting for her mouth to explode into flames from the chilli, but the flavours in her food were subtle and she knew instantly she didn't have the wrong plate. Which meant he clearly had a mouth lined with asbestos.

'Is there any more?' Alessandro speared the last prawn. 'You don't seem to be eating yours.'

'I am. And there isn't any more.' She hadn't thought for a moment he'd eat what she'd served him. Clearly his mouth was as tough as the rest of him.

Feeling aggravated, Tasha finished her food. 'Why did you fall anyway? Was the horse too difficult for you?'

He accepted the slight with a flicker of a smile. 'The horse wasn't difficult. I lost concentration for a moment, but that was long enough for the guy on the opposite team to bring us down. My ankle took most of the weight. My ribs took the rest.' He leaned back against the sofa, his eyes closed.

She wondered why he'd lost concentration.

'You were trapped under the horse? Ouch. So no physical activity for the rest of the summer?'

His eyes opened and he studied her from underneath lush, dark lashes. 'Depends what you mean by physical activity.'

Staring into those dangerous dark eyes, her mouth dried. 'I meant polo and surfing.' Tasha felt the heat slowly spread through her body and wished she'd never mentioned physical activity. Even injured, the man was deadly. 'You look tired. Do you want me to call your security team to help you from the sofa to the bed?'

'No. I have the crutches and I can manage.'

'Independent, aren't you?'

'You could say that.'

Torn between wanting to see him suffer and not wanting him to exacerbate his injuries, Tasha tilted her head. 'The crutches won't be much use while your ribs are so bruised. We might need to think of other options.'

'This is fine.' Shifting to the edge of the sofa, Alessandro picked up the crutches and stood up, taking his weight on his good leg.

Tasha flinched.

That had to hurt.

'Alessandro—'

'I can do it. Just give me space.' There was a stubbornness in his tone. A grim determination to succeed despite the agonising pain. Reluctantly impressed, Tasha stood there, careful not to touch him and distinctly unsettled by how much she wanted to do just that.

'Look, I could call one of those burly security guards—'

'It would help if you could check the route to my bedroom is clear. So far I haven't mastered doing this with obstacles.' His face was chalk-white as he slowly eased his way forward. 'I'll just use the bathroom on the way so that I don't have to make two journeys.'

Tasha watched as the muscles in his powerful shoulders flexed and knew that every movement had to be causing him agony. 'I think you need help.'

He cast her a look that told her he'd be long dead before

he'd accept help from anyone. A crooked smile flickered at the corners of his mouth. 'You're offering to assist me in the bathroom? Now, that could be interesting.'

Trying to work out how the atmosphere had shifted to intimate, Tasha felt her face turn scarlet. 'I just don't see how you're going to manage to do what you have to do without help.'

His eyes lingered on hers for a long moment. Mockery mingled with something else that she didn't even want to put a name to. 'You want to come and watch how it's done, *tesoro*?'

He'd called her that at seventeen and her heart rushed forward, doubling its rhythm. '*Don't* speak Italian.'

'Why not?'

'Because…' Her mouth was dry. 'Because I don't speak it and it's rude to talk a language someone doesn't understand.'

'It's my native tongue.'

'I know. But you're fluent in English so that's no excuse.' She scowled at him. 'I just don't want you falling and fracturing more bones. I'm not sure my patience with this whole nursing thing is going to last that long, so you'd better heal quickly.'

He shifted the position of the crutch. His knuckles were white where they gripped the handles. 'I won't lock the door. If I find myself in trouble, I'll shout and you can come to my rescue. But not on a white charger. I've had enough of horses for one week.'

Pinned to the spot by that dark, sexy gaze, Tasha felt as if she were the one who had eaten the chilli. Her entire body was caught in a fiery rush of heat and suddenly she didn't feel like the one in control. 'Fine,' she croaked, 'leave the door unlocked. Good idea.'

Feeling the heat in her face, she moved through to his bedroom and cleared the suitcase off the bed. His bed was enormous and faced out towards the sea.

How many hearts had he broken in that bed?

Trying to push aside disturbing images of Alessandro's strong body tangled with a slender female frame, Tasha ripped the duvet back so that he could get into the bed and wondered why on earth she'd volunteered for this job. Why had she ever thought she could make his life difficult? The herbal tea had been moderately irritating but the chilli hadn't even registered on his taste buds, and all her digs about surfing hadn't had much impact either.

And now she was stuck here with a man who made her think things she didn't want to think. It had always been like that, she remembered crossly, even as a teenager. When Alessandro had walked into the room there had never been any confusion. She'd known she was a woman.

If she really wanted him to suffer then she needed to do something drastic.

What was a man like Alessandro likely to be missing more than anything?

Tasha gave a slow smile as she thought about the other items in her shopping bags.

Time for Plan B.

The pain in his ribs was excruciating. Even small movements resulted in blinding agony, as if a burning-hot poker was being forced into his chest.

But at least it distracted him from the parts of his life he was trying to forget.

Taking advantage of the privacy of the bathroom, Alessandro gave in to the pain.

He balanced himself against the washbasin and reached for a glass. To add to the pain in his ribs and his ankle, his mouth felt as though someone had started a bonfire. Chilli, he thought, gulping down water. When he'd taken the first mouthful of food he'd thought she must have made a mistake but then he'd seen her eating hers happily. Clearly she liked her food hot. Not wanting to offend her, he'd forced his down, eating it as quickly as possible. If she walked out, he'd be back in hospital and there was no way he was going back to hospital. So he'd forced himself to eat with enthusiasm the food she'd prepared.

He drank deeply, wondering how long it took nerve-endings to recover. There wasn't a single part of his body that wasn't burning.

Frustrated by his own weakness, accustomed to being at the peak of physical fitness, Alessandro used the bathroom and then clenched his jaw against the pain and hobbled back towards the bedroom, trying in vain to find some way of distributing his weight so that the movement didn't exacerbate his injuries.

Tasha had turned back the duvet and smoothed the sheets.

Never before had his bed looked so inviting, but the short distance from the door felt like running a marathon. It didn't help that she was watching him, those cool eyes steady on his face.

'Aren't you taking your nursing duties a little too seriously?' He wished she'd turn away so that he could give in to the pain. 'You're off duty once I go to bed.'

'I'd better help you undress.'

Was she serious? Marvelling at the discovery that extreme pain didn't seem to interfere with sexual arousal, Alessandro gritted his teeth. For his own sanity he knew he didn't dare let her touch him. 'I'll manage.'

'How? At least let me help you change your shirt for pyjamas.'

'I don't own pyjamas.'

'I thought you might say that, so I bought you some when I was out shopping.' Pleased with herself, she picked up a bag and produced a pair of pyjamas.

Distracted from the ache in his loins by the flash of vivid colour, Alessandro blinked. '*Pink?*'

'It was the only colour they had.' Her expression was

anxious. 'Oh, dear. Are you one of those guys who believes wearing pink makes them less masculine? Sorry. I hadn't thought of that. Only I know some guys wear pink shirts these days and I thought these might be OK…'

Was she winding him up? His swift glance at her face suggested nothing but concern. Wondering just how far he was going to have to go not to offend her, Alessandro reminded himself that without her he'd be back in hospital.

Her generosity was the reason he'd be sleeping in his own bed tonight.

All he had to do was keep his hands off her. Which shouldn't be that hard, surely, given that every movement was agony.

'I don't have a problem with pink.' He eyed the pyjamas in disbelief, wondering which idiot had thought there was a market for such a vile creation. 'But I don't think they'll fit over the cast.'

'Leave that to me.' Beaming at him, she picked up a pair of scissors and cut a slit down one of the legs. 'There. Simple.'

Reflecting on the fact that the wretched garment now looked more like a dress than trousers, Alessandro manoeuvred himself onto the bed and let the crutches fall to the floor. Pain lanced his side and he sat still, breathing slowly, hoping it would pass. The helplessness was driving him mad.

'I'll help you take off your shirt.' Tasha sat next to him on the bed and gently eased off his shirt. As she exposed his chest, the breath hissed through her teeth. 'I've never seen bruises like those, Alessandro. How are you still walking around?' Her tone altered dramatically. Light and flirty gave way to crisp concern.

'I'm fine. To be honest, walking isn't any more painful than breathing.' He was taken aback by the change in her. The girl had gone and in her place was a doctor. A concerned doctor. Her fingers gently traced the bruises and when he glanced at her face he saw that her expression was serious.

'Does this hurt?'

'No.'

She gave him an impatient look. 'Honest answers only, please. A man wearing pink is allowed to express his true emotions even if the resulting language is colourful.'

'All right. It hurts like crazy and I want to punch something?'

'And when I do this?' She pressed lower down and Alessandro swore long and fluently.

'OK.' She didn't blink. 'Now I know you're telling the truth.'

The pain was a blinding, agonising flash. Once again he had that sick dread that the doctors might have missed something. Something that was going to keep him bedridden for longer than a fractured ankle and a few broken ribs. 'Are you trying to kill me?' He spoke through his teeth and she straightened, her hair sliding over her shoulders.

'Actually, no. I'm checking you over. I don't like the look of those bruises. Just sit still. I'm going to check your breath sounds.'

'I've already been examined by about a hundred doctors. They kept wheeling in yet another expert to give an opinion.'

'Sorry, but the only opinion I trust is my own.' She disappeared and reappeared a moment later with a stethoscope in her hand. 'Good job I packed this in my box of tricks, although I haven't listened to an adult's chest for quite a while.'

'If that's supposed to fill me with confidence, it doesn't.' It was a lie. Strangely enough, he was relieved to have her opinion. He remembered Josh telling him that Tasha had astonishing instincts to go with her sharp brain. He had no doubt that she was a skilled doctor. Unfortunately that didn't make things any easier and he sat still while she touched the bruising, trying not to think about how her fingers felt on his skin. 'Do you have to prod me?'

'I'm checking there's no underlying trauma. Those bruises are very impressive. Must hurt a lot.'

Alessandro spoke through his teeth. 'Not at all.' As if the pain wasn't enough, he also had the extra hit of sexual arousal. As she tilted her head, her hair slid forward and brushed against his arm. He tried to move backwards but every movement felt as though he were being slammed into a wall.

'Bones have a lot of nerve-endings,' she murmured. 'That's why it's painful.'

'Thanks for the explanation.'

'Generally, when someone breaks a bone, the treatment is to immobilise it. We can put your ankle in a cast to protect it. Unfortunately we can't do the same thing for your ribs.' Tasha put the stethoscope in her ears. 'Every time you breathe, you hurt yourself again.'

'Can't they strap my chest or something?'

'No. Now stop talking while I listen.' She narrowed her eyes and moved the stethoscope on his chest. Her hair whispered across his arm. 'Breathe in for me.'

Alessandro did and almost passed out. Pain skewered him and darkness flickered around the edges of his vision, muting the lust.

Her eyes locked on his. 'Breathe in and out through your mouth.'

Was she trying to torture him?

But when she finally removed the stethoscope from her ears, her expression was serious. 'Your breath sounds are fine, but I'm going to keep an eye on you. To answer your question, they actually did used to strap chests in the old days, but not any more. It impedes movement and stops you breathing deeply—you can't shift the secretions in your lungs and you can end up with a vile infection. Then you're back in hospital on yet more antibiotics.'

The word 'hospital' was enough to make him ride the pain and breathe deeply. 'I get the message.'

'Don't worry—a young, fit guy like you can cope with a couple of broken ribs and heal quickly. It's older patients who suffer.' Digging her hand into her pocket, she pulled out her phone. 'I'm just going to call your doctor. I want to add in a drug.'

'I'm already swallowing the contents of a pharmacy.'

'I want to give you a non-steroidal alongside your pain-killers. I don't know why he didn't give you that. You don't suffer from stomach problems, do you?'

'I've never suffered from anything,' Alessandro growled, 'until a horse fell on me.' Watching Tasha talk on the phone, he found his eyes lingering on the curve of her cheek and the thickness of her eyelashes. She was brisk and professional, giving her opinion bluntly and firmly to a man at least twice her age. Impressive, he thought. And he could imagine her working with children. As a teenager, she'd had an irrepress-ible sense of fun. Remembering some of the tricks she'd played on her brothers, he allowed himself a faint smile.

'OK, so that's done.' She slid the phone back into her pocket. 'In the morning I'm going to pick you up some extra tablets. I think it will help and so do the guys at the hospital. They should have thought of it, but sometimes it takes a woman to get these things right. Now, then—pyjamas.'

'I can dress without your help.' Alessandro, who had never felt awkward with a woman in his life before, suddenly felt awkward. She was behaving as if they had no history. As if—

Tasha picked up the pink pyjamas and dangled them in front of him, her expression bored.

'I've seen it all before, Alessandro. I'm a doctor.'

'You haven't seen m—' He was about to say that she hadn't seen his body before, but then he remembered that she had. And he'd seen hers. *All of hers.*

And he didn't want to mention that. If she was going to act as if nothing had happened, so was he.

He looked at her cautiously, but her face revealed nothing but professional concern.

'I want to examine the rest of you. Lie back for me.' Her expression serious, her hands moved down his body, sliding and pressing. 'Does this hurt?'

'Everything hurts.' Feeling her cool fingers on his abdomen, Alessandro sucked in a breath. How low did she intend to go?

Lust slammed through him and Alessandro grabbed the duvet and pulled it higher, ignoring the avalanche of pain that rained down on him. 'I'm fine. I can manage. Go to bed. You must be tired.' He wished she'd step back a bit. Her scent was playing havoc with his libido and this close he could see the smoothness of her skin. *How the hell could a guy be aroused when his broken ribs were virtually impaling his lungs*? 'Goodnight, Tasha. Thanks for all your help.'

'If the pain changes, let me know.'

The pain had changed. Suddenly it was all concentrated below his waist and it had nothing to do with being trampled by a four-legged animal. 'Get some sleep.'

'Don't hesitate to wake me up if you need to.' She walked briskly across the room to close the blinds.

'Leave them—I prefer to keep the doors open.'

'You won't be able to sleep.'

He didn't tell her that he rarely slept. 'I'll be fine. I like the fresh air.'

'Well, if you change your mind, just shout out.' Her hips swayed as she walked from window to door. She held a stethoscope in her hand but she walked like a seductress. 'I hope you have a really good night's sleep. I've chosen the bedroom right across the hall and I'll leave the door open so I'll hear you if you shout.'

Great. There were three guest bedrooms, the other two at the far end of the house. Couldn't she have chosen one of those?

After she left, Alessandro spent a frustrating and agonising fifteen minutes removing his shorts. Exhausted, he didn't bother replacing them with the pyjamas. Instead he flopped back against the pillows, drained of energy.

He lay without moving until a noise from across the corridor made him look up.

Tasha was walking across the guest room towards the *en suite* bathroom, undressing as she walked. First she pulled off the scarlet jumper and dropped it in a heap. Her full breasts pushed against a silken wisp of a bra. When her hands moved to the snap of her jeans, Alessandro wanted to groan out a request that she stop, but he couldn't make a sound and the jeans went the way of the jumper and this time the lace was so brief it was almost irrelevant.

His muscles tensed, sending spasms of pain shooting down his bruised body.

Finding it impossible to breathe, Alessandro wondered if one of his broken ribs had suddenly punctured his lung. There was no air in the room. He was suffocating. He lifted his hand to undo his collar and then remembered that he was naked.

As he watched, she stretched upwards to clip her hair on top of her head, the movement accentuating her lean, flat stomach and her long, slim legs. He felt like a voyeur at an erotic floor show. Clearly she'd forgotten that she had both doors open. Either that or she was just assuming he was asleep.

If he called out, he'd embarrass her, and he couldn't look away because his head refused to move.

Telling himself that any moment now she was going to lock the bathroom door, Alessandro kept watching. And he was still watching when she turned her back to him, unfastened her bra and stepped out of her knickers.

CHAPTER FOUR

MEGAN'S hand shook as she opened the door that led to the neonatal intensive care unit.

All day she'd been in a daze of happiness. A daze of happiness that nothing could blunt—not even the knowledge that technically she'd slept with a married man.

Married, but not together, she told herself, wondering why the fact that Josh and Rebecca were almost divorced didn't make her feel any better.

Her head was in a spin and she'd found it almost impossible to concentrate.

She'd thought of nothing else all day, ever since that knock on the door that had sent Josh springing from the bed before they'd had the opportunity to talk about what they'd shared. She had no idea who had been at the door, but whoever it was had been important enough to make sure that Josh didn't return.

Megan had waited for twenty minutes then dressed quickly and exited the on-call room quietly. Her heart had been working double time all the way back to the paediatric ward but she was fairly confident that no one had seen her.

She'd spent the rest of her day stopping herself from checking her phone every two minutes to see if Josh had called. It was like being a teenager all over again.

The extended silence made her jittery and sent her imagination into overdrive.

Was he embarrassed? Did he regret what they'd done?

Reminding herself that Josh was a senior doctor whose working day was ridiculously intense and demanding, she tried to rationalise the fact that he hadn't called. She told herself that it wasn't surprising that he didn't want to publicise their relationship. They were colleagues after all, and affairs between colleagues could so easily become messy.

Having convinced herself that she wasn't likely to see him that day, it came as a shock to see Josh sitting at the computer at the nurses' station.

Megan felt a tiny thrill of excitement bloom inside her.

He wasn't avoiding her. He was here, on her ward.

Her heart pounded against her chest and she was relieved that the other staff appeared to be occupied elsewhere.

Just for this first encounter she wanted to be alone with him. She didn't want to share the memories of the night with anyone but Josh.

Remembering the look he'd given her just before he'd left the on-call room, she gave a little smile and her stomach fluttered with anticipation.

'Hello, Josh.'

'Ah, Megan, I'm glad you're here. We had an emergency delivery in the department. Thirty-four-weeker.' He turned to her, his tone crisp and professional. 'Showing signs of respiratory distress, so we've transferred him to you.'

There was nothing intimate in his gaze—nothing to hint that they'd spent the night together.

Taken aback, Megan glanced behind her but there was no one within earshot.

The baby was ill, she reasoned, and he was an exceptional doctor. Josh would never put his personal life before the well-being of a patient.

Slowly, she put her bag on the floor, controlling her disappointment. 'Was it a normal delivery?'

As he told her, she found herself looking at his hands and the dark hairs dusting his forearms. Those same hands had touched her. Everywhere. *Held her.* It had been genuine, she had no doubt about that. She still remembered the look in his eyes as he'd driven her wild.

That knowledge gave her confidence. 'Josh—'

'I need to get back.' He rose quickly to his feet, interrupting her before she could finish her sentence. 'You might want to spend some time with the mother. She's very upset. The whole thing took about twenty minutes from start to finish. Precipitate doesn't begin to describe it.'

It was a verbal dismissal but it may as well have been a physical slap for the pain it caused.

'Of course.' Megan pushed the words through stiff lips and stood frozen to the spot as he walked past her, careful not to touch. He was as cold as he'd been eight years before. It was as if their night together hadn't happened.

She wanted to say something. She wanted to grab his arm and demand to know what was going on in his head. She wanted to know why he was hurting her like this.

But his face was a frozen mask and her pride kept her hands by her sides as she let him walk away.

Tasha took her time strolling towards the shower.

He was watching her. She could almost feel the heat of his eyes on her back.

Get a load of that, she thought happily as she stepped into the shower. Flat-chested? *I don't think so.*

From the moment she'd decided to do her striptease, her heart had been hammering. First she'd checked he was awake through the crack in the door, then she'd choreographed her walk across the room to ensure that he witnessed every move.

After that all she'd had to do was not give in to temptation and look round. She'd done everything in her power to push up his blood pressure. What she hadn't done was ask herself why she would want to.

Until now.

Muttering to herself, she turned the shower to cold.

Ten years hadn't done anything to make him less attractive. Unfortunately. In fact, he'd filled out in places where it counted. His shoulders were wider, his chest stronger and his arms thickened with muscle. Less of the boy and more of the man. Too much more of the man.

Despite the cold water, her body felt scorching hot again and she wondered why on earth she'd agreed to this.

Another one of her stupid ideas.

She'd thought her feelings for him had been no more than a childish crush. She'd thought the pain he'd caused would have inoculated her against his lethal charm. She'd thought she was immune. If you'd been infected with something once, you shouldn't catch it again, should you?

So why the explosion of chemistry?

Tasha gave a groan of frustration and turned off the shower.

Her brother was right. She needed to get out more.

Wrapping herself in a huge towel, she opened the bathroom door and risked a glance towards his bedroom. It was in darkness. The feeling of superiority drained out of her. If he'd been watching her, he wasn't now. He wasn't lying there tortured with unfulfilled desire after seeing her in her underwear.

He was asleep.

Which said it all. You couldn't torment a man who didn't even bother looking.

Feeling cross and hot and all sorts of things she didn't want to feel, Tasha flopped onto the bed and rolled onto her stomach, burying her face in the pillow. It wasn't supposed to be this way. She was supposed to have taken one look at him and wondered what she'd seen in him. She wasn't supposed to be having the thoughts she was having now. Why couldn't he be a total wimp like all the other men she met on a daily basis? Her last relationship had floundered after less than a week when the doctor in question had taken to his bed with a dose of man-flu. Tasha, who had endless patience with sick children, had been exasperated by his dying-duck impression but she'd dutifully made hot drinks, dished out tablets and made sympathetic noises until finally calling a halt, reasoning that there was no future in a relationship where one of the partners wanted to strangle the other.

Why couldn't Alessandro provoke the same feelings of irritation?

Why didn't she want to strangle him?

'Ugh.' Blocking out images of his broad shoulders, she burrowed under the pillow. The man had to be in agony. The bruises on his chest were the worst she'd ever seen. But had he uttered a murmur of complaint? No. In fact, he'd been so stoical about the whole thing it had been a struggle to persuade him to take painkillers. She wanted him to be a wimp, but he was anything but. And as for the chilli...

Clearly he liked his food hot.

Tasha thumped the pillow angrily and rolled onto her back. So he was tough. So what? That just proved the man had no nerve-endings and she already knew that. A man with the slightest sensitivity wouldn't have treated her the way Alessandro had treated her.

Had she seen a flicker of remorse?

Had he apologised?

No. And she hadn't exactly progressed in her plan to make him suffer. In fact, so far her plan had totally failed to get off the ground.

Wishing she hadn't wasted her limited finances on sexy underwear, Tasha rolled onto her back and stared at the ceiling.

So far she'd failed spectacularly to make him feel remotely guilty for the way he'd treated her, but she couldn't very well back out now without exposing herself to relentless questioning and teasing by her insensitive brother. Which meant she was stuck here.

She lay in the dark, unable to sleep, wondering how

someone with a chest that bruised had somehow managed to get himself to and from the bathroom without help. It hadn't just been the physical strength that had impressed her, it was the mental strength. Somehow he'd pushed through the pain.

He didn't just look like a warrior, he had warrior mentality.

There was a hardness to him that hadn't been there ten years before. He wasn't the same person.

And neither was she.

Tasha was pondering on that when a loud crash echoed around the house.

She was out of bed in a flash, her mind already working through various scenarios. If he'd fallen out of bed, it could have seriously aggravated his injuries. They'd need an ambulance. Paramedics… 'Alessandro?' Sprinting into his bedroom, she saw a lamp lying on the floor where he'd knocked it off the bedside table. On the wall in front of him a football match was being played out on the wide-screen TV and he was watching avidly, his hand locked around the remote control.

'Tash, you're standing in front of the screen!'

'You're watching sport?' Her heart was hammering and she felt weak at the knees. 'You frighten the life out of me and then all you can say is "You're standing in front of the screen"?' Incredulous, she rescued the lamp and waited for her heartbeat to reach a normal level. 'I thought you'd fallen out of bed. I thought you'd broken the rest of your ribs and your skull to go with it.'

'I knocked the lamp off when I was reaching for the remote control.'

'It's two in the morning. What is it with men and the remote control?'

'I wanted to watch sport. I couldn't sleep.'

Him too?

Only she'd been lying there thinking about him while he'd

been thinking about football. The knowledge scraped at her nerves and strengthened her resolve. 'Is it the pain?' Tasha straightened the lamp. 'I thought you'd fallen.' And she'd been terrified of what a fall could do to his broken ribs. Not that she cared, she told herself quickly, but she didn't want to be stuck here nursing him any longer than she had to be.

'It isn't pain. Go back to bed, Tasha. I'm sorry I disturbed you.' He didn't shift his gaze from the screen, watching un-blinking as the crowd roared its approval. He was a typical man, obsessed with sport, just like her three brothers. She could walk across the room naked and he wouldn't look up because some feat of sporting prowess was being enacted on the giant plasma screen.

Why had she bothered buying expensive lingerie to drive him wild? she thought crossly. She may as well have worn her ancient Mickey Mouse T-shirt.

The glass doors were still open onto the terrace and a cool breeze wafted into the room. 'Shall I close these now?' She walked across the room. 'You must be freezing.'

'I like the cold air.' Something in his tone made her look at him closely and it was only because she was trained to notice subtle clues that she realised he wasn't actually watching the game. True, his eyes were fixed on the screen, but they were blank. Empty.

And suddenly she knew that the football was an excuse.

Tasha switched on the other lamp and for a fleeting second saw the expression on his face. The humour was gone and in its place was exhaustion and pain. She hesitated and then sat down on the chair, hating herself for not just being able to walk away. It wasn't that she cared, she told herself quickly. It was because he was in pain. She'd never been any good at watching someone in pain. 'You look rough.'

'Go to bed, Tasha.' It was a dismissal she chose to ig-nore.

She wondered whether he was thinking about his injury or the loss of his brother.

'Things always seem worse at night,' she said casually.
'I see it on the ward with both the kids and the parents.
There's something about being in the dark. It makes you
think too much.' And she knew that sometimes it helped to
talk to pass the time. She'd spent hours keeping frightened
kids company at night, playing cards, chatting quietly while
the rest of the ward slept. 'What were you doing back in
Cornwall anyway? I imagined you in some gilded palace,
doing prince-like things.'

'You imagined me?' His head turned and she wanted to
bite her tongue. Suddenly she was staring into those dark
eyes and everything inside her melted, just as it had when
she was a teenager.

'Just a figure of speech. You're the crown prince.' Suddenly
she felt awkward, and she wondered why she found it so much
easier to talk to children than adults. 'I was sorry to hear
about your brother. That must have been very hard for all of
you.'

'It's life.' His voice was hard and she floundered, wondering how it was possible to want to comfort and run at the
same time. 'What are you doing here, Tasha? Why did you
really volunteer to look after me?'

Her heart jumped in her chest. So he wasn't just brave, he
was as sharp as a blade.

It wouldn't do to forget that.

'I wanted to help.'

'Really?' The bleak, cold look in his eyes had been replaced by smouldering sexuality that made it impossible to
breathe or think. Time was suspended. In the background
the crowd roared its approval at some amazing feat of sports-
manship but neither of them looked towards the screen. They
were looking at each other, the chemistry a magnetic force
between them, drawing them together.

And then he turned his head and closed his eyes. 'Go to
bed, Tasha.'

Embarrassment drove her to her feet. Another minute and

she would have kissed that mouth. She would have leaned forward and—

Oh, God.

'Right. Yes. Good. Well—try not to knock over any more lamps.' She fled to the door, wondering what it was about this man that affected her so badly.

She was a career-woman. She was dedicating her life to her little patients. The only thing she was interested in was getting another job as fast as possible.

This time when she walked into her bedroom she closed the door firmly behind her.

The dark rage inside him mingled with frustration. The inactivity was driving him crazy. Almost as crazy as living with Tasha. Even when she wasn't there, she was there. He smelt her perfume, spied a pair of feminine shoes discarded next to a chair.

And now she was surfing. Alessandro watched from the terrace as she carved into the wave, graceful and perfectly balanced. It was like watching a dancer. Some bolder tourists had chosen to visit the beach to take lessons on the soft sand and then try the bigger surf created by the rocks. They huddled in groups, learning to stand on the board, learning to balance, practising the 'pop-up'. Then they ventured into the water and spent the time falling off their boards in the shallows.

Tasha had none of those problems.

Watching her was sheer poetry. He turned away from the window, envying her the opportunity to push herself physically. Before the accident he would have been out there with her. Or maybe not *with* her, exactly. He frowned, not sure how he felt about having her there. She was the reason he was home, and those new painkillers had certainly taken the edge off the agony. But other parts of him weren't faring so well. The inactivity was driving him mad.

As were the phone calls from Miranda.

She wanted to visit.

But he wasn't ready to see her.

Wasn't ready to make the decision everyone wanted him to make.

Driven by a burning desire to recover as fast as possible, he hauled himself to the bed and started the exercises the physio had shown him.

He worked without rest, channelling all his anger and frustration into each movement, pushing himself hard.

By the time Tasha arrived back in the apartment, he was in agony. Still in her wetsuit, her feet bare, she stood and looked at him.

'Did you take your painkillers before you started?'

It cost him to speak. 'No.'

'That's what I thought. Let me tell you something about pain—once it comes back, it's harder to manage. The trick is to head it off before it returns. You should have waited for me. I was going to do the physio with you.' Dropping her towel and her bag on the floor, she walked over to him. Her hair lay in a damp rope over her shoulder and she smelt of the sea. 'The surf is fantastic.'

Her enthusiasm and sheer vitality sprinkled salt into his wounds. 'I saw you. You took a risk with that last wave.'

'I don't think you're in a position to lecture me about risk given that you lay down under a horse.' She glanced down at his ankle. 'How's that feeling?'

'It's fine, thanks.' Speaking required energy he didn't possess and she gave him a knowing smile.

'Fine? Yeah, I bet. Why don't you sit down and I'll check you over.'

Despite the agony, his entire body heated and he reflected on the fact that having Tasha as his private nurse was the worst torture anyone could have invented. 'You already checked me over.' *And he'd had a sleepless night as a result.*

'Sorry, but while I'm in charge, I'll check you whenever I feel it's necessary.' Cool and calm, she faced him down.

'You're my responsibility. No one dies on my shift, got that?'

'I have no intention of dying.'

'You might, if you carry on being uncooperative.' Her smile managed to be both threatening and sweet as she gestured to the bed. 'Lie down.'

It was an awkward manoeuvre. 'When will they take this damn thing off?'

'That cast is holding your joints in the right position while they heal. When the surgeon is happy that your bones are healing, they'll remove it. Usually about six to eight weeks. So that gives you at least another month. Better get used to it.'

'And once it's removed?'

'Intensive physio—hydrotherapy—'

'Hydrotherapy?'

'Basically exercising in the water.' Gently, she pushed him back against the stack of pillows. 'Good for strengthening muscle without stressing bone and joint.'

Alessandro lay on the bed and tried to ignore the pain licking through his body. He wondered if she planned to change out of the black stretchy wetsuit before she examined him. She looked like Catwoman. 'I just want to be fit.'

'You will be, but it's going to take time.' Tasha reached behind her and unzipped the back of her wetsuit slightly. 'If you're worried that you'll never be fit again, don't be. I've seen your X-rays and I've talked to your surgeon. There's no reason why you won't be back to normal in a few months providing you're sensible. If you do the wrong thing now—if you push it when you should be resting—you'll just do damage. You need to take it steadily and do as you're told.'

Relief mingled with humiliation that she'd read him so easily. 'I'm not good at doing as I'm told.'

If he were, then he'd have bowed to pressure and married.

'I know, but if you want to be fully fit again, that's what

you're going to have to do.' Tasha dropped her hands from the zip. 'I need to get out of this gear and take a shower. Then I'll give you a massage to try and relax those muscles of yours. Don't move until I come back.'

'Shower.' Alessandro closed his eyes, not daring to think about the word 'massage'. 'Now you're torturing me.'

She paused, her hand on the doorhandle, a frown in her eyes. 'You could take a shower if you wanted to.'

He gave a sardonic smile and gestured to his cast. 'Oh, yeah—easy as anything.'

'Not easy, but possible. We just have to cover it in plastic to protect it.'

There was a long, pulsing silence. 'You're offering to help me in the shower?'

'That's why I'm here.'

Alessandro wondered if he was the only one feeling warm. Suddenly he wished he hadn't suggested it. Nurse, he told himself. She was offering as a nurse, not anything else. 'I was joking. I can manage.'

'Well, you can't shower on your own, no matter how macho you are.' Her voice was mild. 'But if you don't want a shower, that's fine. I don't want to push you if you're shy.'

Shy?

It had nothing to do with being shy and everything to do with the fact that she was standing in front of him wearing a form-fitting black wetsuit.

'Yeah.' His voice was a hoarse croak. 'That's right. I'm shy. So we'll give the shower a miss for now.'

As she strolled away from him he took comfort in the fact that at least there was one part of his body that appeared to be working normally.

By the end of two weeks, Tasha had reached screaming pitch.

As plans went, this one had backfired big time.

The tension that had been there on the first day seemed to grow with each passing minute.

If revenge was supposed to be pleasurable then she was definitely doing something wrong because she was in agony. The only one suffering was her.

Instead of giving her the opportunity to be aloof and distant, she was being sucked deeper and deeper into his life. His lack of mobility inevitably meant that she did everything from physio to answering the phone.

Even as she had that thought, the phone rang again and Tasha rolled her eyes and answered it, wondering which of Alessandro's many female friends it would be this time.

A brisk voice informed her that the Princess Eleanor wished to speak to her son, but before Tasha could hand over the phone a cool, cultured voice came down the line.

'Are you his nurse?'

Tasha frowned. 'Well, no, actually, I'm a—'

'Never mind. I'm better off not knowing.' In a cold, unemotional tone she demanded to speak to her son and Tasha passed the phone over without question, feeling defensive and irritated and about as small as a bacterium.

Just what was his mother implying?

She'd been expecting to be asked for a clinical update on progress, but clearly his mother didn't consider her worth speaking to.

Angry with herself for caring, Tasha busied herself tidying up and tried not to listen to the conversation, but it was impossible not to pick up the tension between the two of them, even though the conversation was conducted in Italian.

Alessandro replied to what appeared to be a barrage of questions in a similar clipped, perfunctory tone and afterwards he flung the phone down onto the sofa, picked up the crutches and struggled onto the terrace. The loud thump of the sticks told her everything she needed to know about his mood.

Startled by the lack of affection between mother and son,

Tasha stared at his rigid shoulders for a while and then followed him outside. Was she supposed to say something or pretend it hadn't happened? This wasn't her business, was it? And she wasn't supposed to care...

Torn, she stood awkwardly. 'Can I get you anything?'

'No. Thanks.' He kept his gaze fixed on the surfers in the bay. 'Not unless you can conjure up a new, fit body. I need to heal instantly so that I can get back to my life.'

A life he clearly hated.

'I know it feels frustrating, but if you rush things you'll just do more damage.' She tried to put herself in his mother's shoes. Alessandro was her only surviving son. To hear about his accident must have given her a shock. Perhaps it was anxiety that had put that chill in her tone. 'Your mother must be worried.'

'She's worried I'm not doing my duty. Apparently while I'm "lounging" here, enjoying myself with pretty nurses in attendance—that's you, by the way...' he threw her a mocking smile '...my image is suffering.'

So that explained Princess Eleanor's frigid tone on the phone. She'd assumed there was something going on between the 'nurse' and her son. Irritated rather than embarrassed, Tasha glanced at the bruises visible through the open neck of his polo shirt. 'Does she know how badly you were hurt?'

'Yes. Josh called her while I was in Theatre the first time.'

'And?'

'And she said it was no more than I deserved for indulging in high-risk sports. My accident is badly timed. I had fifty official engagements scheduled over the next month, including opening the annual May ball at the palace.'

'Oh. Well, perhaps she's worried that—'

'Tasha, she isn't worried.' He cut through her platitudes, his dark eyes hard and cold. 'My mother only worries about two things—duty and responsibility. My love of polo was bad enough. Having injured myself, I've committed the cardinal sin of making life very inconvenient for her.'

'You're her son and I'm sure that—'

'Let's get one thing straight.' Alessandro shifted his position so that he was facing her. 'As far as my mother is concerned, the wrong son died. It's because of me that Antonio is no longer Crown Prince. I can't bring him back so I'm expected to fill his shoes...' He hesitated and then muttered something under his breath. 'In every way.'

Tasha frowned. *In every way.* What did he mean by that? 'It wasn't your fault. Why are you blaming yourself?'

He turned away abruptly and Tasha felt the tension flowing from him. Darkness surrounded him like a force field and suddenly she knew that the change in him, the hardness, was all to do with the death of his brother.

Her insides softened. 'Do you want to talk about it?'

'No.'

'But—'

'Not everything can be healed by good nursing, Natasha.' The bitterness sliced through her own defences and she stretched out her hand and touched his arm.

'Is that why she rang? To tell you you've made her life difficult?' Anger glowed inside her and suddenly Tasha wished she hadn't passed him the phone.

She should have screened the call.

'She rang to order me to see my advisers, who apparently have a plan for, and I quote, "pulling something positive" out of this disastrous mess I've made.' A cynical smile tilted his mouth. 'Apparently an injured prince may appeal to a certain age group, so she thinks there may be some mileage in media interviews. So that's my contribution to society—providing entertainment for bored housewives.'

'Next time I'm going to tell her you're asleep and can't be disturbed.' Part of her wondered why she felt the urge to rush to his defence and clearly he was asking himself the same question because he stared at her for a long moment.

The hardness left his eyes and he lifted a hand and touched her face. The attraction flickered between them, live and dangerous.

Tasha tried to speak, tried to move, but her body seemed to have shut down and Alessandro gave a low groan, slid his hand behind her head and brought her mouth down on his in a hungry, explosive kiss.

Heat burst through her. Last time she'd kissed him it had been a childish experiment, a desperate desire to grow up fast. There was nothing experimental about this kiss. It was hot and sexual and the explosion of desire gripped her so fiercely that she moaned against his seeking mouth and dug her fingers in the front of his shirt.

It was only as she felt him flinch that she realised how much she must be hurting him. The backs of her fingers were pressed against his bruised chest and she'd leaned into him, instinctively drawing herself closer to his hard body. *Closer to heartbreak.*

'Damn you—no.' Angry with herself, and even more angry with him, she pulled back quickly. 'I didn't want you to do that. I came out here to give you sympathy and support.'

'I don't want sympathy or support. I want you.' He spoke with the assurance and conviction of someone who'd never been turned down by a woman in his life, and she started to shake.

'Don't start that, Alessandro.' She virtually spat the words. 'Don't start all that smooth talk, seduction thing—I'm not interested.'

'Tasha—'

'Age may have given you wider shoulders and longer legs but it obviously hasn't given you a conscience. Do you honestly think I'd put myself through that a second time? Do you think I'm that much of a masochist?' Her voice rose and she saw his dark brows rise in astonishment. 'I'm not interested, Alessandro. I don't want you to kiss me, I don't want you to touch me—' She broke off, aware that her voice was shaking as much as the rest of her. And he was looking at her as if she'd gone mad. *Oh, God, she was overreacting.* She should have laughed it off. Or said she didn't feel anything. Or… Her hands raised, she backed away. 'Coming here was *such* a mistake. I should have said no when Josh asked me. I should have…' She breathed deeply, struggling for control. 'I should have said no.'

'Tasha, wait a minute.' He reached for her but she slapped his hand away and he was forced to grab the rail to regain his balance.

It was a measure of her dedication as a doctor that she made sure he was stable before she walked away.

'Touch me again and I'll break your other leg.' She turned and stalked out off the terrace, her heart crashing against her ribs and terror in her heart.

CHAPTER FIVE

TASHA sat on the bed, her knees drawn up against her chest like a child protecting herself. Her heart was pounding with reaction to the adrenaline surging around her body. The doctor in her recognised the physiological process.

Fight or flight.

The kiss licked like fire through her body, as if that one single touch had set in motion something that couldn't be stopped. She rubbed her hands down her legs, trying to kill the sensations that engulfed her. Why had she let him do that? *Why?*

It wasn't as if she was short on self-discipline. She could say no to chocolate, she'd never been drunk in her life and she'd worked relentlessly to achieve the highest grades possible in her exams. So why couldn't she apply that same single-minded focus to staying detached from Alessandro?

Furious with herself, Tasha thumped her fist on the mattress.

There was something about him that just drew her in. She felt out of her control and that part of it infuriated her more than anything.

Impulse was her greatest fault, she thought savagely. She was a scientist, wasn't she? Impulse shouldn't be part of her make-up, and yet she couldn't seem to stop herself acting on her instincts. First she'd resigned from a job she loved and now she was getting herself involved with the last man in the world any woman in her right mind would get involved with.

So what was she supposed to do next?

She couldn't carry on nursing him, could she? She didn't trust herself.

She was going to have to leave.

She was going to have to make some excuse and—

The door slammed open with a violence that sent it crashing into the wall. Alessandro stood there, his eyes dark as a storm, one hand against the doorframe to balance himself. 'What the hell is going on, Tash? If you feel like that, why did you agree to help me?'

'Get out!' She wasn't ready to face him. *Didn't trust herself to keep him at a distance.*

'I'm not going anywhere. Not until we've had an honest conversation.'

'Honest? What do you know about honest?' It was a struggle to keep her voice even. 'One minute you—you—make a woman feel as though she's the only female alive in the world and then the next minute you—'

'The next minute I…?'

'Just forget it. I don't know why we're even talking about this. *I don't want to talk about this.*'

'We're talking about it because it's obviously on your mind. And it seems to have been on your mind for a long time.' He hobbled into the room, his jaw clenched against the pain, his muscles pumped up and hard. 'That first day in the hospital, I asked you if the past was going to be a problem and you said—'

'I know what I said.' Her voice rose. 'I don't need you to repeat it.'

His gaze was steady on hers. 'If you hate me that much, why did you agree to help me?'

'I don't hate you. I don't have any feelings for you whatsoever.' She threw out the words, knowing them to be untrue. But she badly wanted them to be true. She badly wanted to have no feelings for him. In fact, it was essential for her emotional well-being that she had no feelings for him.

'Which brings me back to the same question—why did you agree to help me?'

'Because I'd messed up my job and I was at a loose end. Because I wanted to prove that you didn't mean anything to me any more, and...' she breathed deeply '...I wanted to see if you were sorry.'

He looked at her for a long moment and then his eyes narrowed and he gave a humourless laugh. 'Ah. Now I understand. You thought you'd punish me, is that it? The strip show was for my benefit. All the "look at me" surfing sessions were designed to make me suffer. All of it was designed to make me suffer. What we shared wasn't water under the bridge. You weren't indifferent. You were getting revenge.'

'It wasn't revenge.' Tasha felt her face grow scarlet as she defended herself. 'I wanted to prove to myself that you were nothing more than a childish crush. The way I felt about you back then was— Actually, I don't even want to think about it. It's just too embarrassing. And, yes, I was angry with you. You behaved like a complete and utter bastard.'

'I know.'

'And then you—' His words penetrated her brain and she broke off and stared at him. 'What did you say?'

'I said I know. I know I treated you horribly.'

'Y-You do?' Stunned by his blunt admission, she stared at him. 'You knew that?'

'Of course. That's why I was so surprised when you waltzed blithely into my hospital room and offered to help me out. Frankly, I was expecting a black eye from you, not assistance.' He watched her cautiously. 'Clearly I was right to be suspicious of your motives.'

'But—' Anger shot through her. 'If you knew you'd behaved horribly, why didn't you ever say anything? You could at least have said sorry.'

'That would have defeated the purpose.'

'The purpose?' Tasha stared at him blankly. 'I don't get it.'

'The purpose was to make you hate me,' he said gently. 'If I'd apologised, it wouldn't have worked, would it?'

'You—you *wanted* me to hate you? Why?'

He gave a crooked smile. 'Because every time I walked into a room you looked at me as though I was the only person there. Because you thought you were in love with me. You were crazy about me, and—'

'All right, all right.' She held up her hand like a stop sign. 'Can this get any more embarrassing? Enough! I know exactly how I behaved. There's no need to rub it in.'

'I was going to say, "and I was crazy about you".' He spoke the words so softly she wondered if she'd misheard.

'You—'

'I'd never been with anyone who behaved as normally around me as you did.'

'I hero-worshiped you.'

'I know, and that was sweet, but the best part was that you were such fun. You were so unselfconscious. The first time I visited you kept trying to remember to call me Your Highness and then you just gave up and called me Sandro, and you were the first person who had ever done that. And you were so beautiful…' He shifted position awkwardly, unconsciously trying to ease the pain. 'Too beautiful. Josh introduced you as his kid sister but it didn't take me long to realise you weren't a kid. Especially when you wore those bikinis.'

Tasha watched him, her heart thumping. 'I wanted you to notice me.'

The corners of his mouth flickered. 'I noticed you.'

'And then there was the ballgown.'

'I wondered when we were going to talk about that. That night at the ball—' his eyes glittered '—I couldn't believe Josh had agreed to take you. The only way I'd kept my distance was because I kept telling myself you were a kid. And

Josh kept telling me you were a kid. And then suddenly you were standing there in this scarlet dress that made you look like a sex goddess—'

'You remember what I was wearing?'

'And suddenly telling myself that you were a kid didn't seem to be working.' His eyes were very dark. 'It didn't help that you were so wildly determined to lose your virginity that night. To me.'

Mortified at the memory of how brazen she'd been, Tasha covered her face with her hands. 'Do we have to talk about this? Isn't there just a nice deep hole I can jump into?'

'I wanted you, too.'

'Oh, sure.' Still cringing, she shook her head. 'Which is why you kissed me senseless and…' *He'd touched her,* she remembered. *Everywhere.* The memory sent fiery heat streaking through her. 'And then you walked away.'

'And why do you think I walked away, Tash?'

His intimate use of her name made her heart thud. 'Because you discovered I was flat-chested? Because I had no idea what I was doing?' His skill had left her trembling and boneless whereas she'd fumbled awkwardly, unsure of herself and of him.

'I stopped because it was the right thing to do, and that is probably the only time in my life I've done the right thing, so you should be grateful, not angry,' he confessed in a raw tone. 'I didn't know if you were a child or a woman. Damn it, I went into your bedroom to give you a message one day and your bed was covered in stuffed toys! One minute you were doing your homework, the next you were wearing a tight red dress designed to drive a man out of his mind. I wanted—well, never mind what I wanted. But I knew I had to do something drastic. That night of the ball I'd promised myself I was going to behave like a real prince. I was going to dance with you and not do anything else. But then we went out to the garden to get some fresh air and the next minute—'

'You don't need to spell it out.'

'Believe me, walking away without looking back was the hardest thing I've ever had to do. And for what it's worth, I'm sorry I hurt you, but at the time I couldn't see any other way. I wanted you to hate me.'

'You could have just told me you weren't interested.'

'I was interested. There was a chemistry between us I'd never experienced before. It was crazy, and—' He broke off. 'You were seventeen. Apart from anything else, it was barely legal.'

A warm glow burned low in her stomach. *He'd wanted her, too.* Tasha wrapped her arms around herself. 'Plenty of people have sex at seventeen.'

'You had your head in the clouds and your eyes on the stars. You were still more of a child than a woman and I had no idea how to handle someone like you. The women I mixed with were usually my age or older—heiresses, society princesses who'd been fed cynicism and experience with baby milk. You were different.'

'And it didn't occur to you to have that conversation with me?' Tasha swung her legs off the bed and stalked over to him, her eyes boring into his. 'I had a brain, Sandro. And a mind of my own.'

'I did the decent thing.'

'*Decent?* You broke my heart, Sandro. You…' She spread her hands, appalled. 'What the hell is decent about making a girl feel totally rubbish about herself? Please tell me that.'

'I didn't make you feel rubbish. I saved you from making a big mistake.'

'*Saved* me? Do you think you could have "saved" me before you ripped off my red dress?' Her face was scarlet at the memory. *The humiliation.* 'Then when I was totally vulnerable and ready to trust you with anything and everything, you suddenly backed away and told me to come back when I'd grown a chest. But that wasn't the worst of it. The worst of it wasn't struggling to get my ballgown back on so that a bunch of strangers didn't see me naked—and you broke the zip, by the way, so I never actually managed to get it back on—the worst was when you walked away from me straight into the arms of a tall, skinny blonde. When you kissed her I thought I was going to die.' It was good to remind herself what had happened, she thought grimly. Good to remind herself why she wasn't going to be seduced by the chemistry again.

'Tasha—'

'You knew I was watching, didn't you? At the time I assumed you didn't know I was still there, but now I see you did it for my benefit. You *wanted* me to see you kiss her.'

There was a stillness about him. A hardness about his eyes that she hadn't seen before. 'I've told you—I wanted you to hate me and forget about me. You were a kid.'

'Did I feel like a kid when you stripped me naked?'

'What do you think would have happened if I'd taken you that night?' His tone savage, he took her chin in his fingers and lifted her face to his. 'Think.'

'We would have made love,' she whispered. 'You would have been the first.'

His fingers tightened on her face. For a moment they stared at each other, sharing the memories through that single look. 'I would have broken your heart.'

The air dragged through her lungs and each beat of her heart felt painful. 'You did that anyway. But I should be grateful. Because of you I buried myself in my books. I gave up on men.'

'That's not what I heard.' His eyes were fixed on hers, his breathing heavy. 'Josh told me you were engaged once—'

Great. More humiliation. 'That didn't work out.' Trying not to think about the fact he'd obviously discussed her with Josh, Tasha pulled away from him. 'I'm not great with relationships. I'm the first to admit it.'

'That makes two of us.'

'You have endless relationships. I read about them all the time in the paper.'

'Those aren't relationships.'

'Right.'

'For what it's worth, I'm sorry I hurt you, Tash. I should have handled it a different way.' He adjusted his balance. 'Forgive me?'

'No! I don't forgive you.'

He was standing close to her. 'There's always been something between us and it hasn't gone away.'

'I'm older and wiser now.'

'You're still the same Tasha,' he breathed. 'Feisty, emotional, warm, giving—'

'Be quiet. I don't trust you when you're nice.'

'I'm always nice, *tesoro*.' His soft, velvety voice wrapped itself around her senses and she felt her willpower crumble.

'I'm still really angry with you,' she choked. 'I'm always going to be angry with you.'

'Even if I say sorry? *Mi dispiace.*'

She felt the warmth of his hand against her head and the heat of his body close to hers. He was a breath away from kissing her again and her eyes closed.

'No, Alessandro—please don't...' There was a tense silence and all she could hear was the sound of her own breathing. 'I mean it—I don't want you to touch me.'

For a moment she thought he was going to ignore her and then she felt his hand drop and he moved away. 'All right.' His voice was hoarse. 'I won't touch you until you ask me to.'

Disappointment mingled with relief, and the confusion of it infuriated her.

It wasn't logical to be disappointed when she was the one who'd asked him to move away.

'That will be never.' Tasha opened her eyes and looked at

him, feeling as though the whole centre of her balance had shifted. 'I'd better find you another nurse.'

'Why? Last time I looked my leg was still in a cast and my ribs were still bruised.'

'I don't think I can do this,' she said desperately. 'I thought it would be easy, but it isn't. We're— You're…'

He was still standing close to her. The warmth of him, the scent of him, wound itself around her insides and sent anticipation skittering through her.

She swayed towards him and then she saw the dangerous burn of heat in his dark eyes and remembered how long it had taken her to recover last time she'd fallen for this man.

She was hopeless at relationships, wasn't she? She didn't want one. She had a career she loved. And she had to concentrate on sorting out the mess she'd made of her professional life.

'You hurt me, Alessandro.' Tasha forced the words past her lips. 'I have more self-respect than to let you do it again. I'll stay and look after you because I gave my word, but it's not going to be any more than that.'

'We thought maybe a carefully placed interview with a celebrity magazine, Your Highness, focusing on your hopes for the future…'

As his advisers droned on, Alessandro stared out of the window towards the waves. It was early morning and there was only one surfer in the waves.

Tasha. She was out there again, enjoying the swell beneath her board and the spray on her face.

Seeking distraction…

It had been three days since their conversation and she'd kept their interaction on a strictly professional level, but that didn't alter the tension that added an edge to the atmosphere whenever they were in a room together.

'Your Highness?'

Alessandro dragged his gaze from contemplation of the surfer. 'Sorry?'

His advisers exchanged glances. 'We were suggesting ways in which you could potentially raise your profile even though you're…' one of them cleared his throat and looked at Alessandro's leg '…incapacitated.'

'Featuring in a celebrity magazine?' Alessandro didn't bother to conceal his contempt for the idea. 'I don't think so.'

'It would be—'

'Shallow and useless,' Alessandro snapped. 'I don't want to be portrayed as some royal layabout. I run a successful multimillion-dollar business.' Or he had until his brother's death. Now a select team ran it in his place and he was only involved in the major decisions.

'The important thing is that the people want to see *you*, Your Highness. They want to know their prince. They'll pay an enormous sum for the interview.' His chief adviser named a figure that made Alessandro shake his head in disbelief.

'They'll pay that much to take pictures of me lying on the sofa with my leg in plaster? The world has gone mad.'

'The money would be given to your favourite charity, Your Highness, and that would be excellent publicity.'

'And both contrived and manipulative.' Alessandro felt bitter distaste for the workings of the media. 'If they have that kind of money to throw around then let them just donate it to the charity in the first place. Cut out the middle man.'

'Her Highness, the Princess Eleanor wants—'

'I know what my mother wants.' His tone cold, Alessandro stared at the thick file they'd brought with them. 'What do you have there?'

'We've outlined proposals for various ways of support-ing charity and generally raising your profile in these…' the man's hands trembled slightly as he pushed the file across the table '…difficult and limiting circumstances. The ideas have been approved by the palace. The one that Her Highness particularly wanted us to draw your attention to is—' He broke off, a sheen of sweat on his brow.

'Is?' Alessandro's silken prompt made the man flinch.

'Is the suggestion that you announce your engagement, sir.'

It was like being caught in an avalanche. The cold slammed into him, suffocating him and chilling him right to the bone.

When he didn't speak, the man cleared his throat. 'It's been a while, Your Highness, and everyone assumes—'

'I know what everyone assumes.' Alessandro barely recognised his own voice. He leaned back against the sofa, suddenly exhausted. 'Leave the file. I'll read it and tell you what I intend to do.'

'Yes, Your Highness.'

They left and Alessandro stayed where he was. The file remained unopened.

The thought of allowing sycophantic journalists and photographers into his private life made him cold inside. But the thing that made him coldest of all was the prospect of announcing his engagement. The last thing he wanted was marriage. Given the choice he would have stayed single rather than risk the sort of relationship his parents had. But he didn't have the choice, did he? It was up to him to produce the next generation to rule the Mediterranean island of San Savarre. It didn't matter whether he liked it or not.

Filling his brother's shoes.

He needed to talk to Miranda. He needed to *see* Miranda. But instead of seeing Miranda's sleek blonde hair and elegant clothes, he saw Tasha putting chilli in his food, undaunted by royal protocol. *Hope I'm not supposed to bow or curtsey.*

Tasha, walking away from him.

Since their heated, tense exchange they had hardly seen each other and Alessandro knew that she was staying out in the surf as long as possible to avoid him.

Telling himself that it was probably a good thing,

Alessandro hobbled through to the bedroom and turned on the television in the hope of distraction.

By the time she arrived back from her session in the waves, he'd pulled himself together and he focused hard on the screen as she whirled through the apartment like a tornado, singing to herself as if nothing had happened between them.

Alessandro watched her steadily. *She was putting on an act.*

'Hi, there, hopalong!' she called to him as she stripped off the jacket she'd put on over her wetsuit and walked jauntily towards her bedroom. 'Surf's up today and this time I'm not saying that to make you want to thump me.'

'Tasha—'

'Need to get out of my wet things!'

He had to admire her performance. If he hadn't known better he would have said she was indifferent. But he knew she was far from indifferent. Watching her breeze through the house, he wondered how long she was going to keep up the pretence that nothing was happening between them. 'When I finally get this damn plaster off my leg, I'll join you.' They were going through the motions. Talking about surfing, even though that wasn't the topic uppermost in their thoughts.

He heard the soft hiss of water as she turned on the shower and immediately he started thinking about Tasha naked. And thinking about Tasha naked—

Cursing softly, he picked up the remote control and flicked on the sports channel.

'How did your meeting go?' She was standing in the doorway, wearing a T-shirt and a pair of shorts. Her hair was still wet from the shower and her feet bare. 'What do they want you to do?'

Get married.

'The usual stuff. Palace promotion. I'm afraid I'm not very good at being told what to do. I've always been a bit of a rebel

that way. Antonio was the dutiful one. He was the Good Son.'
He felt the bed give as she sat down next to him.

'You must miss him terribly. I know you were close.' Her
voice was soft and for the time being she seemed to have
abandoned her act. 'I can't begin to imagine how I'd cope if
I lost a brother.'

'We both had our roles. I was the bad boy. Even as kids
it was the same. It never occurred to me I'd have to play his
role. The truth is, I'm not good at it. No matter how much my
parents would like me to be, I'm not my brother.' Alessandro
wondered why he was telling her this. He never talked about
it. Not to anyone.

But talking to Tasha had always been easy. She had a way
of making a person spill the contents of their minds.

'No, you're not your brother. You're you, an individual.'
She hesitated. 'I suppose you have to find a way to do it that
suits you. A way you're OK with. I mean, Josh and I are both
doctors but we're not the same. We don't approach things the
same way. He's very analytical whereas I'm more emotional.
But I don't think either one of us is better or worse than the
other. We're just different.'

'The problem is, my parents don't want different. If they
could have chosen, I would have been the one who died in
that car.'

'Don't say that.' She sounded shocked and then her forehead creased into a tiny frown. 'The other night when we
were talking—you said it was your fault…'

Had he said that to her? 'Forget it.'

'But—'

'If you want to help me, you can fetch that big fat file from
the table in the living room.' Alessandro gave a humourless
laugh. 'I have to go through it and pick out which duties I'm
up to performing. I need to kiss some babies in public.'

And he needed to finally announce his engagement.

'Kiss babies? Sounds like a recipe for disease transmission
to me. I'll warn infection control. Now, lie back and let me

take a look at your ribs to see how quickly you're healing. It
will give me some idea of what you're capable of doing. It's
no good opening a hospital and then finding yourself as a
patient.'

Remembering what had happened the last time she'd
touched him, Alessandro's eyes narrowed warily. 'No need.
I'm fine.'

'I'm the one who's going to tell you if you're fine.' She
pushed him back with the palm of her hand. 'And wipe that
look off your face. I'm in doctor mode. I don't think about
sex when I'm in doctor mode. And, anyway, I told you I'm
not interested.' Ignoring his protests, she unbuttoned his shirt
with brisk fingers. The fact that there was nothing lover-like
about her expression did nothing to lessen his libido.

'What about the patient?' Alessandro gritted his teeth.
'What if the patient starts thinking about sex?'

'That would be seriously perverted. After all, I'm hurting
you. The bruising is better.' Frowning, she trailed her fingers
lightly over his chest. 'Does this hurt?'

'It depends which part of me you're asking about.'

'Don't be disgusting. This is why I chose to be a children's
doctor.' But her voice was mild as she slid her fingers up to
his shoulders and pressed. 'Does this hurt?'

'If I say yes, will you stop?'

'It obviously doesn't hurt as much as before because you're
not doing that clenched-teeth thing. I think you're definitely
on the mend.'

'Good, then can we—?'

'I just want to listen to your breath sounds.' She'd left her
stethoscope on the table by his bed and as she reached for it
her hair tumbled forward, brushing over his arm. 'I'm just
going to—'

'So am I.' Driven past the point of control, Alessandro
cupped her face in his hands and brought her mouth down on
his. Her lips opened under his and he tasted shock mingled
with sweetness. For a moment he thought she was going to

pull away, but as his tongue slid against hers he felt her moan and tighten her grip on his shoulders. There was a delicious inevitability to the kiss that simply added to the excitement. It was the culmination of the tension and anticipation that had been building between them since the morning she'd walked into his hospital room.

Apparently forgetting all her protests about not wanting him to touch her, Tasha ripped at his shirt, hesitating as he gave a grunt of pain when her fingers made contact with bruised flesh. 'Sorry...' She panted the word against his mouth and pulled back but he grabbed her, his fingers hard on her arms.

'Don't stop. For God's sake, don't stop,' he groaned, his mind at war with his senses. 'Do you want to stop? You didn't want to do this—'

'Changed my mind—' Their mouths clashed, the kiss exciting and erotic, and he rolled her onto her back and then swore fluently as pain overtook him.

'This is—'

'A challenge. I have a better idea.' Desperate, she pushed him back gently and straddled him, her hair falling forward, brushing his bare chest. Her eyes were like dark, dangerous pools. 'I'm the one in charge. If I hurt you, tell me.'

'I think that's supposed to be my line.' Alessandro pulled her head down to his and took her mouth with explicit intent, tasting sweetness and a desperation that matched his.

'God, you're beautiful.' He groaned the words against her lips. 'How did I keep my hands off you all those years ago?'

'You didn't.' Frantic, she tore at his clothes and he tore at hers until only flimsy underwear separated them.

Panting, breathless, they kissed like two crazy people. They were so wrapped up in each other that they were oblivious to anything but the heat they were creating. Which was why they didn't hear the sound in the distance.

'Tasha? Alessandro? Anyone there?' Josh's voice came

from the living room of the house and Tasha froze as if she'd been shot. Her eyes flew open and she dragged her mouth from the seductive pressure of his.

'Ohmigod!'

'Oops.' Hiding his frustration, Alessandro gave her a crooked smile and stroked her hair back from her face. 'It's your brother. That's not great timing. You might want to put your clothes on, *tesoro*. I don't want him to see you naked.'

CHAPTER SIX

'THIS is *all* your fault! I told you not to kiss me.' Tasha yanked her top back over her head and freed her hair. 'Stay there. You're not safe to be around. I was in doctor mode. How the hell did we end up naked?'

'Because the chemistry doesn't go away just because you're clutching a stethoscope. I want you, Tasha. Make no mistake about that.' His smooth, possessive declaration stopped her breathing. For an injured man he was far too threatening.

'I…' confused, she tumbled off the bed, grabbing her clothes. Glancing briefly at him, she collided with dark, burning eyes and felt her insides melt. 'No.' It was both a plea and a protest. 'Just—no.'

She'd promised herself that she wasn't going to do this. That she wasn't going to fall under his spell again.

She was a career-woman. She had a five-year plan and it didn't include falling for a wicked, sexy prince. She'd had herself under control. She'd been doing really well.

Until he'd kissed her…

'Damn you, Sandro. I need to get dressed before he comes looking for us.' Her face burning, Tasha grabbed the rest of her clothes, desperately conscious of those coal-black eyes following her every move. The heat was still in the room, simmering between them like a blast from the sun.

If he was bothered by the fact that her brother was in his house, he didn't show it. But Alessandro wasn't the sort to run from anything, she knew that. In fact, that was part of the problem. He had too much of the devil in him.

And that devil had drawn her just as it had when she was a teenager.

In her haste to drag on her clothes, Tasha couldn't untangle her jeans and they were halfway up her legs when her brother tapped on the door and opened it.

Tasha gave a whimper of horror. She didn't know which was worse—her brother seeing her semi-naked, or her brother seeing her semi-naked with Alessandro.

'Hey, you guys—I thought I'd drop by and see if you've killed each other yet...' His voice faded as he saw them and for a moment Tasha stared like a rabbit at oncoming headlights.

Oh, dear...

'Hi, Josh.' Hands shaking, she finally managed to zip her jeans. She felt as mortified as she had when Josh had caught her kissing the captain of the football team when she was sixteen. 'We weren't expecting you.' She tried to sound casual, as if dressing in Alessandro's room was an everyday occurrence. With any luck Josh would decide to turn a blind eye.

But one look at the flat, disapproving line of her brother's mouth told her this wasn't going to be her lucky day.

'What the hell are you doing?' Josh's voice was tight and the shock in his eyes turned dark as approaching storm clouds as he turned his gaze on Alessandro, who stared right back at him.

'Seducing your sister. If you have a problem with that, take it out on me, not her.'

'You—' Josh was across the room in a flash and Tasha hastily planted herself in front of Alessandro.

'No!' Her legs were shaking and she was mortified at being caught kissing, but most of all she was mortified that she'd been kissing Alessandro in the first place.

That definitely hadn't been part of the master plan.

'Josh, calm down! It's nothing to get into a sweat over.' Actually, it was, but the sweating was going to have to wait for another time because at the moment her brother looked dangerous and she felt a twinge of real fear.

'Calm down? *Calm down?*' Josh closed his hands over her arms and moved her bodily to one side, his voice thick with anger as he confronted his friend. 'I arrange for my sister to nurse you and this is how you repay me?'

Tasha bristled. 'Excuse me! I do have a mind of my own, you know. You might have been the one who suggested it, but—'

'Shut up, Tasha.' Josh growled the words. 'This isn't your business.'

Alessandro shifted his leg. 'It certainly isn't yours, my friend.'

He should have looked vulnerable, but he didn't. In fact, somehow he managed to look physically intimidating, even with broken bones and bruised ribs, Tasha thought absently. She wondered whether his natural air of command was something to do with being royalty or whether it was just the man.

Warrior Prince.

Josh was red in the face. 'It has everything to do with me. She's my sister!'

Tasha opened her mouth to protest again and realised that neither man was taking any notice of her.

Their eyes were fixed on each other in full combat mode. Alessandro stared Josh straight in the eye, the challenge blatant. 'And this time she's way above the age of consent. I repeat—it has nothing to do with you.'

This time? Tasha frowned at that remark but she didn't have time to dwell on it because the two men were squaring up for a fight.

Josh stepped forward, his expression ugly, his hands clenched. 'And that's all it takes for you, is it? She's old enough so that makes it OK? Well, I've got news for you,

Alessandro, it doesn't make it OK. And she's leaving here right now.' Without turning his head, Josh pointed his finger at the door. 'Pack your bags, Tasha.'

Tasha raised her eyebrows, assuming he was joking. When she realised he wasn't, she put her hands on her hips and threw her head back. 'I will *not* pack my bags! Are you deranged? Listen to you!' Her own temper spilled over. 'I'm not six years old, Josh. I'm a grown woman, and if I want to kiss a man, I'll kiss him and I don't have to ask your permission first.' She vented her anger on Josh, even though she knew deep down that most of it should be directed at herself.

She'd been stupid, stupid, stupid…

'You're my sister.' His tone was raw and angry. 'Don't argue with me. Go and pack. This is between Allesandro and I.'

'Oh, for God's sake, will you listen to yourself? *"This is between Allessandro and I,"*' Tasha mimicked his tone. 'What are you going to do, Josh? Challenge him to a duel? Pistols at dawn? This is the twenty-first century. Get over yourself.'

'This isn't your business, Natasha.'

'Well, *excuse* me—' she emphasised each word '—but I was the one naked with him, not you. I think that makes it my business, not yours.'

Josh gave a low growl. 'You were *naked* with him?'

Yes, and she had no idea how it had happened. Clearly at some point during the burn of chemistry, her brain had disconnected itself from her body. But she didn't want to think about that right now. 'So what if I was? *What is your problem?* You do not just barge in here and tell me what to do. Do I ask you what's happening in your love life? Do I lecture you or ask you who you got naked with last night? When I saw you coming out of that on-call room a couple of weeks ago, having had a night of hot sex, did I demand to know who was in the room with you?'

Alessandro raised an eyebrow. 'Hey, Josh, you had a night of hot sex? Good man.'

'Shut up!' Brother and sister spoke simultaneously and Tasha stabbed Josh in the chest with her finger.

'I wanted to ask who she was, but I didn't because I respect your privacy and your ability to make your own decisions. I understand that you're an adult. If you want to have a one-night stand in the on-call room, that's up to you.'

There was a tense, frozen silence.

Josh's face had turned from scarlet to grey. 'It wasn't a one-night stand. And this isn't about me, it's about you.'

'Precisely.' Tasha folded her arms and pursed her lips. 'Which makes it my business, not yours. If I want to sleep with a man, I'll sleep with him. I don't need your permission.'

Josh's shoulders sagged and suddenly he looked exhausted. 'Fine.' His voice was brittle. 'You're right, of course. I apologise.'

Startled by the sudden change in him, Tasha frowned. One minute he was yelling at her and the next he looked as though his brain was on another planet. 'So—when I need a knight in shining armour, I'll text you.'

Alessandro started to laugh. 'I hate to break it to you, Josh, but I think your baby sister is all grown up and slaying her own dragons.'

Josh was still looking at Tasha. A tiny muscle flickered in his cheek and he shook his head slightly, as if trying to focus. 'Just as long as you know he will break your heart,' he said shakily. 'You'll fall in love, because that's what you do, and he'll smash you to pieces. I don't want that for you. I don't want you loving someone you can't be with. I wouldn't wish that on anyone.' There was an anguished note to his tone that killed Tasha's anger like water on flame.

Instinct told her there was more to her brother's words than a throw-away comment.

I don't want you loving someone you can't be with.

Suddenly she knew that his explosion of emotion was

driven by something deeper than her own indiscretion. Something much more personal.

'Josh...' Her voice faltered. 'I—'

'I'm just telling you to be careful, that's all.' Cutting her dead, he blanked the emotion and walked to the door. 'I'll leave the two of you alone. I'm sorry I interrupted. And who am I to give advice on relationships? It's a subject I know nothing about.'

His departure was more painful than his arrival.

Tasha felt her heart clench. Her brother was suffering and she sensed that his anguish went much deeper than concern about her.

Was this about the woman in the on-call room?

'Wait!' Tasha sprinted after him. 'Don't just walk off—for crying out loud, Josh, will you *wait*?'

He kept walking, talking over his shoulder as he strode through Alessandro's double-height living room. 'I need breakfast. I've been working all night. I have to get back to the hospital.'

'I'll make you breakfast.' Catching up with him, she caught his arm. 'The kitchen here is like a spaceship and I can do amazing things with eggs. Please.'

'I need to be on my own.' He shook her off and she saw the emptiness in his eyes as he detached from her. 'I'm sorry I disturbed you.'

Tasha felt a flash of exasperation but this time it was fuelled by real concern for her brother. 'It wasn't like that, Josh—honestly, it was nothing.' She didn't know what it was and she hadn't had time to work it out, but at the moment her priority was Josh. 'I want you to stay. I haven't seen you properly since I arrived. Let's chat. Catch up.'

'Sit down, Josh.' Alessandro's slightly accented drawl came from behind them. Tasha realised that while she and Josh had been arguing Alessandro had hauled himself from the bed and was now gripping the doorframe. His shirt—*the shirt she'd ripped*—hung loose around his body, exposing his bronzed muscled chest. 'I'm going mad trapped in this place. I need male conversation.'

Tasha gave a faint smile. 'Men don't have conversations. They just exchange sporting results.' But she was relieved that Alessandro had added his voice to hers.

Josh looked undecided and the look he gave Alessandro was cold. 'I should go—'

'There's a wealth of difference between what one should do and what one chooses to do,' Alessandro drawled. 'Sit down. Your sister isn't a bad cook, providing you keep her away from chilli.'

Tasha opened her mouth and closed it again. This wasn't the time to give him a lecture on the emancipation of women.

Josh relaxed slightly. 'Are you going to promise not to touch my sister again?'

'No.' Alessandro's tone was calm and he lifted his hand as Josh's eyes flared. 'But I promise to stop if she asks me to. Fair enough?'

Josh's mouth was a tight line. 'I don't think—'

'Hello? I'm over here!' Exasperated, Tasha waved at both of them. 'You don't need to talk about me as if I don't exist. In fact, you don't need to talk about me at all. Let's just drop the whole subject.' She was relieved to see her brother sprawl on the deep leather sofa.

As he ran his hand over his face she realised that he hadn't slept in a long time.

The sunlight pouring through the floor-to-ceiling windows simply accentuated the shadows under his eyes and the pallor of his skin. Why had it taken her so long to notice how awful he looked?

Because she'd been too busy getting her clothes on.

'So...' She sank down on the sofa next to him and curled her legs underneath her. 'You look wrecked.'

'Thanks.'

'Have you been working nights or something?' Even

as she asked the question, she dismissed it. Josh never had any trouble coping with work volume, so it couldn't be that. Which meant it must be a woman. But the split with Rebecca had been mutual...

Using a process of elimination, she mentally ticked off the options and decided that it had to be something to do with the woman he'd had in the on-call room.

She'd thought at the time that he was behaving oddly.

Suddenly she wished she could send Alessandro into the kitchen so that she could question her brother in private.

'So how's the leg?' His expression slightly less black, Josh looked at his oldest friend. 'Are you healing?'

'Yes, but not fast enough.' Alessandro limped over to the other sofa and sat down. He'd mastered the art of keeping his movements as smooth as possible to reduce jarring. 'I'm hoping this cast will be off soon, then I can get back to normal duties.'

'Palace giving you a hard time?'

'They are not amused,' Alessandro said lightly, a sardonic smile on his face. 'I'm supposed to be earning my keep, not "lounging" around here.'

'You can't do much with your leg like that.' Josh's gaze flickered to Tasha. 'Except mess with my sister.'

'Let's not go there again.' Alessandro leaned back against the sofa. His shirt flopped open, revealing smooth bronzed skin and well-defined muscle. Feeling suddenly dizzy, Tasha was about to tell him to button it up when she realised that he couldn't because she'd ripped the buttons.

Concern for her brother mingled with the realisation that the chemistry between her and Alessandro was as powerful as ever.

So much for the childish crush theory. So much for proving to him that she was indifferent.

Satisfied that they weren't going to kill each other, Tasha used the excuse of breakfast to escape to the kitchen.

Behind the safety of the closed door, she took refuge in

mindless cooking to keep her mind off Alessandro. She didn't want to think about Alessandro. She wanted to know what was wrong with Josh.

People said women were complicated, but at least women usually talked about their problems. Frustrated and grumpy, she chopped fruit into a bowl and then remembered she was feeding men and fried a stack of bacon.

Walking back into the living room with a heaped tray, she found the two men deep in conversation about sport. The earlier argument might never have happened.

They were lifelong friends, of course, and the bond showed as they talked easily, barely acknowledging Tasha as she deposited the tray on the table.

'Hello? Earth to Neanderthals,' she said cheerfully. 'I've cooked it, but I draw the line at actually forking the food into your mouths. That bit you can manage yourselves if you really concentrate.'

'Thanks, Tasha.' Josh sat forward and helped himself to bacon. 'I can't be long. They're holding a prince-and-princess party on the children's ward this afternoon and I promised to dress up as a prince. Which means I have a pile of work to get finished this morning.'

Tasha felt her insides tighten at the mention of the children's ward. She missed it dreadfully.

Being with Alessandro had distracted her slightly from her life, but now reality was back with full force. What if she couldn't find another job? What if she'd messed everything up for good?

Oblivious to her anxieties, Alessandro was laughing at Josh. 'You trained for all those years to pretend to be a prince?'

'It isn't funny. I should have said no.'

'So why didn't you?'

He hesitated. 'Because a friend asked me. There are some kids who have been on the unit for ages—they're bored and need some distraction.' Josh bit into his sandwich. 'Someone came up with the idea of having a prince-and-princess tea party so that they can dress up. Tiaras—that sort of thing. Because I'm not officially working today, I'm supposed to arrive halfway through dressed as Prince Charming.'

Tasha slid her hands round her mug of tea. 'You're kidding.'

'I did Father Christmas last year.' Josh wiped his fingers on a napkin. 'What's the difference?'

'Is that a serious question?' Alessandro was still laughing. 'One is fat and wears a red coat. The other is suave and capable of slaying dragons.'

Tasha sat with the mug halfway to her mouth, watching the way Alessandro's eyes shone and his cheeks creased when he laughed.

He was the sexiest man she'd ever met.

It was just as well Josh couldn't read her mind.

'No dragons at our tea party. This bacon is good, Tasha. I can't remember when you last cooked for me. Usually you glare at me and tell me it's not women's work. Are you all right?' Josh frowned at his sister. 'Why are you staring at Alessandro?'

'I'm keeping an eye on his colour,' she said smoothly. 'If he does too much, he gets tired.'

'He didn't look that tired when I arrived.' His tone dry, Josh helped himself to more bacon. 'He looked as though he had all his faculties. He won't need you for much longer.'

Tasha wondered if her brother was having another dig. 'I'll stay until he's able to cope without help.'

'Have you applied for any jobs?'

Tasha leaned forward and stacked the plates. 'Not yet.'

'Why not?'

'Because I don't know what I'd say in the interview about why I left my last job. I'm worried everyone is going to think I'm a troublemaker.' Tasha rescued the ketchup before it could tumble onto the floor. 'I miss medicine. I miss the kids. I miss being part of a unit. I miss—all of it. I'm a doctor. I want patients.' Aware that Alessandro was no longer smiling, she suddenly wished she hadn't said anything. 'Sorry, it's just that I had this great career plan and then—*poof*—I managed to blow the whole thing. Well done, Tasha.' She knew that her light tone hadn't fooled them. 'Anyway, I don't know why we're talking about me. I already have a job for the time being. Preventing Alessandro from trying to run before he can walk.'

'I can tell you're a paediatric doctor. You're treating me like a kid.'

He wasn't a kid at all. He was a grown man and she was horribly aware of every bronzed, handsome inch of him. She'd thought her anger would keep her safe, but her anger had vanished. She'd thought her feelings were all from the past. But the explosion of passion that had erupted between them had nothing to do with the past and everything to do with the present.

Fear flashed through her. If she let him, he'd hurt her again. Just as he had the first time. And she wasn't going to let a man do that to her...

The sooner she found herself a paediatric job, the better.

'You shouldn't feel insecure. You're a good doctor, Tasha.' Josh stole the last piece of bacon. 'Remember that little girl you saw on the unit that day you came to my office to tell me you'd resigned? Turned out you were right. It wasn't hay fever. She had a congenital heart defect.'

Alessandro looked bemused. 'I didn't think Tasha worked on your unit.'

'She doesn't. But she walked past this girl and saw something that none of my doctors had seen.' Josh gave a smile. 'She's very intuitive, my baby sister.'

Snapping out of her dream, Tasha stared at him. 'The girl had a congenital heart defect? You're sure?'

'She's already seen the cardiologist. You probably saved her life.'

'Oh.' She felt an ache of sympathy for the child and the

mother. 'I wish it had just been hay fever. Poor little thing.'
Suddenly she missed her job even more. She wanted to be
the one looking after the child, supporting her and helping
her through a difficult time. She could make a difference,
she knew she could.

'This prince-and-princess party…' Alessandro eased his
leg into a more comfortable position. 'That must be something I can help with.'

Josh glanced at him with a frown. 'You?'

'You should be saving lives, not dressing up as a prince.
I don't have your medical skills, but I can do the prince bit.'
His tone was loaded with irony. 'I've never dressed up in a
cloak or worn a crown, but if it would help the kids I can do
it. Provided someone keeps the paparazzi at a distance. I'm
doing it for the children, not the press.'

'Why keep them at a distance?' Tasha jumped to her
feet. 'It's a brilliant idea. Your mother wants some good
publicity—what better than the prince visiting the children's
ward? You can autograph stuff for them. They can have pictures taken with you. They'd love that. I'll come with you.'
Better to be on the children's ward as a visitor than not be
there at all, she reasoned.

'How far from the car to the ward? I can't walk that far
on this damn leg of mine.'

Tasha opened her mouth to suggest a wheelchair but took
one look at the set of his jaw and closed her mouth again.
Alessandro would drag himself across the ground by his
fingernails before he'd agree to use a wheelchair.

'It's a great idea. We can drop you right outside. And Tasha
can come with you.' Josh nodded. 'I'll have a word with the
staff and let them know you're coming.'

'I've been thinking about a job in NICU. Is there someone
there I could talk to?'

Alessandro frowned. 'What's NICU?'

'Neonatal intensive care unit.' Josh shifted in his chair.
'Talk to Megan Phillips.'

Tasha noticed that her brother's tone had altered and wondered if it had anything to do with Megan. Glancing up, she met Alessandro's steady dark gaze. Clearly he was thinking the same thing. He smiled and that slow, sexy smile connected straight to her insides. Her stomach swooped and plunged, the chemistry between them as electrifying and terrifying as ever. Staring into his mahogany eyes, she opened her mouth to speak but he spoke first.

'You've got me through the worst bit. Thanks to you, they let me out of that hospital. I can manage now. If you want to leave, leave.'

He was giving her a choice. And she knew it wasn't just about caring for him.

He was making her decide whether to leave or not.

Both men were looking at her expectantly and Tasha swallowed. She didn't know how she was going to answer until the words left her mouth.

'I'm not in the habit of letting people down. I'll stay until you're fully mobile, just as I promised.' It was easy to convince herself that that was the reason she was staying. 'But I do need to be looking for a full-time job. I thought I'd explore NICU—except that I'm not sure I'll get a reference.'

'You will. I made a few phone calls this week.' Josh leaned back against the sofa. 'Turns out you had a lot of support at the unit. Questions are being asked. People are enraged that you were allowed to resign.'

'Really? Why didn't you say so before?' Tasha brightened. 'Enraged? Oh, I'm so pleased.'

Alessandro lifted an eyebrow. 'You want people to be enraged?'

'I want them to care that I've gone, yes. I'm human enough to want that. And I'm human enough to need to be told I did the right thing—that others would have done the same. I would love an apology from him,' she sniffed, 'but I doubt I'll get that.'

'You won't. They guy's an idiot. Forget about him.'

Josh leaned forward. 'So, about the prince-and-princess party...'

Energised by the knowledge that people were supporting her, Tasha reached for her handbag. 'Leave that to me. I'm going to pay a visit to the dressing-up shop in St Piran. Alessandro and I will see you back at the hospital.'

He'd given her the opportunity to leave and yet she'd chosen to stay.

Alessandro watched Tasha as she gathered bags and put them in the car. Her coat was buttoned from neck to hem and he wondered why she was wearing a long coat when it wasn't cold.

'I've bought tiaras and all sorts of props that should be useful.' She slid his crutches into the boot. 'Be careful as you get in. Sit down, then I'll move your legs.'

She gently moved his leg into the car and helped him with his seat belt. 'Is that comfortable?'

It was agony, but even agony wasn't enough to dampen his response to her.

'Alessandro?' She lifted her eyes to his face and chemistry immediately flickered between them. Flushing, she drew back sharply. 'Right. Well, if you're not too uncomfortable then we'll get going.'

'Tasha, listen—'

'The kids are waiting.' The car door slammed and Alessandro winced as pain rocked through his leg. Fine. So they'd go through the day pretending they hadn't stripped each other half-naked.

'Did you agree to stay with me just to annoy your brother?' He watched her as she slid into the driver's seat. 'If you want to take a job at the hospital, you should take it. I can manage.'

'I promised to look after you until you're out of the cast and that's what I'm going to do. And, anyway, I don't really want to work in the same hospital as Josh. You've seen what he's like. He'll be banging on my door, questioning every decision I make. We'd drive each other crazy.' She drove fast and Alessandro found himself clenching his teeth.

'Do you know these roads well?'

'Yes.'

'Good, because if there are any surprises behind that blind bend, you're about to smack into it head first.'

She shifted gears smoothly. 'Do I make you nervous? Big, tough guy like you?'

An image of tangled metal lodged itself in his head. 'I'm not a good passenger.' He didn't elaborate but she immediately trod on the brakes.

'Sorry,' she muttered. 'I didn't think.'

Her sensitivity surprised him, although it shouldn't have. She'd always been sensitive, hadn't she? *Too sensitive.*

He braced himself for her to question him about the accident that had killed his brother but instead she smoothly changed the subject.

'Did you notice anything strange about Josh?'

'Strange in what way?'

'You didn't think he was tense and on edge?'

'He'd just caught his sister naked with a man.' He watched as the colour bloomed in her cheeks. 'That was reason enough for him to be tense.'

'Yes, but it wasn't that. It was something else. Something personal. Did you see his face when he made that little speech about loving someone you couldn't be with?'

'He's worried about you.'

'I'm not sixteen years old.' This time her gear change was vicious. 'Why do men always think a woman has to be in love? This is the twenty-first century. I don't want love. The most important thing to me is my career. And, anyway, a woman can have sex without being in love.' The words spilled out of her and he watched her steadily, wondering why he wasn't convinced.

'We didn't have sex, Tasha.'

The gears crunched again. 'I'm well aware of that. All I'm saying is that if we *had* had sex then it wouldn't have had anything to do with being in love, and I can't imagine why you'd even think that. Women can have sex like a man. Without emotional involvement. I don't want emotional involvement.'

'Right.' Alessandro tried to imagine Tasha doing anything without emotional involvement, and failed. Her emotions were involved in everything, from cooking chilli to handling her stethoscope. 'So, if that's the case, why are you worried about what Josh said?'

'There's something wrong with him. He's been acting really strangely since I caught him in the on-call room that day I came to see you…' Without breaking the conversation she flicked the indicator and turned into the hospital car park. 'And I know he had someone in the room with him, but he was hiding the fact. He didn't want me to know. But when I saw him, he looked all lit up inside. As if something special had happened. There was an energy about him that I haven't seen for years.'

'So maybe he's found someone. What's wrong with that?'

'Nothing. But today he didn't look like that. He looked exhausted.' She pulled into a parking space and gnawed at her lower lip with her teeth. 'He looked awful, Sandro.'

'He works hard.'

'I know, but he always has. Josh has endless reserves when it comes to work. It's something else. Something to do with a woman, I'm sure of it.'

Looking at her troubled expression, Alessandro wondered why it was that women had to analyse everything in such depth. 'Maybe he's met someone and she's married.'

'Josh would never have an affair with a married woman.'

'He was married himself. Still is, isn't he?'

'His relationship with Rebecca has been dead for ages.'

Alessandro felt the cold trickle down his spine. 'That's what marriage does to people.'

'Do you really believe that?'

'How many happy marriages have you seen?'

She hesitated. 'Just because we haven't seen them, it doesn't mean they don't exist.'

'Does it matter? I thought you said you could have sex without emotional involvement.'

'I can. But that doesn't mean I don't believe that happy marriages don't exist.' She snapped her seat belt and Alessandro watched her for a moment.

'If you're worried about Josh, why don't you just ask him what's wrong, instead of subjecting yourself to all this guesswork?'

'I've tried—obliquely. But he dodges it. And then this morning...' she retrieved her bag '...he just seemed really stressed about something.'

'He'd just seen you naked with me,' Alessandro drawled. He knew from past experience that was sufficient reason to stress Josh. 'In case you hadn't worked it out, your brothers are very possessive of you. Particularly Josh.'

'Maybe we should invite him round for supper so that we can chat properly. I could cook something.'

'Something with chilli?'

She grinned wickedly. 'I don't know how you ate that.'

'The eating it was fine. It was putting out the fire afterwards that was the problem.' Alessandro eased his leg out of the car, clenching his jaw against the pain as Tasha lifted the bags out of the boot.

As he straightened up she slung a cloak around his shoulders.

'All hail, Prince Alessandro. Welcome to the Kingdom of Sick Child.' She curtseyed deep and he stared down at the velvet cloak in wry amusement.

'What on earth is this?'

''Tis your finest clothing, sire. Otherwise known as

prince's-cape-from-dressing-up-shop.' She stood up. 'Don't you dare refuse to wear it—took me ages to track it down. There's a cute crown to go with it. They threw it in free.' As she rummaged in the bag, Alessandro glanced around the car park to check that there were no photographers.

'There is no way am I wearing a velvet cloak and a plastic crown to walk across the car park.'

'Not even for sick children? They might be watching from the window.' She batted her eyelashes but Alessandro didn't flinch.

'If they're watching from the window, they can't be that sick.'

'I just want you to make an entrance.' As she spoke she slid off her coat and Alessandro almost swallowed his tongue as he saw what she was wearing.

'What—?'

'How do you do, Your Highness? I'm the Princess Tasha.' She beamed at him and gave a quick twirl. The shimmery pink dress swirled and floated around her slender frame. Still smiling, she reached into the bag and pulled out a tiara. Ducking down to look in the wing mirror, Tasha slid it into her hair and adjusted it. 'Just need to fit the crown jewels. There. Perfect. How do I look?'

Alessandro ran his tongue over his lips, grateful for the cloak.

When he didn't reply, she frowned at him. 'Do I look like a princess?'

'No.' His voice came out as a hoarse croak. 'At least, you don't look anything like the ones I've met.' And he'd met a few. *Too many.*

Her face fell and she took another sneaky look in the mirror. 'I thought I looked cute.'

'You do look cute. But princesses don't generally look cute. In my experience they're usually hard and cynical.' He gave a crooked smile. 'Comes from having contact with too many wicked princes, I guess.'

'See? *That's* why I'd never want to be a princess. If I can't be the fantasy version, I'm not interested.'

He loved her energy and her sense of fun.

He loved the fact that she treated him the same way she treated everyone else.

Alessandro dragged his eyes away from the twist of hair that had come loose from the tiara and decided that the sooner she went back to work as a doctor, the better for his sanity.

He wondered what would have happened if Josh hadn't arrived in the house when he had. *Would either of them have stopped?*

'Let's go. I don't want to stand around wearing a velvet cloak and a crown for longer than I have to. If the press sees me, I'm never going to live this one down.'

'You'll be accused of being typecast,' Tasha said cheerfully, dropping the car keys into a silky pink bag and waiting while he balanced himself. 'Do you want a hand?'

'No, I've got it.' Leaning on the crutches, Alessandro struggled into the hospital and onto the children's ward.

Balloons were tied in huge clusters and a red 'carpet'—a long piece of scarlet fabric—stretched along the corridor to a brightly painted playroom.

'Welcome, Your Highness.' A nurse in a long flowing dress swept a deep curtsey and Alessandro was about to say something flippant when he saw a little girl in a wheelchair, watching him with tears in her eyes.

Disconcerted, he watched her cautiously.

Great. He'd been here less than five seconds and already he'd made someone cry. Suddenly he wished he hadn't interfered. He should have let Josh do it.

Tasha reached for his arm but he shrugged her off and limped across to the child. He'd volunteered for this so he was going to do it. Without help.

'Hey, there—that's a very pretty dress you're wearing.'

Her face turned the colour of a tomato. 'Are you a real live prince?'

'I am.'

'Is that a real crown?'

Alessandro remembered that Tasha had said you should always be honest with children so he shook his head. 'No, it's plastic. Fake. The police get jumpy if I walk around Cornwall wearing a real crown.' Seeing her face fall, he searched his brain for inspiration. 'But I do have a real one. At home.' Leaning forward, he whispered in her ear. 'If you ever visit my country, I'll give you a private tour of the state jewel collection.'

'You will?' Her eyes went huge. 'Do you have alarms and guard dogs and stuff?'

'All of that. And bodyguards.' Seeing how thin she was, Alessandro felt his heart twist. Suddenly he felt guilty moaning about breaking his ankle. Yes, he was bruised and broken but he was basically fit and healthy, whereas this child... 'How long have you been in hospital?'

'This time? Three weeks.'

'There have been other times?'

'I come in a lot. Sometimes my blood goes wrong.' Her tone was matter-of-fact and she reached out and stroked his cloak. 'The other kids thought it would be an actor or one of the doctors dressed up. You know, like Father Christmas. They always say it's Father Christmas but really it's just a fat man in a beard. They're not going to believe you're a real prince. Do you have proof?'

Caught off guard, Alessandro glanced at Tasha. 'Do I have proof?'

'Absolutely. I brought the proof with me and I have it right here.' Throwing the little girl a dazzling smile, Tasha reached into the bag on her shoulder and pulled out a scrapbook. 'Have a look at this. Here's Prince Alessandro at a royal function at the palace... And he...' she pointed '...he's opening a hospital. Just look at those crowds!' It seemed she'd thought of everything, and as she turned the pages for the child, Alessandro stared at the pictures of himself at various royal events.

Something shifted inside him. Somehow he'd managed to hide his feelings in front of the cameras.

'Wow. Everyone wants to take your picture. Is this your horse?' The little girl pointed to a photograph of him playing polo, and Alessandro nodded.

'He's my favourite horse. His name is Achilles.'

'Do you wear a cloak when you ride him, like Prince Charming?'

'Er—no. I wear pretty standard stuff—breeches and boots.' He gave an apologetic smile and she beamed and took his hand.

'What happened to your leg?'

'I fell off my horse.'

'Ouch.' She peered at the cast. 'You need people to write on that. It's very clean. You need messages and pictures and stuff.'

'You're right, I do.'

'I can help you with that. Can I wheel my chair down the red carpet with you?'

Alessandro looked at the flimsy strip of red fabric and wondered if it would survive. 'Sure. Let's give it a go.'

Who would ever have thought he was so good with children?

Tasha watched as Alessandro handed another little girl a pen so that she could draw a pony on his cast.

Here, in the relative privacy of the children's ward, she saw a different side of him. He was patient, natural, amusing and, most of all, interested.

She'd expected him to try and keep the encounter as short as possible. Instead, he'd settled down amongst the children in the playroom and seemed intent on giving them as much time as they wanted.

'It was generous of him to dress up and play the part.'

Tasha turned to see a young doctor watching her.

The woman smiled. 'I'm Dr Phillips. Megan Phillips.'

Tasha dragged her eyes from Alessandro and stood up quickly, hand outstretched. 'Hi. I'm Tasha O'Hara.'

'Yes, I know. You're Josh's sister.' Something in the way she said it drew Tasha's full attention.

'Josh mentioned you.' She noticed the other woman tense slightly. 'I told him I'd love to talk to you about working in NICU.'

'Oh—right.' Visibly flustered, Megan gave a brief smile. 'Well, I love it.' She went on to detail the pros and cons and Tasha stared at the other doctor, noticing the dark shadows under her eyes. *Shadows uncannily similar to the ones under Josh's eyes.*

With a woman's intuition, Tasha sensed that Megan and her brother were a great deal more than just colleagues. She wondered whether the beautiful, fragile-looking doctor was the woman causing Josh stress.

'Well—it's great to meet you, Megan. Thanks for the inside info.' She decided to do some digging. 'So, how long have you known Josh?'

'A while. We first met at university.' Megan avoided eye contact. 'Not that we hung out together or anything. Josh was Mr Cool—but you know that, being his sister.'

Tasha certainly knew Josh had broken a lot of hearts. She wondered whether Megan's had been one of them.

'If you were at university with Josh, then you must know Alessandro, too.'

Megan gave a brief nod of her head. 'I knew him by sight, that's all, because he was part of Josh's group. I didn't exactly move in their circle. I certainly didn't know he had such a way with children.' The insistent sound of a bleep had both women reaching into their pockets.

Tasha spread her hands in apology. 'It's you, not me—I can't get used to the fact I don't carry one any more.' And it felt strange, being in a hospital and not working.

'I'd better answer this—I slipped off the unit so that I could catch you.' Megan checked the number. 'I expect we'll bump into each other again soon. Maybe we could grab a coffee or something.'

'Yes. I'd like that.' Tasha watched the other woman hurry away from the ward and made up her mind that they were definitely going to meet again. There was something about Megan's pallor that tugged at her heartstrings.

She looked like someone who needed a friend.

Tasha turned back to Alessandro, to find him being swarmed over by children.

Remembering the bruising on his ribs, Tasha strolled over and gently lifted one over-eager toddler onto the cushions. 'Don't climb on the prince. You might damage him and then he won't be able to slay dragons.'

'She doesn't weigh anything.' His tone gruff, Alessandro rescued a little girl in a fairy costume who was about to tumble onto the floor. 'Who were you talking to? She looked familiar.'

'That's because you were all at university together.'

'Really?'

'That's Megan Phillips. Do you remember her?'

'Not the name, but I know the face from somewhere. Can't think where. I met a lot of people at university. Are you going to draw on my plaster?' Gently, he lowered the child onto the cushions and handed her a pink crayon. 'Go ahead.'

Tasha frowned. 'She knew you.'

'Without meaning to sound conceited, a lot of people know me.' He shifted his leg to give the children better access to his cast. 'It doesn't mean I know them.'

In other words, women always flocked to get close to him because of who he was.

'She knew straight away that I was Josh's sister,' Tasha mused, 'which means she must know Josh pretty well. I can't imagine he exactly spends his time waltzing around the hospital talking about me.'

'They work together. They probably chatted in the hospital restaurant over a stale chicken sandwich.'

'Prince Alessandro?' A small girl with her hair in bunches and wearing thick glasses squinted up at him. 'It's time for our story. Will you read it?'

Tasha watched as Alessandro smiled and scooped the child onto his lap.

He was a natural. And he possessed exactly the right combination of strength and warmth.

Strength.

Meeting his eyes, she stared at him for a long moment, wondering what would have happened had Josh not arrived when he had.

She and Alessandro would finally have slept together.

Tasha swallowed. She didn't know whether to feel regret or relief.

CHAPTER SEVEN

'REALLY, we should have invited the press. It would have been a perfect photo call. Even your mother would have approved.' Tasha kept her tone light but underneath she was shaken up. His gentleness with the children didn't fit with the image she had of him as an arrogant playboy.

'If I'd invited the press then I would have been accused of being manipulative.' Alessandro hobbled through to the kitchen, propped himself on one crutch and grabbed a cold beer from the fridge. 'I don't want to be in the newspapers at the expense of some poor family who is going through hell. Neither do I want an innocent child's private trauma broadcast to the world. I don't subscribe to the school of thought that we should all know everything about everyone.' He slammed the fridge door shut, snapped the top of the bottle and drank while Tasha stared at him in amazement.

'What's got into you?'

He lowered the bottle slowly. 'How do you do it?' His tone was savage. 'How do you go there day after day and work with those poor kids? Doesn't it break you apart, seeing them sick?'

She was stunned by the emotion in his voice. 'Yes, sometimes. It isn't always easy, but it's almost always rewarding. And the reason I go in there and work with those kids is because most of the time I make a difference. I'm not saying I can cure them all—' her own voice shook slightly '—but I do everything I can to make a horrid experience better. Some doctors think it's just about throwing the right treatment at a child, but they're wrong. *How* you treat the child is almost as important. Say the wrong thing and suddenly they're twice as scared and anxious.'

Alessandro drained his beer and thumped the empty bottle down on the shiny surface. 'I'm never complaining about my ankle again.'

'Actually, you haven't complained. Not once. Even when you've been in agony,' she muttered. 'You're brave.'

'Brave?' He gave a humourless laugh. 'Brave is that little girl who is never going to walk, or that boy who's on his tenth operation. They humble you, don't they? I mean...' he licked his lips '...we adults moan about the slightest thing. We moan about the weather, our workload, our family, but those kids—they're stuck in bed when they should be out playing with their friends and not even thinking about the way their bodies work, but they don't complain. They're smiling and getting on with it. That sweet little girl without the two front teeth—'

'Hattie?'

'Yeah—the one waiting for a transplant. Do you know that her mum travels two hundred miles to be with her—then she drives home when little Hattie's asleep so that she can spend some time with her two teenagers?' He dragged his hand through his hair and shook his head in disbelief. 'Then drives back again before Hattie wakes up in the morning. Can you imagine living like that?'

'Exhausting. Mentally and physically. Which is, I presume, why you offered her the use of your helicopter.' The generosity of the gesture still shocked her. 'I saw her mother crying and assumed she'd had bad news or something. Then she told me you'd promised to ferry her backwards and forwards until Hattie is discharged. She was completely overcome.'

'It was nothing.' He dismissed his contribution with a

frown. 'It will give my pilot something to do. Do you come across cases like that often?'

'When parents have to travel a long way? Yes. Especially in a rural area like this. And St Piran's is a specialist unit so I expect they take kids from a wide distance.'

Alessandro let out a long breath. 'How long until she gets her transplant?'

'I think they're exploring live donor. Her mother was telling me that a cousin might be a match. In the meantime she needs the dialysis to stay healthy.'

'She seemed so small and fragile.'

'Yes, well, that's probably because the kidneys play a role in the metabolism of growth hormone—chronic kidney disease can limit physical growth.' Tasha helped herself to an apple from the fruit bowl. 'Not that I know anything about Hattie's particular case, of course. I'm just talking generally.'

'If I throw money at it, can I make it go away?' His rough question brought a lump to her throat.

He cared.

'No. But you've already made it easier. She has her mum with her until she goes to sleep. That's a really big deal when you're eight.'

'You're wasted here, looking after me.' He leaned his hips against the counter, his expression serious. 'You should get out there and use that training of yours.'

'Are you trying to get rid of me?'

'No, but I could see how skilled you were with those kids and I know that's what you should be doing. Have you lost your confidence? Is that what's going on here? This whole thing with that idiot you used to work for—has it shaken you up?'

Startled, she felt her breath catch. 'Maybe,' she croaked. 'Just a little.' It was better to tell herself that than believe that she was there because of him. 'I'm still afraid no one will want me. But I've started looking. There just aren't that many speciality doctor posts around right now.'

'What's your dream? Ultimately you want to be a consultant?'

'That's why I worked my butt off in medical school.'

'What about marriage?' His voice was gruff. 'Family? Kids? When you were seventeen that was what you wanted. You wanted the whole fairy-tale. What happened?'

'I grew up. The whole fairy-tale thing bombed.' She gave a careless shrug. 'Anyway, I always thought Cinderella should have picked up her own shoe instead of expecting someone else to pick it up after her. And who in their right mind is going to marry a man she met when she was asleep? If I'd been asleep for a hundred years, I'd want to get out there and party, not walk down the aisle with a stranger.' Tasha bit into the apple, horribly conscious of him. Even with broken ribs and his leg in a cast he was indecently sexy.

'Tell me about Hugo.'

She choked on the apple. 'How do you know about Hugo?' Looking at his face, she scowled and threw the apple into the bin uneaten. 'Josh, presumably.'

'What happened?'

'I don't know.' Irritated, embarrassed, she shrugged. 'The usual. I fell for a guy. He wasn't serious. Only that time I learned my lesson.'

'Which was?'

'A girl has to be in charge of her own happy-ever-after. And it doesn't always have to include a man. I discovered that having a career can be every bit as exciting as sex.'

There was a tense silence.

'If you believe that, maybe you've never had really good sex.'

Her heart doubled its rhythm. 'Or maybe I just have a really great career.'

'Maybe you do. But shouldn't it be possible to have both?'

'Maybe. But there are plenty of broken marriages in my business. Just look at Josh and Rebecca.'

'I don't want to talk about Josh.'

She felt his gaze right through her body. 'I think I'll just—'

'No.' Somehow he crossed the kitchen before she could move towards the door. 'Don't run off. Not this time.'

Tasha backed herself into the kitchen counter. 'Look, whatever you're going to say, I'm not—'

'I was going to say that you're beautiful.'

The words stole her breath. 'Oh. Well, in that case—'

'You were beautiful at seventeen but you were a child then…' His voice was husky. 'Now you're a woman.'

But she felt like a teenager, with her heart pounding and her breathing shallow. 'Sandro—'

'I want you, Tasha.' The words were thickened with emotion. 'But it's your choice. I'm not in a position to throw you over my shoulder and influence your decision. You can walk out of that door, or you can walk into my bedroom.'

Oh, dear God…

Slowly, her eyes lifted to his and her heart tumbled as she met the intimacy of his gaze. His eyes were dark pools of desire. And serious. There was no humour there. No mockery. He was an adult, making an adult decision, and he was asking her to do the same thing. She could walk away. *She could say this wasn't what she wanted.* Or she could…

'On second thoughts, forget the bedroom.' His mouth came down on hers and he kissed her. Desire punched hard and deep and Tasha slid her hands over his shoulders, feeling male muscle flex under her fingers as his mouth plundered hers with erotic purpose.

Dizzy, she remembered that Alessandro had always known how to kiss. It was obvious that the intervening years had done nothing but polish his performance.

Engulfed by sexual excitement, she felt his hand slide to

her bottom, pulling her hard against him, and she tumbled blindly into a well of sensation.

Somehow—and afterwards she couldn't even remember how they'd done it—they made it to the bedroom, still kissing, and Tasha found herself on the bed, staring up into Alessandro's burning eyes.

'Do you know how long I've wanted to do this?'

'About as long as I've wanted you to do it.' There was no pretence between them. No shyness or coyness. And the sheer honesty of it took her breath away.

For a brief, intimate moment he looked down at her, and then he lowered his head and took her mouth again, tasting her, exploring her intimately. And she kissed him back with the same fevered hunger, taking everything he offered and more.

His hands made short work of her shirt and she felt the last two buttons ping onto the floor as he finally lost patience.

'I'll buy you another.'

'Don't bother.' Tasha matched his desperation, tearing at his shirt the way she had only that morning when Josh had interrupted them. It was choreographed madness as they stripped each other.

Naked, they rolled together and Alessandro gave a grunt of pain as her elbow encountered his bruised ribs.

'Sorry.' She braced herself on her hands, murmuring against his mouth. 'I'm really sorry. Just lie still and don't move. I'll do it all.' Before he could protest, she kissed her way down his body, her mouth infinitely gentle as she explored his bruises and moved lower.

This time his groan had nothing to do with pain. 'Tasha…'

She felt his hands slide into her hair but she didn't stop and then heard the change in his breathing as she explored him intimately.

Her intention had been to drive him wild but in the end she

couldn't wait, and she slid up his body and straddled him, her hair tumbling forward onto his chest. 'Am I hurting you?'

'Yes—' his reply was thickened '—but not in the way you mean.' His hands gripped her hips and he shifted her over him, taking control despite her superior position.

Wildly excited, Tasha was about to move when he moaned something against her mouth.

'What?' She dragged her mouth from his and tried to focus on him. 'Sorry?'

'Condom.' He reached out a hand towards the drawer by the bed and she realised that the thought of contraception hadn't crossed her mind. 'We should—'

'Yeah.' *She was a doctor, for goodness' sake.* And it hadn't even crossed her mind. Fumbling in the drawer, she grabbed protection and then they were kissing again, hands and mouths frantic as they feasted on each other.

His hand was between her legs and Tasha felt the skilled stroke of his fingers as he drove her higher and higher.

'Sandro…' She panted his name—heard the growl of frustration deep in his throat, and then he was inside her and the sheer size and heat of him punched the breath from her body.

She came immediately, the explosion so intense and violent that she dug her fingers hard into his shoulders, holding on as everything collapsed around her. Dimly, through the burning fever of blind lust, she knew she should apologise for hurting him, but his hands were on her and he took her hard, each powerful thrust sending her spiralling up towards the peak she'd just left.

This time when she hit, she took him with her and she sobbed his name as he drove into her hard, bringing ecstasy tumbling down on both of them.

He lay on his back with his eyes closed, drained of energy. 'If I'd known it was going to be that good, I would have done it years ago and risked being beaten to a pulp by your brother.'

'So you're basically admitting you're a wimp.' She lay sprawled next to him, one leg across his. Her fingers trailed over his abdomen. 'You have an incredible body, have I told you that?'

'As a matter of interest, which bit excites you the most? My broken ribs or the leg that's in plaster?'

'All of it. I love a vulnerable man.' Smiling, she pressed her lips to his chest. 'You're helpless.'

He captured both her wrists in one of his hands and anchored her hands above her head. 'Not that helpless, *tesoro*.' He rolled, ignoring the protest of his injured ribs. 'Do you know how long I've waited to get you naked?'

'About as long as I've waited for you to get me naked.' She stared up at him, her gaze mirroring the desire he felt. 'If I'd known you were that good at sex, I wouldn't have wasted the last couple of weeks tucking you into that bed on your own.'

'So we need to make up for lost time.' He lowered his mouth to hers, thinking that he'd never been with a woman who made him want to smile and ravish her at the same time.

'When the physio told you to take more exercise, I don't think this is what she had in mind.' With a smooth movement, she wrapped her legs around him and Alessandro hesitated, his hand locked in that glorious, tumbling hair.

'You do know I'm rubbish at relationships, don't you?'

'Me too.' She dragged his head down towards hers. 'Which is why we're going to make the most of this one while it lasts. Now shut up and kiss me.'

'Two skinny lattes, both with a double shot, please.' Tasha stifled a yawn as she dug her purse out of her bag and paid for the coffee. Glancing at her watch, she realised she'd had less than two hours of sleep the previous night.

'Any pastries with that?' The girl placed the coffee on the tray and Tasha looked longingly at the croissants and muffins, wondering whether carbs would wake her up or put her to sleep. Her brain too fuzzy to make a decision, she glanced over her shoulder towards Megan, who had bagged the only empty sofa in the coffee shop. 'Croissant or muffin?'

'Neither.' Megan recoiled and patted her flat stomach, but Tasha ignored her.

'I've got to have something or I'll pass out. I'll get a croissant and we can share.'

She wondered what Alessandro was doing. Was he still with his advisers? *Was he thinking about her?*

'You look absolutely exhausted.' Megan's gaze was concerned as Tasha set the tray down and sank onto the sofa next to her. 'Aren't you sleeping?'

Tasha picked up the knife and sliced the croissant in two. 'Er—not that much.'

'Is Alessandro a demanding patient?'

Demanding? Tasha lifted her coffee and hoped her blush didn't give her away. Yes, he was demanding, and over the last two weeks he had driven her almost mad with his demands, but not in the way that Megan clearly meant. 'I'm just worried about the future. Don't know what to do about my job.' She told Megan the story, surprised by how easy it was to talk to her.

'Tasha, your job prospects are good.' Megan picked up her coffee. 'Between you and me, everyone knows that consultant you worked for is an idiot. Everyone is probably cheering you on.'

'Well, it would be nice to be cheered on from within a job.' Tasha nibbled her croissant. 'Still, at least Josh found me temporary employment. He's not bad, as brothers go.'

'He's an amazing doctor.' Megan spoke with real warmth and Tasha watched her over the rim of her cup, noticing the pink streaks on Megan's cheeks. Her brain slotted together the clues. She remembered Josh's reaction when he'd mentioned Megan's name and the way Megan's face had lit up when she'd talked about Josh on the ward.

'So…' Tasha kept her voice casual '…you know all my secrets. Tell me something about you. Are you married?'

It was the simplest explanation for her brother's behaviour. Why else would he be holding back?

'No.' Megan picked up her spoon. 'Not married. You know how it is with this job. It's hell on relationships.'

'That's true enough.' So if Megan wasn't married, what was the problem? Maybe Megan wasn't interested. 'Personally? I wouldn't have a relationship with another doctor. All those dinners in the bin.'

'I'd be fine with it. In fact, I think it makes it easier if you're both doctors—you both understand the issues.'

'Josh is terrible at remembering social engagements when he's working.'

'That's the person he is,' Megan breathed. 'He focuses on what's important.' She looked up and her eyes shone. 'He's a brilliant doctor.'

Knowing that she was looking at a woman in love, Tasha felt a flash of delight, quickly followed by exasperation.

Josh and Megan were in love. No doubt about it. So why hadn't they got it together?

Was her brother letting his toxic relationship with Rebecca influence his future?

In which case she needed to give him a sisterly prod.

'I can't believe you've been back to the ward every day since the pirate party.' Josh refilled his wine glass as the setting sun sent a rosy glow over the living room. 'When you volunteered to help out with the prince-and-princess party I expected you to be there under sufferance for two hours and then leave, not go back for three weeks running!'

'Alessandro has appointed himself chief wish-fulfiller.' Tasha pushed the casserole towards her brother, careful not to look at Alessandro. She didn't dare look in case they gave themselves away. And she wasn't ready to tell Josh yet. He'd overreact and worry about her. He'd want to know what it all meant—where it was going. And the truth was, it wasn't going anywhere.

The relationship was intense and physical, but she wasn't fooling herself that it was anything other than great sex.

'I never knew you were this domesticated.' Josh filled his plate a second time.

'Took me ages to make it so you might as well eat it. Today our prince arranged for some football player or other to come and spend some time with one of the boys. I have no idea who he was but he had a fit body. The nurses were as interested as little Toby.'

'Which football player?'

Alessandro mentioned a name that had Josh's eyebrows lifting in disbelief.

'You're kidding. How on earth did you persuade him to come?'

'He just picked up the phone,' Tasha said dryly. 'Alessandro is nothing if not persuasive. All those years of being in command, I suppose.'

Lounging in his chair at the far end of the table, Alessandro gave a dismissive shrug. 'I knew he was in the UK. It was nothing for him to spend a few hours with a sick child and it meant a lot to Toby. The little guy has been to hell and back lately.'

And Alessandro had been there every step of the way, giving whatever support he could.

Tasha felt her heart twist as she remembered the look on Toby's face as his hero had strode onto the ward holding a football signed by all the members of the England team. 'How do you know all these footballers, anyway?'

'I know a lot of people.'

'Top athletes always know each other.' Josh cleared his plate. 'That was great, thanks.'

Top athletes? *Was Alessandro a top athlete?*

She knew he played polo, but as it wasn't a game she knew anything about, she had no way of knowing whether he was any good or not. Somewhere in the recesses of her mind she had a vague recollection of Josh once telling her that Alessandro could be the best if he put his mind to it, but at the time she hadn't really paid much attention.

As the two men talked about sport, Tasha thought about the time they had spent together this past month. Alessandro had proved a real hit on the children's ward and had spent hours with the children, talking to them and finding out what they enjoyed most and what their dreams were. Then he'd proceeded to try and make each and every dream come true.

'Megan Phillips thinks he's a hero.' Dropping the name casually into the conversation, Tasha poured herself a glass of water. 'He distracted a child for her yesterday while she took bloods.'

Josh's expression altered. 'You've met Megan?'

'Well, of course. She popped down to the unit on that first day to chat to me and we've got together since then. We went for a coffee together a week ago. She's lovely. The sort of woman you're instantly friends with, even though you've only just met each other.'

Josh put his fork down slowly. 'You went for a coffee? You chatted?'

'Er...yes. Generally when we women go for a coffee we don't sit in silence. Neither do we discuss sporting results.' Tasha gave the two of them a meaningful smile. 'Women know how to talk properly.'

Her brother was very still. 'What, exactly, did you talk about "properly"?'

'Oh, this and that. I don't remember the specifics.' She kept her answer intentionally vague, but the look on her brother's face confirmed what she'd suspected from the moment she'd met Megan Phillips—that there was something going on between Josh and the beautiful paediatrician. 'She really likes you.'

Alessandro sucked in a breath. 'Of course. *That's* where I know her from! It's been driving me mad.' He sat forward and thumped his glass down on the table, a triumphant gleam in his eyes. 'Megan was the one you spent the night with at that party when we were at university! New Year's Eve—that's it! We were celebrating because you were the new hotshot of the emergency department and my team had just won a trophy. You spent the night flirting with this gorgeous girl in a red dress.'

Tasha held her breath.

A tense silence settled across the room. 'I flirted with a lot of women. I don't remember.'

Alessandro smiled, man to man. 'You mean you don't want to remember. Your ego took a real bashing that night. Normally all you had to do was stand there and fight them off, but she wasn't interested. You had to work really hard for once in your life. It warmed my heart to see it.'

Tasha closed her eyes briefly. Why did men do this? Why was their form of communication either ribbing each other or punching each other?

Josh was still. 'I'm surprised you can remember, given that you had your hands full with that blonde from Radiography.'

Wishing she'd never prompted this conversation, Tasha pushed her plate away.

'You were Mr Cool, who was never going to succumb to a woman.' Alessandro was still laughing. 'And then the next morning you looked dazed—Megan Phillips got to you in a way no woman had ever got to you before. And it scared the hell out of you. I saw her around for a few months and then she just vanished. And you couldn't find her. It was a mystery.'

'There was no mystery.' Josh stood up abruptly. 'Nice dinner, Tash. I need to go.'

'Wait.' Alessandro sounded puzzled. 'You look like hell. And she looks like hell, too. You've obviously got something serious going on. So why aren't you doing something about it?'

Josh arched an eyebrow. 'You're giving me advice on relationships?'

'I just don't see the problem.'

'No. You don't.'

'I'm the first to admit I'm rubbish at relationships. That's because I've never felt anything for a woman, whereas *you*—' he emphasised the word '—obviously really care for Megan, so just give in to it! Accept that it's over for you and get on with it.'

'Well, you're such a romantic pair,' Tasha pushed the words past her dry lips, wondering why Alessandro's frank admission that he'd never felt anything for a woman should make her feel this sick. She knew that, didn't she? *So why did hearing him say it hurt so much?* 'I can't imagine why an intelligent woman like Megan would look twice at either of you.' She stacked the plates noisily and then caught sight of her brother's white face and paused. Anxiety shot through her. *She'd never seen Josh like this.* And Josh was her priority right now. 'Alessandro's right, though,' she said gently. 'Why not just finally give in and admit how you feel about Megan? What's wrong with that?'

Alessandro leaned back in his chair. 'Yes, go on. Admit that Mr Cool has fallen hard. Why not?'

Josh curled his fingers over the back of the chair, his jaw clenched, his face an unhealthy grey colour. 'Because my wife is pregnant.' He looked at them then, his eyes blank and soulless. 'That's why not.'

CHAPTER EIGHT

ALESSANDRO woke suddenly and glanced at the clock. Four-thirty a.m.

Outside it was still dark and rain was lashing the windows.

Turning onto his side, he saw that he was on his own in the bed. And then he saw Tasha standing on the balcony, apparently oblivious to the weather as she stared across the beach.

With a frown, Alessandro eased himself out of bed and limped across to her. For the first time in weeks the movement didn't leave him in agony.

He was healing.

Soon the cast should be off and he could begin intensive physio. He'd no longer need a nurse, which was just as well because he knew that Tasha had short-listed at least three jobs and she'd told him that she intended to get her applications off shortly.

And he had some big decisions to make.

'What are you doing out here?' Screwing up his face against the rain, he realised that she was wearing nothing but one of his shirts. 'It isn't exactly Mediterranean weather. Your climate sucks.'

She shrugged him off. 'Go back to bed, Alessandro.'

Hearing the ice in her tone, Alessandro stilled. Underneath

the soaked shirt, her shoulders were stiff. 'Are you going to tell me what's wrong?'

For a moment he thought she wasn't going to answer and then she turned sharply, her hair swinging around her shoulders, her eyes fierce. 'Why the hell are we doing this? I mean—*what* are we doing?'

The question was so unexpected that for a moment he didn't answer.

Programmed to recognise trouble when he saw it, Alessandro chose to keep it light. 'Standing on a draughty balcony in a howling wind and a thunderous rainstorm. We'll probably catch pneumonia. I suggest you come back inside while there's still a chance we'll live.'

'I don't want to go back inside.' She turned away from him. 'Just go back to bed, Alessandro.'

The storm of emotion he sensed in her was greater than the one swirling around them.

'Tell me why you're upset.'

'Why would you even care? You've never felt anything for a woman in your life, remember?' She threw the remark back at him and he flinched.

'That was just banter with your brother.'

'No, it wasn't. It was the truth. You never *have* felt anything for a woman in your life. Why do men do that?' She reached up and pushed her sodden hair out of her eyes. 'I mean, what is so cool about staying single and not committing?'

Alessandro stilled. 'You tell me. You're single. And I haven't seen you making a commitment.'

Her eyes flew to his and then she turned away. 'Just ignore me. I don't know what's wrong—it's just this thing that's happening between Josh and Megan.'

He knew a lie when he heard one.

Josh had been right, Alessandro thought grimly, when he'd said that his sister wasn't capable of not becoming emotionally involved.

Gently, he closed his hands over her shoulders and turned her to face him. 'Tash, look at me.'

She glared at him fiercely and tried to pull out of his grip. 'Just go back to bed. I'll be fine.'

'We're going to talk about this.'

'No, we're not.'

'At least tell me if this is about us or Josh?'

'I'm worried about him.' She was rigid and tense and then the next moment she leaned against him and buried her face in his chest. 'I've never seen him like this. He's so big and tough. Nothing bothers him. There's nothing he can't handle. But tonight he looked really...defeated.'

Alessandro hesitated and then stroked his hand over her head. 'You're right that he's big and tough. He'll handle it.'

'The truth is, I don't think he's ever really been in love before. But with Megan—it's real, Sandro. He really loves her. And she really loves him. Did you see his face when he told us Rebecca is pregnant? What a mess. What a complete and utter mess. When two people love each other that much, they should be together, no matter what the obstacles.'

He wondered if she realised what she was saying.

Feeling cold, Alessandro folded his arms around her and held her close, ignoring the rain that trickled down the back of his neck. Through the thin fabric of his shirt, her body felt warm and soft. And vulnerable.

She might talk blithely about sex without commitment, but she wanted love to exist.

She wanted it badly.

He gave a shiver.

He'd kidded himself that their relationship could be superficial. That both of them could walk away. But Tasha didn't do superficial, did she? Whatever she said to the contrary, she wanted the whole fairy-tale, just as she had as an idealistic teenager. Maybe she didn't even realise it herself, but it was perfectly obvious to him.

'Don't worry about Josh. He'll sort it out.'

'How can he? The woman he's about to divorce is having his child and there's no way Josh would *ever* leave his child. Never. Not after what happened to us as kids.' She lifted her hands to her face and he realised that the raindrops were mingling with her tears.

'Don't cry.' For some reason her tears disturbed him more than the realisation that she hadn't changed. Tasha wasn't a crier. 'Damn it, Tash—don't cry.'

'Sorry.' Her voice was thickened as she scrubbed at her face with her hand, 'I'm really sorry, but I love my brother and I hate to see him in this situation. He should be with Megan but I know Josh will never divorce Rebecca now she's pregnant. And she knows that.' She sniffed. 'That's why she did it. I know Josh is to blame too, but why would any woman want to have a baby with a man who doesn't love her? And quite honestly I don't think she loves him either. She just likes the idea of being married to a doctor. I just don't get it.'

Cold spread through his body as he thought of his own parents. 'A loveless marriage isn't exactly a rare occurrence, *tesoro*. People marry for many different reasons.'

Like political convenience.

'But what about the child? When Dad left…' her breathing was jerky '…I thought it was all my fault. I assumed I'd done something. Parents splitting up, parents who don't want to be together—it's the pits. I know Josh will love that child, I know he will. But if he doesn't love Rebecca and she doesn't love him…' She looked up at him, her eyes swimming with anxiety. 'That can't be good, can it? My parents split up and look how screwed up I am. And yours stayed together and you're screwed up, too.'

Alessandro gave a humourless laugh. 'Thanks.'

'All right, maybe you're not screwed up exactly, but you don't let yourself get close to a woman, which is sort of the same thing.'

'You and I have been pretty close lately.'

'Physically,' she mumbled. 'And we were thrown together

by circumstances. I don't want to talk about us. I want to talk about Josh. I want to wave a magic wand.'

Alessandro smoothed her hair away from her face. 'Josh has to work this out, *tesoro*. You can't do it for him.'

'I want him to be with Megan.' Her voice was desperate. 'You say they met all those years ago and it was special—think of all the time they've already wasted. They should be together for ever.'

For ever.

The words chilled him to the bone more effectively than either the wind or the rain. Alessandro took her hand. 'Let's go back inside.'

Tasha stood under the shower, waiting for the hot needles of water to warm her numb skin. She hadn't realised how cold she'd become, standing on the terrace while the rain sheeted down. She was freezing.

And, as if that wasn't bad enough, she'd made a total fool of herself.

All that talk of love and happy-ever-afters. It was a wonder Alessandro hadn't freaked out and tossed her off the balcony.

She needed to redeem herself fast. Salvage her pride before it ended up in a disorderly heap like last time.

Turning off the shower, she wrapped herself in a warm towel and walked through to the bedroom.

Crossing her legs on the bed, she switched on her laptop, intending to continue her search for jobs. But the moment the search engine appeared on the screen, she found herself typing in '*Prince Alessandro of San Savarre*'.

Glancing quickly towards the door, she checked that Alessandro was still occupied making hot drinks in the kitchen, then clicked the search button.

'Great,' she muttered. 'Over six million results. What on earth is he doing with you, Tasha?'

But the answer to that was all too obvious. He was enjoying

convenient sex while he was trapped in Cornwall. Soon he'd be back to his old life, playing polo and presiding over state occasions.

She ignored all the references to his role as Crown Prince and instead clicked on a result that said 'Sporting Legend'.

As she read, she realised how little she knew him.

He was a top polo player. One of the best in the world, with the potential to be *the* best in the world.

Tasha scrolled down the other results.

The Prince of Polo.

Alessandro the Great.

As she scanned the articles, the same words were repeated over and over again—'exceptional', 'the best', 'generous'. No wonder his injuries had been so frustrating for him. He was an athlete at the top of his game.

Absently, she scrolled down and clicked on another article hinting at trouble at the palace—the Princess, his mother, had expressed her disapproval at her son's sporting endeavours and insisted that he spend more time at home on royal duties.

Frowning, she clicked on an image of him accepting a cup for his team. He looked bronzed and handsome, his eyes burning with the fire of achievement.

Everyone was in agreement that the wild prince of San Savarre had astonishing talent.

Talent that he wasn't allowed to use.

Clicking again, she stared at a picture of him at a charity ball, dressed in a black dinner jacket with a tall, slender blonde on his arm. This time the caption read, *'Prince or Playboy? Will Alessandro of San Savarre ever settle down?'*

Her stomach ached.

They looked perfect together.

Regal. The only thing that spoilt the picture was the expression on Alessandro's face. There was no missing the adoration in the woman's eyes but he looked bored and desperate, as if he'd rather be anywhere else.

I've never felt anything for a woman in my life.

Tasha stared at the image on the screen and then glanced at the name of the woman.

Miranda.

She relaxed slightly. Wasn't Miranda the woman who had been engaged to his brother?

Tasha cursed herself for even caring. She knew only too well what a heartbreaker he was, didn't she? No woman held his attention for more than five minutes. It probably didn't help that he'd been fed a diet of female adoration from his cradle.

He wanted her now, but she didn't fool herself that he would want her once the cast was off his leg and they were no longer trapped together in this small, safe world they'd created.

Panic rushed through her.

She wasn't going to do that again. She wasn't going to jeopardise her career for a relationship.

Still fiddling, she followed another link and saw images of a car wreck.

Apart from his tension in her car the other day, his feelings about the accident were something he didn't reveal. And yet it had changed everything for him.

According to the report, his brother had been alone in the car the night of the crash.

Tasha was still puzzling over that when she heard his footsteps. Quickly she exited the site and deleted the search history. No way did she want him knowing she was looking him up. That would be beyond embarrassing and she'd already embarrassed herself enough with all that talk of love and soul mates.

'I made hot chocolate. I thought you needed warming up.' Alessandro hobbled up to her. 'Are you job-hunting again? I thought you already had interviews lined up.'

'I was just playing around. Thanks for the chocolate. How did you make it with one hand?'

'I can do a lot of things with one hand. Want me to show you?'

'Not right now.' Shaken by a flare of sexual awareness, she flipped the laptop shut and put it on the bed. 'I need to have a serious think about jobs. After all, you have your appointment at the hospital tomorrow and it's very likely that they'll take that cast off. You'll be fully mobile again soon. I need to find myself a job.'

'So you're still Tasha the career girl, then.'

'Absolutely. What else?'

'Out there on the balcony you seemed to be extolling the virtues of love and family.'

'Ugh—for goodness' sake, Alessandro, I'd had a drink! Several drinks, actually. I always get morose after a glass or two of wine.' She put her laptop on the floor and finished her hot chocolate. 'And anyway I was talking about love for Josh, not love for me.'

'Right.' The way he was looking at her said that he didn't believe her and she decided to shift the focus of the conversation.

'Can I ask you something?'

'Sure.'

'Why do you think your mother blames you for the accident? You weren't even in the car that night.'

He put his mug down slowly and for a moment she thought he wasn't going to answer. 'I should have been.' His tone was bitter. 'I should have been the one driving.'

'Why?'

'Because he'd been drinking.'

Tasha put her mug down slowly, realising that those words had great significance. 'You were there?'

'We were both at a fundraising ball. I told him that he was too drunk to drive but he didn't listen.' Alessandro's expression was bleak. 'Antonio never listened, but that probably

wasn't all his fault. My brother was treated as the golden
boy from the moment he was born. He was used to issuing
commands, not receiving them.'

'So he ignored you. Why wasn't he being driven in a fancy
bulletproof limo?'

'Because he wanted to visit a woman. And she wasn't the
woman he was planning to marry.'

'And he was supposed to marry Miranda, right?'

A tension rippled through his powerful frame and
Alessandro sent her a strange look. Tasha was still trying to
interpret that look when he turned away.

'I should have stopped him. Taken the keys. Knocked him
unconscious. Something.'

'Hold on a minute.' Tasha frowned for a moment and then
sat down next to him. 'If he hadn't been sneaking off, or if he
hadn't been drunk—are you saying that's why your mother
blames you? Because you didn't stop him driving when he
was drunk?'

'She's right to blame me.'

'No, sorry, but she isn't. Antonio made his own decisions
and it sounds as if they were all bad ones.' Tasha was out-
raged. 'You can't be blamed for what he did.'

Alessandro lifted his head and looked at her, a faint smile
playing around his mouth. 'Beautiful Tasha—one minute
you're as gentle as a kitten and the next you're a tiger.'

'I just hate injustice, and if she's blaming you then that's
unjust.' She sighed and took his hand. 'When someone dies,
people look for someone to blame. It's part of the grieving
process. They want an explanation—a reason. I see it all the
time at the hospital. That doesn't mean anyone *is* to blame.
And you're not, you know you're not.'

'Do I?'

Her hand tightened on his. 'Yes, you do. It's also normal
to feel guilt. And that's what's happening to you. But lay out
the facts, Sandro. Take away the emotion. Are you really to
blame?'

There was a long silence and his hand closed over hers. 'Perhaps not.'

'Definitely not.'

'Tasha—about what you said on the balcony…'

'I was waffling. Take no notice of anything I say when I'm upset. And you're right—this is one thing Josh has to sort out by himself.' She deliberately chose to focus her attention on her brother's relationship rather than theirs. 'We should get some sleep. I'm surfing in the morning and you have that magazine interview.'

A faint frown touched his brows. 'You don't have to leave the house just because I have an interview.'

'Easier if they don't know about us.' Tasha slid into bed and flipped off the light. 'I'll go down to the beach as soon as it's light.'

'Tasha—'

'What?'

'I haven't told anyone about that before.'

She pulled up the covers. 'It wasn't your fault, Sandro. You weren't responsible. He was an adult and he made his own decision. You know it's true.'

He hauled her close. 'My ribs are healing.'

All of him was healing. Soon he wouldn't need her any more.

Once his cast was off and his mobility increased, he'd be able to cope alone.

She'd go back to paediatrics.

Back to her career.

And she was fine with that.

Absolutely fine.

'How does it feel?'

Alessandro moved his leg cautiously, aware that Tasha was watching him closely.

The answer was that it felt strange without the cast. It also felt strange to think that soon she'd be moving out. 'I feel surprisingly good considering I've had it in plaster for so long. The surgeon says that the bones are healing well but they want me to use the swimming pool as much as possible to build the muscle back up.'

And then he'd be returning home to San Savarre. No more delaying tactics.

It was time to face his future.

Distracted by that bleak prospect, it took him a few moments to realise that Tasha had asked him a question and was waiting for the answer. 'Sorry—I missed that. What did you say?'

'I asked if they're arranging for a physio to come to the house.'

'I told them I had you.'

Her gaze turned from concerned to exasperated. 'Sandro, I'm not a physio—'

'But you're a bright girl and you can talk to the physio. She'll do a session with us and then you can take it from there.' It was unsettling to acknowledge that his real reason for not accepting more help was that he didn't want anyone intruding on the little cocoon they'd created.

'Pool running is good.' Tasha whipped a notebook out of her bag and made a few notes. 'You wear a buoyancy aid and move through the water—I'll see if I can borrow the equipment.'

'You see what I mean? I don't need a bunch of different people traipsing through the house when I have you.'

She lifted her eyes from the notebook. 'So you're officially mending.'

'Apparently.'

Their eyes met and he knew what she was thinking because he was thinking the same thing. That this was the end.

They were both moving on.

As someone who did 'moving on' better than most,

Alessandro waited for the rush of relief that inevitably followed the demise of a relationship.

It didn't come.

'They're pleased with the rate of healing.' He maintained the conversation, even though his mind was elsewhere.

'So—that's that, then. You're not going to need a nurse for much longer.'

A nurse? No. He didn't need a nurse.

But that didn't mean—

Making a decision, Alessandro took a deep breath. 'There's something I need to say to you.'

'It's perfect timing.' Her smile was dazzling and she interrupted before he could say what he wanted to say. 'I have an interview on Friday. The job looks really interesting and apparently it's a very progressive department so they might even be able to cope with me.'

The news that she had an interview landed like a thud in his stomach. 'Tasha—'

'How honest do you think I should be about why I left my last job? My natural instinct is to tell the truth, but I have to admit that my natural instinct sometimes gets me into trouble— Oh!' Her flow of speech was cut off as Alessandro crushed his mouth down on hers.

Her lips were warm and sweet and what had begun as a silencing exercise fast turned into a sensual feast. 'God, you taste fantastic.'

'Sandro…' She moaned his name and slid her arms around his neck. As the kiss heated up Alessandro found it hard to remember what he'd wanted to say.

'Wait.' He dragged his mouth from hers, trying to focus through the burn of raw lust that heated his body. 'We have to talk.' He felt the tension ripple through her and wondered why she would react like that when she didn't even know what he was going to ask.

'No, we don't. You don't need to say anything.' Eyes closed, she muttered the words against his mouth. 'We always knew this was just for now. You're moving on. I'm moving on. No worries—although I have to admit I'm going to miss the sex...'

Alessandro pulled his mouth from hers. Her words should have brought him nothing but relief. Instead, tension spread across his shoulders. 'I'm not ready to move on. That's what I'm trying to tell you.'

Her eyes opened slowly. 'You're not?'

'No.'

He stroked his thumbs over her cheeks, thinking that she had the most beautiful eyes he'd ever seen. 'At the weekend I have a high-profile wedding to attend. The Earl of Cornwall's daughter.'

'Is this in an official capacity?'

'Yes. And I want you to come.'

She stared at him for a long moment. 'Me?'

'Yes.'

'You want *me* to come?'

Alessandro stared at her in exasperation. 'Why are you repeating everything? Yes, I want you to come. What's so strange about that? We've spent the past six weeks together.'

'Oh—yes.' She cleared her throat and glanced around self-consciously, apparently only now realising that they could easily be overheard. 'So you're taking me for my medical abilities?'

'No. I'm taking you because I want to take you. I can't stand the formality of these occasions. I particularly hate weddings. I'd love your company.'

'But if it's an official appearance, shouldn't you be taking a princess with blonde hair and a haughty expression?'

'I'm taking you.'

Her eyes were wary. 'Am I expected to call you Your Highness in public?'

'No.'

'Are you going to be mobbed by adoring women?'

'It's a wedding,' he drawled, 'so hopefully not.'

She bit her lip and tilted her head to one side. 'So what would I have to wear?'

Alessandro smiled. If they'd reached the point where she was asking what to wear, it meant that she was definitely coming. 'It will be dressy. It's being held in a castle. Wear something glamorous.'

'A wedding in a castle?' Tasha pursed her lips but couldn't hold back the twinkle in her eyes. 'Sounds pretty downmarket. Might be boring.'

'It *will* be boring.' He sighed. 'All weddings are boring, so kill that shine in your eyes right now.'

'Are they madly in love? How did they meet? Was it romantic?'

'Tasha—'

'Sorry. Just asking. Good. Fine. Boring old wedding.' She gave a tiny shrug. 'I'll find something boring to wear, then.'

'I can't believe he's taking you to the Earl of Cornwall's wedding.' Megan gave a disbelieving laugh. 'That's…huge.'

'I'm the one who's huge compared to all those breedy aristocrats.' Tasha stared down at herself in dismay. 'Can I lose a stone by Saturday?'

'You don't need to lose a stone. You look fantastic.' Excited, Megan hugged her. 'I'm so pleased for you. I know how much you like him.'

'I hear a "but" in your tone.' Tasha extracted herself. 'You think he's going to hurt me.'

'No.' Megan bit her lip. 'But any man as rich and gorgeous as him is bound to attract non-stop female attention. And he does have a reputation.'

'It's someone else's wedding, not ours,' Tasha said blithely, 'so his reputation isn't an issue.' Not for anything would she admit how she felt about him. Not even to Megan, who had become a real friend over the past few weeks.

The only subject they never discussed was Josh. Whenever her brother's name was mentioned, Megan instantly changed the subject.

'Well, he certainly isn't hiding you away. Every time I open a newspaper I see another article about that wedding. It's very high profile and by taking you he's making a statement about your relationship.'

Tasha felt her heart bump against her ribs. 'You think he's making a statement?'

'Of course. You've been living in this little cocoon together, but now he's taking you out in public.'

'As his nurse.'

'Nurses don't usually wear glamorous dresses and have sex with their patients.'

Tasha choked. 'When I first met you, I thought you were dignified and delicate.'

'I'm practical,' Megan said dryly, grabbing Tasha by the arm. 'Come on. We're supposed to be finding you something to wear.' Without giving her the chance to argue, Megan dragged her towards St Piran's most exclusive boutique.

'You have to be kidding. I can't afford this place.' Tasha dug her heels in like a horse. 'I don't have a job, remember?' She'd told Megan everything that had happened at her last hospital and had been relieved when the other doctor had stoutly declared that she would have done the same thing in the same situation.

'Isn't he paying?' Megan paused in front of the heavy glass doors. 'Tasha, he's a prince. He's loaded and he's the one who invited you to this wedding. If he expects you to dress up in something glamorous and photogenic, he should pay.'

'He wanted to pay. I refused.'

'He offered to buy you an outfit and you refused? Are you mad?'

'No, I'm independent.' Tasha scowled at her. 'Do you know how many women fling themselves at him? Loads. And most of them just do it because he's a prince and rich and—well, you know. I don't want him ever to think our relationship has anything to do with who he is.'

Megan stared at her for a long moment. 'Tasha, he *is* a prince. You can't get away from that.'

'No, he's a man,' Tasha said firmly. 'These last few weeks—it's been so normal. He's just a regular guy. Well, maybe not a regular guy exactly because he's super good looking and devilishly charming and most of the regular guys I meet are complete no-hopers. But he doesn't act like a prince. To me he's just Sandro.'

Megan looked as though she wanted to say something else but in the end gave a brief smile and shook her head. 'Yes. Of course. I'm the last person to give advice to anyone on anything of a romantic nature.' It was the closest she'd ever come to admitting that her relationship with Josh was a disaster.

Tasha didn't even know if Megan was aware of Rebecca's pregnancy and she felt torn, knowing something about her brother that she couldn't share with her friend.

But she decided that it wasn't her place to say anything.

It was up to Josh to deal with it the way he believed was best.

Megan was smiling at her. 'I can completely understand why you want to buy your own dress and be independent. So let's do it.' Without giving Tasha a chance to argue, she pushed open the doors that led into the boutique, leaving Tasha no option but to follow.

Deciding that Megan wasn't as fragile as she looked, Tasha slunk in after her. 'I hate this sort of shop—they always look at you as though you have no right to be here.'

Megan lifted her head and smiled at the frosty-faced assistant. 'My friend is going to the wedding of the Earl of Cornwall's daughter. She needs something special. The photographs will be everywhere so it's a super opportunity to publicise the boutique.' She drew breath. 'Which is why you're going to give us a generous discount.'

Tasha cringed, but the sales assistant hurried over, as did her colleague.

'You are in absolutely the right place. We have several things that would be *perfect* for you.'

'Excellent.' Megan smiled. 'Let's get started. Tasha, go and take off those jeans.'

CHAPTER NINE

'SO THE Earl of Cornwall's daughter obviously doesn't believe in keeping a low profile.' Tasha blinked as another flashbulb exploded in her face. 'Whatever happened to quiet, intimate weddings?'

'Arabella describes herself as a socialite. She believes she has a duty to be seen.'

'Except that everyone here seems to want to see *you*.' Tasha flinched as a photographer leaned forward over the barriers and pointed his camera towards her. 'Whoa—unless you're airbrushing, that's too close. Please pull back to the next county. Remind me why I didn't specialise in plastic surgery rather than paediatrics?' She kept her tone light, but it was impossible not to feel self-conscious surrounded by an endless stream of beautiful women who seemed completely at home in front of the cameras. It was also impossible not to be aware that the crowd was chanting Alessandro's name.

'Is this why you were invited?' Hating herself for feeling daunted by the crowds, Tasha moved closer to his side. 'Does having you here get her more publicity?'

'Yes.'

'Don't you hate that?'

'Being the star attraction?' A sardonic smile touched his mouth. 'Of course not. Much more entertaining than being on the polo field.'

'Don't be sarcastic. This is exciting.' She slipped her hand into his and he looked down at her, his eyes glittering dark and dangerous.

'You look beautiful. If I throw you over my shoulder and take you behind the nearest large bush, what do you think will happen?'

Her stomach tumbled. 'I'll black your eye and the press will get some interesting photos. Forget it, Sandro. I'm all dressed up. I want to stay dressed up for a while at least. I want to enjoy the party.'

'Dr O'Hara—can you look this way? Can you tell us who your dress is by?' a photographer shouted across to them and Tasha froze.

'How do they know my name?'

'Arabella will have provided them with a guest list.'

'They want to know who my dress is by.'

He lifted his broad shoulders in a dismissive gesture. 'So tell them.'

Tasha leaned closer to him. 'I would if I knew,' she muttered. 'You're going to have to look in the back and see if there's a label or something.'

Alessandro looked at her in astonishment and then started to laugh. 'You don't know who designed your dress? Why did you buy it?'

'Because it's pretty and it looks nice on me. Why else?' Tasha glared at him, affronted. 'And I don't see what's so funny about that. Why are you laughing?'

'Because you, Dr O'Hara, are an original.' Cupping her face in his hands, he kissed her slowly and deliberately, ignoring the multiple flashes that lit the sky like a firework display. 'That's tomorrow's picture.'

'What? The back of my head? Now you've smudged my make-up,' Tasha grumbled, but her heart was racing as she saw the look in his eyes. Behind the flare of desire there was something else. Warmth. Intimacy. *Love?* 'I have a feeling that kiss is going to stimulate interest in more than the designer of my dress.'

'I have a feeling you could be right.'

Remembering the chill in his mother's voice, Tasha shivered. 'Are people going to mind that you've brought me?'

He took her hand in a firm grip. 'I don't care what other people think. Come and meet the bride.'

The day passed in a haze. Tasha was introduced to what felt like a million people, but the only person she was aware of was Alessandro, who didn't leave her side. Whenever anyone called him for a photograph, he hauled her with him, as if they were surgically attached. He acted as if they were a couple.

Something shifted inside her.

Hope sprang through her natural defences.

If their relationship were just about sex, she wouldn't be here, would she? He wouldn't be holding her hand in full view of the wedding guests and smiling down at her with warmth in his eyes.

By choosing to bring her he was making a public declaration about their relationship.

Feeling ridiculously happy, Tasha floated through the ceremony and the speeches, barely hearing a word. Instead her brain was racing forward and she conjured a picture of herself in a wedding dress.

Princess Tasha.

In a dream, she greeted the guests eager to be introduced to her, but her real focus was Alessandro, who looked spectacularly handsome in an Italian suit.

By late evening she'd grown so used to the sound of helicopters arriving and taking off that she barely glanced up when another arrived. It wasn't until she saw the change in body language of the guests that she looked over her shoulder to see who was attracting such attention.

Spying more suited security men, she glanced at Alessandro. 'Someone important?'

'You could say that,' he drawled. 'It's my mother.'

Tasha stilled as she watched the elegant woman move

across the perfectly manicured lawn, flanked by security guards. 'Did you know she was coming?'

'Yes.' His tone was flat and Tasha stared at him in exasperation.

'And you didn't think it was worth mentioning?' Suddenly she felt grubby and self-conscious. 'If I'd known… I don't think your mother exactly approves of me—'

'Who I choose to spend time with is none of her business.' Still holding her hand tightly, he stepped forward as Princess Eleanor approached him. 'Mother.'

Mother.

Tasha winced. It was so formal.

'Alessandro.'

Still holding Tasha's hand firmly, Alessandro drew her forward. 'I'd like to introduce you to—'

'We'll talk indoors.' His mother's tone was colder than the champagne and she turned to the bride, who was almost swooning with delight that she had royalty in attendance at her wedding. 'Arabella. You look beautiful. Alessandro, I want to talk to you. Alone.'

'I want to talk to you, too. But Tasha comes with me.'

Without sparing Tasha a glance, his mother transferred her chilly gaze from his face to his leg. 'Do you still need a nurse?'

'She isn't here in her capacity as nurse.'

'I know why she's here, Alessandro. I'm not stupid. And neither is Miranda.' The woman spoke in a low voice that couldn't be heard by anyone around them, the gentle smile on her face giving no hints to the observer that the situation was anything but completely harmonious. 'And your little plan has worked, so there's no need to overplay your hand. Now, let's go inside so that we can work on damage limitation. Natasha, I'd like you to come too. I think it's best if you hear what I have to say.'

Tasha threw a bemused look at Alessandro but he was staring at his mother. His face might have been carved from marble. 'I agree. We'll go inside.' Without waiting for her agreement, he strode towards the wing of the castle that had been allocated for the use of guests.

'Ow—you're hurting me.' Tasha twisted her hand in his and he released his grip slightly.

'Sorry.'

'Look, maybe you should have this conversation with your mother without me there.'

'You need to be there.'

'Yes, she does.' They entered a wood-panelled library and two security men closed the doors so that they were alone. Princess Eleanor delicately removed her silk gloves. 'Natasha, isn't it? And you're his nurse.'

'Actually I'm a—'

'It doesn't matter. Did he tell you why he invited you here today?'

Tasha frowned, thinking that it was an obvious question. 'He needed to take someone to the wedding. This sort of event isn't much fun on your own.'

'Indeed.' The older woman's smile was chilly. 'But Alessandro doesn't attend these events to have "fun".' She spoke the word as if it were a disease. 'He attends because that's his job—to be seen. He's here to represent San Savarre. And the person by his side should also be representing San Savarre—'

'Tasha is my guest.' Alessandro interrupted in a cold, hard voice that made Tasha look towards him in astonishment. She'd never heard him use that tone before. He sounded... *regal*? Very much the one in charge. 'Unless you want me to walk out of that door and not look back, do *not* insult my guest. Tasha, would you give us a few moments, please? I've decided I do need to talk to my mother on my own.'

'Sure. No problem.' Feeling about as welcome as a virus in an operating theatre, Tasha made a rapid exit. The two stony-faced security men were standing guard outside the door and she slid past them and made her way to the ladies' room, hoping to avoid the inevitable gossip and speculation.

What did Alessandro need to discuss on his own?

And why was his mother looking so disapproving?

She was about to replenish her lipstick when she heard female laughter outside the door. Anxious to avoid everyone, Tasha slipped into one of the cubicles and locked the door.

'I mean, he's utterly gorgeous,' a female voice said, 'so you can hardly blame him for not wanting to settle down.'

'He is gorgeous, but an utter bastard. Fancy bringing another girl to the wedding of the year.'

'You have to feel sorry for her. He's just using her to send his ex-girlfriend a message.'

Tasha opened her mouth. She wanted to alert them to the fact that she was there so that they'd stop talking, but no sound came out.

'It's a double blow to Miranda. First she loses Antonio and now Alessandro. I mean, he hasn't even ditched her for someone royal. Or even someone well connected. That girl he's with is just ordinary—like you or me.'

'Not like you or me.' Her friend gave a catty laugh. 'She didn't even know who designed her dress.'

'That's probably because it's the first time she's ever worn a designer dress.'

'And it will be the last. I'm sure he only brought her here to make a very public point to his mother. Judging from the bodyguards outside the library, they're having the conversation right now. What wouldn't I give to be a fly on the wall? Can I borrow your lip gloss? I left mine at that nightclub last weekend.'

'Do you think she knows that he was supposed to be marrying Miranda?'

Tasha frowned. No, that wasn't right. Miranda had been his brother's fiancée.

'Little Miss Ordinary? Shouldn't think so. If she doesn't

know her dress designer, she's hardly going to be up on palace politics, is she?'

'I thought it was common knowledge that everyone is waiting for an official announcement of the engagement between Alessandro and Miranda.' There was a pause. 'Does this shade look too red on me?'

'No, it's perfect. I heard she's been looking after him.'

'Oh, well, the poor thing is in for a rude awakening when she discovers what he's like. Still, this will probably still be the most exciting thing that ever happens in her life. She's just a nurse.'

Alessandro and Miranda?

Alessandro and Miranda?

Shaking all over, Tasha exited the cubicle. 'Actually, I'm a doctor,' she said, her voice robotic, 'but some of my best friends are nurses, so I'd be grateful if you didn't talk about them as if they're second-class citizens. Next time you fall off your horse, it may be one of them saving your life. And, just for the record, that shade is definitely too red for you. It's very ageing.' Without pausing, she swept out of the room, grateful that whoever had designed her dress had given her sufficient fabric with which to make a dignified exit.

He was supposed to be marrying Miranda. His brother's fiancée.

The tears lodged in a lump at the back of her throat, she continued to walk even when she heard Princess Eleanor calling her name.

'Natasha.'

Tasha thought about pretending she hadn't heard, but then turned, her expression blank. 'I'm just leaving, Your Highness.'

'I need to tell you a few things about Alessandro.'

'Actually, no, you don't. I'm the one who needs to tell you a few things about Alessandro.' As the last thread of her control snapped, Tasha's temper bubbled over. 'Do you know that he doesn't sleep at night because he blames himself for his brother's death? Do you know that he believes that you would have preferred him to be killed? He's living with that, and you're not doing anything to stop it.'

Shocked, the woman stared at her. 'Do you know to whom you're speaking?'

'Yes.' Tasha's lips tightened. 'I'm speaking to a woman who hasn't called her son once in the past six weeks except to nag him about official duties.'

'I have a responsibility towards my country.'

'You also have a responsibility towards your son.'

The other woman straightened her shoulders. 'You seem very concerned about Alessandro's well-being.'

'I'm a doctor,' Tasha said smoothly. 'I'm trained to deal with the physical and the psychological. And, by the way, that child playing over by the tree looks as though she has measles. You might want to remove her from all those people because she'll be infectious. Excuse me. I'm leaving now.' Wondering whether she was about to be arrested for insubordination, Tasha turned away, continuing her walk towards the exit.

Damn and double damn.

Her heart was hammering, her palms were damp and her hands were shaking.

She'd lost her temper again.

Wasn't she ever going to learn?

'Tasha! Tash!'

Hearing Alessandro's voice behind her, she quickened her pace. The last thing she wanted was to speak to him.

When a strong male hand closed over her shoulder, she shook him off. 'Let go of me.' Furious, she whirled around and faced him. 'You are an utter bastard and I hate you. I hope your bloody horse falls on your other leg and breaks it.'

He stared at her, stunned. 'You're upset about the way my mother spoke to you and I don't blame you, but—'

'I'm not upset with your mother. I'm upset with you for not

telling me the truth.' Steaming mad, Tasha turned on him, eyes blazing. 'Why the hell didn't you mention Miranda to me? I knew she was engaged to your brother. Why didn't you mention that you'd taken over that role, too?'

His expression altered instantly and she suddenly felt like sobbing.

Instead, she punched him in his bruised ribs. 'Damn you, Sandro. I wanted you to deny it. I—I hate you.'

'You don't understand—'

'I understand perfectly. You were laid up in Cornwall so you thought you'd have some fun. And that's fine, because I had fun too. But you didn't need to bring me here and use me to send some message to your girlfriend.' Her voice rose but she didn't care. 'You used me. If you wanted me to come to this wedding so that you could send your girlfriend some sort of message, you at least should have had the decency to tell me.'

A muscle flickered in his jaw. 'That isn't what I was doing.'

'Don't lie to me, Alessandro. I want to go home and I want to go home now.' Before she made even more of a fool of herself in public.

'Before you go, my mother would very much like to talk to you again. If you still want to go after that, I'll take you myself.'

'I don't want you to take me yourself. I'm perfectly capable of driving.' Snapping the words out, Tasha dragged her shoulder out of his grip. 'And I don't need to talk to your mother. Everything that needs to be said has been said.'

Suddenly she felt herself crumbling. 'Why did you bring me? It was cruel, Alessandro. Really cruel.'

He stood in perfect stillness. 'I wanted to see whether you would enjoy yourself.'

'Enjoy being mocked? Enjoy being ridiculed? I'm not that much of a masochist.' Her voice felt thick as she struggled to push the words past the tears. 'So now we've established that you should have brought someone else, I'd like to leave.'

Seeing a pack of journalists approach, Alessandro snapped his fingers and a sleek black car appeared from nowhere. 'Take Dr O'Hara back to my house. We'll talk later. In private. There are things I want to say to you.'

'Nothing I want to hear.' Tasha climbed into the back of the car, stumbling over the hem of her dress. The moment the car pulled away, she leaned forward and gave the driver a different address.

She had no intention of going back to Alessandro's house ever again.

It was over.

Josh rapped on the door of Megan's cottage. It had been weeks since he'd slept properly. Not since the morning he'd arrived home to find Rebecca waiting in the kitchen.

He'd been thinking about nothing but this moment—*trying to find another way.*

But there was only one way.

A seagull shrieked overhead and he could smell the sea. Normally he would have breathed deeply and enjoyed his surroundings, but there was nothing normal about today.

When Megan opened the door it took all his self-control not to drag her into his arms for one last time. 'Hi. I should have called, I know, but—'

'Come in.' She stood back and he saw hope flicker in her eyes.

It made it all the harder to step over the threshold because he knew he was going to kill that hope dead for ever.

Once before she'd trusted him with her heart and he'd broken it.

He was about to do the same again.

Blissfully unaware of what was coming, Megan walked in front of him to the kitchen. The house overlooked the beautiful sweep of Penhally Bay. He knew she'd had countless offers from developers. He also knew she'd never accept any of them. The house had been her grandmother's and for Megan the emotional ties were as powerful as the lure of the idyllic surroundings.

'Can I get you something to drink?'

'Just water. Thanks.'

'Water?' She gave a hesitant laugh. 'Josh the party animal drinking water?'

He ran his hand over the back of his neck, thinking of all the times he'd broken bad news to patients. It never came easily, but somehow he managed it. Because this was personal, it was almost impossible to form the words. 'We have to talk.'

'I agree.' Calm, she lifted a jug from the fridge and poured a glass of filtered water.

Josh watched as the water sloshed onto the side and then suddenly realised she wasn't as calm as she pretended to be.

'Do you want lemon? Ice?'

'For God's sake, Megan—' He prised the jug out of her hand even as he brought his mouth down on hers. He felt her gasp of shock and then she was kissing him back, her fingers curling tight into the front of his shirt as if she was afraid he was going to vanish.

It was crazy, insane, stupid, but he couldn't stop himself. His hands were buried in her hair and he was kissing her with a desperation that went bone deep. 'I love you.' He groaned the words against her mouth, 'I love you, sweetheart.'

'Oh, Josh…' Her voice broke and she made a sound somewhere between a sob and a laugh. 'I—'

'I love you so much, which is why this is the hardest thing I've ever had to do.' With supreme difficulty, he drew back, forcing himself to do what had to be done. 'That night we spent together was incredible—'

'I know that, Josh.' Her voice was whisper-soft. 'I know, and—'

'No.' This time his voice was harsh, and he stepped back from her because he knew that if she stopped him now he'd never be able to say what needed to be said. 'You have to listen. You have to let me speak.'

Her eyes were startled. 'All right. Speak.'

'That night was so special. You have no idea.' He raked his fingers through his hair. 'When I left you that morning you were all I could think about.'

A tiny frown touched her forehead and she gave a bemused shake of her head. 'Josh, what on earth is wrong? You're making me nervous, I—I don't understand. Why shouldn't you love me? Why shouldn't I love you? I know it's been a bumpy road getting here, but—'

'I can't be in love with you.' He clenched his jaw as he saw her flinch.

'But—'

'Rebecca is pregnant.' His tone was raw and the words burned his chest. 'She's having a child.'

Megan stood very still. Behind them sunshine poured through the window but neither of them noticed. 'But…that's good, surely? It means she's moved on. She has another relationship.' Her voice faltered. 'Josh? Why are you looking at me like that? What's wrong?'

He couldn't remember ever crying. When his father had walked out he hadn't cried. Even that night Megan had been brought into A and E and he'd failed to save their baby, he hadn't managed to cry. But this time, for some reason, the obstruction in his throat was an immovable object.

'Megan…' He couldn't form the words. It was the hardest thing he'd ever had to say. *The hardest thing he'd ever had to do.* 'It's my child. Rebecca is having my baby.' He watched as the hope in her eyes turned dull. Watched as love drained away, leaving nothing but pools of pain.

'But—if that's true then it means…' Tears glistened in her eyes and she gave a sharp gasp and backed away from him. 'You told me the marriage was over. You told me—'

'It was.'

'But you were still having sex with her?' Her voice rose and she wrapped her arms around herself in a gesture of self-protection. 'We clearly have a very different idea about what constitutes "over". Oh, my God.' Agitated, she paced to the far side of the room and pressed her hands to her mouth. 'I would never have slept with you that night if I'd thought you were still together.'

'We weren't together.' Josh walked over to her but she whirled round, her eyes fierce.

'Don't touch me!' She backed away, the sob lodged in her throat. 'How *could* you? *How could you do that?* You were sleeping with me and your wife at the same time?'

'No!'

'She's pregnant, Josh.'

'It was just one night, weeks before you and I...' He sucked in a breath and spread his hands. 'I can't even explain it—'

'I suggest you don't even try.' The chill in her voice was agonising to hear.

'It was a mistake. Megan, she did it on purpose. She wanted a baby. This was her way of keeping us together.'

'You told me the marriage was over. You told me it was mutual.' The tears slid down her cheeks. 'But you had sex with her, Josh.' She was crying openly now. *'You had sex with her.'*

The memory brought a bitter taste to his mouth. 'It was just once.'

'Is that supposed to make it OK? Because I can assure you it doesn't. It's not OK, Josh.' She scrubbed the tears from her cheeks with her hand and the frantic attempt to hide her distress was more disturbing than any accusation she could fling at him. 'You say you love me and then you tell me this? How do you think that makes me feel?'

Josh closed his eyes. 'Megan—'

'She can give you the one thing I can't give you.' Her voice cracked and she lifted her head to look at him, resignation in her eyes. 'She can give you a child and I can't compete with that.'

'I love you, Megan. And I'm telling you that because I don't want there to be any misunderstanding about what happened here. I truly love you, but no child of mine will grow up as I did, without a father. I won't do that. I have to make this work. For the child's sake.'

'Yes. Of course you do.' Her lips were stiff and her voice was a flat monotone. 'You're going to make it work, I know you will. You'll be a very happy family, you, Rebecca and the baby. If you don't mind, I'd like you to leave now.'

Josh opened his mouth to fight that request and then realised that she was holding herself together with difficulty. And so was he.

With one last look at her trembling frame, he turned and strode out of her cottage.

A happy family?
Not in this lifetime.

CHAPTER TEN

FURIOUSLY angry, Tasha stormed out of the car. It was dark, and the familiar smells and sounds of Penhally Bay should have soothed her throbbing head. Instead she just wanted to punch someone.

Remembering her manners, she leaned back into the car and thanked the driver.

'You've been brilliant,' she muttered, 'and thank you for taking me to the house to collect my stuff. Sorry about the ranting and raving during the journey. Just forget everything you heard me say.'

Alessandro's driver cleared his throat. 'Actually, it was quite a revelation. Usually His Highness's female friends depart crying. I keep tissues in my glove compartment.'

'Maybe you could add a shotgun.'

'Most women aren't like you, Dr O'Hara.' The man gave a regretful smile. 'Unfortunately. It's been a pleasure driving you these past few weeks.'

'Thanks, Mario. I just hope your bastard boss—sorry, I mean *His Royal Highness*—doesn't fire you for giving me a lift here.'

'No worries, Dr O'Hara. I'll get your cases from the boot.' Mario moved round the car but Tasha was already there.

'I've got it.' She hauled the cases out of the boot so violently that the driver took a step back.

'They're heavy—'

'You'd be amazed how much weight I can lift when I'm steaming mad.'

Alessandro had humiliated her publicly. Again.

She'd trusted him...

Later she knew it was all going to hurt badly, but right now she was running on adrenaline in pure undiluted fury.

She took her surfboard from Mario and tucked it under her arm. 'Thanks.'

'Are you sure you'll be OK?' Concern in his eyes, he watched as she hitched the once-glamorous dress up around her waist. 'I'll just wait while you check your friend is in.'

'No need. I know she's in. I just texted her. Thanks for bringing me here and for being so kind.'

'You're welcome. You have my mobile number. If you need to go anywhere, call and I'll come and pick you up.' With a last concerned look at her face, he drove off and Tasha heard the door of the cottage open.

'Tash?' Megan stood in the doorway and Tasha turned and strode towards her, dragging her cases behind her.

'Thanks so much for letting me come here. I couldn't stay at Sandro's, and if I went to Josh's he just would have said I told you so, and then I would have given him a black eye. And to be honest—' She stopped in mid-rant as she saw the look on Megan's face. 'Oh, my God—what happened to you? You look—you're— *Megan*?'

Megan's eyes were red. 'I don't think you can stay, Tasha,' she said stiffly. 'This is so awkward, but—'

'This is about my brother, isn't it?' Scowling, Tasha yanked her cases through the door, breaking a wheel in the process. She leaned her surfboard against the wall of Megan's hall. 'You can say anything you like and I'm just going to nod and agree with you. He's the one who made me go and look after Alessandro. If it weren't for him, I wouldn't be in this mess.' She kicked the suitcase upright and slammed the door firmly behind them. 'Let's lock it and unplug the phones.'

'I don't need to unplug anything,' Megan said wearily.

'Josh isn't coming back. It's over. He isn't going to come round ever again.'

'No wonder you hate him.'

'I don't, that's the trouble.' Megan's voice cracked and she cleared her throat quickly. 'I love him. I've only ever loved him. All my life. I know you probably can't imagine that, but it's true.'

Stunned by that confession, Tasha slipped her arms around her. 'Don't let him do this to you. No man is worth it. Not even my stupid big brother.'

'I wish I could feel as angry as you.' Megan blew her nose hard. 'I feel as though someone has gouged out my insides with a knife.'

Tasha winced. 'That's not good. I'll try and help you feel angry. It's easier. First you need to stop focusing on the reasons you love him and focus on the bad stuff.'

'I can't bear to think about that.' Megan pulled away. 'And I'm being so selfish. You must be devastated. Do you want to tell me the details?'

'I found out that the Crown Pig Alessandro is virtually engaged to some thin, blonde European princess called Miranda or some other stupid name. He doesn't want to marry her because he doesn't believe in marriage so he used me to send her a clear message that their relationship is over. That's why he invited me to the wedding.' Tasha crashed around Megan's kitchen, helping herself to a bottle of wine from the rack. 'I'm so angry I need to break something, but I can't break anything in your house.'

'Go ahead. It's the least of my worries.'

Tasha glanced at her friend's red eyes. 'How long have you been crying?'

'You don't want to know. It's embarrassing.'

'You'll be dehydrated. You need to drink something.' Tasha popped the cork on the wine and filled two glasses to the brim.

Megan's laugh bordered on the hysterical. 'The usual cure for dehydration is water.'

Tasha gave an airy shrug and handed her a glass. 'This will do fine. It's liquid. Cheers.' She tilted her glass against Megan's, worried by how fragile and broken the other girl looked. 'Drink. To sisterhood. And the therapeutic properties of blazing anger.' *She wasn't going to think about her own pain. She was going to blast her way through it and keep busy.*

'He slept with his wife.' Despite her protests, Megan drank half the wine without pausing. 'She's pregnant. But I expect you already know that.'

Tasha stilled. Guilt shot through her. 'Look—'

'It wasn't your job to tell me. It was his.'

'I know it looks bad, and I'm not trying to defend my brother, but knowing Rebecca as I do I can tell you it was all her doing.'

'It couldn't have been *all* her doing, Tasha.'

'Well, that's true of course. He should have said no. But he's a weak, brainless man.'

'Josh is strong and clever.'

Tasha looked at her with exasperation. 'You're focusing on his qualities again.'

'Sorry. It's just—I really did think he loved me.'

Tasha sighed, wondering whether the truth would make the pain worse or better. 'He does love you. I know he loves you. And if it's any consolation, I'm sure Rebecca was lying in wait on the bed in a skimpy set of underwear or something. Slut.'

'They were married.'

'Their marriage has been over for a long time. She was playing games.' Realising that she was probably making things worse, Tasha picked up the wine and topped up Megan's glass. 'Let's just forget it. Your life is a mess and my life is a mess. You can be sad and I'll be angry. Whatever works. Do you have any chocolate in the house? That's good for either mood.'

'There's a large box of Belgian chocolates given to me by grateful parents.' Her cheeks pale, Megan sipped the wine. 'Do you want them?'

'Urgently. We'll share the box.' Tasha tripped over the hem of her dress and cursed fluently. 'I just need to get a pair of jeans out of my suitcase. I'm going to break my neck if I stay in this.' And break her heart because the dress reminded her of Alessandro. She'd dressed with such hope, never once imagining that this would be the outcome. Because she'd been so careful not to dream, somehow the pain was all the more acute.

Anger, she reminded herself. *Anger was easier.*

Megan looked at the dress. 'We had such fun choosing that. I thought it was perfect.'

Tasha retrieved her suitcase and delved inside for a pair of jeans. 'It was a ridiculous amount of money for something I was only ever going to wear once. And now it's just a reminder of a completely terrible day. I'm going to give it to the charity shop.'

'Do you know the worst thing? When Josh came here today, I thought he was going to tell me he loved me. And he did. Two minutes before he told me his wife was pregnant.'

Still clutching the jeans, Tasha stared at Megan's ashen face and bloodshot eyes and wondered if she could have done something to make it easier. 'I don't know what to say. Right now I want to seriously hurt him.'

'I think he's already hurting.' Megan climbed onto a chair and lifted a box of chocolates from the top shelf of a cupboard. 'If I read this situation in a book, I'd think it was ridiculous. Why does life have to be so hard? Start eating. I'm just going to go and wash my face.'

Tasha stood, staring out across Penhally Bay, feeling numb and exhausted.

When the phone in her bag suddenly rang she scrambled

to answer it, heart racing. When she saw that it was Josh, disappointment thudded through her.

She'd thought—

Her finger hovered over the answer button and then she heard Megan coming back down the stairs and she lifted her chin and switched her phone off.

'Which one of them was it?' Megan's voice was hard and Tasha shrugged and dropped the silent phone back into her pack.

'Doesn't matter.' She helped herself to a chocolate. 'Thanks.' She hesitated. 'What are you going to do, Megan?'

'You mean how am I going to carry on working at St Piran's with Josh there? How am I going to cope with seeing Rebecca pregnant?' Megan dropped onto the edge of the sofa, her fingers plucking at the edge of her cardigan. 'I don't know. I honestly don't know. And how about you? You're living with Alessandro.'

'Not any more. No way am I going back there. I collected my things on the way.' Tasha wriggled out of the dress and winced as the zip tore. 'Oh, dear. Good job I wouldn't have wanted to wear it again.'

'You can stay here as long as you like. It's been years since I had a flatmate.'

'Seriously? I can stay? I was sort of hoping you'd say that. Are you sure it wouldn't be an imposition? Just until I find a job.' She wondered how long it would take for the pain to fade. *Never again*, she vowed as she tugged on her comfortable jeans. She just wasn't going to do this again. She was rubbish at relationships.

'Stay as long as you like, although I suppose that might be awkward for Josh.'

'That's his problem, not mine.'

'But soon you'll be an aunty and…' Megan leaned back against the sofa and closed her eyes. 'God, what a mess. The awful thing is I haven't just lost him, I've lost you. How are we going to stay friends? It's going to be so awkward.'

'I'm used to awkward. You're talking to the girl who told her consultant to get a backbone.'

Megan gave a choked laugh. 'I was forgetting that. You're so gutsy.'

'It's not guts, it's an uncertain temper,' Tasha muttered gloomily. 'And while we're on that subject I probably ought to warn you that I might be arrested for treason. I yelled at Princess Eleanor. And then I punched Alessandro.'

'Oh, Tasha…' Megan started to laugh and Tasha found herself laughing too.

'Will you visit me in prison?'

'You've got to admit it's funny.' Still shaking with laughter, Megan wrapped her arms around her ribs. 'You spent all that time trying to help him heal and then you bruise him again. I'm so glad I met you. Where would we be without girlfriends?'

'We'd be stuck with men and then we'd go slowly mad.'

Megan sprang to her feet and reached for a DVD. 'Let's eat chocolate and watch back-to-back trashy movies.'

'Sounds good to me.'

Megan hugged the DVD to her chest and then turned to look at Tasha. 'I was pregnant once.'

Tasha spilled her wine over her jeans. 'Meg! You can't just make confessions like that without warning.' Without taking her eyes off her friend, she put her wine glass on the carpet. 'Who was—? Oh, God, I'm soaking. Oh, never mind.' Ignoring her wet legs, she bit her lip. 'It was Josh's, wasn't it?'

Megan nodded. 'We had a one-night stand—years ago. He didn't know I was pregnant.'

'But—'

'I lost it. At twenty-three weeks.' Megan drew in a deep breath. 'It was Josh who saved my life. But he couldn't save our son. He was just too little—too sick.'

Tasha felt the tears spill down her cheeks. 'Oh, Meg, I—I'm so sorry. Josh never— I didn't know. I had no idea.'

'Josh only found out recently, although he'd suspected for a while. That morning you banged on the door of the on-call room—'

'You'd spent the night together.'

'I told him then. He overheard something.' Megan shook her head. 'It doesn't matter. It's all in the past now.'

'Is something like that ever in the past?'

'Maybe not. I still ask myself whether the whole thing was my fault.' Megan spoke quietly. 'When I found out I was pregnant I panicked. It wasn't what I wanted. Or at least it wasn't what I wanted right then—and nature took me literally.'

'No! You know that isn't what happened. It wasn't your fault.'

'I developed complications, and…' Megan breathed slowly '…now I can't have children. I'm infertile. I lost our son. So perhaps it's just as well for Josh that he's having this baby with Rebecca.'

'No.' Tasha hugged Megan. 'Josh wants to be with you, I know that.'

'Well, that's never going to happen.' With a sniff, Megan pulled away and fed the DVD into the player. 'You rang me in a state of misery and since you've arrived all I've done is moan. It's the wine. Never give me wine. And stop being so unselfish. Moan to me about Alessandro.'

But Tasha discovered she didn't want to moan, or even talk about what had happened with Alessandro. It was all too raw. And she felt so foolish. Foolish for believing that what they'd shared was real. 'I don't really want to talk. But I do have a question.'

'You want to know why Alessandro behaved like that?'

'No!' Affronted by the suggestion she wanted to talk about Alessandro, Tasha glared. 'I want to ask you if you happen to know who designed this dress I've just ruined. Everyone seems to think I ought to know.'

* * *

Tasha slept badly and awoke early to hear a rhythmic banging sound coming from Megan's kitchen.

With a groan she rolled onto her stomach and stuck her head under the pillow but the banging continued. 'What *is* she doing?' Giving up on sleep, Tasha slid out of the bed and padded barefoot downstairs.

Megan was in the kitchen, attacking a chicken fillet with a rolling pin. 'Good morning.' The rolling pin smashed into the meat again. 'Sleep well?'

'Er—not particularly.' Tasha winced as the sound resonated through her brain. 'Megan—'

'I'm preparing something for our supper.'

Tasha glanced at the clock. 'It's seven in the morning.'

'I'm pretending the chicken is Josh's head.'

'Ah. And is that helping?'

'I think it might be.' Megan gave the chicken an extra-hard thwack and the fillet split in two. 'Oh, dear.'

'It's OK. It will taste the same.' Her head throbbing, Tasha pushed her hair out of her eyes. 'If it's all right with you, I'm going surfing.'

'At this time of the morning? You'll have the beach to yourself.'

'That's the way I like it. Are you working today?'

'Fortunately not. I have two days off.'

Tasha saw that the scrubbed kitchen table was covered in pages from the internet. 'Australia?' She picked one up. 'You're going on holiday to Australia?'

'Not holiday, no.' Megan gave the chicken one more *thwack* for good measure. 'I'm looking at jobs. They need paediatricians, you know. We could both go.'

'To Australia?' Tasha started to laugh. 'I actually think that's a totally genius idea. Let's do it. Are there men in Australia?'

'Apparently, but it's a big country, so if we're really careful we should be able to avoid them.'

'Great. When I get back from surfing, we'll look at it together.'

Tasha thought about it all the way down to the beach and was still thinking about it as she walked onto the damp, cold sand. Just as Megan had predicted, the beach was empty. The wind blew her hair across her face and she heard the plaintive shriek of a seagull.

For a moment she felt a pang at the thought of leaving St Piran, but then she reminded herself that she wouldn't have been working in St Piran anyway. She would have had to go wherever the jobs took her. And that may as well be Australia. Maybe that far away, it wouldn't hurt so much. Presumably the antipodeans weren't remotely interested in a European principality so she was unlikely to be turning on the news and finding herself looking at pictures of Alessandro.

Trying to block it all out, Tasha plunged into the sea, feeling the cold bite through her wetsuit. Australia had some of the best surfing in the world. She could visit the Barrier Reef—maybe learn to dive.

Somehow try and forget about a certain tall, arrogant prince who had played a starring role in her dreams for far too long.

Ignoring the heavy ache in her chest, she paddled out and took up position just outside the breaking waves. Then she sat up, straddling her board as she stared out to sea, waiting for the right moment.

Could she grow to love Australia the way she loved Cornwall?

Her cheeks were wet and she realised that the sea water had mingled with the flow of her tears.

Furious with herself for crying, she turned the nose of the board to catch the oncoming wave, focusing on the sea and not her feelings. The surge of water lifted her and she paddled hard and then hopped up on the board. She dropped down the face of the wave, feeling the speed build, and she rode the water, arms outstretched, knees bent. As she angled along the face of the wave for that single moment there was nothing else in her mind but the rush of speed and the sheer exhilaration of being carried by the erupting swell of water.

She turned and paddled back into the waves, repeating the exercise until she was exhausted.

Wondering whether Megan had finished bashing the chicken, she finally lifted her board under her arm and walked across the cool sand towards the little path that led towards the cottage.

It was the car she noticed first. Long and black, with darkened glass. Bulletproof glass.

Alessandro stood against the car, watching her, four powerfully built bodyguards positioned at strategic positions around him.

They looked so incongruous in this beautiful, wild place that Tasha almost laughed. But she discovered that she couldn't.

As their eyes connected she felt her heart ache as the pain she'd locked away burst free.

Horrified to feel a lump in her throat, she turned her board, deliberately intending to head back out to sea, but his voice travelled across the sand.

'Tasha, wait.'

She closed her eyes, clenched her jaw and kept walking.

Last night she'd held it together and she was proud of the way she'd handled herself. No tears. No begging. Just anger and dignity. She didn't want to sully an otherwise perfect performance.

'Tasha.' He growled her name. 'If you walk away, I'll assume you're a coward.'

She stopped dead and anger shot through her like a live flame. Furious, she turned. 'Coward?' She stalked back to him, eyes blazing. 'You're calling me a coward? Sorry, but were you or were you not the one who invited me to the wedding for the express purpose of sending a message to your fiancée?'

'Miranda isn't, and never was, my fiancée.'

'*Almost* fiancée, then.'

'I would never have married her.'

'But she didn't know that, did she?' Tasha pinned a sweet smile on her face. 'So you thought you'd give her a stronger message. Using me as the messenger.'

'That wasn't what I was doing.'

'Oh, really? Then why did you take me?' She glared at him and he sucked in a breath and glanced over his shoulder towards his bodyguards.

'Walk with me for a few minutes.'

'No way. What the hell are you doing here, Sandro?' The name spilled easily from her tongue and suddenly she was back in his bedroom, in the intimate world they'd created. And she knew from the sudden blaze of awareness in his eyes that his mind was in exactly the same place.

'I'm flying to San Savarre tonight.' Alessandro's expression was grim and serious. 'There's something I want to say to you before I leave.'

'I've said everything I want to say.'

'Fine. I'll do the talking.'

'How did you find me, anyway?'

'I asked my driver where he dropped you. How's Megan?'

'She's doing just fine,' Tasha said coldly, knowing that Alessandro might well speak to Josh. 'Now, just say whatever it is you want to say so that I can get on with my life and you can get back into your bulletproof car.'

'I came to apologise for last night.'

'And you needed bodyguards for that? Now who's the coward?'

Alessandro's mouth flickered at the corners. 'Walk with me.'

She lifted an eyebrow. 'Is that an order?'

'No, it's a request.'

Tasha hesitated and then shrugged. 'All right. If you're

finally going to apologise, this I have to hear.' She put her board down on the path, horribly conscious of his powerful shoulders in the perfectly tailored suit. Dressed formally he looked remote and intimidating, nothing like the man she'd shared midnight picnics with after hot sex. 'Make it quick. Megan is expecting me back.'

'Why didn't you go back to my house?'

Tasha gave an incredulous laugh. 'Er—isn't it obvious? Excuse me, but this is a waste of time.' She turned away but he grabbed her wrist and dragged her close to him.

'I didn't take you to the wedding to make a point.' His voice was lethally soft. 'I took you because I wanted you with me. And because I wanted to see whether you enjoyed yourself at something like that. You're not like most of the women who attend that sort of thing. '

'Thanks for the reminder.' She felt his fingers hard on her wrist and tried to tug herself free. 'I studied for seven years in medical school and I'm still studying—but nowhere in my research have I ever found a benefit for memorising dress designers. I couldn't care less who made my stupid dress. So you were probably right to dump me.'

'I didn't dump you. You dumped me.'

'You made sure I dumped you.'

'No.' He hauled her against him. 'That's my life, Tasha. That's what I do. I go to weddings, I attend fundraising events, I open hospitals, I go on state visits.'

'Why are you telling me this?'

'Because if our relationship is going to work, you need to know what you're getting into.' He drew in a breath. 'I did take you to that wedding to make a point, but it wasn't the point you obviously thought I was making. It was nothing to do with Miranda or anyone else. It was to do with you and me. I wanted to show you my life. This last six weeks—it hasn't been real, Tasha. Yes, we spent time together, and it was special. But we were cocooned in our own little world. I wanted to know if you'd still want to be with me in the other world I inhabit.'

All the air had gone from her lungs. She felt as though she was the one with the broken ribs. 'You—'

'I'm sorry if you felt humiliated.' He took her face in his hands, his eyes holding hers. 'That was never my intention. I know you're not interested in the whole designer-dress thing, that's one of the reasons I love you. But a huge part of my life is attending events. I needed to know that you wouldn't hate the life.'

Tasha felt dizzy. 'Whoa…' Her voice cracked. 'Rewind. Somewhere back there you said something I didn't quite catch.'

A smile touched his mouth. 'I said I love you. I've never said that to a woman before. Ever. Frankly, I never thought I would. But spending that time with you showed me I was wrong. I love you.'

The words had the effect of a drug. Tasha's head spun. She felt decidedly strange. 'If you…love me, why didn't you say something sooner?'

'Because love isn't enough. It isn't that simple. Not for me.' He pushed a strand of hair out of her eyes. 'I'm very aware that when you marry me, you'll have to take on all of it. Not just me, but the whole royal role. It's a lot to ask of anyone.'

'When I…?' Tasha blinked. 'Excuse me, but could you stop saying these completely shocking things with no warning? There's absolutely no way on this planet I'd marry you.'

His eyes held hers. 'Why not?'

'Well, because you're…' Flustered, she waved a hand vaguely. 'And I'm…' She pressed her fingers to her forehead. 'Just—give me a minute here. Yesterday your mother was looking at me as if I were a virus. Now you're suggesting marriage?'

'It may surprise you to learn that my mother is your biggest supporter.'

'You're right. It would surprise me. She turned me to ice with a single glance.'

'Yes, she's good at that. It's her way of keeping people at a distance. But you impressed her, Tash. You were tough. You stood your ground. And she likes the fact that you have your own career.' He gave a short laugh. 'And the fact that you have no idea who designed your dress.'

'Precisely. I have my own career.' Her heart was hammering. She didn't know whether she was feeling terror or excitement. 'I'm not giving that up for anyone.'

'I'm not asking you to. I wouldn't want you to. You're a very talented doctor. I've seen that in the time we've spent at the hospital. I've heard the way people talk about you. But we have hospitals in San Savarre. In the capital we have a brand-new hospital with state-of-the-art equipment. And consultants who are interested in being progressive.' He paused, a wicked gleam in his eye. 'We also have beaches. Incredible surfing. Endless sunshine.'

Seduced by the picture he painted, Tasha glared at him. 'That's not playing fair.'

'I don't want to play fair. I want you.'

Her breath lodged in her throat. 'Well, that's a shame because I hate you.'

'No, you don't. If you hated me you wouldn't have moved in and helped me. You wouldn't have stormed off last night. You stormed off because you love me and I hurt you. I upset you.' He drew breath. 'And I'm sorry. I should have come clean with you.'

'Yes, yes you should.' Tasha faltered. 'So—so you were seeing if I behaved myself at the wedding? You were thinking, Does she use the right knife and fork?'

'No. I was thinking, Could we do this together? Could we have this life?'

'I overheard some girls talking—'

He nodded. 'I thought you might have done. It happens, Tash. When you're a public figure everyone assumes they know everything there is to know about your private life. They think they know you. But they don't. But now I understand why you were so angry.'

'Sometimes I overreact,' Tasha muttered, her face pink. 'Just a little. When it's something I care passionately about.'

'That's all right with me. I'm happy to be someone you care passionately about.' He slipped his hand into his pocket and pulled out a small box. 'I would have followed you yesterday, but I needed to discuss it with my parents.'

'Discuss what?'

'The fact that I was going to ask you to marry me.' Sure and confident, Alessandro flipped open the box and extracted a glittering diamond ring. 'I can't go down on one knee because with this damn ankle I don't think I'd ever be able to get up again.'

Staring at the ring, Tasha lost the ability to breathe. 'Sandro—'

Without pausing, he took her hand and slid the ring onto her finger. 'I want you to marry me. I want you to be my wife and I want to live our lives together.'

'But—'

'For God's sake, Tash, just say yes, will you? For once in your life could you not argue with me?' He took her hands in his and his fingers were cool and strong. 'Princess Tasha. Josh told me you wrote that a few times on your textbooks.'

'That's two reasons I have to kill him when I next see him.'

'Don't do that. He's going to be my brother-in-law.' Alessandro drew her against him. 'I never thought I'd want to get married. I never thought I'd find a woman I wanted to spend the rest of my life with. And then I found you. Being with you feels…right. It always did, even when you were seventeen.'

Melting inside, Tasha lifted her face to his. 'Don't ever mess me around. If you step out of line, I'll hurt you.'

'But at least you'll be able to put me together again afterwards,' Alessandro drawled, smiling as he lowered his mouth to hers. 'I'll take my chances with you. I've always enjoyed dangerous sports.'

'Wait a minute.' She put her fingers against his mouth, delaying the kiss. 'You haven't told me about Miranda. She's the one everyone was talking about. Call me insecure, but I want to know about her.'

He hesitated and then pulled back slightly, his expression serious. 'Miranda was my brother's fiancée, as you know. We were good friends. I hated the way my brother treated her and for a while...' he shrugged '...other people thought it would be neat if we got together. And maybe she thought it, too. But it was never going to happen. She's always been like a sister to me, but I felt as though I owed her something. But I also knew that to go into a marriage without love was the wrong thing to do. You helped me see that.'

'Me?'

'It was the way I feel about you that made up my mind. So the other night I had a long chat with her. It was the most honest talk we've ever had. I told her about you and how I felt.'

'And now she wants to kill me.'

'She wants to meet you.' Smiling, he lowered his forehead to hers. 'You're going to like each other. She didn't really want to marry me any more than I wanted to marry her. We just gave each other support after Antonio died.'

'I yelled at your mother about that.'

'I know.' He gave a low laugh. 'Thanks to you, she and I also had the most honest conversation we've ever had. It cleared the air.'

'So I'm not going to be arrested for treason or whatever and thrown in your dungeons?'

'I might throw you in the dungeons if you don't give me an answer soon.'

Tasha placed her hand against his face and looked at him for a long time. What she saw in his eyes brought tears to her own and happiness burst free inside her. 'Yes,' she muttered. 'I'll marry you. Just don't expect me to call you Your Highness.'

His mouth came down on hers and they kissed until her heart was hammering and her brain was blurred.

Finally Alessandro lifted his head. 'Let's go somewhere more discreet before our most private moment is captured on film by some photographer with a long lens.'

'Wait…' Tasha hesitated, torn between what he was offering and loyalty to her friend. 'I honestly don't think I can leave right now. Megan is in a mess—she's thinking of going to Australia. Making a new life away from Josh and Rebecca.'

'She doesn't have to go that far to make a new life. We need paediatricians in San Savarre. She could rent out the cottage here and make a new life for herself in the Mediterranean.'

Tasha stared at him, touched by his generosity. 'But Josh is your friend. And my brother. Will it be awkward?'

'Josh loves Megan,' Alessandro said quietly. 'He's crushed with guilt. I think right now he'd support any idea that would stand a chance of making her happy. Why don't you invite her? It would be nice for you to have a friend there. She can have an apartment in the palace. I'm not saying it will be easy for her, but at least she won't have to worry about the basics.'

Smiling, Tasha held out her hand. 'I love you, Your Highness, have I told you that?'

'No, but from now on I expect you to do so on an hourly basis.' He lowered his mouth to hers. 'And that's a royal command.'

ST. PIRAN'S:
THE WEDDING!

ALISON ROBERTS

PROLOGUE

'CODE ONE, DR Phillips.' The registrar slammed down the phone as he swung his head. 'Theatre Three.'

Megan's pager began sounding at precisely the same moment, with the particular sound reserved for an absolute emergency.

The surge of adrenaline made everything else irrelevant. Even signing her resignation. Her ticket to finally escape.

She dropped her pen on top of the paperwork and leapt to her feet.

'Let's go.'

A code one was a life-threatening emergency. A life was at stake. More than one life, potentially, if Megan was being summoned. For a paediatrician to be called in with the same paging system used for something like a cardiac arrest meant that a newborn baby could be in need of specialist resuscitation. For it to be happening in Theatre meant the baby was arriving by emergency Caesarean. There were no scheduled Caesareans for the St Piran's maternity department today so this one must have come in via the emergency department.

The registrar, Matt, was keeping pace with Megan as she ran for the elevator.

'Suspected uterine rupture,' he said.

Megan nodded, holding her finger on the button as if that would speed up the arrival of the lift. Then she turned away.

'Stairs,' she snapped. 'It'll be quicker.'

'She'll be bleeding out, won't she?' Matt was right behind her. 'The baby won't stand much of a chance.'

'Depends.' Megan was taking the stairs two at a time. 'Internal blood loss can sometimes slow down or even stop simply because it's filled the available space and that puts pressure on ruptured vessels. The real danger comes when you open that space and release the pressure.' She blew out a hard breath as she pushed open the fire stop door on the theatre suite level. 'But you're right. It's critical for both of them.'

The main corridor in St Piran's theatre suite was deceptively quiet. The flashing orange light above the door of Theatre Three was a beacon. But so was something else that Megan hadn't expected to see.

A lone figure, at the end of the corridor, in front of the tall windows. A figure that stopped pacing and was now poised, reminding her of a wild animal sensing danger.

There was no mistaking the intensity of the stare Megan knew was directed at her.

'Get some scrubs on,' she ordered Matt as they reached the door to the change rooms. 'Then go in and make sure we've got everything we might need on the resus trolley. Check the incubator. I'll be right there.'

The figure was moving towards her. It might only be a silhouette because of the background light of the fading day beyond the windows but Megan knew exactly who it was.

Josh O'Hara.

Oh…*God*…

Why now? When she'd successfully avoided being alone with him for months.

Ever since that final, devastating kiss.

She could have avoided it now, too. Why hadn't she gone straight into Theatre with her registrar?

Because there was only one reason why Josh would be pacing the corridor like this. Why he wouldn't be in the Theatre with a case that would have been in his emergency department only minutes ago.

Megan was holding her breath. She'd never seen Josh look this tense. Distraught, even. Not even when he'd come to tell her that he loved her but they had no future.

Or…maybe she had. Once. So long ago now that the memory of his face was only a faint chord in the symphony that nightmare had been.

They'd had more than one turning point in their star-crossed history, she and Josh.

Clearly, this was another one. The third.

Bad things came in threes, didn't they?

That meant that this had to be the last. Of course it was, because escape was only days away for Megan now. She'd be on the other side of the world very soon. Just not quite soon enough.

Megan sucked in enough air to be able to speak. 'It's Rebecca, isn't it?'

His wife. They might not be living together as man and wife at the moment but they were still married.

A single nod from Josh. God, he looked terrible. He always looked like he could use a shave but right now his face was so pale it looked like he hadn't been near a razor for a week. And he must have been virtually scrubbing at his hair with his fingers for it to look so dishevelled. The expression in his eyes was worst of all, however. Blue fire that was born of desperation. Guilt. Despair.

And shame, perhaps, for what he had to beg for?

'The babies…' The words came out strangled. 'Please, Megan. Do your best for them. They…they won't let me in.'

Of course they wouldn't. He was far too emotionally involved. This was his family in Theatre Three. The whole family. As if it hadn't been hard enough for Megan that Rebecca was going to give him a child, she had to go one step further and present him with a complete family. Two babies.

And it might be up to her to save the lives of Josh's children.

The irony would be unbearable if she gave herself even a moment to think of it. Fortunately, she didn't have a moment to spare. As if any reminder of the urgency was needed, her registrar burst out of the changing room and went into the theatre.

Even then, something made Megan hesitate for just a heartbeat and, without any conscious thought, she reached out to touch Josh's arm in a gesture of reassurance. Not that she needed to touch him to ramp up the tension. Megan opened her mouth to say something but there were no words available.

With a curt nod, she turned away and went to throw on some scrubs.

Of course she would do everything she could to save his family. She would do it for any of her patients but if heroics were called for in this case, she wouldn't hesitate.

After all, it was Josh who had saved *her* life all those years ago.

That touch on his arm was almost enough to utterly unravel Josh.

His breathing ragged, tiny sounds escaping that could

have been the precursors of gut-wrenching sobs if he couldn't pull himself together, Josh went back to his pacing.

Back to the window end of the corridor where he was far enough away to keep his agony private but close enough to see who came and went from Theatre Three.

He got his breathing back under control and silent again but guilt was still threatening to crush him.

This was his fault. If Rebecca died, he would know where the blame could be laid. Why had he allowed himself to be pushed so far away? In recent weeks she had refused to see him. Or talk to him even. The only information he had been given had been that Rebecca was 'fine'. That her GP was looking after her, with the implication that he was doing a better job than Josh ever had.

God…if it hadn't been so hard, he would have been able to ask the questions that might have told him something wasn't right. He might have given in to the urge to turn up on her doorstep and make sure she was 'fine' for himself.

As recently as this morning, he'd thought of doing exactly that on his way to work but it had been all too easy to talk himself out of it. He hadn't really wanted to start his day by stopping by his old house, had he? If he was really honest, he wanted to avoid laying hands on the woman he'd once loved but should never have married.

But the way he felt about Megan had been the reason he'd married Rebecca at all, wasn't it?

Oh…*God*…the threads of his life were so tangled. So confused… The pain of his childhood, knowing how much his mother had loved his father and seeing how she'd been destroyed bit by bit as she had been cheated on time and again. The conviction that, if this was what love was all about, he wanted nothing to do with it.

Knowing that he was falling deeper in love with Megan

with every passing minute of that night they'd spent together.

Turning his back on her and everything that that kind of love could lead to.

Marrying Rebecca because he had been lonely. And because it had been safe. He had liked her. Respected her. Loved her the way you could love a good friend. A *safe* kind of love.

Had he allowed himself to be pushed so far out of Rebecca's life because it had been so hard to face the irrefutable evidence that he'd cheated on Megan by having sex with Rebecca that one, last time? When he'd known the marriage was over and it was only a matter of time before he and Megan could finally be together.

But Megan believed he had cheated on his wife when he'd gone to *her* bed.

He couldn't blame her for hating him for it.

At least he'd had the chance to save Megan's life that time, ironically in not dissimilar circumstances, but right now he'd been rendered useless. He couldn't even try to save Rebecca.

Did people think he wouldn't *want* to?

She was the mother of his children, for God's sake. Still his wife, even if it was in name only.

He had loved her once.

Just…not the way he'd loved Megan.

A part of him, so ruthlessly and successfully squashed months ago, was still capable of reminding him that he still loved Megan in that way. And always would. Not that Josh was going to acknowledge the whisper from his soul. It was a love he had chosen to forsake.

For his career and his sanity, that first time.

The second time it had been for his unborn children.

What would he have left if things weren't going well in Theatre Three?

He'd lose his wife.

His children.

And he knew what that pain was like. It was years ago now but the memory of holding that tiny scrap of humanity in his hands would never leave him. He'd known, on some level, that it had been his own son that Megan had lost that day. That he had been holding. It was too neat a fit, not only with the dates but with the power of that night. The connection that had felt like it would last for ever. The kind of connection that made it feel right to create a baby. Make a family.

He'd lose Megan again, too, if things weren't going well in Theatre Three.

No. A fresh wave of pain ramped up the confused agony Josh was grappling with.

He'd already lost Megan. Months ago.

Something made him stop the caged-in prowl back and forth across the corridor end. Made him freeze and whip his head sideways.

Of course it was Megan. In green theatre scrubs now, with her hair covered by a cap. Moving decisively from the door of the changing room to the one beneath the flashing orange light. She didn't look in his direction.

Despite, or perhaps because of, the overwhelming emotions he was having to deal with, Josh allowed himself to be distracted from the agonising, lonely wait for just a heartbeat.

Baggy, shapeless clothes like theatre scrubs did nothing to stop Megan being the most beautiful woman Josh had ever known. It didn't matter what she wore. Scrubs.

Tattered old jeans. The gorgeous gown she had worn as a bridesmaid in a royal wedding party.

Oh…no…Tasha. Josh reached for the mobile phone clipped to his belt. He needed to let his sister know what was happening. She could be the one to break the news to their mother.

What time would it be in San Saverre?

As if it mattered. Tasha would want to know the trouble that both her brother and her best friend were in right now.

Her loyalty would be tested. She knew the empty space he was in now, having sacrificed a relationship with the woman he truly loved for the sake of his children. To keep a marriage, even in name only, so that he wouldn't repeat history by being the kind of man their father had been. She would know how devastating it would be, being faced with the prospect of losing those children.

But she would also know how hard this had to be for Megan. To be expected to save his babies that were being carried by another woman. The babies she could never have given him because losing *their* son, all those years ago, meant she could never have another child.

Josh had to stifle an audible groan.

He was a reasonably intelligent man. He was damned good at the job he did, running the emergency department of St Piran's.

How was it that he always messed things up so badly when it came to his relationships with women?

He could save lives.

But he was just as good at breaking hearts.

It was his fault Rebecca hadn't had medical help in time to prevent this catastrophe.

His fault that Megan had become pregnant with his first child.

His fault that she'd lost the baby. That she'd never have another.

No wonder Megan had blanked him at Tasha's wedding. He'd done it to her, hadn't he?

Twice.

Every time he'd come to a point in his life where he was losing control…faced with the absolute vulnerability of loving someone—*Megan*—enough to give them the power to make or break him…he had frozen. Backed away and stayed with what he knew. What seemed to work.

He was an emotional coward.

Or a control freak?

As a modus operandi it was fine as far as his career went. Kept him on top. Moving forward. He could deal with a thousand people professionally and win acclaim. But he didn't seem to be able to deal with even one person on an intimate level and not cause serious harm.

What made anybody think he would be a good father?

Maybe he'd end up just like his own father had been. Worse than useless.

Maybe he would fail *all* his children before they even had a chance of life.

No.

The word was wrenched from deep inside Josh.

These babies couldn't die.

Megan wouldn't let them.

The baby looked dead.

Delivered to Megan's area of the theatre seemingly within seconds of the emergency surgery starting, the nurse laid her limp burden down under the lights, gave the paediatric team a grim glance and moved swiftly back towards the main table. Another baby would be delivered almost as quickly.

The resuscitation protocol was automatic for Megan. Airway, breathing, circulation, drugs.

She couldn't allow the fact that this was Josh's baby anywhere near the conscious part of her brain. Even a hint of distraction, let alone panic, could be disastrous.

'Suction,' she ordered.

Making sure the newborn's head was at the correct angle to keep the airway open and holding the end of the soft tubing at a length that couldn't go too far and trigger a laryngeal spasm, Megan cleared away any possible obstruction. Against the soft chugging of the suction machine, Matt was gently stimulating the baby's body by rubbing the skin with a warmed towel.

To one side of them, the tension was escalating.

'Pressure's dropping again.' The anaesthetist's tone was a sharp warning. 'Ectopic activity increasing.'

'We've got to get this second baby out. Where the hell's the suction? I can't see a damned thing…'

On Megan's side of the theatre the baby was showing no signs of starting to breathe.

'Bag mask.' Megan's order was clipped.

With the tiny mask covering both the mouth and nose of the infant, she gently depressed the soft bag to deliver the tiny amount of air needed to inflate the lungs. Again. And again.

'Not pinking up,' Matt noted.

'He's in shock.' Megan signalled for a technician to take over the bag mask. 'Start chest compressions, Matt.'

'You going to intubate?' Matt was already slipping his hands around the tiny chest, keeping his thumbs in front ready to start compressions.

'In a minute.' Megan could see over her registrar's shoulder. The second baby was lying on a towel a nurse was holding flat on both hands as the cord was cut. She was close enough to be able to see if there were any signs of life.

There weren't.

They needed a second paediatric team in here but there hadn't been one available. It was up to Megan and Matt here. At least they had a second resuscitation trolley set up.

'Keep up the CPR,' she instructed Matt. 'One hundred and twenty beats per minute. He may need some adrenaline. We'll need to cannulate the umbilical vein as well as soon as we can. Let's see where we are with baby two.'

Baby two was a girl. Just as flat as her brother was.

Or maybe she wasn't. After the first puff or two of air from the bag mask, the tiny girl gave a gasp and began trying to breathe on her own. It wasn't enough, though. The heart rate was still falling.

At ten minutes the Apgar score for both babies was still unacceptably low. They needed intubation, stabilisation and transfer to PICU—the neonatal intensive care unit.

They were both alive, however, and Megan was fighting to keep them that way.

The battle on the other side of Theatre Three was not going so well.

Part of Megan's brain was registering the increasing tension as she slid a small tube down the first baby's airway to secure ventilation. The obstetric surgeon had found the torn abdominal artery but too much blood had been lost. The fluid replacement and the drugs being used were not enough. Rebecca's heart had stopped.

CPR continued on the mother as Megan checked the settings on both incubators and watched the recordings being taken on both babies reach a level that meant it was safe to transfer them to PICU.

As the second incubator was wheeled from the theatre, she heard the defeated note in the surgeon's voice.

'Time of death…sixteen forty-three.'

November in Cornwall could provide a bone-chillingly grey day with an ominous cloud cover that threatened a torrential downpour at any moment.

The rain held off for the duration of Rebecca O'Hara's funeral but the background was suitably grim for the final farewell of a young mother who had never had the chance to see her babies.

'I hope nobody gets too sick today,' somebody muttered as the congregation filed into the chapel. 'Looks like practically the entire staff of St Piran's is here.'

There were whispered conversations in every pew.

'Who's that sitting beside Josh?'

'Tasha. His sister. The one that married the prince. I didn't know she was pregnant.'

'No. On the other side. The older woman. Is that his mother?'

'Yes. Her name's Claire. I heard that she's planning to move to Penhally to help him look after the babies.'

Further up the aisle, St Piran's CEO, Albert White, was sitting with a member of the board of directors, Luke Davenport.

'Thank goodness the babies are doing so well,' he muttered. 'Josh looks wrecked enough as it is.'

'It's all so sad.' Luke's wife, Anna, tightened her grip on her husband's hand. 'All of it. Rebecca was so unhappy for so long. I think she really believed that the babies would make everything all right.'

She exchanged a glance with her husband. One that suggested that—given enough time—maybe things would be all right eventually.

For Josh, anyway.

At the very back of the church, a woman noted for her tendency to gossip wasn't about to rely on meaningful glances.

'You'll see,' she muttered to the colleague sitting beside her. 'Now that the wife's out of the way, he'll be married to his fancy piece in no time flat. You just wait and see.'

'Shut up, Rita,' her companion hissed.

For once, Rita did shut up. She spent the next few minutes watching as the final people squeezed in to take up the last of the standing room at the back of the church. She'd been watching the congregation ever since she'd arrived. Early.

'Where *is* Megan?' Rita finally had to ask. The organ music was fading and the funeral director was taking his place to start the service.

'Haven't you heard?' The person on the other side seemed amused that Rita was out of the grapevine loop for once. 'She left St Piran's yesterday.'

'Where's she gone?'

'Africa.'

'She's coming back, though…isn't she?'

'Doubt it. Her resignation was permanent. She's joined *Medécins San Frontières*.'

'But—'

'*Shhh.* Leave it, Rita. It's over.'

CHAPTER ONE

Almost two years later

WHY ON EARTH had she come back here?

Penhally, Cornwall, on this November day seemed grim. Grey and bleak.

And so *cold*. Megan was quite sure the temperature was a single digit and having come from an African summer where a cool day could still be thirty degrees Centigrade, this was like being inside a fridge.

It didn't help that she'd lost so much weight in recent weeks, of course. Dengue fever took a huge toll, especially the second time around. Her old coat hung so loosely on her that Megan could wrap it around her body like a blanket. Which was exactly what she did as she stood there, shivering, a suitcase by her feet, looking out over Penhally Bay as the taxi disappeared down the hill.

The sky was a deep, ominous grey and looked ready to unleash a torrent of rain at any minute. The sea looked equally menacing with whitecaps on the steel-grey water, moored yachts rocking on the swells and huge breakers crashing onto dark, wet sand. Seagulls circled overhead and the sharp, plaintiff notes of their cries echoed perfectly how Megan was feeling.

It was too cold to stand here in the street, that was for

sure, but the view as she turned towards the cottage was just as dispiriting. The gate was barely visible in the wild growth of what had been a neatly trimmed hedge. The small garden was a wilderness but not high enough to disguise the coils of long-dead plants in the hanging baskets on either side of the front door or the broken panes in the lattice windows, some of which had curled pieces of cardboard trying to fill the small squares.

How long had it been since the last tenants had gone? Since she'd fired the rental agency who had failed to fix the issues like the broken pipes that had driven the tenants away? At least six months, but Megan had been too far away and too busy to cope with the hassle of putting new arrangements in place. Angered too by the flood of queries coming in from developers who were always waiting in the wings like vultures to get their hands on such a desirable piece of real estate.

And then she'd been too sick.

It was a ridiculously hard effort to push the gate open and drag her suitcase along the flagged path now choked with weeds and the branches of perennials like lavender that looked like they hadn't been cut back since she'd left two years ago. Megan felt the prickle of tears at the back of her eyes. This had all been so pretty once. Not that she'd ever managed to keep it as picture-perfect as her grandmother had but she'd tried her best to keep it the same.

To preserve the memories of how it had been in her childhood, when this cottage and her beloved gran had been the most precious things in her life.

And that, of course, was what had brought her back now.

This was where her roots were.

Not that she'd actually been brought up here. No... After her parents were tragically killed in a car accident,

Megan had gone to live with her grandmother in London. But Gran had been brought up in Penhally and that was where she'd taken Megan for a seaside holiday, every summer. They'd rented this very cottage, year after year, and the memories of those weeks had always been tinged with the rosy perfection of being the best time in the best place in the world. The cottage had been the home of her heart for as long as she could remember.

When she'd been so dreadfully ill, nearly losing her life after losing the baby, Megan had been forced to finally tell her grandmother the truth. Despite being already frail, Gran had gathered up all her strength, wrapped it all with the unconditional love she had for her granddaughter and declared that they needed a new beginning, starting with a seaside holiday. When she'd found that their beloved rental cottage was on the market, Gran had simply moved their lives back to her home town and, by doing so, had allowed Megan to put the pieces of her shattered life back together.

So this cottage and its memories, the sea and the village all added up to *home*. And home was the place that drew you back when you needed comfort. A safe place to recover and reassess your life.

Besides, the cottage badly needed sorting out. It would have been unforgiveable to let it crumble into some sort of ruin. Megan could hear the kind of 'tsking' sound her grandmother would have been making as she pushed open a front door stiff with disuse and stepped into a space that felt just as cold as it was outside. A space that reeked of damp and mould and mice.

Oh…*hell*…

This was far worse than she'd expected.

It wasn't just the evidence of appalling neglect. The horrible smell of the rubbish left by the tenants littering the hallway or the ominous sound of trickling water coming from the kitchen. Or was it the bathroom upstairs? Probably both.

It wasn't the knowledge that there would be no electricity on yet and it mightn't even be safe to have it turned back on until she found someone to check the wiring. It wasn't even the wave of incredible weariness as Megan contemplated the energy it would take to sort any of this out.

No. It was the feeling of being so alone.

The result of the emotional punch of the memories of *not* being alone in this house.

Not that Josh had ever stayed here. But this was where it had ended, wasn't it? Her feet seemed to be literally treading memory lane. Taking her down the hallway and into her kitchen while her head and her heart conjured up the figure of Josh following her.

Her feet crunched through pieces of broken glass on the kitchen floor.

Her heart had been broken long ago. How on earth could it still hurt this much?

Because it was here that Josh had prised that jug of water out of her hands? Just before he'd kissed her as if it was the end of the world and she was the only thing that mattered to him.

Here that Josh had told her how much he loved her?

When he'd told her that he couldn't be in love with her any more because his *wife* was pregnant.

She could actually hear echoes of his voice.

I love you so much, which is why this is the hardest thing I've ever had to do...

It was just one night, weeks before you and I...

I love you, Megan...but no child of mine will grow up as I did, without a father. I won't do that. I have to make this work...

Yes. That had been when her heart had really broken.

With the realisation that Josh had been lying to her when he'd told her the marriage was over. When she realised he'd still been sleeping with his wife at the time as he'd shared *her* bed.

That was when she'd known that it was truly all over. When any hope had died. She had known that, despite the love they had for each other, they could never, ever be together. Nothing could change that. If Rebecca's death hadn't even made a dent, then being back in Penhally certainly wasn't going to. That sense of betrayal was clearly still there. She'd thought she'd got over it all but the pain she was feeling right now was proof that she'd only managed to hide from it.

The chirrup of her mobile phone announced a text message. It was from Tasha—the only friend she'd really kept in touch with over the last couple of years. Maybe because Tash had also left Penhally. Or because she'd understood. How ironic was it that Tasha was Josh's sister?

U there yet? The message read. *How's it going?*

Megan's breath came out in a snort of wry amusement as she pulled off a woolly glove and tapped a response.

Just got here. Bit messy.

Would Tasha wonder what she was referring to? The house? Her emotional state? Her life?

Maybe she knew. *Hugs*, came back. *U OK?*

I will be. Thnx. Call u soon.

Tasha would be worried about her. Her friend had been dubious about the return. Why not come somewhere sunny to recuperate? she'd suggested. Like San Savarre? Or London, which would be close enough to make sorting things out a little easier and she wouldn't be so alone because Charles would be there, wouldn't he? Being with such a good friend who knew the whole story would be the best protection from being vulnerable to ghosts from the past.

She could cope, Megan had assured Tasha. It wouldn't be for long. Yes, she knew that Josh had moved from the smart St Piran town house he'd shared with Rebecca and was living closer to Penhally now. Of course he had moved. He'd needed a bigger house and a garden for the children and for his mother, who'd gone to live with them. By tacit agreement, she and Tash rarely talked about her brother but in those early days Megan had needed to know that the babies had survived their dramatic entrance to the world and had gone on to thrive. She hadn't really needed the later snippets that had told her Josh was a perfect father to little Max and Brenna. Or that his emergency department at St Piran's hospital was considered to be the best in the county.

Or that there were no women of any significance in his life. That he'd taken some sort of vow not to mess up anybody else's life.

His children and his career were all that mattered to Josh now. He probably wouldn't even be interested that she was visiting the area. There was no reason for their paths to cross other than the fact that this was a small village.

Megan closed her eyes to the view of Penhally Bay she still had in front of her through the kitchen window.

Maybe it was time to really let go of the past.

All of it.

Sell her grandmother's cottage and move on for ever.

If the memories were this hard to handle, how on earth did she think she would cope if she actually met Josh again?

The sooner she got out of here the better.

Maybe she didn't even need to think about fixing up the cottage. It wasn't as if it would make much difference to the kind of money a developer would be happy to offer.

She did need to find a place to stay for the night, however, and she really didn't want to contact any old friends from St Piran's even though she knew they would be happy to help.

The information centre in the village should be able to direct her to somewhere that would have a room available. Too weary in both body and spirit to face carrying her suitcase, Megan locked it into the cottage, taking only her shoulder bag as she set off to walk down the hill.

When she went back through the gate, however, the small path down to the beach caught her eye.

Just a look, she told herself. A glimpse into part of her past that wasn't associated with Josh. If she could feel the sand beneath her feet and close her eyes and breathe in the salty air, maybe she could remember something happier.

A summer's day, even. Building sandcastles and collecting shells and pieces of seaweed. Sitting on the damp sand with her bare legs stretched out in front of her, waiting for the thrill of the last wash of a wave to foam around her. Running back to the cottage to show Gran her new treasures.

Maybe it should have been running into Josh unexpectedly that she should have prepared herself for.

The dog on the beach was large enough to be quite frightening as he came loping towards Megan with a piece of driftwood clamped between his jaws. In the periphery of her vision, however, Megan could see a woman and children who had to be the dog's family because the beach was otherwise deserted. Nobody with children would have a vicious dog, would they? Besides, his teeth were occupied with the large piece of driftwood. And his tail was wagging in a very friendly manner.

'Crash!' The woman called firmly. 'Come back here.'

Crash? The name was unusual enough to ring a bell.

He'd only been a gangly, half-grown puppy then, of course, but Megan could remember him wearing a big, white ribbon around his neck at a summer beach wedding. Luke and Anna Davenport's wedding.

It wasn't Anna coming towards her now, though.

'I'm so sorry.' The woman, bundled up warmly in a coat, hat and huge scarf, was very apologetic. 'He's a bit too friendly, so he is. But he wouldn't hurt a fly.'

She had a strong Irish accent and the lilt took Megan immediately into a space she really didn't want to be. Was everything and everybody here going to make her think instantly of Josh? She took a deep breath and focused on the dog.

'It's fine,' Megan said. 'I don't mind.' To prove it, she scratched the dog behind one of his ears, which was easy to do because Crash was leaning on her leg. 'Isn't this the Davenports' dog?'

'Indeed it is. We mind him during the day when they're both working. The children love him to bits, so they do.'

The children were half hidden behind folds of the woman's coat as she held their mittened hands. Megan could see cute hats with ears on them and bright plastic boots. A pink pair with red flowers and a green pair with eyes that made them look like frogs. The owner of the frog boots peered out from the folds of coat.

'Cash naughty,' a small voice pronounced.

Crash wagged his tail harder.

The woman looked down to smile at her charges. 'Say hello, children.'

But the children said nothing. Neither did Megan. Her gaze had also dropped and she could see that the children were no bigger than toddlers. That they seemed to be close enough the same size as each other to be twins.

And…oh, God…the cheeky smile on the little boy's face

had a charm out of all proportion to his age. His eyes were too dark to determine their colour but they were so...alive. His face danced with mischief and Megan could feel the pull of a personality that went past being cute or attractive.

It was the kind of pull that made it impossible not to get sucked in.

To fall in love.

The kind of connection that could be overwhelming. That had the capability of derailing, if not destroying, a life.

Megan sucked in a deep breath. How ridiculous to be... what, *afraid* of a child?

But it was more than that, wasn't it? Much, much more.

Her gaze jerked up again and now she could see past the folds of the scarf and a woollen hat pulled low over her forehead. She could see a woman who looked to be well into her sixties but could be younger because those lines suggested a life that had not been easy. Behind the spectacles she wore, Megan could now see the colour of her eyes and her heart skipped a beat. She knew who had inherited that shade of indigo blue.

'Oh, my goodness. You're Josh's mother...Claire O'Hara?'

'Indeed I am.' Claire blinked in surprise. 'Have we met?'

'Just once. At the hospital. When the twins were still in the intensive care unit. The day before...'

The gaze Claire O'Hara directed at Megan was intense. And then it turned distinctly wary. 'Oh...You're Megan Phillips. The doctor. I'm so sorry. I didn't recognise you. It was such a terrible time...the day before poor Rebecca's funeral and...'

'There's no need to apologise.' Megan was still caught

by the undertone she couldn't fail to have missed in the older woman's gaze. Recognition of more than her identity.

Had Josh filled her in on his star-crossed lover history?

Unlikely. But this was a small village and St Piran's hospital grapevine was robust thanks to people who loved to gossip, like that dreadful woman—the ward clerk in the NICU...what was her name? Ruth? No...Rita.

Oh...Lord. Had Josh's mother heard about the way they'd met, way back when Megan had been a final-year medical student? That she'd become pregnant after a one-night stand with Josh, who hadn't been remotely interested in seeing her again? That he'd saved her life but that their son had been too premature to survive?

That baby—Stephen—had been Claire's grandson.

Even if she hadn't caught up on ancient history, she couldn't have missed the scandal of the way she and Josh had been drawn back to each other when he'd moved to St Piran's.

"Poor Rebecca", she'd said. Because her daughter-in-law had been badly treated by her husband, who had given up on their marriage and had been more interested in another woman? That Megan was the "other woman"? And that, in the end, they hadn't been able to keep their hands off each other?

Or maybe she felt sorry for Rebecca because she'd died knowing that Josh was only staying in the marriage for the sake of the children.

Megan was acutely embarrassed. Ashamed, even. The way she might have felt if Claire was her own grandmother and she'd disappointed her beyond measure. It had been a mistake to come back here. A dreadful mistake.

Except that Claire wasn't eyeing her as if she was the cause of all her son's troubles. 'And you look...different,' she continued. That wary expression had completely gone now. Claire's face actually creased with a kindly concern. 'You're so pale, dear. Are you all right?'

'I'm…um…fine.' Megan nodded for emphasis and then tried to cover her embarrassment at the undeserved sympathy by looking down and smiling at the children. They stared back, wide-eyed and still shy.

'This is Max.' Claire smiled. She turned her head. 'And this is Brenna.'

They were so impossibly *cute*. Small faces with perfect features and she could see now that their eyes were as blue as their grandmother's and their father's. She wondered if the hair beneath the animal hats would be glossy and black and so soft to run your fingers through it, just like Josh's. Or had they inherited their mother's blondeness?

Josh's children. Josh and Rebecca's children. Living proof that he'd gone back to his wife's bed after his marriage was supposedly over, leaving him morally available to Megan.

Maybe something of how hard this was showed in her face.

'Up,' Brenna demanded, dropping her grandmother's hand to hold both arms in the air. 'Up, Nan. Pick me *up*.'

Claire had to let go of Max's hand to pick Brenna up. Max immediately toddled off, at some speed, towards the waves. Crash loped after him.

'*Max*. Come back. We have to go home now. It's starting to rain.'

It *was* starting to rain. Big, fat, icy drops of water began pelting the small group on the beach.

Claire tried to put Brenna down to run after Max but the little girl shrieked a protest. Crash had dropped his lump of wood and was circling Max, who looked determined to get closer to the wild surf.

'I'll get him.' Megan dropped her shoulder bag and took off.

It took only seconds to reach the toddler but the burst of energy it took was enough to make Megan feel faint. She really wasn't fine at all, was she?

It was just as well that Max's little legs had also exhausted their energy reserves. He grinned at Megan. 'Puddle?' he asked hopefully.

Oh, help…he was totally irresistible with that crooked little smile and the hopeful expression on his face.

'Not today, sweetheart.' She scooped up the toddler and held him in her arms. 'It's not sunny enough, is it?'

Her steps almost faltered as she carried the child back to Claire. She was holding Josh's son. The closest she had ever come to holding the child she could have had herself. The shape of the soft little body cuddling into her was delicious. When Max wrapped his arms around her neck to hang on tighter, Megan felt a flash of pain in her chest, as if her heart was cracking. An old scar, perhaps, being torn open?

Thank goodness it was raining. If any tears escaped, at least nobody would know except her. All she wanted was to grab her bag and escape the moment she got back to Claire, but how could she leave her now? The rain was coming down harder and she had to get two small children and a very large dog off the beach and—presumably— into a car. Or was Josh now living this close to Penhally beach? To her cottage?

'The car's not far,' Claire said. 'Just down the road a bit.' She put Brenna down and took a leash from her coat pocket, which she clipped to Crash's collar. Holding the lead with one hand, she held out her other hand to Brenna. 'Can you walk now, pet?'

'No-o-o. Up.'

Relief that Josh wasn't going to turn out to be a close neighbour made Megan take a deep breath.

'Let me help,' she said. 'You're getting wet and you've got a bit of a handful here.'

'Don't I know it?' Claire picked Brenna up, managing to keep hold of the leash. 'And there I was thinking that it would make my day easy if I gave them all a quick run on the beach before we did our messages in the village. I don't know where these tots get their energy from.'

Megan had to hide a smile as she found herself struggling to keep up with Claire on the way back to the car. Limitless energy was clearly an O'Hara trait.

Not that she could leave Josh's mother to cope alone once they reached the car either. The wind had picked up and was threatening to blow the heavy doors closed and it was a mission to strap two wriggling toddlers into their car seats and then shove a folder double stroller out of the way to make room for a big dog to jump into the back hatch of the station wagon.

Finally, everything seemed to be sorted but as Claire reached up to pull the hatch down, she suddenly stopped. She closed her eyes and bent her head, her breath escaping in almost a groan.

'Are you all right?'

'Oh, I'm fine, I am. Just need to catch my wind.'

But Megan could feel a prickle of awareness. One that she'd learned never to ignore.

'Sit down for a minute,' she said. 'Here…' She pushed the stroller further back and guided Claire to sit on the edge of the car floor. Crash shuffled sideways to make room. The car was pointed into the wind and with the hatch cover still up they were fairly well protected from the weather. 'You are a bit short of puff, aren't you?'

'It's the cold, that's all.'

But Claire was virtually gasping for air. She started loosening the woollen scarf around her neck but abandoned the action to start rubbing the top of her left arm through her coat sleeve.

'Have you got any pain in your chest?' Megan asked.

Claire shook her head. 'It just gets…tight…that's all. In the cold…and…if I hurry.'

'But your arm hurts?'

'Only an ache… It's nothing… Goes away…'

Except it didn't seem to be going away this time. And Claire's face looked grey. Even as Megan watched with mounting alarm, beads of perspiration appeared beneath the edge of the woollen hat.

'Go.' A small voice came over the top of the back seat. 'Go, Nan. Go-o-o…' The plea trailed to a miserable sound. Beside Max, Brenna began to cry.

Claire tried to stand up but had barely begun moving before she collapsed backwards.

'I don't…I don't feel very well…' She tugged harder at her scarf and it came away and rippled to the ground.

'Do you have any history of heart problems?' Megan asked. 'Do you carry spray for angina or anything?'

'No…I'm fine…' Claire's face was crumpling. She looked terribly afraid. 'I *have* to be,' she whispered.

Megan had stripped off her gloves and was feeling for Claire's pulse. The rapid, uneven beat made it very clear what had to be done. She reached for her shoulder bag to find her mobile phone.

'I'm calling an ambulance,' she told Claire calmly. 'You need medical attention.'

'No…I'll be fine… Just give me…a minute…'

But the emergency services had answered Megan's call with commendable swiftness and she was already describing their location.

'Cardiac chest pain,' she told the dispatcher. 'Radiating to the left arm. Arrhythmia.'

'You're a doctor?' the dispatcher queried.

'Yes.'

'An ambulance is on its way. Are you able to stay with the patient?'

In case of a cardiac arrest?

'Of course.'

Megan made Claire as comfortable as she could while they waited for the ambulance. She took off her own coat to provide the older woman with some extra warmth. Picking up the scarf, she saw why it had been difficult for Clair to loosen. It had become caught on a necklace chain, which had broken.

Not that she pointed that out to Claire but, to prevent a possible treasure being lost, she put the chain into her own coat pocket, leaving the scarf in the back of the car. Her actions were brisk and organised but automatic because she was busy providing as much reassurance as she could, knowing that any stress could make this much worse. If Claire was, as she suspected, having a heart attack, then anxiety could tip the balance and stop her heart completely.

Would she have the strength herself to keep up CPR until an ambulance arrived?

Thank goodness she didn't need to find out. The ambulance arrived only minutes later and the crew had Claire on a stretcher and attached to a monitor within a very short time. She had an oxygen mask on by the time the rhythm settled on the screen of the life pack and a paramedic was preparing to insert an IV line.

'Marked ST elevation,' her crew partner noted. 'Looks like an infarct all right.'

'Are you on any medication?' the paramedic asked

Claire. 'Are you allergic to anything that you know of? Have you had any aspirin today?'

Claire was shaking her head in response to all the questions. Things were happening too fast for her to find any words. The children in the car were both crying loudly now but Megan was still holding Claire's hand.

'It's going to be fine,' she reassured Claire yet again. 'These people are going to look after you and make sure you get checked out properly at hospital.' She turned to one of the crew members. 'Claire's son is Josh O'Hara at St Piran's. He may well be on duty at the moment so you might like to let him know in advance who you're bringing in.'

'Will do.'

Megan tried to let go of Claire's hand but the grip tightened. She leaned closer to hear the words that were being muffled by the oxygen mask.

'But who's going to…look after the children?'

Megan felt a cold chill run down her spine. No. She couldn't offer to do that. It would be too hard. The scars were still too fresh. Best not to go near anything that might pick at them. Her life was taking a new direction now. Having it derailed would be a disaster.

The paramedic was busy with her other hand. 'Sharp scratch coming, Mrs O'Hara.' She slid a cannula into a vein. 'There. All done.'

Claire lifted the hand that Megan was still holding, trying to pull the oxygen mask away from her face. 'I can't do this…the children…'

Her partner was leaning over Megan. 'Chew up this aspirin for me,' he instructed Claire. 'I'll give you a sip of water to wash it down.'

Megan was in the way. She tried to pull her hand free but Claire's grip tightened.

'Please…' Claire's face looked alarmingly grey. Getting

stressed was making her condition rapidly worse. 'Can't you help?'

'Yeah…' The paramedic gave Claire a very direct glance. 'Can you drive?'

'Yes, but—'

'You could follow behind the ambulance, then. I'm sure there'd be someone else to look after Doc O'Hara's kids once you got there.'

Claire was nodding. 'Please, Megan…'

'Otherwise we'll have to bring them in the ambulance. Or wait for back-up.' The paramedic was sounding impatient now. 'And we really need to get going.' The look he gave Megan was a direct warning. Hold this process up any further and if anything goes wrong between here and the emergency department of St Piran's, she would have contributed.

Megan was caught. She couldn't walk away. There were two crew members in the ambulance and one of them had to drive. If the other had to care for two toddlers, there would be nobody left to care for Claire. And she could get worse. Go into a cardiac arrest, even.

Her nod was jerky. 'I'll do it,' she said tightly. 'Are the keys in the car?'

'Yes…oh…*thank* you, lovie.' Claire finally let go of her hand but her eyes filled and tears rolled down her cheeks.

Megan closed her eyes for a heartbeat. There was no help for this, so all she could was do her best to cope with it. At least she had a kind of advantage here. She knew there was a high likelihood that she would have to see Josh and she would have a few minutes to at least try and prepare herself emotionally for that.

No doubt Josh would prefer to avoid this encounter as much as she would. And he probably wouldn't have the luxury of any warning.

Megan opened her eyes and smiled at Claire. 'Try not to worry,' she told her. 'I'll be right behind the ambulance. I won't let anything happen to the children. You'll see them again very soon, I promise.'

The back door of the ambulance slammed behind her after Megan had climbed out.

The vehicle was pulling out onto the road as Megan checked the fastenings on the car seats, fastened her own safety belt and started the car, surprised to see how shaky her hands were.

The beacons on the ambulance were flashing and the siren began to wail as the vehicle picked up speed. Megan wasn't going to try and keep up with it. Not on a wet road when she was feeling shaky. Certainly not with two precious children in the car.

She didn't need to follow that closely anyway.

The route to St Piran's was written on her heart, like everything else about this place.

CHAPTER TWO

'INCOMING, DR O'HARA.' The nurse's voice came from just behind Josh's shoulder as he scrolled through the images on the computer screen.

He grunted an acknowledgement, still focused on the screen. Surely something had shown up on the MRI of his earlier patient to explain her acute neurological symptoms?

'Status two.' The nurse sounded oddly nervous but, then, she was new and had only just learned that flirting with him was likely to earn disfavour. 'Sixty-year-old woman who looks like she's having an infarct.'

'Put her straight into Resus, then. Is Ben around?'

'Yes…but…'

The back of Josh's neck prickled as he turned his head. 'But what?'

'The patient is your mother, Dr O'Hara.'

The prickle ran down the entire length of his spine now, turning icy cold. Josh was on his feet and moving before he gave the action any conscious thought.

'How far away?'

'ETA five minutes. They're coming from Penhally.'

They? Were the children in the ambulance as well? This couldn't be happening. Not now, when his life was exactly the way it was supposed to be. The children, the house, his job—none of it would have been possible without his mother's help.

An infarct? Claire O'Hara had never had a day's illness in her life. She'd never smoked. She was as slim now as she'd been in her twenties. Her blood pressure was fine. She had energy to burn.

Or did she? Had she been pushed too far by him taking up the amazing offer of her helping him to raise the twins?

If this was yet another disaster in his life, could the blame be laid, yet again, at *his* feet?

Ben Carter, another emergency medicine consultant at St Piran's, was already in the resuscitation area. The defibrillator was being tested. A twelve-lead ECG machine was standing by. He glanced up and saw Josh.

'Don't panic,' he said quietly. 'We don't know exactly what we're dealing with yet.'

'Status two infarct,' Josh snapped. 'Unstable. What the hell happened? Have you had any details? Where was she? Did she...*arrest* somewhere?'

'No. That much I do know. She's status two because she's throwing off a few ectopics. She's on oxygen and she's had aspirin, GTN and morphine. Her breathing's improving.'

'Improving? My God, how bad *was* it?'

'Josh...' Ben stepped closer to put a hand on his colleague's arm. 'I've got this, OK? It'll be good for Claire if you're here but you need to stay calm.'

'What about the children? Were they with her?'

'I don't know.' Ben was looking past Josh now. Towards the double doors sliding open to admit a stretcher and ambulance crew. A nurse was pointing them towards the resus room. He turned to a nurse. 'Has the cardiology registrar been paged?'

'Forget the registrar,' Josh said. 'Get Anna Davenport down here. This is my *mother*, for God's sake.'

Claire looked terrified as she was wheeled into the resus room.

'Josh…' she gasped, reaching out a hand. 'Thank heavens you're here.'

'Of course I'm here.' Josh took hold of the hand. He knew he was getting in the way as the ambulance crew transferred Claire to the bed and gave Ben a handover but, for the first time in years, his mother needed *him* instead of the other way round. He kept his eyes on her face as the staff stripped away the clothing from her upper body and started adding extra dots so they could take a more comprehensive recording of the electrical activity in her heart. Ben was drawing off bloods for urgent analysis.

'Let's sit you up a little bit, Mrs O'Hara,' a nurse said, slipping another pillow behind Claire. 'And I'm just switching the oxygen over to this plug on the ceiling so we can get rid of the portable tank. No, don't take your mask off.'

Claire ignored the nurse, pushing the mask clear of her mouth. 'The twins, Josh…they're…'

'Please keep your mask on.' The nurse gently moved Claire's hand. 'It's important that you get some oxygen at the moment.'

'I can hear you.' Josh leaned closer. 'What about the twins?'

'They're fine.' The paramedic was loading the portable oxygen cylinder back onto the stretcher. 'The doctor who called the ambulance for Mrs O'Hara said she'd be bringing them straight here. She can't be far behind us.'

'A doctor?' Josh was confused. 'Was she at the medical centre?' Getting treatment, even, for some condition she'd never let him know she had?

'No. She was at the beach. With the children and a big dog.'

'Crash. Oh, no…' The woman coming swiftly into the resus room sounded as though she was starting a conversation with an old friend. 'What's he been up to now, Claire?' She was smiling down at her patient. 'More importantly, what on earth have you been up to?'

The smile was reassuring but Josh could see the concern in the face of the head of the cardiology department. Concern that increased as a technician handed her the sheet of paper from the twelve-lead ECG machine. Ben was also reading the ECG over her shoulder.

'What is it?' Josh forgot his confusion about a doctor being on scene when Claire had become ill. He hadn't missed the significant glance passing between Anna and Ben.

'Left anterior,' Anna said calmly. 'ST elevation of up to three millimetres. Have we got anything back on the bloods yet? Cardiac enzymes? TNT?'

Josh had to take a deep breath as he heard Ben relay the earliest results. He didn't want to let Claire know how serious this could be. An infarct that knocked out part of the left ventricle was more likely to have serious consequences. Every minute counted now so that they could save as much cardiac function as possible.

Anna had turned to Claire. 'You're having a heart attack, Claire,' she said gently. 'But there are things we can do to minimise the damage it might be doing to your heart. I'm going to take you up to the catheter laboratory and we can see exactly where the blockage is in your coronary arteries. We'll clear it if we can and might put something called a stent in to keep the artery open.'

'You're going to…operate on me?' Claire's face was as white as the pillow behind her.

'Not exactly. You'll be awake. We put a tiny tube inside an artery and that goes into your heart. It's very clever.'

'And Anna's very good at it,' Ben put in. 'You'll be in the best hands, Claire.'

'We'll give you a sedative,' Anna added. 'You'll be awake but it won't hurt and we won't let you get too anxious.'

'No.' Claire shook her head. She tried to peer past the medical team crowded around her bed. 'I can't go. Not yet. She said I'd see the children again. Very soon.'

'*Who* said?' Josh could feel the tension of this whole situation spiralling upwards. They couldn't let Claire get any more upset because there was still a definite risk of her rhythm degenerating into a fatal arrhythmia. Who had his children? Where were they?

'She does.' Claire's lips were trembling. 'The doctor.'

'*What* doctor?'

'The one who…looked after them…when they were born.'

'Megan Phillips? But that's impossible. She's in Africa.'

'Not any more.'

Josh froze as he heard the voice coming from behind Ben and Anna on the other side of the bed. Everybody turned to see who was at the entrance to the room. Holding the handles of the double stroller that contained the twins.

'*Daddy.*' Both Max and Brenna's faces lit up with smiles as they spotted their father. They held up four little arms.

But Josh didn't even see the plea. His gaze was locked on the woman behind the stroller.

Oh, my God…

Megan.

For just a heartbeat, the world stood absolutely still.

Nothing else mattered.

That his mother was dangerously unwell. That he had two tiny, defenceless children calling for him. That he was the head of a department of St Piran's Hospital that was gaining widespread recognition as a centre of excellence in emergency medicine.

None of those things could even exist in the space Josh was sucked into for just a second.

A space of such intensity, it pulled the oxygen from the air around him and made it feel impossible for him to breathe.

The space he'd been in on that New Year's Eve party when he'd met Megan properly for the first time. When he'd sensed the power of truly falling in love. The power that had held his mother captive and broken her life.

He'd been there again in the trauma of that emergency when it had looked as though Megan might die. When he'd sensed the power of what a parent's love for a child could be as well, and had vowed never to let that power control him either.

During the course of that one, incredible night when he'd shared her bed for only the second time—just before he'd found out he was going to become a father.

On the day he'd had to do the hardest thing in his life, and tell her it was all over.

In that moment when he'd had to beg her to do her best to save the lives of Rebecca's and his children.

Daddy.

The echo of the word penetrated the space. Grounded Josh instantly. He was where he needed to be. Living his life the way it had to be lived.

The way he *wanted* to live it.

Nothing could be allowed to change that. Somehow, he had to resist the incredible pull that that space could exert. It felt like his life was depending on it. It was almost ironic to have his mother in the same room. The example he'd grown up with of the damage that that kind of love could inflict.

Stepping towards the newcomers, Josh was aware of the tension around him. The kind that came from a collective holding of breath, waiting to see what was going to happen.

Their story was hardly a secret, was it? Not that Anna or Ben knew that he'd slept with Megan while he'd still been married. While his wife had been in the early stages of pregnancy with the twins. But everybody knew their early history by now. And if anybody had missed the way they'd been drawn back to each other when he'd first come to St Piran's, the hospital grapevine would have filled them in. Maybe everybody *did* know about that night in the on-call room.

Oh…Lord…Tash knew everything. How much did his mother know?

Josh pulled the barriers of his professional image around him like a force field.

'Megan… What a stroke of luck you were there for my mother when she got sick. And thank you so much for taking care of my children.'

He stooped to release the safety straps around the twins. Not that he squatted down fast enough to miss the change of expression on Megan's face. Had she been holding her breath like everyone else in here? Hurt by his deliberate focus on his own family? Himself?

He hadn't even asked her how she was despite some alarm bell ringing faintly in the back of his head. As he stood up, with a twin under each arm, he couldn't help taking another look at her. That warning bell hadn't been a false alarm. She looked…terrible.

So thin. So pale. Something was wrong. Her emerald-green eyes looked dull enough to be frightening.

Except that Josh had no right to have an emotional stake in Megan's wellbeing any more.

And even if he did, this wasn't the time. Or place.

He held her gaze for the briefest moment, however. He couldn't help it. He knew his concern would be transparent but that didn't matter either. He tried to send a silent message.

We'll talk. Soon.

'The babies…' Claire's voice wobbled. 'Let me give them a kiss before I have to go.'

Megan's heart was hammering in her chest.

How ironic would it be if she provided another cardiac emergency for Josh to deal with?

What had she expected to happen here? A moment of pure fantasy where the existence of anyone else—including his mother and children and colleagues—simply evaporated? And Josh's face changing as though he was witnessing a miracle? That he would come towards her in slow motion and sweep her into his arms? Kiss her again just like he had that last time…?

Maybe some tiny, secret part of her had hoped exactly that.

It didn't mean that she'd wanted it to happen, though. Or that she could have coped with going down that track. It was the last thing she wanted when she'd fought so hard to find her new direction. A completely different track.

Josh had done exactly the right thing. Been professional. Cold, almost. But then, when she'd been trying to process that, feeling dizzy and bewildered, he'd looked at her again. *Really* looked at her. And she'd known that this wasn't it. This moment couldn't count as their first meeting after a long absence.

That had been postponed due to unforeseen circumstances.

Circumstances that were slightly chaotic right now, as staff bustled around, taking care of Claire and preparing to move her to the catheter laboratory even as Josh gave her the chance to kiss and cuddle each of the children. Max grabbed one of the wires attaching an electrode to the cardiac monitor and pulled it free, which set off an alarm. The sound frightened Brenna, who clung to her father and had to be persuaded to give her grandmother a quick kiss.

Meanwhile, Megan simply stood there, clutching the handles of the stroller. She could hardly walk out, could she? Not when these people were old friends. How rude would it seem to Ben and Anna if she just left?

Besides, she felt frozen. Watching Josh. Seeing the easy way he held his small children and talked to them. Knowing that his light tone and smile was an act. That the way those lines had deepened around his eyes advertised how much stress he was under right now.

And…he looked as gorgeous as he ever had. His palpable charm hadn't changed either and it was being directed towards the twins right now and they looked as if they were being won over by that lazy smile as easily as she always had. He must have raked his fingers through his hair a fair few times to get it looking so rumpled, and to her horror Megan could feel the urge to smooth it with her own hands. To push that wayward lock back from his forehead and cup his face with both her hands so that she could really look and discover every tiny change that time had wrought.

She gripped the moulded plastic handles of the stroller

more tightly. Forced herself to smile in response to Ben's greeting.

'We'll have to catch up. I'd love to hear about Africa. You here for a while?'

No. She needed to escape as fast as she could.

'I...I'm not sure yet.'

Ben's pager sounded and he excused himself hurriedly. Megan wished she had one clipped to her own belt. A reason to disappear.

But she couldn't leave quite yet. Anna needed to know that her dog was locked in the back of Claire's car out in the car park and the cardiac surgeon had been busy on the phone for the last few minutes, juggling her responsibilities so that she could join the cardiologists and be involved in this emergency angioplasty case.

Anna finished her call and nodded at someone. A loud clicking noise announced that they had disengaged the brake on Claire's bed. It was time to move.

'You coming up with us, Josh?' Anna queried. 'Not that you can stay in the cath lab, of course, but you're welcome to come in while we set up.'

Ben stuck his head back into the room.

'You're covered here, mate. Give me a call later and we'll sort out what happens tomorrow.' He smiled at Claire. 'I'll come up and see you in the ward later. You'll be feeling a lot better by then.'

Josh stood there, holding a twin on each hip.

Megan stood there, holding the handles of the empty stroller.

As Ben vanished, Josh's gaze shifted to settle on Megan. So did Anna's.

The whole room seemed to pause and the atmosphere was electric. Josh couldn't take the twins with him to go with his mother. Everybody was clearly waiting for her to make an offer to help out.

It was too much to ask. Way too much. Josh had plenty of staff here, didn't he? Any number of nurses who would probably fight for the chance to earn his appreciation by babysitting.

But Josh was looking at her and it was like that graze of a glance he'd given her when he'd picked the twins up. The one that recognised *her*.

Not as a separate person.

As part of what they had once been. Together.

With a huge effort Megan broke the eye contact as she tried to marshal the wild tumble of thoughts and emotions in her head. She looked at Anna.

'I've got Crash outside in Claire's car,' she said. 'What would you like me to do with him?'

'Oh…help…' Anna caught her bottom lip with her teeth.

'Sorry, love.' The beeping of the monitor recording Claire's heart rate increased its tempo noticeably. 'It's my fault. I took him to the big beach for a run with the twins and—'

'It's OK.' Anna's gaze flicked to the monitor. 'Don't you worry about anything, Claire. I can sort this. Oh, help…if only Luke hadn't left already. I could have called him to take Crash *and* the twins home.'

'Did Luke decide to go, then?'

Josh had moved towards Megan. He put Max down and began fitting Brenna back into the stroller. Max turned around and headed back towards Claire's bed.

'Not so fast, cowboy.' Anna scooped the toddler up and came towards the stroller as well. She was close to Megan again, but her gaze was on Josh. 'Yes,' she told him. 'He'll be halfway to New Zealand by now.'

Megan blinked. New Zealand? This whole situation was starting to feel surreal. Anna noticed her expression.

'Luke's father has had a stroke. It doesn't sound too bad but his mother is freaking out completely. When he checked flights late last night, he found he could get a ticket for a dawn flight leaving Heathrow. He drove to London at one a.m.'

'Of course he wants to support his mother. I'll think of something else.' But the desperate note in Josh's voice was so uncharacteristic it told Megan just how tightly he was hanging on here. Did he feel like his world was collapsing around him?

His mother was seriously ill.

His ex-lover had appeared in his life again.

He had a child-care issue on his hands.

Who could he turn to?

Another silence. Megan couldn't ignore the trouble Josh was in here.

Just because he'd broken her heart…because they could never be together…it didn't mean that she had to stop caring, did it?

Even if it did, it didn't mean that she was capable of stopping.

'I can look after them,' she said quietly. 'All of them.'

Both Josh and Anna's faces lightened instantly.

'I couldn't ask you—'

'Would you really?' Anna spoke over Josh's exclamation.

'I can't take them home, though,' Megan added. 'My cottage is a bit…uninhabitable at the moment.'

'Take them to my place,' Anna suggested. 'The key's just upstairs in my office. You know where our cottage is, don't you?'

'Yes. You had your wedding on the beach just down the hill.'

Josh was shaking his head. 'It would be better to take the twins home. My keys are right here. And they might be happier if they have their own stuff around.'

Meaning that they might not want to be with her? A complete stranger?

The look Josh gave her was apologetic. As if he was reading her mind.

'I mean, there's all their toys. And the food they like. And their PJs and beds if things don't…'

The unspoken warning that things might not go as well as expected was enough to make them all suddenly anxious to get going.

'Fine.' Megan nodded. 'I'll take them home to your place, Josh. Only…'

He turned his head, already moving to go and find his house keys.

'Only I don't know where you live.'

'Anna can fill you in.' Josh kept going.

Anna smiled. 'That's easy. Josh bought the Gallaghers' farm, next door to my place. On the St Piran side. Crash has a basket on the veranda. He won't wander—it's always been his second home.'

Josh was back, thrusting a set of keys into Megan's hand.

'Thank you *so* much.' Stooping swiftly, he touched the twins' heads. 'Be good for Megan,' he told them. 'I'll be home soon.'

Claire's bed was moving past them now, with most of the staff disappearing as well. Any moment now and Megan would find herself alone with Josh's children and the keys to his house in her hand.

How surreal this all was had just gone off the Richter

scale. Was she the only person who found this unbelievably bizarre?

No. Claire was watching Megan as her bed was manoeuvred through the door of the resus room. There was concern in her face. And sympathy? Something else as well.

Maybe a message. One that said: *You can do this. We all know how strong you are.*

It wasn't true. Nobody around here knew how strong she had become over the last two years. Maybe if she'd had that kind of strength way back, none of this would have happened, but at least she had it now.

She *could* do this.

And if she succeeded, it would prove to everyone just how far she had moved on with her life.

She could prove it to Josh.

She could prove it to herself?

CHAPTER THREE

How WEIRD WAS this?

To be going home to his children, knowing that Megan Phillips was there. Looking after Max and Brenna, like a stand-in mother.

In his house.

Like a stand-in wife?

No.

Josh wasn't going into that space. The idea of he and Megan being together had died a long, long time ago.

The moment he'd told her that Rebecca was pregnant.

Parking his car next to where the family wagon was, Josh walked towards the rambling, old farmhouse that looked out over the ocean. It was far too dark and drizzly to see anything, especially in the welcoming glow of the house lights, but he could hear the sea and the wash of waves was a familiar, comforting pulse of sound.

Crash was on the veranda. Watching. Ready to protect his second home from any intruder. His tail began waving as soon as Josh climbed the steps, however, and a damp nose nudged his hand in welcome.

He let the big dog into the house with him as he entered.

Josh knew he needed some moral support. He just didn't realise how much until he walked inside and could smell hot food and hear the sound of voices and could feel...

Could feel Megan's presence in his house. Even before he entered the big, open-plan living area where the children were snuggled up on the couch on either side of Megan, listening to a story.

Josh had to pause for a moment. To listen to the soft lilt of Megan's voice. To soak in the tilt of her head and the way his children were tucked into the crooks of her arms as if it was the most familiar, and loved, place in the world for them.

Dear Lord…if things had been different…it could have been *their* son listening to Megan reading that story. Getting sleepy and needing to be tucked up in bed. Leaving his parents to have a quiet evening together bathed in that flickering firelight.

That soul-deep yearning had been successfully buried for years now.

But it hadn't gone away, had it?

Perhaps it was fortunate that Crash didn't get stopped in his tracks and mesmerised the way Josh had been. The dog padded far enough into the room to interrupt the story.

'*Cash.*' Max wriggled free of Megan's arm and slid down from the couch, running to throw his arms around the big animal.

'*Daddy.*' Brenna also wriggled free and made straight for Josh, who was glad of the need to move and pick his daughter up. He had to give her a good cuddle and kiss as well and that covered a few more awkward seconds. And when he looked up, Megan's gaze was on Crash.

'Sorry,' she said. 'I didn't realise he was allowed inside. I shouldn't have left him out in the cold like that.'

'That's his spot,' Josh assured her. 'It means Anna can drop him off or collect him without worrying about disturbing us.'

Us.

God…it sounded as if he was including Megan.

'She'll be here to pick him up soon,' he added hurriedly. 'She had a few things to catch up on and wanted to check on Mum again.'

'How is she? Did James get to see her in the end?'

Josh nodded. 'Yes. He agrees that bypass surgery isn't necessary. Anna put in four stents and everything's looking great. The damage should be minimal and Mum will be able to come home in a day or two.'

'That's wonderful.'

'Yes. I'm sorry it all took so long, though.'

'No worries. You said it might.'

He hadn't thought it would take this long, though. That phone call to update Megan on progress and fill her in on what the children might need had been hours ago.

'Thank you so much,' he said now. 'I don't know how we would have managed it you hadn't been there.'

Megan turned her head away. 'I'm sure you would have managed just fine.'

Of course they would have.

Just like Josh had managed when Megan had finally walked out of his life, physically, months after her emotional departure.

Just when he'd needed her most.

'When did you get back from Africa?'

'Today.' Megan turned back, a wry smile shaping her mouth.

Welcome home.

The words hung there, unspoken.

Josh cleared his throat. 'Max, don't let Crash lick your face, mate. Come on…it's high time you two were in bed.'

Megan closed the story book and put it on the table beside the couch. 'I'll leave you to it.'

Josh had scooped up Max as well. He had to peer over two small heads to catch Megan's gaze.

'Couldn't you stay for a few more minutes...?' He had barely had the chance to thank her properly, let alone talk about anything other than today's drama. He should let her leave but... His mouth seemed to be moving of its own accord. Producing words that weren't getting filtered through any of the usual channels.

'For a coffee or something?' he was saying. 'To... I don't know... I don't feel like we've even said hello yet.'

A long pause this time, during which Megan got slowly to her feet.

Was it his imagination or did she close her eyes and dip her head a fraction, almost as if she was praying for strength?

Whatever it was, it lasted only a heartbeat and then she spoke very quietly.

'I'll put the kettle on, then.'

Megan was sitting at the kitchen table with a half-empty mug by the time Josh returned.

'Sorry. That took a bit longer than usual. I think they're missing their gran.'

Megan smiled. 'I'm sure she's missing them as well. They're...gorgeous kids, Josh.'

'They are, aren't they?' He tried not to sound too full of pride as he went to the mug on the bench beside the kettle.

'I didn't finish making your coffee.' Megan was watching him. 'I didn't know whether you still took it black or... or if you'd started having sugar or something.'

'Same old,' Josh said lightly. 'Some things never change, do they?'

Their eye contact was fleeting but significant. Things

did change over time. Little things, like how you had your coffee. Big things, like how you lived your life.

Megan was looking around as if she was trying to find a way of changing the subject.

'This place is wonderful. I'd never have thought of you living on a farm, though.'

Did she think of him, then? Josh found it unexpectedly hard to take his next breath. His chest felt tight with some nameless emotion. Relief? *Hope*? He fought to shake it off.

'It's not a farm any more. Doug Gallagher died suddenly eighteen months ago and June decided to sell up.' He poured boiling water into his mug. 'The neighbours on the other side wanted the land but not the house so she subdivided. We've only got about three acres or so around the house. More like a big garden than a farm.'

'Must be perfect for the kids with all this space and the beach just across the road.'

'Seems to work well.' Josh sat down at the end of the table, at a right angle to Megan.

It felt too close.

It didn't feel close enough.

He had to close his eyes for a moment. To focus and get through the wave of confusion.

'It is perfect,' he heard himself saying aloud. 'I'm lucky enough to have the perfect life.' Who was he trying to convince here? Megan or himself? 'It's a bit further away from work than the apartment,' he added, 'but that was no place to try and raise children.'

'No.' The mention of the St Piran's townhouse he had shared with Rebecca had chilled the atmosphere, and Megan's tone, noticeably. Or had it been his declaration that he had the perfect life? One that didn't contain her? Maybe he'd gone too far in erecting protective boundaries.

'I needed to get away, anyway,' Josh added quietly. 'To make a fresh start.'

Megan seemed to be finding the colour of her remaining coffee fascinating. 'As you do,' she murmured.

The tiny silence couldn't be allowed to continue because anything could have taken root and flourished enough to get spoken aloud. Things like…

I've missed you. So, so much.

It would be much safer to stick to less personal topics but there was something personal that Josh couldn't ignore any longer.

'Are you OK, Megan?' Oh, help…the query sounded far too intimate. Dangerous territory. He had to back off fast. 'Physically, I mean?'

He couldn't read the glance he received in response. Women were so good at that. Making you feel like you couldn't have stuffed your foot any further into your mouth if you'd tried.

'I'm getting over a rather nasty bout of dengue fever. Second one in a six-month period.'

'Sounds horrible.'

'It's certainly not pleasant. I'm having a bit more trouble getting my energy level back this time. And I'm still getting a bit of joint pain.'

Josh didn't like that. It made him feel like he did when one of the twins got sick. Or fell over and skinned a knee. The feeling of needing to make it better.

'Do you need anything? Anti-inflammatories or…multivitamins or something?'

Megan shook her head. 'I'm fine, Josh. I just need a bit of time, that's all.' She glanced up and her face was amused. 'I'm a doctor, remember? I can look after myself.'

The amusement made her face more alive. Brought a

hint to her eyes of the kind of sparkle they used to have. Josh wanted to keep it there.

'Doctors make the world's worst patients,' he reminded her with mock severity. 'Sometimes they have to be told exactly what they should be doing.'

To his disappointment, the amusement faded from Megan's eyes and she sighed. 'I *have* been told,' she said sadly. 'That's the only reason I left Africa.'

'The *only* reason?' The question popped out before Josh could stop it and it earned him another one of those inscrutable looks.

'I need to sort my cottage out. It's turned into a bit of a mess.'

How ridiculous was it to feel disappointed? What had he expected? That Megan would say she'd come back because she'd wanted to see *him*? He wouldn't have wanted that, anyway.

Would he?

A wave of something like confusion made Josh's next query tentative. 'Are you planning to live in it again?'

'No.' The head shake was decisive. 'But renting it out hasn't worked out so well. I might have to sell up.'

And then she'd have no ties to Penhally left at all. That was a good thing.

Wasn't it?

'Where will you go?' Josh could feel himself frowning. 'Back to Africa?'

'I can't. Not if I stay with MSF, at least.'

'Why not?'

'I've got immunity to two types of dengue fever now. I'm also female and Caucasian. It puts me in a high-risk bracket to get the haemorrhagic form of dengue and that can be fatal. It's not a risk that MSF is prepared to let their medical staff take.'

Josh felt his gut tighten. 'Surely it's not a risk *you'd* be prepared to take either?'

Megan's silence spoke volumes. She wanted to go back, that much was crystal clear.

Why? What would make anyone want to risk their lives like that? Something was nagging at the back of Josh's mind. A cryptic conversation he'd had with Tash a while back. Not that they ever talked about Megan these days— he'd made sure it had been a no-go subject ever since the wedding—but she'd said something about how happy Megan was finally. And she'd had a smile that suggested...

'Is there someone in Africa?' Josh heard himself ask. 'Someone...special?'

'You could say that.' Megan nodded and she had the same sort of smile on her face he remembered Tash having. A...loving kind of smile.

Josh had to look away. He gulped down a mouthful of coffee and tried to think of something...*anything*...to change the subject.

He didn't want to hear about the new love of Megan's life.

It was good that she was happy.

It wasn't as if either of them would ever consider being together. Not now.

Josh had to regain control of what was happening here. Of his life. He'd almost lost it today, what with his mother's health scare.

With seeing Megan again.

But the shock was wearing off. Those odd frissons of confusion were fading. Knowing that Megan had moved on to someone else should be all he needed to put things back into perspective.

To help him remember what it had been like two years ago.

There was anger in the mix, deep down, wasn't there?

Anger that Megan had not believed him when he'd said that his marriage was truly over before he'd gone to her bed. That sleeping with Rebecca that one, last time had been nothing more than a moment of weakness. Of feeling guilty and sorry for the woman who'd made the mistake of marrying him.

That anger had helped a lot in those months of Rebecca's pregnancy when he had been struggling with having had to end things with Megan before they could even get started properly.

And then his world had collapsed around him. Rebecca had died and he'd been left with two tiny, fragile babies and he'd been facing the impossible.

And what had Megan done?

Walked out and gone to the other side of the world.

She hadn't even gone to the funeral.

No. Josh couldn't think of a way to change the subject. All he could do was sit there and stare at Megan.

She had found someone *else*?

Thank God Anna chose that moment to arrive at Josh's house to collect Crash.

They could both hear the front door opening and closing again. And Anna's cheerful call.

'It's only me. Anyone downstairs?'

Even though she was avoiding eye contact, Megan could feel the way Josh had been staring at her. As though he was shocked that she could have moved on with her life?

What the hell had he expected her to do? Sit and watch him raise Rebecca's children and pine for what might have been?

'In the kitchen, Anna.' Megan grabbed her coffee mug and pushed her chair back. She should have left Josh's house long ago. She shouldn't have come in the first place. Right now, she couldn't remember what it was she'd thought she was going to prove by doing so.

Whatever it had been, it felt like she had failed.

When she'd seen him gather Brenna into his arms and hold her like that. Pressing a kiss onto her soft, dark curls... The shaft of pain had felt like the knife that was permanently lodged in her heart had been twisted violently.

Their son had never known his father. Never had a cuddle or been kissed so lovingly. Stephen had never had a chance.

She and Josh had never had a chance.

And it was so...*unfair.*

'Gosh...' Anna breezed into the kitchen. 'It's raining cats and dogs out there now. Thanks for letting Crash inside.' She was grinning. 'Not that it's going to be easy dragging him away from your nice fire to go back to our cold cottage.'

'Want some coffee?' Josh sounded brusque. 'The kettle's still pretty hot.'

'No... My slow cooker is calling. I threw the makings of a beef stew in there this morning and it should be extremely well cooked by now.'

'It's been a long day,' Josh agreed. 'Did you get the chance to check on Mum again?'

'Of course.' Anna's smile was relaxed. 'She's fine, Josh. No pain and her rhythm's back to normal. I told her she's going to end up being in far better health from now on. Give her a week or two and she won't know herself. Oh, and I saw Ben in the car park. He said to tell you that ED's covered for the next couple of days. He's not expecting to see you anywhere near St Piran's unless you're coming in to visit your mum.'

'Thanks. I'll certainly need to be at home tomorrow.

I'll have to sort out some extra child-care arrangements to take the pressure off Mum for a while.'

Megan had already rinsed out her mug but she did it again to avoid turning around and becoming a part of this conversation. Just because she'd stepped into the breach today it didn't mean she wanted to continue spending time with Josh's children.

In fact, she really *didn't* want to spend any more time with them. Or with him.

'I'd better be going,' she said brightly. 'And let you both get on with having your dinners.'

'I can drop you home,' Anna offered.

'No... I'll call a taxi.'

'Don't be daft. It's only a few minutes down the road to your cottage. You'll be waiting ages for a taxi in this weather.'

'I'm not staying at my cottage.'

'Why not?' Josh was frowning. 'Oh...you said it was uninhabitable, didn't you? How bad is it?'

'Pretty bad. Some pipes burst and the place got flooded months ago. The tenants moved out and left all their rubbish behind. There's no power. Probably no water either, except for what's still leaking out of the pipes.'

'Good grief...' Anna looked horrified. 'No wonder you can't stay there. Have you found somewhere in the village? I can drop you there.'

'I...um...haven't found anywhere yet. I was on my way to do that when I met Claire at the beach.'

'So it's my fault you haven't found somewhere to stay.' Josh was pushing his fingers through his hair in a gesture that Megan remembered all too well. 'You can stay here. We've got plenty of room.'

Megan could feel her jaw dropping. Stay under the same roof as Josh for a whole night for the first time in her life?

Wake up and have breakfast with him? And his children? Why was fate throwing this stuff at her? Just how far did she have to go to prove she had moved on from Josh?

'Don't be silly.' It was Anna who spoke. Not that she could have read any of Megan's thoughts from her expression because she had moved to the door to summon Crash. She turned back to Megan with a smile. 'It's perfect timing. I'll be lonely while Luke's away and our spare room is all set up.' Her smile widened. 'Do you like beef stew?'

'I...ah...' Megan was shaking her head. Anna's cottage was just down the road. Next door to Josh. It was still too close for comfort.

'Just for tonight,' Anna said persuasively. 'You can sort out something else if you want to tomorrow, when it's not dark and raining. You look exhausted, Megan.'

She was. Emotionally as well as physically.

Just for one night? That's all it would need to be, wasn't it? She might even decide to sell up and be leaving all of this behind her by tomorrow.

'And it'll give us a chance to catch up.' Anna was looking wistful now. 'I've missed having you around, Megan.'

The persuasion was working. Megan felt far too weary to make any further protest. And she would enjoy Anna's company. The company of female friends was something she had missed badly after leaving here.

'OK,' she agreed. 'Just for tonight. Thanks, Anna.'

'Hooray...' Anna threw her arms around Megan and hugged her. 'It's so good to see you again.' She stepped back, still beaming. 'Isn't it, Josh?'

Megan didn't turn her head to see what reaction Anna's assumption that Josh was happy to see her had provoked but she got an inkling by the curiously raw note in his voice.

'Yes... It is.'

* * *

What else could he have said?

No, it was excruciatingly painful to see Megan again.

He'd thought he had it all finally sorted and now he was feeling like his perfectly ordered world had big cracks in it.

He would have preferred to never have laid eyes on her again.

But he couldn't have said any of those things in front of Megan. And they weren't even true. Not the one about preferring to never see her again, anyway. It might have been easier, certainly, but he would have always wondered where she was. How she was. Who she was with.

In the wake of both women and Crash leaving the house, Josh ransacked the fridge for enough leftovers to make himself a meal. He thought enviously of the hot beef stew Anna and Megan would be eating by now. Or was he more envious of Anna having the opportunity to find out more about Megan than she would ever be prepared to tell him? What would they be talking about?

That new *special* person in Megan's life? The one she was prepared to risk her life for by going back to Africa?

It should be *him*.

The thought came from nowhere and hit Josh like a sledgehammer. It wasn't framed as a regret. Or any kind of desire.

It was just there. A statement of fact. *He* was the person Megan should be with if she was going to be with anyone. Always had been. Always would be.

How could she get past that so easily?

Because it wasn't true for her? Maybe it never had been. She'd found it easy enough to condemn him for sleeping with Rebecca, hadn't she? She'd never shown the slightest sign of forgiving him. Not even when he'd found himself at the most harrowing point of his life as a single father with premature twins.

At least his mother had been there for him. She had provided the glue that had let him stick his shattered life back together. It might present a very different picture from what he had imagined would be his future but...dammit... it was a good life.

Good enough, that was for sure. Better than most people had. He had a brilliant job. A wonderful home. His mother reminded him regularly how lucky they all were. How different it was from the cramped flat in London where she'd tried to raise him and his siblings after his father had finally walked out on them all for good. He was so lucky to have his mum here to help, too. Family. And he had two amazing children who were more important than anything else could ever be.

Including Megan?

Yes. Josh shoved his plateful of food into the microwave and set it to heat.

He'd made that decision long ago. The moment he'd known he was going to become a father. When he'd vowed not to be like his own father. He was well on the way to honouring that vow now. He couldn't—*wouldn't*—let anything undermine that.

Maybe he needed to take a new vow now. Not to be like his own mother. To try again and again in the name of love, only to be hurt beyond anything remotely acceptable. Because it wouldn't only be him who got hurt now, would it? It could be his children. His mother even. And that would turn him into his father again. God...life could be a complicated business sometimes.

A new vow wasn't really needed, was it? He could stick to the original one and he'd been successful so far.

Josh turned away from watching the plate go round and

round inside the microwave. He had time to ring the coronary care unit at St Piran's and check on how his mother was doing. The sooner life got back to normal for them all, the better.

As if to underline the resolution, a faint cry came from upstairs. One of the twins had woken and needed comfort.

Josh left the kitchen.

'I'm coming,' he called. 'It's OK, darling. Daddy's here.'

Where he needed to be. Where he *wanted* to be. You could only live in the present, couldn't you?

You had to trust that the future would turn out all right.

And you had to let go of the past.

CHAPTER FOUR

PALE SUNLIGHT WAS filtering through the curtains in Megan's room when she woke up the next morning from one of the best sleeps she'd had for a very long time.

Perhaps the red wine she had shared with Anna over the meal of beef stew and crusty bread could take the credit. Or maybe it was the cathartic effect of having a heart-to-heart conversation with another woman, including more than a few tears being shed. The lullaby of the sound of surf had probably had a calming influence as well.

Whatever the reason, Megan was astonished by how good she felt as she luxuriated in that boneless relaxation of waking slowly from a very deep sleep, stretching cautiously and revelling in the fact that her joints were not giving even the slightest twinge. And then it occurred to her that it was November in Cornwall and for the sun to be high enough to be coming in her window meant that it had to be—

Good grief…ten a.m.?

Discarding the borrowed nightwear, Megan dressed in yesterday's clothes and hurried out of the room, although she knew Anna must have left for work long ago. Sure enough, there was a note propped up on the kitchen table with a set of keys beside it.

Wanted to let you sleep as long as possible.
Help yourself to breakfast. There's cereal, toast and
eggs around.
I got a ride to work so here are my car keys. You can
drop them in to me later which will give everybody
else a chance to say hi ☺
Love, Anna.
PS—you're more than welcome to stay again tonight.
Your turn to cook?
PPS—enjoy the sun while it lasts!

Crash was nowhere to be seen. Back at day care at the O'Haras'? Thank goodness Anna hadn't asked her to drop him off. Megan didn't think she was ready to see Josh again yet. Maybe she never would be.

He had the perfect life. A job he loved. A fabulous home. Family around him. His mother and…and his *children*.

Megan had none of those things right now.

But…she did have plans, didn't she? She needed to hang onto that and decide what the next step should be.

Mulling over her options while she had a cup of coffee and toast didn't make things any clearer. Washing up her dishes, Megan looked out towards the little bay over the road from the Davenports' cottage. The surf still looked pretty wild but the clouds were white and billowing today, moving fast enough for the sun to make frequent appearances.

Getting a little bit of exercise and a blast of fresh, sea air was irresistible. Megan put her warm coat and gloves on and borrowed one of Anna's woolly hats to keep her hair from driving her crazy.

Gusts of wind strong enough to douse her with salt spray and almost knock her off her feet made it a struggle to walk in one direction on the beach but when Megan reached the end of the bay and turned around, it suddenly felt like she was flying. She held her arms out wide and laughed aloud from the childlike joy of it.

Seagulls were swirling overhead, riding the strong air currents, and they sounded as if they were shrieking from the excitement of it all. Megan didn't shriek but she was still laughing by the time she got back to her starting point and she'd never felt more alive. As if her blood was actually fizzing in her veins. She had to stop for a minute then to catch her breath and she looked up and down the bay, hugging herself with both arms.

She loved it here. So much.

The buffeting in the cold air and the fresh, sticky feel of salt spray she could taste on her lips had done more than restore her zest for life. It seemed to have had a cleansing effect as well. Not that Megan could have said exactly what had been blown away.

Maybe the disappointment of finding the home of her heart virtually derelict.

The backwash of the emotional disturbance that seeing Josh again had caused.

Or maybe doubts about the big decisions she needed to make about her future.

Whatever it was, right now it had gone and Megan was left feeling at peace.

At home.

She couldn't deny the sense of belonging to this little corner of the world. Could she really turn her back and walk away for ever?

It would be an easy way out, that was certain. But would she always miss it? Be haunted, as Charles warned her might happen, by thinking she had left unfinished business behind?

Worse than that, now that she'd seen the cottage, would

she be left thinking she had dishonoured the memory of her grandmother—the woman who'd always been there for her? Who'd taken a frightened four-year-old and guided her towards adulthood with infinite wisdom and warmth?

'What should I do, Gran?'

The only sound in the wake of her plea for advice was the crash of the surf. Even the seagulls were silent for a moment. Megan took a last, deep gulp of salty air before turning to leave the beach.

She couldn't leave. Not yet, anyway. The sustaining memories held in this place were bigger than the heart-breaking ones. It was a sanctuary she couldn't afford to throw away if there was another answer. And she owed it to Gran to fix up the cottage as much as she could before she made any final decision.

Resolutely, Megan began walking back to Anna's cottage, wrapping her coat around her body to keep warm and sticking her hands in her pockets to keep the wind from sneaking into any gaps.

Even through the woollen gloves, she could feel something in her pocket. A small, hard object. She remembered what it was as she pulled it out. Claire's chain, which had caught on her scarf and broken yesterday. It was only now that Megan registered what was hanging on the thin silver chain. A tiny, silver shamrock.

Very Irish, she thought with a smile. And probably treasured. Was Claire fretting about losing it? She could take it in when she returned Anna's car keys. On the way, she could sort out a rental car for herself and find some tradesmen to come and start urgent work on her cottage.

By mid-afternoon, with the sun already taking a bow for the day, Megan pulled into the doctors' car parking area at St Piran's feeling weary but satisfied with her day.

She sat in Anna's car for a minute after turning off the engine. Just because she could. Because today was so different from yesterday and she could take her time. Because that awful stress of being afraid of what she would find here was gone.

Megan knew that Claire was going to be fine. She would probably have a new lease on life now and be healthier than she'd been in a long while.

She knew that she didn't have to imagine what it would be like to see Josh again. To wonder if her feelings would be strong enough to turn her carefully reconstructed world upside down. To be afraid that he might actually hate her for walking out of his life when he'd badly needed his friends.

And, as it was with the cottage, she could accept that this hospital was an important part of her personal history. That it held a lot of memories worth treasuring and that avoiding it was not only immature but it could lead to regrets.

Locking the car, Megan walked towards the sprawling, modern structure that housed a renowned medical facility. A helicopter was approaching, hovering just before coming down on the heli-pad. Such a familiar sound here because the A and E department had the reputation of being able to handle anything and it was the first choice in the area for any major trauma.

Thanks to Josh.

Children were also brought here rather than to other hospitals within easy flight distance because the paediatric department was equally first rate. They had the facilities, equipment and dedicated staff to cope with any traumatic or medical emergencies.

It was so familiar.

And so different from what Megan had been forced to

get used to in a developing country that had far too little available in the way of facilities, even basic equipment and supplies, and far too few staff. It had been so easy to feel that she was making an important contribution there but was saving a little life in Africa any less satisfying than saving one here?

No. Parents were parents the world over and they all loved their children. It was just…different. The challenges were different and often unbearably frustrating because it could be purely luck that made something available there that would be taken totally for granted here, like an incubator or even antibiotics.

There were familiar faces to be seen on her way to the cardiology ward, including one of the midwives Megan had known well.

'Brianna…hi.'

'Megan…I heard you were back in town. How are you?'

'I'm fine. And you? Obviously back at work?'

'Only part time. The twins are setting new heights in being "terrible twos".' But Brianna was smiling, clearly loving motherhood.

Twins. There was something in the air around here. Reminders of Josh around every corner? Megan could feel herself trying to pull a protective layer around her heart. Putting up some 'road closed' signs.

Brianna was still smiling. 'I've got to run. Home call to make to a new mother. But I'd love to catch up. Are you back for good?'

Megan shook her head with more emphasis than necessary.

'Oh, shame. We could sure use you. Did you know there's a consultant paediatric position being advertised as we speak?'

Again Megan shook her head. She hadn't known. Didn't really *want* to know, in fact.

'I'm just visiting,' she said, forcing a smile. 'But we should definitely have a coffee or something.'

Just visiting. The words echoed in her head after she'd said goodbye to Brianna. They felt wrong, somehow.

Did she still belong here, in the same way that part of her would always belong to Penhally? Did she belong in Africa now, where part of her heart would always be? Or maybe she needed to be somewhere that she had belonged to long ago. London.

Megan didn't know and it was a disturbing feeling. As if she was drifting.

Lost.

At least the map to the cardiology ward was well remembered and easy to follow. Megan found Claire sitting up in bed, reading a magazine.

'Oh, my dear…' Claire's smile lit up her face. 'I'm so pleased to see you. I don't know how I'm going to thank you. Josh tells me you probably saved my life.'

The heartfelt gratitude was embarrassing but it was impossible not to return such a warm smile.

'I've got something else you might be pleased to see.' Megan fished in her pocket. 'The chain was broken but I had it fixed for you today when I was in Penhally.'

'My chain…' Claire took it from Megan almost reverently. 'Oh…'

'It looked like it might be special.'

Claire nodded, her face misty. 'My Joshie gave it to me for Mother's Day. He bought it with the first money he earned from his paper round. I think he was about six or seven.' Claire pressed the hand holding the chain to her heart. Her smile was rather wobbly now. 'Sorry,' she sniffed. 'It's all a bit…'

'Emotional. I know.' Megan's smile was sympathetic. 'You've been through rather a lot in the last twenty-four hours. I understand completely.'

More than Claire would know, in fact. Megan had been on a bit of a roller-coaster herself. She watched as the older woman's fingers trembled, trying to open the catch on the chain.

'Can I help?' She took the chain and Claire bent her head forward so that she could fasten it behind her neck. When she leaned back on her pillow her face was disconcertingly close. Those blue eyes so familiar.

'Thank you, lovie. Please…sit down for a minute. Have you got the time?'

'Of course.' Megan took off her coat and perched on the edge of the chair beside Claire's bed. She couldn't help casting her eye over the monitor still recording an ECG and up at the IV pole, where the bag of fluids was empty. Did she still need a line in and fluids running to keep a vein open in case of emergency?

'You're looking good,' she told Claire. 'Are the doctors happy with you?'

Claire nodded. 'I'm allowed to go home tomorrow as long as I behave myself today. They're going to do a…an echo-something-or-other in the morning.'

'An echocardiogram?'

'That's it. They did tell me what it would show but it all sounded very technical.'

'It gives them a way of looking at your heart and seeing how well it's pumping. They can measure the blood that comes out with every beat and give it a number. It's a percentage of the blood that was in that part of the heart. They call it an ejection fraction.'

Good grief…Megan knew she was hiding behind professionalism here. Avoiding talking about anything too personal because this was Josh's mother. The grandmother of Rebecca's children.

Claire seemed to see straight through her. She leaned forward and patted Megan's arm.

'I'm so glad you've come back,' she said softly. 'Josh will be too.'

But she hadn't come back. Megan opened her mouth to reiterate her visitor status but Claire was nodding.

'You're a star,' she told Megan. 'I saw your picture. In that refugee camp. You were holding a dear little baby and there were so many children all around you.'

Megan's eyes widened. 'Where on earth did you see that?'

'In that newsletter thing that comes from the organisation you work for. What's it called again?'

'Medécins Sans Frontières,' Megan said faintly. 'The MSF. Doctors without borders.'

'So it is.' Claire's gaze was oddly direct. 'Josh gets it delivered every month.'

'I…ah…' Megan had no words. Josh had been following where she was and what she'd been doing for the last two years? That was…unexpected. Flattering? Confusing, that was for sure.

'He needs things to keep him interested.' Claire's tone was almost offhand. 'Poor man, all he's got in his life are the children and his work. It's not enough, is it?'

Megan could only stare at Claire, her jaw still slack. What was Claire trying to say?

She didn't have to wonder for more than a heartbeat.

'He'd never admit it for the world.' Claire's voice was no more than a whisper. 'But he's lonely, so he is.'

Megan took in a slow breath and tightened her jaw. Lonely? With two gorgeous children and his mum living with him? With his job and all his colleagues? His *perfect* life?

He was *lonely*?

And she was supposed to care about that?

For heaven's sake, Josh O'Hara didn't have to be lonely if he didn't want to be. He could have any woman he wanted. Back when she'd first met him, when he'd been no more than a talented but very junior doctor, he'd had the reputation of being a notorious womaniser. He'd been a legend. To have him even noticing the naïve bookworm of a final-year med student that Megan had been at the time, let alone focusing his well-deserved legendary skills in the bedroom on her for a whole night, had been unbelievable. When he'd been back with his ultra-cool friends days later and had ignored her, she'd known exactly how easily replaceable she'd been.

So what had changed? He was still impossibly good looking. In that unfair way men were capable of, he was only getting more attractive as he got older. He was still supremely confident, with good reason, given the accolades the emergency department of St Piran's Hospital regularly garnered. He was a prime example of pure alpha male and Megan could be absolutely sure that no woman in her right mind could be immune to the lethal Irish charm with which he could capture anybody he fancied.

So, if he *was* lonely for feminine company, why wasn't he doing something about it?

And why did the mere thought of him being lonely echo in her own heart like this?

Because, despite the new directions in which she had taken her life, she was lonely too?

Did she really think she could move on and find a way to ignore the person-shaped hole in her life that would never be filled?

There was no point in allowing that train of thought. If Josh was lonely, it had nothing to do with her. She couldn't allow it to. With a huge effort Megan focused on what was right in front of her.

An IV line that had blood backing up its length because the bag of fluids was completely empty and exerting a vacuum effect. She reached out and pushed the call bell.

'You need your IV sorted,' she told Claire. 'And I should really be getting going.'

It wasn't a nurse who answered the call bell. It was Anna.

'Hey…' She grinned at Megan. 'You called?'

'Hardly needs a consultant cardiac surgeon to remove a cannula or hang some more fluids but this is good. Saves me having to page you to give you your car keys.'

'How did you get on? Was it useful?' Anna glanced at the IV tubing taped to Claire's arm.

'Enormously. Thank you so much. I zipped all round Penhally and sorted out some contractors to start work on the cottage. They're charging like wounded bulls but the plumber and electrician both said they could start tomorrow.'

'Fantastic.' Anna was eyeing the monitor beside Claire's bed. 'It's all looking great,' she told her patient, 'but I'd rather keep your IV in for a bit longer. Think of it as an insurance policy against any complications. If it's there, we won't need it. Now…where's the trolley? Ah, there it is…' She moved to the corner of the room but turned to look at Megan as she pulled open a drawer. 'If they're not starting till tomorrow, that means you won't be able to stay there yet.'

'Probably not for a few days, no.'

'So you'll stay and keep me company?'

'If you're sure…' Being so close to the beach was as

much of a draw card as Anna's company. 'And, yes, I'd be delighted to cook tonight. I'm going to go and pick up my rental car now and will do some shopping.'

'Oh…' Claire had been following the conversation, looking from one younger woman to another and back as though following a tennis match. Now she was beaming. 'You'll be just down the road, then, lovie. You'll have to come and have a cuppa, so you will.'

Anna excused Megan having to respond. She'd come back with a new bag of saline from the trolley drawer but exclaimed in frustration when she went to hang it on the hook.

'It's past its expiry date. It shouldn't even be in the trolley. That really isn't good enough.' Discarding the bag, she went back for another one.

Megan's jaw dropped. 'You're not going to throw it out, are you?'

'Have to. It expired a month ago.'

'But that's such an arbitrary date. You can see it's all right.' Megan held the bag up to the light. 'No goldfish swimming around. This stuff lasts for ever. It's only salty water. We wouldn't hesitate to use it in Africa.'

'Plenty more where that came from.' Happy with the new bag, Anna was changing over the giving set, pushing the spike into the port on the bottom of the bag. 'And not only fluids. I'll bet there are hundreds of things like cannulas and syringes that have to be discarded at every stocktake because they've gone over the date. Hospital policy. Hey…maybe we should gather them all up and post them to Africa.'

'That's not a bad idea. In fact…' Megan felt a fizz of real excitement '…it's a *brilliant* idea. My clinic would be over the moon to get a crate of supplies like that.'

'We could do some fundraising, too.' Claire didn't want

to be left out of the discussion. 'There's plenty of grannies like me in the district and we'd love a good cause to have a bake sale or something for.'

'Oh, I couldn't ask you to—'

Claire held up her hand in a stop sign. 'Don't you say another word, lovie. I've been lying here wondering how I was ever going to be able to thank you for saving my life and this is it. I can not only say thank you to you but we can do something for all those poor children in Africa at the same time. It's perfect.'

Perfect. There was that word again. Funny how it was starting to grate.

'Go and talk to Albert White,' Anna advised. 'You'll need the CEO's permission before you start gathering up the old stuff. I'll ask Luke who else you could talk too as well. You could fill dozens of crates if you got some other hospitals on board with the idea.'

If nothing else, the excuse of going to talk to Albert White took Megan away from Claire and her disturbing confidences about her son's state of happiness. It also stopped Megan worrying about the downside of staying longer at Anna's place with it being next door to the O'Haras. It was a godsend to have something other than herself or Josh to think about as she walked through the hospital corridors, and the more she thought about it, the better the idea seemed.

By the time she knocked on the CEO's office door, she was more excited about it than she could remember being about anything for a very long time.

The last thing Josh O'Hara expected to see when he emerged from the lift on his way to visit his mother was Megan Phillips shaking hands with Albert White.

'Josh…' Albert was positively beaming. 'I heard about

your mother. I'm delighted to hear today that she's doing very well.'

'You and me, both.' But Josh was looking at Megan, who seemed to be avoiding his gaze. She looked oddly... nervous? What was going on?

'You're not working today, are you, Josh?' Albert continued. 'Didn't Ben tell me he had things covered in Emergency?'

'I'm just here for a visit.'

'All by yourself? Where are those little ankle-biters?'

'Being babysat by one of Mum's friends from her grand-mothers' group. Only she's a great-grandmother. You remember Rita—the ward clerk in NICU who retired a while back?'

Albert's eyebrows rose. 'Who could forget?'

Josh snorted softly. 'I know. She's a much nicer person these days now that her feet don't hurt from too much standing. Her great-grandson, Colin, goes to the same play-group mine do. They call it "afternoons with the oldies" or something similar. Anyway...'

'Yes, yes. Must get on. I'll leave Megan to tell you the good news.'

Josh stared after the CEO as he bustled away.

'Was he actually rubbing his hands together?' he murmured.

'Probably.' Megan was biting her bottom lip.

'And didn't I see you two shaking hands? It looked like you'd made some kind of a deal.'

'Mmm.' Megan was still avoiding direct eye contact.

Josh sighed inwardly. He had a feeling that whatever it was, it was going to make life a little more complicated for him.

Megan was eyeing the button to summon the lift. Josh

leaned against the wall. She'd have to reach around him to get to the button.

'So…is it a big secret?'

Megan sighed audibly. 'No. And you'll find out soon enough, I suppose. Anna had this idea…'

He listened to the plan of collecting out-of-date supplies like IV gear and drugs and old equipment that was being replaced and donating them to Megan's clinic in Africa. He had to agree it was a brilliant idea but he was only half listening to the words coming out of Megan's mouth. What was even more riveting was the way her mouth was moving. The flicker of real passion he could hear in her voice and see in her eyes.

It had the effect, he thought, that holding a shot of whisky under the nose of a recovering alcoholic might have.

So tempting.

He actually had to fight the urge to put his finger against Megan's lips and stop the words. And then to cover her lips with his own and silence them for a very, very long time…

And then Josh realised that Megan had stopped talking. He tried to pull back her last words from the ether before they evaporated completely.

'I'm not quite sure what this has to do with my department.'

'Albert made me an offer I couldn't refuse.'

'Which was?'

'He'll donate everything suitable that St Piran's can spare. He'll contact his fellow CEOs from other hospitals in the district and get them to pitch in. He'll endorse a hospital fundraiser to cover the shipping costs.' Megan was biting her lip again. 'He'll even throw in a ticket so that I can travel with the load and make sure it gets to the right place.'

Josh shook his head in amazement. 'That's an amazing offer all right.' But he couldn't shake the image of Albert walking away rubbing his hands together as though he'd got the better end of the deal. 'What does Albert get out of it?'

'Me,' Megan said simply. 'I've agreed to work here for the next few weeks to get a big project off the ground. He needed a paediatric specialist to oversee it.'

Josh was grateful for the wall he was leaning on. Now he could understand exactly why Megan had looked nervous. She knew that he wouldn't like this.

'The project's the paediatric triage and observation suite to go into A and E, isn't it?'

It had been a pipe dream for such a long time. The busy emergency department with all the sights and sounds and smells that went with major trauma and life-threatening medical problems was a terrifying place to bring young children, especially when they were sick and even more vulnerable. And often, admitting them to a ward was not necessary but they did need observation for a period of time because, if you had the slightest doubt, you couldn't afford to send them home. A dedicated, child-friendly space that still had the capability to deal with life or death situations would put his department even more securely amongst the best in the country.

'Mmm.' Megan finally looked up. 'I couldn't say no, Josh. I did try, I can assure you.'

Really?

Maybe she was doing this to punish him.

Seeing her again had disturbed his equilibrium markedly. Feeling her presence in his house and seeing her close to his children had made visible cracks in the foundations of his new life. Even when she wasn't there, he could feel the way it *had* been last night. It had haunted him all day.

So much so that he'd accepted with alacrity Rita's offer to babysit. So that he could escape. Not only to visit his mother but to find refuge in the other half of his life.

His work.

How could he handle knowing that he would see her here every day? For weeks?

Megan had found her new life. In Africa. She'd found someone *special*.

Did she want to rub his nose in that? To remind him, on a daily basis, just how much he'd messed up his own life?

It was then that Josh realised he'd been holding eye contact with Megan just a shade too long. That he'd been searching her face for confirmation. But what he saw was something quite different.

Anxiety.

Fear, almost.

Why was *she* afraid?

'I could try and talk to Albert again,' Megan said quietly. 'If it's a problem.'

Josh could feel his head moving. Not in assent. He was slowly shaking it from side to side in a negative response.

Because he knew why Megan was afraid. She didn't want to be working near him any more than he wanted her to be. Because she was unsure about whether she could handle it.

And she could only be that unsure if she still felt the same way about him as she had before she'd walked away two years ago. Before he'd ended things to stay in his marriage and be the father he'd had to try and be for his children.

But he wasn't married any more, was he?

Was that going to make a difference? Could he afford to even think about letting it make a difference?

Josh had no answer to that internal query.

   And maybe that was what he needed to find out. It
might be the only way he could avoid being haunted for
the rest of his life by what might have been with Megan
Phillips.

   He could talk to Albert himself but if the incentive
that had been offered had been massive enough to swing
the deal when Megan was clearly feeling vulnerable, how
could he do anything that might wipe out the reward she
wanted so badly? If she didn't have something like this to
keep her here, she might leave again, and Josh knew that
if she left on such a disappointing note he would never
see her again.

   Besides, the CEO knew what he was doing.

   Megan was perfect for the task.

   Josh was still shaking his head. He added the hint of a
smile as he eased himself away from the wall and allowed
Megan free access to the lift button and escape.

   'It's not a problem,' he said decisively. 'We're lucky to
have you on board. When are you going to start?'

   'In a day or two. As soon as I've got the renovations on
my cottage underway properly. Maybe Thursday?'

   'Excellent.' Josh tried, not very successfully, to widen
his smile. 'See you then, Megan.'

   He walked away. He knew Megan would have pushed
the button for the lift but he also knew that she wasn't
watching for it to arrive.

   She was watching him.

   He could feel it as clearly as if it were her hands and
not her gaze touching him.

CHAPTER FIVE

WHAT *HAD* SHE been thinking?

Megan was shredding salad vegetables with far more force than required as she groaned inwardly yet again.

'I must be crazy,' she said aloud.

'Hardly.' The voice came from her mobile phone, which she had on speaker mode, propped on the kitchen windowsill. 'It's not every day that you get such a generous donation. It'll make a huge difference to the clinic, you know that.'

'But it's not a donation, is it? I'm going to have to earn it. By working…with Josh. He'll be looking over my shoulder the whole time. This is *his* baby. He was talking about it years ago. Before I left.'

'What's really worrying you, Megan?' The male voice was kindly. 'Not being able to do the job justice, or having to work that closely with Josh?'

'I—I'm not sure. It's complicated.'

'Relationships always are. You've got some serious history with Josh, we both know that.'

'It's not just him, Charles. It's the cottage and the hospital and…and Gran. When I think of family, I think of this place. These people. It's…confusing.' She twisted the iceberg lettuce in her hands, dividing it into smaller and smaller pieces.

'Which is precisely why you need to take time to get your head around it all.'

'But maybe that's the wrong thing to do.' Megan was separating lettuce leaves now and pulling at them to break them up even further. 'Maybe I should just pack it all in and come to London. What's the weather like?'

'Cold and grey.' She could hear the smile in his voice. 'I'm sitting beside the fire. I think Mrs Benson's got some roast beef and Yorkshire pudding in the oven for my dinner.'

'Mmm…nice. We're having fish and salad.' Megan eyed the lettuce she'd shredded into minuscule pieces, the tomatoes that had been diced to within an inch of their lives. Cucumber that should be discs but was now tiny triangles. 'I'm not sure it was such a good idea after all.'

'It's healthy. I'm pleased that you're looking after yourself. Oh, there's the bell. I'd better go and present myself in the dining room. Talk to you soon, love. When are you going to start the job?'

'On Thursday. I'm meeting all the contractors at the cottage tomorrow to make a list of everything that needs doing.'

'Don't overdo things.'

'I won't.'

Having said goodbye, Megan scooped the sorry salad into a bowl and turned her attention to crumbing the fresh fish fillets she'd bought in St Piran.

It was all Claire O'Hara's fault, she decided.

Telling her that Josh was lonely.

No. It was her own fault, for remembering what Claire had said in that moment when she could have said no to Albert. When, having come up with his brilliant idea, he'd given her a very significant glance and asked if—given her…ahem…history with Josh—she thought they would be able to work together again.

She could have said no. She probably could have said no and still received permission to collect at least something to contribute to the clinic, but the lure of being able to make a really significant difference had been huge.

And when she thought about working with Josh, all that came into her head was Claire's voice.

But he's lonely, so he is.

Why had he told her that his life was so perfect? Was he trying to protect her in some way?

And why did it bother her so much if he *was* lonely?

Because she understood? Because the words resonated at such a very deep level in her own heart?

Because the kind of love that she and Josh shared would never, ever go away completely—on either side—and because they could never be together, there would always be that empty…lonely space inside.

The fact that they couldn't make it work was sad but it didn't mean that she didn't want Josh to be happy. To close off that lonely space and move on.

Did it?

Charles had been wise, Megan concluded, slipping the fish into the oven to bake. She had to face this head on and find out exactly what was going on in both her head and her heart. She'd promised Charles that she would do that before making those final, irrevocable decisions about her future.

When she was really sure of herself, she could make sure that Josh knew that she was stronger now. That she didn't need protection. That she'd moved on successfully and was on the way to making her life as perfect as possible, too.

Did they both need to believe that in order to finally let go?

* * *

'Did you order this, Megan?'

'What is it?'

The nurse, Gina, started unrolling a large, laminated poster. A line of text became visible. 'It's a paediatric resuscitation chart.'

'Oh…good. That's to go on the wall behind where the IV and airway supplies are going in the main resus area. There should be a paediatric Glasgow coma scale and a classification of shock chart coming as well.'

'OK.' But Gina looked curious as she unrolled the chart a little further. 'Aren't doctors supposed to know all this stuff about weights and drug dosages and things off by heart?'

Megan nodded, looking up from where she was sorting packets of supplies. 'Think of it as an insurance policy,' she said. 'In an emergency situation, the more time you can save and the more accurate you can be, the better.'

Behind Gina, she could see Josh approaching. This new area of the emergency department, taken from part of the plaster room and a couple of offices, was still a mess a week after the transformation had begun. There were workmen installing ceiling tracks for X-ray equipment, putting pipes in for an oxygen supply, sorting lighting and electrical fittings for monitors and computers, and installing phone lines and the fixed furniture like the central nurses' station.

When this exciting project was finished, St Piran's would have a six-bed observation unit where babies and children could stay for up to twenty-four hours without needing admittance to the main ward. They would also have two resuscitation areas. A main one that would have everything needed for a life or death emergency and a second one so that they could cope with more than one serious case at a time. The division between the two areas could be folded back, if necessary, to allow access to the state-of-the-art gear that would be going into the main part.

The whole concept would be something that many hospitals would envy. Josh O'Hara would get the credit for its inception and execution. No doubt it would generate huge publicity and kudos and his already stellar career would skyrocket even further. If he was at all concerned about how the result would affect his own reputation, he wasn't showing it right now. Josh looked relaxed and confident. His shirtsleeves were rolled up and a stethoscope was dangled carelessly around his neck.

It was by no means the first time Josh had wandered out of the main department to see what was happening with the set-up of the new paediatric wing and, of course, Megan had been rattled by the close professional scrutiny that had so many deeply personal undertones but she was finally starting to relax.

The tone of their interaction had been put into place on the first day. This was Josh's territory. The career half of his perfect life. He clearly had no idea that his mother had suggested it wasn't so perfect to Megan and he seemed determined to demonstrate how happy he was in his work.

He talked easily and passionately about the new project, happy to discuss any queries or ideas Megan put forward. He interacted with his colleagues in a totally relaxed manner but she was left in no doubt about the respect he was given as head of department. And she'd seen him, in passing, treating patients. On one occasion holding someone's hand to reassure them, on another leading a full resuscitation on a badly injured trauma victim.

Megan had taken her cue from Josh. She was here as a colleague in a professional capacity, nothing more. To her relief, it wasn't proving as hard as she'd expected. No-

body could know how aware she was of Josh's proximity.
How she could hear his voice across the whole department,
even when he was speaking quietly. How she could sense
his approach when she wasn't expecting him or looking
in the direction from which he was coming. Like she had
when Gina had been showing her the poster.

Megan acknowledged his approach with a tiny tilt of
her head but continued talking to Gina.

'There are so many variables with paediatric patients,'
she said, pleased to hear her voice sounding so steady despite the awareness of Josh infiltrating every cell of her
body. 'And size and weight can make a critical difference
to what size ET tube you might want to grab or, say, how
much diazepam you want to give to treat a seizure.'

Josh was smiling as he stepped closer to Gina. He took
the chart and unfurled it completely, holding it up against
a wall to admire it. The movement made the muscles of
his shoulders move under his shirt and the light caught the
dusting of dark hair on his arms but Megan's attention was
caught by his hands. Watching those long, clever fingers as
they traced the different text boxes on the colourful chart.

'You can't weigh a sick baby or toddler easily,' he was
telling Gina, 'but you can measure their length. Look…'
He pointed to one side of a graph. 'I've got a two-year-old
who's come in in status epilepticus and I want to give him
an initial dose of IV diazepam. Here's his age. A quick
measure shows me he's quite big for his age at just over
a hundred centimetres so he's close to twenty kilograms,
and I can double-check the dose I want to give him here…'
Josh's hand made a rapid swoop towards a new box con-
taining drug dosage information. Something in Megan's
stomach mirrored the swoop.

'Cool.' But Gina was looking at Josh, not the chart, and
the hero-worship was all too obvious.

She was young, Megan noted. And very pretty. It was also quite obvious that Josh had no need to be lonely if he didn't want to be. Not physically, anyway. Something much less pleasant than the previous sensation settled in her stomach. Deliberately, she dragged her gaze downwards and stared at the package in her hand. An ET tube. Cuffed. Smallest size.

'Want me to stick the poster up now?' Gina asked.

'No.' Megan's tone was a lot crisper than she'd intended. She smiled at Gina to disguise her inward turbulence. 'Put it on one of the trolleys in the corner of the observation room. I've got the mural painter in Resus at the moment, checking out how she can work around the fittings that are going in.'

'Mural?' Josh was finally looking at Megan directly as Gina moved away. She could feel it. 'In the resus room?'

She wanted to look up but resisted. Too hard to meet his gaze and still sound completely professional. So she reached for another handful of packages from the carton as though sorting ET tubes was too important a task to interrupt.

She risked a very quick glance upward, so as not to appear rude. 'Not as bright or complicated as the walls and ceiling in the observation area. I'm going for some leafy beanstalk plants with caterpillars on them and butterflies scattered over pale blue walls. A few on the ceiling too, where there's any space.'

'Sounds time consuming. I hope it won't put us behind on the target to have all the radiology gear installed by tomorrow.' She could hear the frown in Josh's voice. She could also feel the intensity of the look he was giving her go up a notch or two. But when she looked up, she found that he was watching her hands, not her face.

What was it about hands? She only had to let her gaze

rest on his, even if they were perfectly relaxed and just curled on the table in the staffroom or on his thigh when he was sitting down on the couch in there for once, and it always gave her that odd curl of sensation. The way it had when she'd been caught watching him trace the information on that resuscitation chart. Was it the memory of touch?

Did Josh get that by looking at *her* hands?

Megan sucked in a quick breath. 'It fits in with the overall philosophy of making this whole area as child friendly as possible,' she said evenly. 'You get conscious patients in Resus too, you know. Trauma victims, for example. If you can distract them from their pain and fear at all, it's going to help not only the assessment but it can potentially improve their status.'

It was quite true. Megan could almost hear Josh talking to the media about it when he was proudly showing off the new facility. Shock, from internal blood loss, he might say, is made worse by how fast the heart is beating. If you can calm a child down, you can slow the heart rate and potentially slow the rate of bleeding. People would lap it up. Everybody who contributed to the fundraising efforts would know that money hadn't been wasted in decoration for its own sake. Parents would feel happier knowing they could take their child into a place that went the extra mile.

Megan managed to smile as she looked up at Josh. 'I'll bet you could distract Brenna from something scary or sore by getting her interested in the big blue butterfly in the corner, or trying to find the yellow caterpillar with green spots on a leaf somewhere.'

The mention of his daughter did the trick. The intensity with which he'd been watching Megan faded rapidly and Josh relaxed. He even smiled back. A real smile that made the corners of his eyes crinkle.

Something crinkled inside Megan yet again.

Rebecca's daughter, she reminded herself, not only Josh's. The child that had been conceived when his marriage was supposed to be over.

'I take your point,' Josh conceded. 'A pretty resus room is commendable. What are you doing there?'

'Sorting airway supplies and deciding how we want to arrange them for ease of access. I'm thinking sets of the most commonly used sizes of ET tubes, cuffed and uncuffed, with guide wires but having appropriate LMAs and needle cricothyroidotomy kits with them as well to cover any complications.'

'Mmm.' Josh seemed to be listening intently and approving of what Megan was telling him.

Except that there was just a hint of a far-away gaze in his eyes. As though he was listening to her voice and thinking of something quite different. Had he remembered that it was her birthday today? Did he even know? And if he did, was that too far into personal territory to be allowable in this new phase of their relationship? Or should that be 'non-relationship'? Megan's train of thought became scrambled enough for her to sigh inwardly and grasp at something to ground her in reality again.

'How's Claire this week?'

'Doing really well, thanks.' Yes, she could see the way Josh blinked and refocused. 'Still getting tired easily but she's managing fine, thanks to her granny group friends. Oh…I had a message for you, in fact.'

'Oh?' Good grief… She was definitely losing the ability to concentrate right now. Was that what Josh had been doing a moment ago? Being so aware of the sound of a voice that the words became almost meaningless?

Funny how you could feel a voice as much as hear it.

'They want to get involved in the Africa project. They're

thinking of starting a toy drive. Mum asked if I could ask you to come and talk to her as soon as possible and tell her the kind of things they should be collecting.'

'Oh…' Megan bit her lip. 'That's very kind of them but, in general, toys wouldn't be the first priority. The really useful things might be exercise books and pencils and paper and crayons and picture books and…' Megan stopped, embarrassed. It was so easy to get carried away and start sounding over excited.

But Josh was smiling. 'That's what you need to tell mum and her cronies. I'm sure they'd be delighted to collect whatever would be most useful.'

'I'll do that. Thanks for passing on the message.' It might be an effort to turn away from that smile but Megan managed. She could even focus on the task at hand again. Out of the corner of her eye she saw Josh stare at her a moment longer but then he, too, turned away, rolling up the resuscitation chart as he let his gaze roam around what was happening away from this corner of the project.

The memories were all there, of course. And that powerful, indefinable pull between them, but it was all manageable. Under control.

It was, Megan mused, like looking at something magical. A tropical pool, maybe, on the hottest of days. Still and deep and so cool looking, surrounded by lush greenery. You knew that if you slipped into the water the sensation would be such bliss you might die from the sheer pleasure of it but you also knew that there were vicious piranhas circling beneath that smooth surface and the pain would be unbearable. The will to survive was enough to keep your feet on dry ground, no matter how uncomfortable or hard that might be.

Gina reappeared from the direction of the main department.

'Dr O'Hara? You're wanted. The condition of that little girl with asthma has deteriorated.'

'Coming.' Josh discarded the poster and began moving but his head turned. 'You've been given practising privileges here again, haven't you, Megan?'

Megan nodded. Albert White had made sure that it was legally covered. What's the use in having expertise like yours in the department, he'd said, if it couldn't be used if needed?

'Would you mind?' Josh was still moving but his head tilted in an invitation for her to follow him. 'She's on maximum therapy already and I thought we had it sorted. A second opinion would be welcome.'

'Sure.' Megan was on her feet and catching up. The thrill of anticipation was due to it having been so long since she'd faced a potential emergency with everything she might need at hand, she told herself.

It had nothing to do with the prospect of working side by side with Josh.

Six-year-old Bonnie was being given a continuous infusion of salbutamol but she was struggling to breathe. She could only manage sentences of one or two words in response to Josh's questions and the outline of her ribs was visible even through the hospital gown due to the effort she was making to shift air.

'What's the oxygen saturation?' Megan queried, her hand on Bonnie's wrist, trying to count an extremely rapid heart rate.

'Down to eighty-six percent,' Josh told her. 'It's dropped. Respiration rate is up from forty to fifty-six.' He was frowning. 'Let's start a loading dose of aminophylline and get a chest X-ray to exclude a pneumothorax.' He raised his eyebrows at Megan, who nodded her agreement.

'We could start her on some positive pressure assisted ventilation, too.' She squeezed Bonnie's hand. 'We're going to change your face mask, sweetheart and give you one that's going to make it a bit easier for you to breathe. It's nothing to be scared about, OK?'

But Bonnie looked terrified. So did her mother, who was sitting close to the head of the bed, holding Bonnie's other hand. Megan moved closer to Josh and lowered her voice.

'We need an arterial blood gas. And we need to get her up to PICU as soon as she's stable.'

Josh murmured his agreement. He was still frowning. Somewhere behind them someone was shouting and a staff member was threatening to call Security if they didn't calm down. An X-ray technician bustled into the resus area and began moving equipment that clanked loudly against something else. An alarm was sounding on some monitoring equipment nearby.

Josh caught Megan's gaze. A gesture with his hand encompassed the undecorated walls with the array of potentially frightening supplies and machinery. 'The sooner we have our unit up and running, the better,' he muttered, 'don't you think?'

'Mmm.' Except it wasn't going to be *their* unit, was it? Megan was never going to work here again on a permanent basis. The realisation gave her a curiously sharp pang of regret.

She was working here right now, though, and over the next fifteen minutes her energies were directed solely to trying to help Josh stabilise Bonnie. Despite all their efforts, however, her condition was getting worse. Single-word responses became no responses at all and the child's level of consciousness was dropping noticeably. The level of oxygen in her blood, having gone up for a brief period, dropped with an alarming plunge. Her fingernails took on a bluish tinge.

'I'm going to intubate,' Josh decided. 'Rapid sequence. Megan, can you pre-oxygenate and then give me some cricoid pressure, please?'

Megan took her position and held the mask over Bonnie's face, turning up the flow of oxygen to try and get as much into her bloodstream as possible before any attempts to breathe were interrupted by the anaesthesia and intubation procedure.

She was ready to push on the front of the now unconscious Bonnie's throat to help Josh visualise the vocal cords and slip the tube into the correct position but his first attempt was unsuccessful. Megan could see the beads of sweat forming on his forehead. She reached above his head to silence an alarm on the monitor that was insistently beeping.

Josh looked up. He didn't have to say a word—the communication was simply there telepathically. If the next attempt was unsuccessful they would have to do something more invasive, like puncturing Bonnie's airway from the front of her neck. They couldn't afford to have her paralysed and not ventilated adequately for more than a few minutes. Megan had more experience with the smaller and sometimes difficult airways of children. She also had smaller hands that were capable of defter movement.

It wasn't anything like an admission of defeat on Josh's part to swap positions. He was simply taking the best advantage of the resources available.

The pressure of needing to perform to the best of her ability was countered by the knowledge that Josh had enough confidence in her to give her the chance. Megan didn't realise she was holding her own breath until she felt herself release it in a sigh of relief when the tube slipped into place and she could hear the air entry into Bonnie's lungs with her stethoscope as Josh squeezed the bag attached to her face mask.

The tension was still there for the next few minutes as they hooked Bonnie up to the ventilator and adjusted settings until they were happy with the way she was breathing and the amount of oxygen that was circulating in her bloodstream. And then Megan went with Bonnie to the paediatric intensive care unit to see her settled in and her care passed to the medical team on duty.

Finally, Megan returned to the main part of the emergency department because she wanted to tell Josh that the little girl appeared to be stable and she was already showing some signs of improving.

Josh was standing beside the triage desk, along with several nurses. He was holding a huge bunch of red roses wrapped in Cellophane. He didn't see Megan approaching because he was reading the small card stapled to the Cellophane.

Red roses. The most romantic of flowers. Who was the lucky recipient? Megan wondered. Or had someone sent them to Josh? Either way, she was experiencing a rush of emotion that was a long way from being pleasant.

Until Josh looked up and smiled at her.

'These are for you,' he said.

The unpleasant heaviness in her belly twisted and tried to break up and form something entirely different. Except that Josh's smile wasn't reaching his eyes.

'Apparently, it's your birthday,' he added.

'Oh… Happy birthday, Megan.' The chorus came from several staff members but Megan barely heard them. If Josh was surprised to learn that it was her birthday today, it meant that the flowers couldn't possibly have come from him.

And that meant…

Josh had her pinned with his gaze. 'So, who's this Charles?' he asked, his tone deceptively casual.

This was it. A defining moment. There was a choice to be made. Did Megan stick to her new plans for her future or was she going to allow the past to hold her back?

Could she finally accept that what she had once wanted more than life itself was never going to happen and take the final step that would set Josh—and herself—free?

There really wasn't a choice to make, was there?

Megan took a deep breath and spoke into the waiting silence, ignoring all the expectant faces around her, except one. She was speaking to Josh here.

'Charles is my fiancé,' she said quietly.

CHAPTER SIX

FIANCÉ?

Megan had a fiancé?

He shouldn't feel this shocked, Josh realised. What had he expected—that Megan would stay single for the rest of her life because she couldn't marry *him*?

The chorus of 'happy birthdays' had turned into a round of congratulations. And questions. Who was Charles? Where had she met him? How long had they been engaged?

'He's a tropical diseases specialist,' he heard Megan telling them. 'I met him when he came out to Africa. He lives in London and…and we only got engaged very recently.'

'Is that why you're not wearing a ring?'

'Ah…yes…'

The hesitation was tiny. It might not have even been significant except for the way Megan's gaze finally moved to meet Josh's intent stare. The contact was brief but he registered two things. That there was more to this engagement than Megan was saying and that she was shocked by the way he was staring at her.

Fair enough. Josh pasted a smile on his face. Fortunately he had long since let go of that bunch of flowers.

'Congratulations, Megan,' he heard himself saying in a perfectly normal voice. 'I hope you'll be very happy.

Now, you'll have to excuse me. I want to go and see how Bonnie's getting on.'

It was a good enough reason to walk out of the department, wasn't it? Josh hadn't banked on being followed, however. He increased his pace.

'Josh...wait...' Megan was closing the gap. 'That's what I came to tell you.'

'What?' He didn't turn his head. 'That you're *engaged*?'

'No...' The word was a sigh. 'That Bonnie's doing well. Tidal volume's increasing and her blood chemistry's improving. She's quite stable.'

'Good. I'd still like to see for myself.' Josh kept walking.

'Josh...' This time the word was a plea. 'Don't be like this...please...'

Her voice was quiet enough to carry no further than his own ears but two nurses coming towards him along the corridor were giving him frankly curious stares. And then they gave each other a significant glance. He could almost hear the newsflash that would hit the hospital grapevine in the very near future.

It's happening again. They can't even work together for five minutes without the sparks flying. What is it with the chemistry between those two?

No. It wasn't happening again. Or it wouldn't be if he could get a grip and stop behaving like a petulant teenager. He forced himself to slow down. To turn and give Megan a direct look.

'I need coffee,' he was saying as the nurses passed them. 'How 'bout you?'

He hadn't banked on the cafeteria being so deserted for once, any more than he had on Megan following him. They ended up sitting at one of the prized tables by the windows and there was nobody to overhear their conversation.

Megan had been very quiet during the walk to the cafeteria and while they fixed their drinks. Now she wasn't even tasting her coffee. She'd sat down at the end of the table, at a right angle to him, the way they'd been in his own kitchen. As though she didn't want the barrier of the table between them. Did she feel like he had? So close but not close enough?

'I'm sorry,' she said. 'I…should have told you about Charles the other night.'

Josh made a noncommittal sound. She had, hadn't she? When she'd talked about that 'someone special' still in Africa?

'It's…complicated,' Megan continued. 'I'd like to explain.'

Josh wasn't at all sure he wanted to hear anything more about Megan's engagement. He averted his gaze. 'Why? What's the point?'

The silence made him look back and the expression on Megan's face made him catch his breath. His question had made much more of a direct hit than he'd intended. She looked…stricken?

Why? Was she embarrassed at letting him know she'd found someone she loved more than him?

Ashamed that this was evidence that she'd found it easy to move on?

Or did she wish that things could have been different?

Megan's lips were moving. They trembled, which made the words sound shaky.

'I don't want you to hate me,' she whispered.

Josh could actually feel something melting inside him.

That anger at the way Megan had refused to believe him when he'd tried to explain how he'd ended up in Rebecca's bed that night. At the way she had walked out of his life at such a dark time when Rebecca had died. He could feel all the resentment he'd clung to just melting. Evaporating.

How could he ever hate the only person he had and ever would truly love?

He had chosen to end things between them. He'd pushed her out of his life so that he only had to think about being a good father and he'd had good reason to do that. The best reason because he'd known how dangerous it was to rely on having a love like that in your life. Having his mother alone and looking older than she should for her years was a reminder he could tap into every day, with the added bonus of remembering what that relationship had been like for himself and his siblings. How it was the children who could be hurt most.

He'd done the right thing. The only thing he could have done, anyway. He'd honoured his vow. But it didn't mean that he didn't want Megan to be happy, did it?

Of course it didn't.

'I don't hate you,' he said aloud. The smile he could feel tugging at his lips came from somewhere very deep. Very tender. It was just there. Kind of like the way his hand moved to cover one of Megan's. 'I could never hate you, Megan.'

He had to let go of her hand. But not quite yet. The warmth and silky feel of her skin was irresistible. His thumb moved over it. The memories of this hadn't done reality justice. He needed to capture it properly.

'Charles is…' Megan's voice sounded curiously thick, as though clogged by tears she was holding back. 'It's not perfect, you know…but…but what we had—it's gone, Josh—and I…I had to try and move on…'

'Of course you did.' The movement of his thumb had become something to comfort Megan now. 'I'm happy for you. Really, I am.'

'You'll move on, too.' He could actually hear Megan swallow.

'No.' Josh pulled his hand away.

It wasn't going to happen because the choice was unacceptable. He couldn't be with Megan because, even if he could somehow exorcise the ghosts of his own childhood, it was too late. She had found someone else. And to be with anyone else would be a shell of a marriage. The way it had been with Rebecca. He'd only end up messing with someone else's life and he'd vowed never to do that again.

'You still blame yourself, don't you? For everything.'

Josh said nothing.

This time it was Megan who, after a long and increasingly tense silence, reached out and caught his hand.

'It wasn't your fault,' she said softly but fiercely. 'I'm just as much to blame for getting pregnant that first time. And I didn't tell you. That was wrong. You thought it might be your son you were trying to save that night in Emergency but even then I didn't tell you. I let you wonder about that and be haunted for years and years. I...I'm sorry, Josh. I know it was a terrible thing and neither of us will ever forget but it's far in the past now. We need to let it go.'

'I married Rebecca,' Josh muttered. 'I can blame myself for making her life miserable.'

'She chose to marry you,' Megan said quietly. 'And, from what I heard, you'd made it very clear that you didn't want children. But you gave up what you *did* want, didn't you? For the children. For her.'

Josh had a lump that felt like it had sharp edges stuck in his throat. Oh, yes...he'd given up what he'd really wanted and it had felt like something was trying to die a slow and painful death inside him during those months when he'd pushed Megan away.

He couldn't tell her that, though, could he? Not when she had moved on and found someone else.

Except...she was still holding his hand. Really holding

it now. Somehow their hands had moved and now their fingers were intertwined. Josh could feel himself being drawn closer. His head was moving. Something in Megan's eyes was pulling him closer and closer.

Any moment now and he would be close enough to touch her lips with his own. In his peripheral vision Josh could see a group of staff coming into the cafeteria. If he kissed Megan right now, it would be all over St Piran's in a matter of minutes. And the worst thing was, he didn't give a damn.

Right up until the realisation hit him that this newsflash would come right on the heels of the news that Dr Phillips was engaged to some eminent specialist from London. Another relationship would be under threat. And it would be his fault.

History would be repeating itself.

Somehow, Josh found the strength to break that magnetic pull. To untangle their fingers and move himself away.

The group of nurses on early dinner break were heading for a table near theirs now.

'So…it's going well, isn't it?' Josh said, a little more loudly than he needed to. 'Our paediatric wing is going to be something for St Piran's to be proud of, don't you think?'

Megan knew instantly that Josh was trying to put them back onto a professional footing that wouldn't attract any more than mild curiosity from other staff.

It was a million miles away from the space they'd been in only seconds ago.

What exactly had happened there? She could have sworn that Josh had been thinking about *kissing* her.

And, dear Lord…all she had been able to think about was how much she wanted him to.

'Hey, Megan…' The midwife, Brianna, was amongst the group of nurses. She veered closer, a packet of sandwiches in one hand and a bottle of water in the other. 'I've been hearing great things about what's happening in A and E.'

'Yes, it's going really well, thanks.' Megan's smile included Josh. They could do this, it was intended to imply. They could put both their conversation and their interaction with each other back onto a purely professional footing.

Brianna was smiling at Josh. 'Is it true that a member of the royal family is going to come and cut the ribbon for the opening?'

'I believe so.' Josh's smile was as lazy and gorgeous as any Megan had ever seen. She could still see the lines of tension creasing the corners of his eyes, though. Could Brianna sense the undercurrents happening here?

Apparently not. 'How exciting,' she was saying to Josh. 'You'll be all over the news on telly. You're going to be *so* famous after this'

Josh's smile faded. 'I'm not interested in being famous,' he said. 'It's St Piran's I want to put on the map. And not because it has the flashest emergency department but because of the standard of care people get when they come through our doors.'

'Mmm…' But Brianna was grinning. 'Maybe we'll all be famous.' She turned back to Megan. 'You'll still be here, won't you? For the grand ceremony?'

'I expect so.' It was only a couple of weeks away, wasn't it? Megan hadn't made any plans to leave before then. In fact, she still hadn't made any definitive plans for what was coming next in her life. Decisions had to be made. Was she using this new project as a means of procrastinating?' 'I've still got a lot of work to do on the cottage to get it back into shape.'

'I saw all the vans parked outside when I drove past yesterday,' Brianna nodded. 'Looks like you've got every tradesman in Penhally on the job.' She glanced down at the packet of sandwiches in her hand. 'Oh, help. I'd better eat or my break will be over. Nice seeing you again, Megan. You're looking a lot better than when you arrived. I think being home must be agreeing with you.'

Being home? Was that how everybody was seeing this visit?

If she was honest with herself, it was how it felt. Breathing in the sea air every morning. Working in a hospital that was as familiar to her as her own home. Being with people she knew so well. People she respected and liked.

Being close to Josh…

She couldn't really call it a comfort zone with the kind of undercurrents she'd been so aware of just a few minutes ago but she couldn't deny the attraction of the familiarity. The feeling of home. A huge part of who she was belonged here and it was going to be a terrible wrench when she left again.

Megan could feel Josh watching her.

'You're not living back in the cottage again, are you? With all that work still going on?'

She nodded. 'I felt a bit in the way after Luke got back from New Zealand. It's not so bad. I can navigate through all the ladders and paint pots. I have hot water and electricity again. I'm going to start on the garden this weekend.'

Oh…help. Should she tell Josh that Charles was planning a visit to come and help? But then she might feel obliged to tell him more about why they'd become engaged and that might lead to a conversation that would take her in the opposite direction from that she needed to go. Bridges might well get burned behind her if that happened and right now those bridges were an insurance policy.

This was the easiest way through it all, wasn't it? She was getting married to someone else and moving away and that would be an end to it all. For good.

But Josh was making a face that suggested even working in her garden was a bad idea.

'I was supposed to tell you,' he groaned. 'And Mum will have my guts for garters if you don't say yes.'

'About talking to her? The toy drive thing? I'll pop in after work.'

Josh shook his head. 'About Saturday. It's the twins' second birthday party. She's decided that you have to be the guest of honour.'

'Oh…I don't think that's…' A good idea? Of course it wasn't. It was a family occasion. A celebration of exactly why she and Josh could never be together.

It was a horrific idea, in fact. No way could she put herself through that.

Except that she made the mistake of meeting Josh's gaze and it was clear that he knew precisely how hard it would be. And not only for her.

'There's going to be lots of people there,' Josh told her quietly. 'And as far as Mum and everybody else is concerned, you saved the lives of Max and Brenna when they were born. Just before…before you left Penhally. And you saved the life of their grandmother virtually the minute you got back. They want to thank you and they've decided that the birthday party is the perfect venue. They'd be very disappointed if you couldn't come.'

Megan swallowed. Hard.

'You don't need to stay long. It's a lunchtime party. You could just come for a cup of tea or something. Please?'

He cared so much, Megan realised. He didn't want his

mother to be disappointed. He was quite prepared to do something that was probably going to be as difficult and uncomfortable for him as it would be for her, for the sake of someone else he cared about. How could she not be caught by that plea when that ability to care about others was one of the things she loved so much about this man?

'OK.' The word was a whisper. 'I'll come. I'll talk to Claire about what time and things when I see her later.'

The warmth of the smile Josh gave her stayed with Megan for some time. Well after they'd left the cafeteria and gone back to finish their day's work. The evidence of how Josh could put the needs of others over his own needs stayed alongside the memory of that smile and they were both on her mind as she drove home.

And then it happened. Not in a blinding flash but bit by bit. Random thoughts that came out of nowhere like pieces of a jigsaw puzzle and floated until she began slotting them into place. When the final picture came into view, it was enough of a revelation to make her pull off the road. Not that there was a patch of beach to walk on here but it was a parking area designed to let people appreciate the wilder parts of the Cornish coastline. Even in the dark, the white foam of the surf as it boiled over the rocks at the bottom of the cliff was spectacular and the sound of the sea loud enough to make coherent thought too hard.

The picture was still there, though.

Josh…unable to prevent himself from doing what someone else wanted him to do so badly.

A marriage that had been in tatters. A marriage that Josh had felt guilty about having embarked on in the first place simply because he'd been lonely.

A woman who had been bitterly disappointed in how

it had turned out. Who had been obsessed by her need to have a baby.

Josh had said that she'd done it on purpose. Because she'd wanted a baby. It had been her way of trying to keep them together.

Had it been a desperate, last-ditch attempt to save her marriage or to try and at least get pregnant?

Had Rebecca planned some kind of seduction and empowered it by playing on her husband's guilt? Megan remembered what Tasha had tried to tell her but she had been too desperately unhappy to listen. The marriage had been over for a long time, she'd said. Rebecca had probably been lying in wait on the bed in a skimpy set of underwear or something.

She'd been playing games.

Just this one more time…

How could Josh have been cruel enough to refuse? If he had, it wouldn't have been the action of a man who cared as much as she knew he was capable of caring.

It had only been that one time. Josh had told her that, too. A *mistake*, he'd said, and his voice had been agonised enough that she knew he'd been telling the truth.

And it had been weeks before he'd come to *her* bed that night. Had it been the final point of his marriage? One that had been definitive enough for Josh to know he had to leave it behind and move to where he really wanted to be?

How could *she* have been so judgmental?

She'd made it all about herself, hadn't she? She'd been so hurt by the idea that he'd slept with Rebecca even on a single occasion when they'd both been caught by the pull of the irresistible tide that had drawn them back together.

Megan had thrown up an impenetrable barrier right there, on the spot. A barrier that had made it unthinkable that she could ever be with this man she'd loved so much because he'd slept with his wife.

Once.

She'd seen the twins as evidence of his infidelity, for heaven's sake. Those gorgeous children who were the only children of his own Josh would ever have. Children he could never have had if he had been with her. They had his genes. His looks. His personality, probably, judging from the little she'd seen of them.

They were half-Josh. How could she not love them, if she let herself?

But she'd run away. Put thousands and thousands of miles between herself and those tiny babies. Between herself and Josh when he must have needed all the support he could get.

And right now, with tears coursing down her face, Megan could see it for what it had been.

A *mistake*.

They'd both made them. The difference was that Josh had known instantly about the mistake he'd made. It had taken two years and being forced to come home for her to recognise hers.

And the saddest thing of all was that there was nothing she could do about it. It was far too late. She'd run and she'd been away long enough for Josh to put his new life together. A life that he was determined to protect for the sake of the people he loved most.

His children.

A life that didn't—*couldn't*—include her.

CHAPTER SEVEN

A BIRTHDAY PARTY for two-year-olds was bound to be an emotional roller-coaster. Shrieks of delight and peals of laughter were punctuated by the odd bout of tears and even a tantrum or two.

Beneath a sea of balloons and streamers, the furniture in the O'Hara house had been pushed back to give more space both for the children to play and for the small crowd of accompanying adults to supervise as well as enjoy a social gathering of their own.

Claire's fellow grannies from the play group were there, including Rita who had brought her granddaughter Nicola Hallet and her great-grandson Colin. Brianna was there with her twin daughters Aisling and Rhianna. Anna and Luke had brought Crash.

'On request.' Anna laughed. 'But he's our fur child and he fits the age group.'

The look that passed between Anna and Luke at that point had more than just Megan wondering if a less furry child was a not-so-distant prospect but there was no chance to ask her friend whether she was keeping a secret.

The party was full on. Timed for the middle of the day so that the young participants could go home for a sleep when it all got a bit much, there were gifts to open and games to play before the food was served.

Megan had offered to help in the kitchen where Claire and her friends were setting out tiny sandwiches cut into the shapes of animals and heating small pizza squares and chicken nuggets, but Claire shooed her back into the living area to have fun. On her way out of the kitchen Megan saw the dessert platters of bite-sized pieces of fresh fruit and two cakes. One a pink pony-shaped creation and the other an impressively green dinosaur with lurid, candy-covered chocolate buttons for spots. She was smiling as she joined the main gathering. Saving the bright food colouring for just before the toddlers were taken home was smart thinking.

Fun was the last thing Megan had expected to have when she'd steeled herself to follow up her promise to attend this party. She had spent the last few days in a state of confusion that had bordered on unbearable. Charles was driving down from London today and he had every right to expect that she would have achieved her purpose for staying on here by now. That she would have come to terms with her past and would be able to face her new future with confidence.

But, if anything, after the startling insight of how much she could blame herself for this whole, sad, star-crossed-lovers' story that she and Josh had created, it had only become harder to untangle the web of memories and emotions. It was much, much easier to let herself become distracted. To be drawn into the moment by concentrating on her work or the new project of collecting donations for the clinic or…amazingly…having *fun*.

Her trepidation had vanished only seconds after she'd walked in, carrying her gifts. It had evaporated the moment the twins had spotted her and come running.

'*Meggy.*'

That they'd been more interested in receiving cuddles

than the brightly wrapped gifts was testament to how they were being brought up, Megan decided. She was the one to use the gifts as an excuse to call time from the tangle of warm little limbs wrapping themselves around her body.

Around her heart.

Josh was right there, a proud smile on his face, when his children remembered to say thank you for their gifts.

And then the children had wriggled back into the festivities and it was just Josh so close. Before Megan had had a chance to centre herself. She could still feel the overwhelming pull of those cuddles. The unconditional love...

'Great choice.' Josh was still smiling but there was a question in his eyes. 'Well done.'

Megan ducked her head. It was almost too much, receiving praise from Josh on top of the emotions his children had just stirred in her. And she didn't want to answer that question. The one about how she felt about these children. Maybe she didn't even want to think about it.

'The assistant in the toy shop has to get the credit,' she said. 'She told me that dress-ups were always a winner at this age.'

So now Max had a bright yellow Bob the Builder hard hat on, a tiny tool belt clipped around his waist and a miniature high-vis vest over his own clothes. And Brenna had pulled on the tutu skirt with the elasticised waist and put the sparkly tiara on her dark curls and was refusing to let go of her wand with the star on the top. She was waving it like a stern conductor as she danced to each burst of music for the game of musical cushions.

All the children followed her lead and were dancing with varying degrees of competence and balance. Josh's smile was as misty as those of any of the watching adults. He was actually forgetting to stop the music so that the children could make a dash for available cushions.

Megan found herself watching Josh instead of the game, knowing that her own smile was also coming from a very tender place in her heart.

Something had changed in the last few days.

Something very fundamental.

The anger had gone, hadn't it? That sense that Josh had betrayed her by sleeping with Rebecca.

And with it had gone the entire foundation on which she'd built her conviction that they could never be together. It seemed to have simply crumbled away.

Where did that leave her now?

Emotionally available?

Not really. There was Charles to consider now. And the pull of what she'd left behind in Africa.

Megan certainly couldn't forget about Africa. It seemed like it was the only thing people here wanted to talk to her about.

Wendy, the grandmother of three-year-old Shannon, couldn't wait to tell her about the bake sale planned for the next week.

'We're hoping to raise over a hundred pounds,' she told Megan. 'We're going to spend it at the bookshop.'

Margaret, who was at the party with two grandchildren, four-year-old Liam and his younger brother Jackson, overheard Wendy and rushed to join the conversation.

'Mr Prachett at the bookshop is giving us a great discount and he's found a line of picture books that have no text but still tell stories. And he's going to donate lots of pencils and paper, too.'

'The school's on board,' Wendy added. 'Every child has been given an exercise book and they're decorating the covers in art class.'

Another granny, Miriam, offered Megan a cup of tea and a proud smile. 'I'm in charge of clothing donations,' she said. 'I've got two huge crates in my sewing room and I'm washing and mending and ironing everything before it gets packed. We're only accepting lightweight items like cotton dresses and shorts and T-shirts. Will that be all right, do you think?'

'I'm sure it'll be wonderful,' Megan responded. It was impossible not to be touched by the enthusiasm and generosity of these women. 'You're all wonderful. I can't believe how this project keeps growing and growing.'

'It's you who's wonderful,' Miriam said. 'We're having fun collecting things but we're still in our own comfort zones, aren't we? With our families safe and healthy around us. You're the one who was prepared to go to the end of the earth to really help.'

Josh was supervising a bubble-blowing contest but was standing close enough to overhear Miriam's words. When he looked towards them, his glance had none of the admiration of the women around her.

'Megan's an angel,' he said crisply. 'Just ask my mother.'

The tone was light enough to make the people around her smile. Maybe it was only Megan who could hear that the words covered something painful. They both knew the real reasons for her heading to Africa two years ago and it hadn't been entirely altruistic, had it?

Would she do it again, knowing what she knew now?

Fortunately, Josh had turned back to the bubble blowing and there were much easier questions to answer.

'What's it like?' Wendy asked. 'In the camp?'

Megan deliberately censored the first impressions that always came to mind. The unbearable heat and filth. The suffering of so many people. 'Huge. Like a fair-sized city, really, with a hundred and thirty thousand people in the camp and another thirty thousand or so around the edges.'

'It can't be an easy place to live.'

Megan shook her head. 'No. It's hot and dirty and there are pockets of violence but it's the disease that's the worst of it. There are probably eight thousand children suffering from malnutrition and so many orphans who lose their parents to things like AIDS. And then there are other diseases like dysentery and malaria and dengue fever to cope with.' She deliberately stopped herself going any further. A birthday celebration was no place to be telling things like they really were. She could do that somewhere else. At one of the fundraising events, maybe.

But the older women were hanging on every word. They tutted in sympathy.

'And the clinic? Is it like a medical centre or a proper hospital? Do you have operating theatres and maternity wards and things?'

'Oh, yes…it's a proper hospital but very different from St Piran's, of course. And we struggle to cope with what we have to work with.'

Megan's attention was caught by what was happening behind Margaret. Brenna was having trouble with her bubbles because she wasn't holding the loop anywhere near her mouth when she was blowing. Josh was crouched beside her. He closed her little fist over the handle of the loop and dipped it into the soapy water and then held it up in front of her mouth. She could see him miming what she needed to do with her lips and breath.

Brenna sucked in a big breath and whooshed it out and a stream of small bubbles exploded into the air. Her face lit up with a grin that went from ear to ear and Megan could see the way Josh's eyes crinkled as he grinned back. Even if she hadn't been able to read the love he had for his daughter on his face like that, she would have been able to feel the glow of it.

'Sorry, what was that?' She'd completely missed something Wendy had been saying.

'I read in the paper that other hospitals are joining St Piran's to donate old equipment and drugs and things. Isn't that marvellous?'

'It certainly is.'

'Dengue fever.' Miriam was frowning thoughtfully. 'That's what you got sick with, wasn't it?'

'I'm much better now.'

'You look it. Must be the lovely sea air around here that's done the trick.'

'Mmm…' But Megan was having trouble focusing on her health or anything else right now. She was still watching Josh and remembering another time when she had read that kind of infinite love on his face. Way before Brenna had been born. Before he'd even known she was a possibility.

That love, seen in the half-light of that on-call room, had been purely for *her*.

And Josh would have seen the mirror image of it on her own face.

She could feel the glow of it all over again. So much so she needed to take off the cherry-red cardigan she had on over the soft white shirt she had teamed with her jeans. Had Josh sensed something of what she was thinking? Was that why he was suddenly there, his hand extended?

'Let me take that for you. I can hang it up with the coats.'

'Yes…' Wendy was nodding with satisfaction. 'You've got a nice bit of colour in your cheeks now, dear.'

Megan could certainly feel that colour, which must have heightened as Josh's hand brushed hers in relieving her of the cardigan. Feeling flustered, she avoided meeting his gaze, but that didn't help because she found herself look-ing at his hand. Holding an item of her clothing.

Oh, help… She had to excuse herself.

'I might see if your mum needs some help in the kitchen,' she muttered.

'See?' Josh had raised an eyebrow. His lazy grin was charming every female within range. 'I told you she was an angel. You could just enjoy yourself, Megan. You don't have to work, you know.'

Megan shook her head with a smile. It must be time to serve the party food and it was just too disturbing, being this close to Josh and remembering things like that mo-ment in the on-call room. *Feeling* things like the way that had made her feel.

Something huge had certainly changed but was it only on her side?

She was only half the equation here.

Josh had built his own foundation to anchor the barrier of them ever being together. The concrete had been poured the day he'd come to tell her that Rebecca was pregnant. Megan had probably added some steel reinforcing rods herself when she'd walked out without even having the courtesy of attending Rebecca's funeral.

He must have been so hurt by that. The subtle edge to that "angel" comment he'd made suggested that it hadn't been buried far below the surface. And maybe it had just added to the anger simmering in the wake of her accusa-tion that he'd been lying about his marriage being over. That he'd treated her like a bit on the side.

Could he ever forgive her for that?

He'd said he didn't hate her.

That he could *never* hate her.

And, when he'd said that, he'd looked…as if he'd wanted

nothing more than to close the gap between them and kiss her senseless.

There was still something there between them, that much was obvious.

A big something.

But was it big enough? Could it be trusted? Did she even want to find out? Or would she end up back at square one, the way she already had when it came to Josh O'Hara?

Twice, in fact.

There had to be a limit on how many times you could go through that kind of emotional trauma and still survive.

The sensible thing to do would be to run. As fast and as far away as she possibly could.

Josh watched Megan making her way into the kitchen. The room instantly felt emptier without her which was ridiculous given the number of people milling about.

Not to mention a very large dog. Crash was being extraordinarily patient with all the small people who wanted to stroke his nose or try to climb onto his back but Luke was hovering nearby.

'Might be time we took off,' he said to Josh. 'I suspect all the Davenports are ready for a blast of fresh air on the beach. If we stay much longer, all these kids are going to start feeding treats to Crash and the consequences won't be pretty.'

Josh grinned. 'Fair enough. Thanks for bringing him.'

The noise level was rising steadily around them, with Shannon staging quite a spectacular tantrum, lying on her back and drumming her heels on the floor. Josh and Luke shared a grimace. 'No wonder you want to escape,' Josh muttered. 'It's enough to put you right off having kids, huh?'

But Luke just smiled. 'Bit late for that,' he murmured.

Josh opened his mouth but was too stunned for any word to emerge. And then it was too late. Small hands were tugging on his trouser leg.

'Daddy...*up*.'

Claire appeared in the doorway as Josh scooped Brenna into his arms.

'Who's hungry?' she called above the noise. 'And who needs some juice?'

Shannon stopped shrieking but the noise level didn't diminish as the tribe of excited, hungry children flowed past Josh towards the kitchen. Luke and Anna used the exodus as a means to slip away with Crash, and Josh watched them go, still somewhat dazed by their apparent news.

It seemed like whichever way he turned, things were changing around him on an almost daily basis. And they had been, ever since the disruption of his mother getting sick.

Ever since Megan's unexpected return?

That she was here in Penhally at all was surprising but the fact that she was still here at this party was startling enough to signify an even bigger change.

'Here...' Claire put a glass of sparkling wine in his hands as soon as he walked into the kitchen. 'Give that to Megan.'

'I'm not sure she'll want to stay long enough for a drink.'

His mother made a sound that Josh recognised from his childhood. He needed to do what he was told. With a wry smile he headed for Megan, fully expecting her to reject the offer. She hadn't wanted to come to this party at all and he couldn't blame her for that. Josh had expected her to drop in only long enough to be polite. To have a cup of tea and say happy birthday to the twins and then find an excuse to slip away from the chaos, like Luke and Anna had done.

But Megan looked more than happy to accept. Her smile was instant. Brief, but happy enough to light up her face.

'What a lovely idea. Thanks, Josh.'

'You're welcome.' The words were polite. They should have come accompanied by a smile to answer hers but Josh's lips felt oddly stiff. His fingers were tingling, too. Had Megan been as aware as he was of that tiny touch of skin to skin as the glass had been transferred?

There was certainly something very different about the way Megan was looking at him today.

About the way she was smiling at him.

Maybe the biggest change of all had happened a few days ago and was only now filtering through. He'd hardly seen her since that conversation they'd had in the cafeteria. Maybe because he didn't trust himself around her? If Brianna and her friends hadn't come in when they had, would he really have kissed Megan?

Did he still want to?

She was smiling again right now. At Claire this time, nodding as she raised her glass to her lips. His mother's expression was anxious. Did she like the wine? Was she enjoying herself? Megan's smile said that she did. And she was. The tip of her tongue appeared as if chasing an errant drop of wine from her bottom lip and Josh was aware of a sudden heat, deep down in his belly. He almost groaned aloud.

Yes. The answer was most definitely yes. For a long, long moment he couldn't take his eyes off Megan's mouth. God help him, but he'd never wanted to kiss anybody as much as he wanted to kiss Megan Phillips at this moment.

Megan's gaze suddenly shifted, jerking up to meet his as if she'd felt the force of that shaft of desire.

It was impossible to look away. To deny what he was feeling.

To one side of him, Brenna was climbing onto a chair, a mangled chicken nugget in her small fist.

'For you, Daddy,' she announced imperiously.

'Mmm…' But Josh couldn't move. Couldn't even look down. Not yet

Not when he could see that Megan knew exactly what he'd been thinking about. How he was feeling.

And she wasn't looking away…

A faint flush of colour had painted her cheeks again and her lips parted slightly. Never mind that the room was packed with people and there had to be at least a dozen conversations going on, adults helping little ones to eat or pouring juice or drinking their wine and chatting to each other.

Far too many people for such a small space and yet, for that instant, it felt like it had in the cafeteria days ago. As if nothing else mattered and he was alone in the world apart from Megan.

'*Dad*-dy…'

Josh lowered his head and obediently opened his mouth. The chicken nugget was posted home accompanied by a squeal of glee from his daughter and the moment was well and truly broken.

That flush of colour seemed to stay on Megan's cheeks after that. Was it the wine? Maybe it was due to the compliments that Claire kept heaping on Megan to anyone who was listening.

'She saved my life, you know. If she hadn't been there on the beach that day, I probably wouldn't be here, celebrating my grandchildren's birthday. She's my angel, so she is. Where's my camera? I need a photo.'

Rita was only too pleased to arm herself with the camera and take a picture of Claire and Megan side by side and smiling.

And then she wanted one of Megan with the twins.

'She was the doctor who saved them when they were born, you know.' Claire had to wipe a tear away. 'My angel, so she is…'

Josh stood back and watched as Claire engineered the picture she wanted. Brenna was happy enough to sit on Megan's knee but Max took a bit more persuasion. He was busy flattening chicken nuggets with his plastic Bob the Builder hammer. His grandmother bribed him by saying that he would be able to blow out the candles on his cake as soon as the picture was taken and in short order there was Megan with both his children on her lap.

Josh suddenly found it hard to take his next breath. Brenna was reaching up, unable to resist the urge to play with the tumble of Megan's hair. She seemed to change her mind at the last moment, however, and touched Megan's face instead. Unusually gentle for such a small child, Brenna traced the outline of Megan's smile.

Claire was dabbing her eyes with her handkerchief as Rita snapped some photos.

She was right, wasn't she? If it wasn't for Megan, this party might not be happening. She had been the person who had been there to hold them and care for them when they had taken their first breaths.

What a different picture that would have been from the happy, family chaos they were in the midst of here. Josh could paint that different picture in his mind all too easily. The bright lights and tense atmosphere. The hiss of oxygen and the beeping of monitors giving alarming readings.

How hard had that been on Megan?

Harder than it had been for him, banished to pace the

end of the corridor and agonise over what might be happening?

Of course it must have been.

He'd begged her to save his babies, knowing that he couldn't face the agony of losing another child. But the child he *had* lost had also been Megan's and, although he'd done his absolute utmost to save the baby she'd named Stephen, he'd failed. And yet he'd expected Megan to do whatever she could to save the twins and he'd had absolute faith that she would. She'd made sure that he'd been left with the gift of life that he'd failed to give her all those years ago.

She must have been devastated at having to be a central player in such an ironic twist of fate. No wonder she hadn't hung around for Rebecca's funeral. She'd already done far more than it had been reasonable to expect and it was thanks to her that he had these precious children in his life.

And that he still had his mother.

His chest still felt tight and now Josh had a lump in his throat as well. How selfish had it been to harbour resentment at Megan for taking off the way she had? To have hung onto the anger that she hadn't believed him when he'd tried to explain the anomaly of sleeping with Rebecca that one last time? How arrogant had it been to assume she would trust him when he'd let her down so badly in the past? Turning his back on her after that first night together.

Failing to save *their* child.

And she had been afraid to tell him she'd moved on and become engaged to another man because she didn't want him to hate her?

As if the kind of love he had for Megan could ever, *ever* flip over to the dark side of that coin.

If anything, in this moment, seeing her here in his house, holding his children, he loved her more than ever.

The power of that first night they'd had together was trickling back faster and faster.

Threatening to drown him.

A power that was becoming intense because this scene felt so *right*. Megan as the mother of his children. It felt as right as it had to create a new life together on the night they had been discovering each other for the first time.

But what could he do about it?

Too much damage had been done. Megan had finally taken definitive steps to move on from it all. What was it he'd overheard someone saying? Oh…yeah…she'd gone to the end of the earth in order to do that. And she'd found someone else there. This Charles that she was now engaged to.

Megan wasn't available so it didn't matter a damn how right any of this felt. He had no right to mess up whatever it was Megan had decided she wanted for the rest of her life. He had to let go.

Be happy for her?

But…what about the change he was so aware of today? The way Megan was looking at him?

Her smile…

The utter confusion Josh could feel seemed to be contagious. Max was suddenly overcome by the emotional overload of the exciting birthday party. He hit his sister with his plastic hammer and Brenna shrieked with outrage and then burst into heartbroken sobs.

Claire tried to rescue Megan but Brenna wasn't having any of it. She wound her arms around Megan's neck and howled more loudly. A kick from her small legs sent Max tumbling off Megan's lap and his face crumpled ominously. Josh moved in to collect his son. He picked Max up and held him tightly, making soothing noises to circumvent an additional meltdown. It would be time enough when things had calmed down to have a talk to him about what it was acceptable to use his new hammer on. It was certainly pointless right now.

'Maybe we'd better postpone the cakes,' Claire suggested, and there was a murmur of agreement from other adults. The twins weren't the only toddlers who were reaching the end of their tethers. The guests began to sort themselves out to go home.

Megan was on her feet. She had her arms wrapped around Brenna and she was rocking the small girl and making the same kind of soothing noises Josh had been making to Max. His son had now recovered his good humour.

'Juice?' he begged. 'Thirsty, Daddy.'

'I'll fix that,' Claire said. 'Can you give out the goody bags for everybody before they go?'

'Sure.' A glance over his shoulder before he moved to the front door to give out the farewell gifts showed him that Brenna was now almost asleep in Megan's arms. Her eyes were shut and a thumb was in her mouth. Her other arm was still wound around Megan's neck, though. There was even a small fistful of that tumble of brown curls, anchoring Megan's head in place.

When he got back to the kitchen, there were only a couple of guests remaining and Max was sitting at the table, eating pizza and staring hopefully at his cake.

'Later,' his grandmother was saying. 'It'll be our tea-time treat.'

Megan was nowhere to be seen.

'She's gone upstairs to put Brenna to bed,' Claire told him. 'Maybe you could check on them?'

'Sure.' But Josh didn't return his mother's smile. Poor Megan. She'd not only attended a party she hadn't wanted to go to, she'd been firmly cast in the role of stand-in mother.

How on earth was she coping with that?

It had been a huge relief when Brenna's sobs had receded and the stiff little body she'd been holding had begun to relax. That boneless sensation of a child falling asleep in her arms had been so sweet Megan hadn't dared risk waking her by accepting Claire's offer to take her. Instead, she'd said she would put Brenna down for a nap herself.

To find Brenna's tiny fingers still clutching a handful of her hair when she eased her onto her small bed was enough to bring tears to Megan's eyes. She really hadn't wanted anyone else to comfort her, had she?

Kneeling beside the bed and leaning in close enough not to have her hair pulled painfully or disturb the toddler's slumber, she gently disentangled the connection, although she needn't have worried about waking Brenna who was deeply asleep now, her head sinking into her pillow. Dark eyelashes made fans above plump, flushed cheeks and a cupid's bow of her mouth made tiny movements as if sucking on something, even though the favoured thumb had been discarded.

For a long moment Megan stayed where she was, kneeling beside the bed. She smoothed some errant curls back from Brenna's face and then simply watched her sleep, marvelling at such perfect skin and the expression of such innocence that made sleeping children look like angels.

So precious.

So vulnerable.

The vice that squeezed her heart was all too easy to recognise and Megan had to close her eyes for a moment and try to take in a deep, steadying breath.

How had this happened?

How, in God's name, hadn't she seen it coming and put a better protective barrier in place?

It was too late now. She'd fallen in love with Brenna.

With Josh's daughter.

Megan heard the soft sound of movement behind her. Or maybe she sensed Josh easing himself silently into the room. Still on her knees, Megan turned her head, knowing that her eyes were bright with tears. That her distress must be written all over her face. She loved a child who could never be hers. And now she was facing the man she loved and *he* could never be hers either.

She could see pain that mirrored her own on Josh's face. He murmured something that was inaudible but the tone was one of pure empathy. He held out his hand to help Megan to her feet and it felt only right that he didn't let it go. That he drew her into his arms and held her.

They were both suffering here. The swirl of their entire history, mixed with feelings that were too powerful to fight. And Megan didn't want to fight any more. She needed this moment. It felt right. As though there'd been something worthwhile in all the pain over so many years.

Because even a moment as perfect as this made it all worthwhile.

And then Megan moved from where her face was buried against Josh's shoulder. She turned her head and looked up to find Josh looking down at her. Neither of them could look away. There was something far too powerful for either of them to fight happening now.

Slowly...so slowly that she could have easily stopped it happening if she'd thought about it for even a nanosecond, Josh's head dipped and his lips came close enough to touch hers.

So softly. The love she could feel in that gentle touch

was so pure that Megan knew she would remember it until she drew her last breath.

And then, faster than thought itself, the touch ignited and the flame of passion licked every cell of her body. Megan could feel her lips parting beneath Josh's, her body arching into his, a tiny cry of unbearable desire escaping her throat. A whimper of need that was so deep it felt like it was tearing her apart.

A tiny part of her brain remained in control, however. Or maybe it was Josh who was still aware that they were standing beside a bed that contained his sleeping child. It was impossible to unleash the passion but equally impossible to drag themselves away from each other. Every time they tried and the contact became light enough to break, they both pressed closer. Went a little deeper each time.

It was a familiar sound that broke the spiral.

Not the whimper of a child waking or the sound of someone coming up the stairs.

It was an electronic chirp. The sound of a text message arriving on the tiny mobile phone Megan had in the back pocket of her jeans.

A second chirp sounded as she and Josh finally stepped back from each other and the noise was just enough of a prompt to break the stunned immobility of the way they were staring at each other.

Megan read her message. She could feel the curiosity emanating from Josh. She couldn't meet his gaze.

A warning bell was sounding in the back of her head. Taking the shape of the thought she'd had what seemed like only minutes ago.

That things were changing and it was dangerous because she could get badly hurt all over again.

That the safe thing to do would be to run. As fast and as far away as she could.

'It's Charles,' she said, her voice totally without expression. 'He's waiting for me at the cottage.'

There was a moment's charged silence.

'You'd better go, then.' The words from Josh were as toneless as her own had been.

Megan still couldn't look at Josh. Nothing was being said and yet everything was being said.

'Mmm.' A strangled sound. 'I'd better.'

He wasn't watching her as she fled. Megan knew that without even turning back. He hadn't moved an inch. He was standing there, his head bowed, his gaze fixed on his daughter.

CHAPTER EIGHT

THAT KISS HAD changed everything.

Maybe that wasn't a good enough excuse for Josh to be where he was now, too late in the evening for it not to seem significant, standing in front of the door to Megan's cottage. But he'd been agonising over it ever since Megan had virtually run out of his house, according to Claire, stopping only long enough to snatch up her bag and jacket.

She'd left her cardigan behind, draped over one of the chairs that had been pushed to one side in the living room, and it had only been found when the children had finally been been put down for the night and Josh and his mother had been clearing away the remnants of the birthday party.

Returning an item of clothing wasn't much of an excuse, but Josh needed to meet this Charles.

To find out what his competition was like?

No. His motivation wasn't that juvenile.

Taking a deep breath, Josh raised his hand and lifted the brass door knocker. He rapped it briskly, three times.

He hadn't been able to think of anything other than Megan since that kiss. The kaleidoscope of memories, emotions and a determination to be honest with himself had swirled around and around in his head, sliding and colliding until *finally* they seemed to have fallen into place.

He had treated Megan abominably, he could freely

admit that. He'd convinced himself he was being strong and doing the right thing but he'd been covering the fact that he was an emotional coward. And, yes, maybe he wasn't doing the *right* thing now but it was the honest thing to do.

He understood why Megan had left him when he'd been at the lowest point of his life, consumed by guilt at the death of a wife he'd never loved enough. Terrified by the prospect of being a solo father to two fragile, ultimately vulnerable, babies.

He had forgiven Megan for that. He had forgiven her for not believing him when he'd told her that his marriage was over. For thinking that he was sleeping with his wife at the same time he'd gone to Megan's bed.

His knock went unanswered. He could hear some classical music coming from inside the cottage but there was no sound of any voices. The thought that he might be disturbing something intimate prompted Josh to lick suddenly dry lips. To take another deep breath. He would try just once more. He rapped three times again, and then added another couple of raps, slightly louder.

The bottom line was that he could forgive Megan anything at all because…he loved her. It was as simple as that. And as complicated. He could even forgive her for marrying someone else and moving on with her life without him if he could believe that she would be happy doing that.

But Josh also understood why Megan had fled from his house earlier today, in the wake of that kiss.

It was still there.

Whatever they'd discovered on that first night together and rediscovered when they'd found themselves working together in St Piran's all those years later was still there.

Stronger than ever, maybe, because it had been denied and locked away.

Because of his stupid, misguided tunnel vision.

How had he ever convinced himself that he could only be the father he was determined to be for his children by denying love or commitment to anything other than them or his career?

He could never be the best father—the best anything, for that matter—without Megan in his life because he could never be the person he could be if he had her by his side.

He could never feel *whole* without her.

And, thanks to that kiss, Josh was convinced that it was the same for Megan, whether she was prepared to admit it or not.

So why the hell was she planning to marry someone else?

Just what did this Charles have that *he* didn't?

Maybe he was about to find out. The door was opening in front of him. Expecting it to be Megan, Josh felt his lips curling into a smile but the smile drained away when he found himself facing the man who had to be Charles. It was an effort not to let his face freeze into lines of…shock?

Whatever he'd expected Megan's fiancé to look like, it wasn't this. Charles was much, much older than he was. Pushing sixty? He had completely grey hair, wire-rimmed spectacles and…and he was wearing a *waistcoat*. He looked like he could be Megan's father. Or a favourite uncle. There was a kindliness about his face and his smile looked genuine but his eyes were sharp. This man missed nothing.

'You *must* be Josh,' he said into the awkward silence. 'Please, come in. Megan's having a bath but she'll be down in a minute, I expect.'

'I…ah…' This was so unexpected that Josh was completely thrown. Just what had he thought he would do when he got here anyway? 'I just came to return this,' he said, holding out the garment in his hand. 'Megan left it behind at the party. Perhaps you could give it to her?'

A hand was extended but not to accept the item of clothing. It was asking for a handshake.

'I'm Charles Cartwright,' the older man said. 'Megan's friend. Please do come in. I've heard so much about you, I'd like to meet you properly.'

Megan's *friend*?

He couldn't walk away now without appearing rude. Besides, Josh's level of confusion was rising. What kind of a fiancé described himself as a friend? Maybe Megan wasn't engaged at all and that was why she wasn't wearing a ring. Had she told everybody she was engaged to protect herself?

Perhaps all he needed to do was convince Megan that she didn't need that kind of protection. That he'd finally grown up and got over himself. That he could be everything that she needed him to be.

That it might not be as easy as it sounded became more apparent with every step Josh took into the cottage.

It was impossible not to remember the last time—the *only* time—he'd ever been here before. There was an air of redecoration chaos and a strong smell of paint that made it feel different now but nothing could erase those memories.

Steeling himself to do the hardest thing in his life.

Putting it off, just for another minute, resisting the urge to pull Megan into his arms from the moment she'd answered the door. Following her into the kitchen after accepting the offer of a drink.

And then he'd snapped when Megan had betrayed her nervousness by spilling the water when she'd tried to pour it. That kiss was seared into his memory just as deeply as today's now was but...they were so different.

The kiss in the kitchen that day, more than two years ago, had been one of desperation. A last kiss, before he had to tell her what he knew would kill the hope and love he could see in her eyes. When he had to say that he couldn't be in love with her any more.

And today's kiss? The only desperation there had been the need to get far closer than they could through a kiss. Far closer than their surroundings and circumstances would allow.

But they'd both wanted that, hadn't they?

The real difference was that today's kiss had been tinged with *hope*.

Or was he imagining that?

Josh's confused whirl of thoughts circled back and tried to start again. Why had he come here? What did he hope to achieve? The only thing Josh was certain about was that he was nervous. More nervous than the last time he'd entered this cottage because then he'd known what the outcome would be.

Now it felt like the rest of his life was hanging by a thread that was so tangled up he had no idea how to start unravelling it.

Charles was leading the way into the living area of Megan's cottage. It was cosy. The curtains had been drawn to shut out the rest of the world and the fire was a soft glow of embers waiting to be tickled back into life with some new fuel. A couple of wine glasses, one with a few mouthfuls of ruby liquid remaining, had been pushed to one side of the coffee table. The rest of the table was completely covered with photographs.

Josh had to step closer. To see what had been going on in this intimate atmosphere?

'Snapshots of Africa,' Charles said from behind him. 'Can I get you a glass of wine, Josh?'

'No… Thanks,' Josh added belatedly, knowing his refusal had sounded terse enough to be rude.

He couldn't look away from the photographs because Megan was in every one of them. Never alone, but often the only white face amongst a crowd of smiling colleagues. Or standing with family groups against the background of a tent city. Working in what looked like an overcrowded and pressured clinic setting. Mostly, with children. Treating them. Surrounded by them. Holding them.

'I brought copies of all the ones I thought Megan would like to have,' Charles said quietly. 'I'm a bit of an amateur photographer.'

'They're very good,' Josh heard himself saying politely.

But they were more than very good. The images were amazingly evocative. They captured the barren landscape, the poverty and suffering, the harsh climate so clearly Josh could feel himself stepping into that foreign world.

There was a profile shot of Megan, wearing her stethoscope, her head bent as she listened to the chest of a tiny child who lay in its mother's arms. One of those heartbreaking children who were all ribs and stick-like limbs and huge, huge eyes.

Megan's hair was piled up and clipped to the top of her head but some of that luxuriant tumble of curls had escaped, as it always did. The stray lock looked black—soaked with perspiration and glued to the damp skin of her neck and cheek. Josh could actually feel the urge to touch the photograph. To try and smooth that lock of hair back from Megan's face. To say something to ease the lines of distress he could see in her fierce concentration. In the lines of the way she was holding her mouth and the creases around her eyes.

He couldn't resist picking up another image. One that made him suck in his breath sharply the moment he saw

it. He couldn't stop staring at it, even though he knew he
was glimpsing something private. A picture Megan hadn't
known was being taken because she was sound asleep,
slumped in an old wicker chair, her head uncomfortably
tilted so far to the side it was virtually resting on her shoulder, but still there was a hint of a smile curving her lips.

She wasn't alone, of course. Tucked under each arm
was a tiny baby, their faces so black against Megan's white
coat and the blankets they were cocooned in. The babies
were also deeply asleep and all three of them looked utterly at peace.

So *happy*.

'Lovely shot, isn't it?'

'Mmm.' Josh could barely produce an audible sound. He
was seeing a part of Megan's life he could never share. A
part of the woman he loved that was completely unknown.

'They're twins,' Charles told him. 'The girl is called
Asha, which means Life. And the boy is Dumi—the In-
spirer.'

'Special names,' Josh murmured.

'Megan chose them. She saved their lives when they
were born and she fought for them every step of the way
after that. Day and night for weeks, it was Megan who
fed them and changed them and cuddled them when they
cried.'

'What happened to their mother?'

'She came into the camp in the late stages of her pregnancy and it was too late to start any treatment for her
advanced AIDS. She died within hours of giving birth.'

'And the babies?' Josh felt his heart sink like a stone.
'Are they…? Did they…?' He couldn't bring himself to
say the words. Megan would have been devastated if—

'They were lucky.' He could hear the smile in Charles's
voice even though he didn't look up from the photo. 'We at

least had the time to give the drugs that can help prevent transmission of the disease from mother to child. Neither of them were infected with HIV during the pregnancy and they were delivered via Caesarean and then bottle-fed, of course. They're both thriving.'

Thank goodness for that. Josh's relief was tinged with a sense of unreality, however. How weird was it knowing that Megan had been living a life that paralleled his own to such a degree? A lone parent figure for fragile twin babies.

'When was this picture taken?' he asked.

'Six months ago, when they were about eight weeks old, I think.' Charles sounded oddly hesitant. 'The twins were the main reason it was so hard to persuade Megan to come home and recover properly from the dengue fever. It would have been impossible if I hadn't suggested—' He broke off suddenly, his head turning. 'Megan...we have a visitor.'

'So I see. Hello, Josh. What are you doing here?'

Megan was dressed again after her bath, in jeans and a warm pullover, but her feet were bare and her hair hung down in damp tendrils that she was still squeezing dry with a towel.

She looked...good grief...*frightened*?

Vulnerable, anyway. Heartbreakingly vulnerable. Because of him. Because he was here and threatening to break...something.

Slowly, Josh put the photograph down. He held out what he was still holding in his other hand. The cherry-red cardigan.

'You left this behind at the party. I thought you might need it.'

'Oh...' Megan came forward to claim the article of clothing. 'Sorry...'

What for? The inconvenience of it needing to be returned? Or for what had happened that had made her flee his house in such a hurry that she'd left it behind?

The moment was astonishingly awkward. It was Charles who cleared his throat and tried to break it.

'Megan's been telling me about all the fundraising efforts going on for the clinic. It's a wonderful thing you're all doing.'

'It's Megan who can take the credit,' Josh said. He had to clear his own throat because his voice came out sounding oddly raw.

'She's also told me about the new paediatric wing for your emergency department. That's going to put St Piran's on the map in a big way. You've got a brilliant career ahead of you, Josh, by all accounts.'

Josh made a vaguely dismissive sound. Yes, he already had, and would no doubt continue to have, a brilliant career.

But it wasn't enough, was it?

Charles was clearly struggling to find a topic of conversation to break the loaded silences.

'And your twins turned two today? Megan tells me they're beautiful children.'

Josh managed to make another affirmative noise. Yes, his children were beautiful. They were everything to him and he would lay down his life in a heartbeat for them, if it was necessary.

But…right now…it still didn't feel *enough*.

He needed something more in his life.

He needed Megan.

At least part of what he was feeling had to be showing on his face. In his inability to even make polite conversation. No wonder Megan was starting to look embarrassed. Stricken, even?

'I'd better go.' Josh started moving but it felt like he

was walking away too soon. That he hadn't touched on whatever it was he'd wanted to achieve by coming here.

'I forgot.' The words came out in a kind of a growl as he swung back to face Megan. 'We're doing a test run of the technology in Paediatric Resus tomorrow. X-ray and monitoring and so forth. You might want to be there to see how it comes together.' He tried, and failed, to smile. 'It doesn't matter, of course. If you're busy.'

The look that passed between Megan and Charles was palpably significant but Josh couldn't read the message. His gut was forming an unpleasantly rock-like mass inside him.

'I'll be there,' Megan said quietly. 'What time?'

'Three p.m. We're hoping that a Sunday afternoon might be a quieter spell. There are a lot of people who want to see if it's going to fly.' Josh forced himself to acknowledge Charles with a smile. 'You'd be most welcome to come too, Charles. You might want to see what Megan's been up to while she's been here.'

'Thank you, but I'm due back in London early tomorrow afternoon.' Charles was smiling back at him. 'And I've got a pretty good idea of what Megan's been up to. She knows I approve.'

Had there been some kind of hidden meaning there? Josh had arrived at Megan's cottage feeling agitated because he'd known something had changed. Or hadn't changed, more to the point, in the wake of that kiss. He was driving away feeling like he'd found more questions than answers.

There was a part of Megan he didn't know. The part that was bound up with Africa. That was *friends* with Charles Cartwright. A very important part. But he was missing something here, and he had no idea what it was.

Josh was still feeling agitated. And confused.

Totally at a loss as to what he could do about any of it, in fact.

The new paediatric wing of St Piran's emergency department was not quite finished but it was still crowded on this Sunday afternoon. The scenario being run of dealing with a child with multiple trauma after being knocked off his bicycle might be a pretence but to the medical staff involved this was no game.

From where she was standing in the second resuscitation area, Megan was close to the junior star of the show who was getting ready to play his part. Thirteen year old Jem, the son of Nick Tremayne, who was a Penhally Bay GP, had volunteered for the role.

'I'm going to be a doctor when I grow up,' he told Megan. 'Just like my dad. I'm already learning first aid. And I've done this for real, too, when I had my accident.'

'I remember.' Megan nodded. How could she forget? That had been when her path had crossed that of Josh's again so unexpectedly. A route that had only led, again, to an emotional disaster.

'I don't remember this bit of it, though,' Jem said sadly. 'I was unconscious.'

'That's what you have to pretend to be now.' His father was helping one of the volunteer ambulance crew to fasten a collar around his neck. 'And no giggling. This is serious stuff.'

'OK.' Jem lay flat on the stretcher, closed his eyes and groaned. He tried it again, obviously hoping for a more dramatic effect.

Josh appeared though the doors leading to the main resus area. 'The paediatric trauma team have been summoned by pager,' he announced. 'On my count these doors will open and we'll take it from there in real time.'

He looked extremely tense, Megan thought. Not surprising, given that there were so many observers here. Word had spread fast. Albert White was here as CEO. There were quite a few of St Piran's consultant staff present, including Luke and Anna Davenport, and Nick had brought some of the other local GPs with him. There was also a reporter from a local newspaper accompanied by a photographer.

The tension was instantly contagious. Never mind any personal issues between them, if a major glitch showed up in this scenario, it could be due to a poor choice she had made about the design and predicted flow patterns.

It wasn't like Josh to be grim, though, even if he was stressed. He didn't smile at Megan when he spotted her. He practically scowled at her, for heaven's sake. So she'd arrived a little later than she'd intended. Did it matter that much? He was also looking less than amused by Jem's acting.

'Cut the sound effects, Jem,' he said briskly enough to sound like a reprimand. 'We can do without the groaning, OK?'

A minute or two later and they could hear Josh's count. 'Three, two, one…'

The doors swung open. Megan followed the stretcher that was supposedly arriving from the ambulance bay and pressed herself into a corner, out of the way. The paramedic who was helping started his handover, describing a serious incident in which a child had been struck by a car at speed.

'GCS on arrival was fifteen. Blood pressure was one-three-five on ninety. Resp rate thirty-six. Oxygen saturation ninety-nine per cent on air.'

As airway doctor, Ben Carter was leading the paediatric

trauma team, consisting of other consultants, registrars, nurses and technicians. He requested another primary survey as soon as their patient was transferred to the bed.

The angle of the lights was checked, monitors switched on and trolleys moved closer. Megan could see the way Josh was following the movement of every person involved. He stood there, completely focused, looking tense enough to snap.

Findings were relayed via Josh, who was directing the scenario.

Strong peripheral pulses.

Pupils equal and reactive.

Tender abdomen.

Obvious midshaft, femoral fracture.

'IV line in and secured.' A registrar had taped a tube to Jem's arm. 'Hanging normal saline. Oh…where's the hook?'

An impatient sound came from Josh's direction as the minor missing detail was noted and fixed.

Ben was ordering blood tests and then X-rays. 'Neck, chest, abdomen and pelvis. We'll need CT on standby given the mechanism of injury.'

A nurse moved to test the phone lines. The X-ray technician manoeuvred overhead equipment. The staff were already wearing lead aprons, although no real X-rays were going to be taken. This was about testing the ceiling tracks and making sure that they could get the images that were needed quickly.

Josh stepped closer as soon as the process looked like it was not going to present any problems.

'The pelvic X-rays have shown fractures,' he announced. 'Your patient's now becoming restless and confused. He's vomited twice and his GCS has dropped below nine. Heart rate is rising and blood pressure is dropping.'

Ben nodded. 'We'll intubate prior to moving him to CT, then.'

Now they would all be able to see how well Megan's choice of positioning for equipment would work. The team had to pull in a ventilator and suction equipment, find ET tubes and laryngoscopes and draw up the drugs.

Megan didn't realise she was holding her breath until it became clear that everything was going like clockwork and then she released it in a long sigh. This was *great*.

The reporter thought so, too. He was scribbling madly on his notepad. The photographer was actually grinning as he took shot after shot.

Why wasn't Josh looking happier?

He almost seemed to be brushing off the congratulations that came in the wake of the successful test run.

'There's still a bit of fine tuning to be done,' Megan heard him tell someone. 'It has to be perfect before we officially open for business.'

'When's that going to be, Dr O'Hara?' The reporter pressed forward as people began to disperse.

'As soon as possible. You'll have to ask Dr Phillips. She's the one in charge of the project.'

The reporter nodded. 'And is it true that we've got a member of the Royal family coming to cut the ribbon? The Queen, even, or William and Kate?'

Josh managed a smile. 'You'll have to ask Dr White that one.'

But the reporter was distracted now. Behind Josh, Jem was sitting up on the bed, peeling off his neck brace.

'That was *so* cool!' he exclaimed. 'I could open my eyes just a crack and see through my eyelashes. I still looked unconscious, didn't I, Dad?'

'You sure did,' Nick told him. 'Good job. It wasn't scary, was it?'

'Nah.'

'What's your name, son?' The reporter asked. 'And how old are you? Can we get a photo?'

'Cool. I'll put this back on.' Jem lifted the neck brace.

'No, just hold it. Let's get your dad in the photo, too. You're Dr Tremayne, aren't you? What do *you* think of this new development at St Piran's?'

Megan decided to escape while she could. Why had Josh tried to deflect credit onto her? This whole project was his baby, everyone knew that. He'd been dreaming of it coming together for years now. Was he not happy with how things had gone today?

Where was he, anyway?

Ben Carter had gone back to his duties in the main department with most of the registrars and nurses who'd been involved in the practice run.

'Josh?' He shrugged in response to Megan's query. 'Hasn't come in here. He's probably lapping up a bit of the publicity. Hey…it went well, didn't it? Good job, Megan.'

She'd write a note, Megan decided, and leave it on Josh's desk. If he had a problem, he could come and talk to her about it.

The last thing she expected to find was Josh himself in his office.

No. Maybe the last thing was that fierce glare she was being subjected to.

'Sorry to disturb you.' She knew her tone was cool. 'I didn't think you'd be in here. I was going to leave you a note.'

'Why? Because you couldn't bring yourself to talk to me face to face?'

Megan gave her head a small, sharp shake. 'Don't be daft. I thought you'd be busy talking to that reporter or something.' The glare was getting on her nerves. She hadn't done anything wrong that she knew about. 'What's up with you today, Josh?'

'What's that supposed to mean?'

'You got out of bed on the wrong side or something. You're…angry about something.'

'Damned right I am.' Josh stalked across the office and pushed the door shut behind Megan. He turned to face her.

'You can't do it.' The words burst out of him.

Megan already knew what the answer would be. Her mouth went dry but she had to ask anyway. 'Can't do what?'

'Marry Charles.'

She sucked in a breath. She'd known that herself last night, the moment she'd seen the two men standing side by side in her living room.

Her lover and her friend.

Her past and her future.

Safety…and danger.

Charles had known it all along, of course, bless him, but he'd been waiting for her to wake up.

Should she tell Josh why the engagement had been mooted in the first place? That it was no longer a realistic option?

No. Dammit. What right did Josh have to glare at her like this? To be telling her what she could or couldn't do?

So she didn't say anything. She just held Josh's angry glare. Her heart was thumping so hard it was probably visible. She couldn't move. Couldn't even breathe right now. The sheer *power* of this man over her was unbelievably stunning.

The moment stretched until it was unbearable. Josh snapped first.

'Why him?' Josh took in an audible gulp of air. He was rubbing the back of his neck with his hand—a sure sign that he was deeply agitated. The expression on his face was…desperate? He opened his mouth again.

'Why not *me*?'

CHAPTER NINE

MEGAN'S BREATH CAME out in an incredulous huff of sound.

'You're not available, Josh,' she shot back. 'And even if you were, you couldn't give me what Charles could.'

The words might be cruel but they were true. It was the reason her plans had gone in the direction they had.

Josh had flinched. 'Which is?'

'Security,' Megan said decisively. But then her voice wobbled and went quiet. 'Love…' she added.

Josh was gaping at her now. 'How can you *say* that? You know how much I love you. *I'm* not the one who's moved on.'

'I…haven't. I…'

But Josh didn't appear to be listening to her. He'd stepped closer. Megan bowed her head as he took hold of both her shoulders. She could feel the strength in that grip. The tension. And yet the touch was still gentle.

'Can you honestly say you don't still love me, Megan?'

She had to lift her chin. To meet a gaze so intense it burned.

No. Of course she couldn't say that.

She didn't need to say anything. Josh had always been able to read her like an open book. She couldn't look away. Neither could Josh. Not a word was spoken but it felt like a whole conversation was taking place. And the tension was leaving Josh's hands. His fingers moved, skimming her neck to touch and then cradle her face.

'Oh…Megan…' The words were a groan. Josh tipped his head until their foreheads were touching and they stood like that for a long, long moment. And then Josh pulled her into his arms. So close she could feel his heart thudding against her own. She could feel his lips moving against her ear.

'I *can* love you,' he whispered. 'If only you'll give me another chance. I've been blind. Stupid. I need you, darling. I want you. I…I love you. *So* much.'

Oh…*God*…

The words echoed in her own heart. They stirred up memories of similar words spoken in the past. And more… So much more. They stirred up memories of those intimate moments. The touch of those hands on parts of her body that had lain dormant ever since. The feel of his lips…and his tongue…on her mouth and her breasts and…*ohh*… the feel of him inside her. The absolute perfection of that connection that she'd never found—never *would* find— with anyone else.

How could she fight that, if there was even a small chance that, this time, they could make it work?

She couldn't. She couldn't fight. Couldn't protect herself any longer. She had to take this risk because if she didn't, she would always wonder if it *could* have worked. If cowardice had made her miss her chance of true love and as happy-ever-after as this life could offer anyone.

'I love you, too,' she heard herself whispering back to Josh. 'I always have. Always will.'

'Oh, thank God for that.'

They loosened their hold on each other just enough to

be able to see each other's faces. Josh still had a worried crease on his forehead.

'What about Charles? Your…engagement?'

'Charles has known all along how I feel about you, Josh. The engagement was only ever a…a means to an end, I guess. He's a friend, that's all. We weren't sleeping together.'

Megan's heart skipped a beat as the words left her mouth. She could see the effect of them on Josh. The knowledge that there was no barrier there any more. Josh wasn't married any longer. He was prepared to make a commitment. The children were being safely cared for by their grandmother.

He could take her hand and go home with her and they could go to bed together and make love. A fresh start.

The beginning of the rest of their lives?

'But… Oh, hell…' Josh groaned. 'Everybody around here thinks it was a real engagement. They'll blame me for breaking it up. There he goes again, they'll say, messing with people's lives.'

'It's got nothing to do with anybody else,' Megan said. 'Except for the children, of course. And your mum. And Tasha.'

'They'll all be thrilled that I've finally come to my senses. They all adore you. Especially Max and Brenna.'

'And I love them, too, but…' It was all too easy to get carried away by the heat of passion, wasn't it? There *were* other people to consider here. 'Maybe we can wait until the dust settles,' Megan suggested slowly. 'We don't have to rush out and tell anyone.'

We need to be sure about this was the silent message she was trying to send. *So that nobody gets hurt.*

Especially her? There was no doubt that Josh was genuine in *wanting* to make this commitment but was he actually *capable* of it? Maybe there was no way to protect herself any longer but, by keeping it a secret, she could keep a shred of dignity if it went wrong. Again.

Yes…the fear was still there. Easily dismissed right now but would it ever go away completely?

I am sure came back in that intense gaze, but then Josh seemed to take a deep breath. Did he want some kind of insurance policy too? Did he have that same tiny flicker of fear? Whatever he was thinking, he was clearly happy to follow Megan's lead.

'Things *are* crazy right now. We've got the official opening of the paediatric ED wing coming up and there's still a lot to do.'

The fact that Josh was happy to agree to her suggestion made that fear flicker a little brighter but Megan doused it. She took a deep breath herself. 'And there are all the donations to pull together and get shipped off. I'm supposed to go and talk to Albert about that tomorrow. He's getting worried about storing all the stuff that's coming in from other hospitals.'

'And Mum's going to be tearing her hair out in the next few days if she keeps tripping over all the cartons piling up at our place.'

Yes. There was a lot to do for the next little while. It would be best for all concerned to postpone that fresh start to their lives. Maybe they both just needed a little time. To trust completely.

Josh was smiling down at Megan. '*We'll* know,' he murmured. 'And that's what matters, isn't it?'

'Mmm.' This *was* all they needed. A little time. And then the fear would burn itself out and things would be perfect. Megan's breath came out in a sigh as Josh lowered his head to kiss her tenderly. 'I…I can't believe how happy I am right now.'

'Mmm.' Josh broke the contact of their lips for just a heartbeat. 'Me, too.'

He hadn't been exaggerating to say that life was crazy right now.

And it was all so damn exciting!

Josh's life as a single father and full-time clinician had always been quite hectic enough, especially at this time of year with Christmas approaching. This year Christmas was barely registering yet, despite the decorations beginning to go up around the hospital.

Everywhere he turned at the moment, people were telling him how brilliant he was and how proud they were to be associated with St Piran's. They also wanted more of him. His secretary was complaining that it was becoming a full-time job trying to schedule all the requests for interviews and television appearances that were being lined up to follow the official opening of their emergency department extension. Not only that, the media had got wind of the hospital's involvement in Megan's project for Africa and somehow he was getting way too much of the credit. He seemed to be becoming the face of St Piran's and people were liking what they saw.

Over the last couple of days Josh had been hounded by a television company that was trying to persuade him to agree to base a reality TV show around the new paediatric emergency unit.

'We'll do a re-enactment of the story leading up to the emergency,' the producer had enthused. 'We'll have all the drama of the medical crisis and then we'll follow up. Interviews with the family and the staff. Real emotional stories, Doc, and we won't shy away from the gritty stuff.

We'd have no trouble selling this worldwide. You'd be a superstar.'

Heady stuff, but Josh wasn't interested. What he wanted was to have an emergency department that was renowned for its excellence. One that would be the first choice for any case that was within range of an ambulance or helicopter.

The local air rescue service was making noises about needing another chopper and more staff to cope with the expected increase in workload the hype over the new facilities was generating. He needed to slot in a response to their request for an urgent meeting.

On top of all that, there had been more than one fundraising event to try and attend. With space on a cargo plane already booked and the deadline rapidly approaching, it seemed like the whole of Penhally Bay and St Piran were at a fever pitch to get their projects completed and packed up.

Josh had a new anxiety as he drove home each day, that the stress of all these unusual activities would be too much for his mother so soon after her heart attack, but, if anything, she seemed to be thriving on it all.

'Dinner's going to be a bit late,' she apologised on this occasion. 'Rita's on her way over to help me with the last of the book bags. She was going to come after dinner but Colin's come down with the horrible cold the whole family's had and she's promised to help out tonight.'

'I can fix dinner, if that would help,' Josh offered. He could see that Rita wasn't going to be the only visitor to the house today. Megan came out of the kitchen in the wake of Brenna, who had heard her father come home and was rushing to greet him. Megan had a washcloth in her hands.

'Warning,' she called. 'Major stickiness coming.'

Josh couldn't have cared less about the sticky hands that were already in his hair as he picked Brenna up for a cuddle. Finding Megan in his house was becoming a regular event due to Claire's pleas for advice on co-ordinating all the community donations for the clinic. If his mother was aware of any change in his relationship with Megan, she certainly wasn't showing any sign of disapproval. Not only was Megan being invited into the house more often, she was being invited to step further into the lives of his children. Helping to feed them. Reading them stories. And more.

'Would you mind getting the children into their bath, love?' Claire asked Megan now. 'I'm getting worried that we won't get this last crate finished and the truck's coming tomorrow.'

Josh surveyed the train wreck of his living area. Max was sitting amongst a pile of beautifully decorated exercise books, trying to tear open a box of crayons.

'No, Max.' Claire rushed to rescue the crayons.

'Mine,' Max declared.

Josh saw Megan trying not to smile. She held out her hand. 'Hey, Max. How 'bout you come and show me your favourite toy for the bath? Is it a duck?'

'No.' Max scrambled upright. 'My *boat*.'

Josh looked at Brenna. 'Do you want Daddy to come and help with the bath too?'

'Yes. Daddy *and* Meggy,' Brenna shouted.

Max sneezed loudly and his grandmother sighed. 'I hope you're not getting Colin's cold,' she told him. 'Let me find you a tissue.'

The doorbell rang as she finished speaking and Claire flapped a hand in consternation, at a loss to know what to attend to first. Megan was really smiling now.

'Don't worry. I can sort the tissue.' She scooped Max into her arms before anyone could protest. Josh followed her up the stairs. He could hear his mother greeting her friend at the door, his daughter telling him something that made absolutely no sense, and even the strains of a Christmas carol coming from the radio that was on in the kitchen.

It sounded like home. Family. And Megan was here in the midst of it all.

A taste of the future?

Megan looked up from turning on the taps as he entered the bathroom. She caught his gaze and her own face lit up.

She understood perfectly.

In no time at all the bath contained two very happy toddlers, who were splashing and crowing with delight as Megan soaped their plump little bodies and then tipped buckets of warm water over them to rinse off the suds. The splashing was getting vigorous enough to make the adults kneeling beside the tub distinctly damp. Stray curls of Megan's hair were sticking to her face and Josh could feel damp strands of his own hair flopping into his eyes. He pushed them back.

'I need a haircut,' he muttered. 'Goodness only knows how I'm going to fit in an appointment before the opening.' His fingers rubbed his jaw as he dropped his hand. 'And I'm going to have to find time to shave more often.'

'You look great.' Megan slanted him a look that ignited a slow burn somewhere deep inside. 'When they see you on telly, women all over the country will be whimpering.'

Josh smiled back. 'Whimpering, huh?' He only had to tilt his body slightly for his shoulder to come into contact with Megan's body.

The eye contact had caught and was holding. Sending some very clear messages.

Oh…help… How long could they keep this up? This knowing that they had made a commitment to each other? That they wanted each other so much that it hurt? The anticipation that was building might be delicious but it was becoming unbearable.

It was just as well Max sneezed again at that point.

'Time to get you out, captain.' Josh caught the plastic tugboat in Max's hands just before it got smacked onto the water to create another satisfying splash. 'Small boys who are coming down with colds need to be tucked up in bed in their PJs.'

'Good thinking.' Megan had a towel ready to wrap around the slippery little body.

Brenna had her arms up, ready for her turn to come out of the bath. Josh wrapped her in a towel and started to dry her.

'Did Mum tell you that Tasha rang?'

'No.' Megan's teeth caught her bottom lip. 'I've been so slack…I've barely been in touch with her since I got back here.'

'You'll get plenty of time to catch up. She's coming over for the opening.'

'Is she?' Megan was guiding Max's feet into the holes of his pyjama legs. 'That's fantastic news.'

'It is. Alessandro can't make it but he's put their private jet at her disposal. Nice for some, huh?' Josh grinned. 'She said she was really coming because she wants to see you. The opening is just a bonus.'

'That's not true. She's just teasing.'

'I know. But she was really thrilled to know that you're still here. And I think she might have guessed about… you know…'

'Did you say something?'

'Not exactly.' Josh focused on doing up the buttons on Brenna's pyjama jacket. 'But she thought I was sounding unusually happy and demanded to know why. I said that things were looking up—that the changes at work were pretty exciting and that Mum had a new lease on life what with the African project. I…um…apparently wasn't very convincing.'

Megan smiled. 'She'll know soon enough. Everybody will.'

'Can't be soon enough for me.'

They had both finished dressing the children in their nightclothes. It was time to move but the pause button seemed to have been pushed again as they shared a long, significant glance.

'I'll get them into bed if you want to head downstairs and see how Mum is getting on. Don't want her overdoing things.'

'She's loving it.' Megan raised an eyebrow. 'I'm starting to wonder where she's going to direct all her new-found energy once this project is finished.'

'Don't worry.' Josh shook his head. 'Wait till you see what Christmas is like around here. She'll have more than enough to keep her busy and happy.'

Brenna had been listening, wide-eyed, to her father. 'Kiss miss,' she said clearly.

Josh caught Megan's laughing gaze. 'Oh, yeah…' he murmured. 'I'm planning to, don't you worry.'

Two days later, the contributions from hospitals all over Cornwall and from the communities of Penhally Bay and St Piran were packed onto a cargo plane and started the long journey to Africa.

Megan watched the plane take off.

She was alone at the airport. Claire would have loved to have come but Max was really miserable with his cold and Tasha was arriving tomorrow and all sorts of preparations needed to be made. There had been no way Josh could take the time to come with her either. The opening ceremony for the emergency paediatric unit was only a few days away now.

That was OK. Megan knew how important Josh's career was to him and making this long drive simply to see a plane take off had been purely sentimental, really, but the project had been hugely significant to Megan.

Life-changing, in fact.

If Anna hadn't come up with the idea in the first place and Megan hadn't run with it, she probably wouldn't have stayed long enough to not only deal with the past but to move past it into a future that was bright enough to blind her.

Was that why she had tears in her eyes that she had to blink away more than once on the long drive home?

Maybe it was partly due to this being the culmination of such astonishing generosity by so many people. It had all been a bit overwhelming, in fact. Especially when she'd seen Albert White early that morning. The CEO had handed her a large white envelope.

'Open tickets,' he'd told her. 'I know the consignment will get held up in customs and so forth for a while, but we know how much you'd like to make sure it gets to its destination and the board of trustees wanted to show their appreciation for the work you've put in over the last few weeks. It's a return airfare,' he'd added, 'because we're hoping very much that you'll want to come back. There's a consultant position in Paediatrics that's still available, you know.'

The envelope was still in her handbag but Megan had no idea when, or even if, she'd be able to make the long trip back to Africa herself.

Did she even want to now?

And what about that job offer?

Did she want to work full time again? Or work at all when she could be a full-time mother to the twins?

That they were Rebecca's children had become insignificant now that she'd opened her heart to Max and Brenna. She already loved them as much as a birth mother could have. You didn't have to give birth to feel like a real mother. Asha and Dumi had taught Megan that.

Another set of twins. A whole world away.

Would she ever see them again?

Why was it that making a choice had to involve some kind of loss? To be with Josh for the rest of her life was more than she could have dreamed of for her future but the joy was tinged with sadness as well.

Life was a funny business.

That sense of loss and sadness was still with Megan when she finally arrived home to a dark, chilly cottage. She flicked on some lights, contemplated lighting the fire but went to her kitchen to make a hot drink first. She dropped her handbag onto the table, ignoring the way it fell open and tried to spill its contents, and busied herself filling the kettle and switching it on.

The knock at her door came just as the kettle came to the boil and Megan knew instantly who it would be.

Any regret over losses made by her choices evaporated under the glow of joy as she went to answer the door.

Josh was leaning against the doorframe, his grin lazy and utterly gorgeous.

'I missed you today,' he said softly. 'Thought I'd pop in and say hello.'

'Oh…that's nice.'

More than nice. Megan was being backed up against the wall of her hallway. Josh kicked the door shut behind him with his foot an instant before his lips covered hers. She reached up to touch his face but found her hands grasped and held on either side of her head, also against the wall.

She was glad of the support because there was no mistaking where this kiss was going and she was melting inside at the onslaught to her senses. No way could her legs have held her up without some assistance.

Josh finally raised his head. 'I couldn't wait any longer.' His voice was hoarse with need. 'I haven't even been home yet.'

'You're with me.' Megan smiled. 'You *are* home.'

She could see the effect of her words as Josh's eyes glazed from the force of his desire. His hands were busy, undoing the buttons of her shirt. A second later and they were sliding inside her bra to cup her breasts. The shaft of sensation as his thumbs brushed her nipples was exquisitely painful and Megan couldn't see straight any more either.

'Not here,' she managed to gasp. 'Upstairs. Bed.'

'Oh, yeah…' Josh groaned. *'Bed.'* He scooped Megan into his arms as easily as if she'd been one of the twins and headed for the stairs. He didn't put her down until he was standing beside her bed and he didn't put her down on her feet. He dropped her, flat on her back, onto the bed and leaned over her, loosening his tie.

'Oh, Megan. You've got no idea how hard it's been, waiting for this.'

'I think I do.' Megan watched Josh hauling off his clothes but she didn't touch her own. Josh could do that, too. When he unbuckled his belt and let his trousers drop to the floor, her breath caught and Megan had the passing impression that it might be possible to die from desire that was *this* strong but even if it was possible, she didn't give a damn.

As the trousers hit the polished boards of her bedroom

floor they made a noise that rapidly became recognisable as the ringtone of Josh's phone.

He made a very impatient sound. 'I'll turn it off.'

Naked, except for his underwear, he shook the trousers to extract the phone from the pocket. He glanced at it.

Megan could swear she felt the world stop spinning right then.

'It's Mum,' Josh muttered. 'She wouldn't ring unless it was important.'

Megan tried, and failed, to ward off a chill of premonition. 'You'd better answer it.'

He did. Megan knew that it was something serious as soon as he began speaking because Josh's voice took on the crisp focus that she'd only ever heard in the emergency department. When something important needed sorting out. The questions he was asking only confirmed her fear.

'When did it happen?

'How long did it last?

'Where are you now?

'Take his clothes off. Sponge him down with some tepid water. I'm on my way.'

Ending the call, Josh didn't pause for a moment. He was doing up the button on his trousers before he even turned back to Megan.

'Max has had a febrile convulsion,' he told her. 'Mum's called the ambulance but she's scared stiff. I have to go.'

'Of course. Oh, poor Max…'

She should be able to see this from a clinician's point of view. To be involved and caring but not panic the way a parent would. But she couldn't. The fear that gripped Megan was that of a mother, desperately afraid for her precious child.

'I'll come too.' Megan pushed herself to a sitting position. She tried to start doing up her buttons but her hands were shaking too much.

And Josh was shaking his head as he pulled on his shirt. 'No need. It's probably nothing. He's had a cold. This is most likely just an ear infection or something.'

But it could be something much worse. Meningitis? Encephalitis?

'Where the hell is my other shoe?' Josh was swinging his head, searching.

'Over there,' Megan told him. 'By the window.'

How could Josh be sounding like this? Like a doctor instead of a parent? This was weird…

Unless he could sense how Megan was feeling? Was he trying to push her back? To remind her that Max wasn't really *her* child?

That Rebecca was—and always would be—the twins' mother?

She had intended to get off the bed and help Josh find what he needed but Megan couldn't move now. She was frozen with something like horror. And there was no need for her to move anyway. Josh was moving fast. Totally focused on what he needed to do.

What he'd needed when he'd arrived here was the last thing on either of their minds.

It'll be all right, Megan told herself. As long as he kisses me before he leaves.

But Josh didn't stop long enough to kiss her goodbye.

He didn't even *look* at her as he rushed out of the door.

He said something but Megan would never know what those words had been because she'd been sucked back in time. To when she'd seen him again, an alarming number of days after they'd spent that passionate first night together. When he'd blanked her, as though that night had never happened.

It felt exactly the same right now.

He'd been about to make love to her and then, in the blink of an eye, it had been as though it had never been about to happen.

As though she hadn't even existed any more.

She didn't *matter*.

She couldn't stay here, on the bed, with her shirt still unbuttoned and her hair a tousled mess. Megan did up her shirt, forcing stiff fingers into action, but didn't bother touching her hair as she went downstairs.

It was ridiculous to feel like this.

Like what? *Betrayed*?

His child was sick. Maybe seriously sick. Of course Max had to be the priority.

But she was supposed to be sharing his life. Why had he shut her out? He hadn't even *looked* at her before he'd rushed off.

She couldn't do anything to prevent that old button being pushed. The one that fired the emotions she'd been devastated by so many years ago. She'd felt so…used that first time. Used and cheap and stupid. Incredibly naïve and so very, very hurt.

What had Josh told her that day he'd come to pass on the news that Rebecca was pregnant? That his children had to be the most important thing in his life. The only thing that really mattered.

Apart from his career, of course.

He'd been far too busy to come with her today. Far too focused on the upcoming public acknowledgement of his brilliant bloody career.

Something far too close to panic was clutching at Megan now as she paced back and forth across her kitchen floor, her arms wrapped tightly around her body. There was no comfort to be found in the hug or the movement, however. Megan shivered. Her home felt cold and empty with the absence of Josh.

So did her heart.

This was exactly what she'd been afraid of. That she would put herself back into this space. Every step she had taken had made her feel closer to Josh. More a part of his family. That the future was safe from the kind of emotional trauma she *knew*, all too well, that he was capable of causing, whether or not it was intentional.

The panic caught and held. Spiralled.

What the hell was she going to do?

With a sob Megan collapsed into a chair beside the table. Her arms flopping onto its surface. Coming into contact with her handbag. Half-blinded by tears, Megan started automatically shoving the spilled contents of the bag back into place.

The last item her fingers closed over was a large white envelope.

With tears still streaming down her face, Megan stared at it blankly. And then she remembered what it contained.

Her fingers trembling, she opened the envelope.

CHAPTER TEN

'SHE'S GONE.'

Josh O'Hara scowled at his sister. 'What do you mean, she's *gone*?'

After a sleepless night, during which Max had been thoroughly checked and declared to be suffering from no more than an ear infection, Josh had taken the day off work so that he could collect his sister from the airport and look after the rest of his family.

Tasha had been desperately keen to see Megan so she'd taken Josh's car and gone to Megan's cottage as soon as she could without offending her family. She'd been gone a couple of hours and had now stormed back into the farmhouse, looking bewildered as she'd made her startling announcement.

Claire came down the stairs, having settled the twins for a nap. 'That paracetamol has worked a treat,' she said. 'Max doesn't even feel like he's running a temperature any more and he went out like a light. He's exhausted, poor lamb, after such a disrupted night. I'm feeling the same myself, so I am. I'm going to make a big pot of coffee.'

She stopped speaking and looked from her son to her daughter and back again.

'What on earth's the matter with you two?'

'Megan's gone,' Tasha said. 'The cottage is all locked

up. I went to the most likely car rental agency and was told she handed in the vehicle and her keys very early this morning. She ordered a taxi. To take her to the airport.'

Déjà vu.

Josh could feel the blood draining from his brain, leaving a confused maelstrom of questions.

Why?

How could she do something like this?

Where had she gone?

What the hell has just happened here?

Snatches of answers were trying to compete.

You blanked her again, didn't you?

When you got the news about Max, she ceased to matter, when only minutes before she'd been the only thing that mattered.

He'd shut her out. Hurt her unbearably and she'd reacted the way she always had. By running away.

Surely by now she felt she could trust him? Running away was... It was verging on cowardly, wasn't it?

The blood was returning now. Boiling back as something like fury began to nibble its way through all the other devastating emotions swirling around.

Both Claire and Tasha were staring at him.

'Kitchen,' Claire commanded. 'We all need some coffee.'

Moving in a vaguely zombie-like fashion, Josh did as he was told. He needed to sit down, that was for sure. To try and get his head around this. Half of him was furious. The other half was numb. Stunned by a blow he hadn't expected.

Didn't deserve?

Maybe he did. For his past stupidity if not for how badly he'd handled this latest crisis.

He barely heard the chatter going on between Claire and Tasha as they made coffee.

'I'll do it, Mum. You sit down. You look exhausted and you've had a heart attack recently, for heaven's sake.'

'I'm fine. Or I will be when I know what on earth is going on around here to make Josh look like the world has ended. Out of the way, Natasha. Or make yourself useful and find some mugs.'

A chuckle from Tasha. 'You certainly sound like your old self. I'm sorry I couldn't come over when you were in hospital. I was feeling a bit sick myself for a few days there and we didn't know what it was.'

'You didn't say.'

'I didn't want to worry you. And I'm fine now, except for first thing in the morning.'

'Oh…' Claire dropped the lid of the biscuit tin. 'Are you…?'

'Yes.' The joy in Tasha's voice made Josh turn his head and tune in properly. 'I'm pregnant. Three months along now.'

'Why didn't you tell us?'

Tasha sat down at the table and sighed. 'I felt bad, you know? About telling Megan. Knowing that she can never have her own babies. It wasn't something I could tell her in a phone call or a text and…and I thought I could tell her face-to-face. Today. She texted me this morning but now her phone's turned off.'

'What did she text you about?' Josh demanded.

'Max.' Tasha closed her eyes. 'She wanted to know if he was OK. I told her everything was fine and I'd see her soon.'

'And?'

'And nothing. That was it.' Tasha shook her head. 'I could have walked past her at the airport without even knowing. Why has she gone? I would have thought the opening of the emergency paediatric unit was just as important for her as it is to you.' She opened her eyes and glared at Josh. 'This has got something to do with you, hasn't it? I know how much Megan loves you. Did you give her a reason to think it was all on again and then do something to show her that nothing had changed?'

It was Josh's turn to close his eyes. 'Something like that, I suppose,' he muttered.

There was a long silence. The groan from Josh broke it. 'I knew it was like this,' he said. 'I was right to want nothing to do with love. It only wrecks your life. Someone always gets badly hurt.'

'Oh, *rot*,' Tasha said. 'Alessandro and I are as happy as any two people could be, thank you very much.'

Claire had totally forgotten about the coffee she was preparing. She sank into another chair at the table, her fingers at her neck, playing with her silver shamrock. She looked troubled.

'Do you love Megan, Josh?'

'Yes. Totally. As much as it's possible to love anyone.' He could feel his face settling into grim lines. 'But what's the point? She's gone. Again.'

'Wasn't she engaged? To that man from London?'

'Charles?' Tasha sounded astonished. 'No *way*…he was just a friend.'

'Not any more,' he told his mother.

Claire nodded. 'It was a second-best thing, then. Like you and Rebecca.'

'What's made her run away?' Tasha asked gently. 'Do you know?'

Josh didn't answer. If he did, he'd have to take the blame, wouldn't he? And he wasn't the only one at fault here. Megan had run away. Blanked him back in the most blatant way possible. He had every right to be furious with her, didn't he? Not that he expected his mother or sister to buy into that. He was outnumbered here, he could feel it.

'If you don't know, you need to find out,' Claire said. 'For a bright boy, Josh, you can be a bit simple sometimes.'

'I would have thought you'd understand better than anyone,' Josh told her.

'What?'

'You loved Dad, didn't you?'

'Yes, of course I did. I wouldn't have married him otherwise.'

'You loved him enough to take him back, time after time, after his affairs. You believed it could work and he just hurt you again and again. Hurt all of us.'

'Oh…' Claire looked devastated. 'You were just a child. I thought I was doing the right thing, trying to keep the family together.' She looked ready to cry. 'How could I not see the damage that was happening?'

'Hey…I turned out just fine,' Tasha put in.

'Joshie was the oldest,' Claire said sadly. 'I leaned on him. I let him see more than he should have seen about how tough things were.' She reached out to touch her son's arm. 'But you can't compare my marriage to what you and Megan have. Have always had, from what I've heard.'

'Why not?' It didn't bother Josh that his mother knew far more than he'd realised. Nothing mattered right now except that he'd lost Megan.

Again. Maybe for good this time.

'The love in my marriage was one-sided,' Claire said sadly. 'Rory was fond of me, certainly, but he didn't *love* me. The balance was too wrong and *that* was why it never worked.'

Tasha was nodding. 'If you have real love on both sides,

it's like a see-saw. Sure, it tips up and down a bit but you can always find the balance and when it's there, it's like a bridge into another world. Not a perfect world but…' Her smile was misty. 'It's as good as it gets.'

Josh knew that world. It was the space he could be in with Megan and no one else.

'You know how much you love your children,' Claire added. 'What that's like.'

Josh's smile felt rusty. 'It's the best feeling in the world.'

'Well, love between parents and children is pretty much a given,' Claire said sagely. 'When you get that kind of love between people who choose to be together, it's different but just as powerful.'

'Yes,' Tasha agreed. She had her hand on her belly. 'And when you combine all the different sorts of love in your life, that's when the real magic happens.'

'Like the sun that can shine through the worst of any weather,' Claire said softly.

'Or at least dry the puddles afterwards.' Tasha laughed. Then she sobered and patted Josh's hand. 'You and Megan have that. Put the past behind you once and for all and start again.'

The numbness was finally wearing off. The fury was still there but part of it was being directed internally now. Josh knew exactly what he needed to do. What he *had* to do. But was it too late?

'I have no idea where she's gone.'

'I think you do,' Tasha suggested.

'And if you don't, you can find out, for heaven's sake.' Claire sounded impatient. 'Ring that friend of hers that she isn't engaged to any more. Find out what plane she got on.' She clicked her tongue irritably. 'What on earth are you waiting for?'

* * *

Bleached, bone-thin cattle stirred the parched ground and made the dust swirl. Fortunately, there was no breeze to shift it any closer to where Megan was sitting beneath a skeleton tree that offered only a hint of shade.

Back at the camp for less than twenty-four hours, she was finding it a struggle to cope with the heat and the smell and how appallingly tired she was. The flight had been incredibly long. Plenty of time to catch her breath and re-flect on her knee-jerk reaction of escaping Josh.

Why couldn't she get past the automatic response? Maybe it had been justified way back after their first night together because she'd had nothing to hang any kind of faith on. Now she *knew* how much Josh loved her.

But she'd known that last time, hadn't she? And then he'd come to her home and told her it was over—that they could never be together. Because the welfare of his chil-dren had to come first.

And it had been the welfare of those children that had sparked this reaction. Did she really think he would have come back from seeing Max at the hospital to tell her that he'd made a mistake and he couldn't include her in his life?

At that moment, yes… Her panic had been caused by the fear of exactly that happening and the only way Megan had thought she could protect herself had been to some-how make it *not* happen.

And now here she was, having ensured that the worst-case scenario was firmly in place. The way she had when she'd made the mistake of not believing Josh when he'd tried to explain about sleeping with Rebecca again?

He wasn't even going to attempt to explain himself this time, though, was he? Megan had turned her phone on first thing that morning only to find her battery was flat. It was charging again now but unless there were texts or calls she'd missed in her travels, she wouldn't be hearing anything today.

It was opening day. The pinnacle, so far, of Josh's career. He'd already proved he could push her away for the sake of his children and Megan knew his career came a close second in his life priorities. It would be almost dawn in Cornwall right now. Was he awake already? Had he had a haircut? Would he shave for a second time, maybe, before heading off to face all the cameras and lights?

Megan shifted slightly, to ease the pins and needles in her arms.

'You're getting to be big lumps,' she told the two babies she held. She kissed one grizzled scalp and then the other, earning a toothless grin from Asha and a wave of two chubby fists from Dumi. 'Big, fat, healthy lumps. How good is that?'

One of the group of Somalian women Megan was surrounded by, Fatuma, was crouched beside her in the shade of the bare tree, holding a child of her own. She looked up and smiled. 'Fat.' She nodded. 'Is good.'

Megan kissed the babies again. 'It is,' she said softly. Speaking in Somalian, she continued, 'Thank you so much for helping to care for them, Fatuma.'

'It is my honour,' was the reply. 'You saved my baby. I help yours.'

Megan nodded gravely. The exchange of gifts was respected.

For a minute both women watched the older children playing in the bare field near the cattle. They all held long sticks and there was a stone that was being scooted across the ground by being hit. Shrieks of laughter could be heard and it was a sound that could, temporarily at least, reduce the grim reality of these surroundings.

Still, Megan sighed.

'I wish they *were* really mine,' she said.

'They are the babies of your heart. They *are* yours.'

Megan nodded again. It was true. She had missed them so much. If she wasn't able to adopt them as a single woman and take them home, she would stay here despite the risk of dengue fever.

'Lots of insect repellent, I think,' she murmured.

Fatuma looked puzzled but then shaded her eyes to look towards where the sun was glinting off the corrugated-iron roof of the clinic buildings.

'Truck coming,' she sighed. 'More and more people.'

Idly, Megan followed her gaze. The truck was one of those ancient ones with a big wooden crate on its flat deck. A crowd of people stood in the crate, filling the space to uncomfortable levels. Not an unusual sight. What was unusual was a face amongst them that simply didn't fit.

A white face.

The truck stopped near one of the camp registration tents and the people spilled out over the back.

The heat suddenly seemed unbearable to Megan. She could feel a trickle of sweat gluing the folds of her shawl to her back. Exhaustion and jet lag seemed to be combining to make her feel very odd. Unwell, even.

Or maybe it was just because missing Josh was so painful it was like having part of herself ripped away. The pain came in waves and this one was strong enough to have her hallucinating.

Imagining that the tall, lean figure leaping from the back of that truck was actually Josh. That he had come to the end of the earth to find her. That he was striding towards her, flanked by an entourage of curious children, through the shimmer of heat and clouds of dust like some kind of mirage.

Blinking didn't make things any clearer. Lack of oxygen wasn't helping but Megan couldn't take a new breath because…

Because it *was* Josh.

Unbelievably, Josh was here. In Africa. Clearly hellbent on finding her. And as he got even closer, she could see the grim lines on his face.

'Megan Phillips,' he growled as soon as he got within range of being heard. 'Don't you *ever* run out on me like that again.'

This was the part of Megan that Josh had never met before.

Having released the pent-up combination of anger at the way she'd run out on him, fear that he might have lost her completely and sheer exhaustion from the hideously long journey, Josh took a deep breath and soaked in the relief of seeing her again.

Crouched on the arid African dirt, with a shawl covering her head and wrapped around her body, Megan was clearly a welcome companion for the other women who were so well shrouded only their faces were visible. Expressionless faces that were regarding him with barely restrained hostility in the silence that had fallen after his heated reprimand by way of a greeting for Megan. Even the children playing nearby were standing still, as frozen as everybody else by this startling turn of events.

'Y-you…you *c-can't* be here,' Megan stammered.

'Why not?' Oh…*God*…she didn't want him to be here?

The woman closest to Megan touched her arm and said something in her own language. Megan answered in the same language. The words were incomprehensible but the tone was clearly reassuring. Her companion got to her feet with graceful ease and, by some unseen signal, all the others followed her lead. The children still clustered around

Josh were shooed away. Someone offered to take the babies from Megan but she shook her head, smiling.

When the crowd had virtually melted away, Megan looked directly at him.

'Isn't it the opening today?' she asked quietly. 'The new wing of *your* department?'

Josh merely shrugged. 'Ben Carter's looking after that. He was happy to cope with all the publicity and I was more than happy to let him have the glory.'

'But…' Megan looked completely bewildered. 'It's been so important to you. You've dreamed about this happening for years.'

Josh stepped forward and crouched down in front of Megan. He wanted to take her in his arms but she still had her arms full of babies. And he still didn't know whether he was welcome here or not.

'It's not as important to me as you are,' he said slowly. 'I've dreamed of being with you a hell of lot longer than having a paediatric wing in my emergency department.'

A spark of what looked like hope flashed in the emerald-green depths of Megan's eyes but then they clouded again. She seemed to be having trouble processing his words.

'The children,' she whispered. 'Oh…*Max*.' She looked incredulous now. He'd left a sick child to come here?

'Max is fine.' Josh was unconsciously using the gentlest tone he had. The one that was so useful to soothe a frightened patient or its parent. 'He's on antibiotics for his ear infection and he'd bounced back, the way children so often do. Mum's looking after them. And Tasha's helping. Getting some quality "auntie" time. And some practice.'

The hint wasn't picked up. He could see Megan swallow hard.

'You're really here,' she murmured. 'You came all this way. For me?'

'For you,' Josh confirmed. 'I needed to apologise for the way I shut you out the other night. I just wasn't thinking and I'm so sorry I scared you.' His smile was crooked. Self-effacing. 'I know it's not much of an excuse but I am a man. I'm not good at multi-tasking.'

A snort of something like laughter escaped Megan. Unable to resist touching her, Josh reached towards her face, wanting to stroke her cheek. His hand became hijacked halfway there, however, caught by a tiny, dark hand. The grip was remarkably tight.

'Hello, there.' Josh smiled at the baby. 'Are you Asha?'

'No. That's Dumi.'

'May I?' Josh moved to pick up the baby. 'I know what it's like, juggling twins.'

Megan said nothing. She was watching Dumi, who gurgled with pleasure and held up both arms when he felt Josh's hands around his body. Josh gazed down at the small face and felt an odd tightness in his chest when Dumi's face suddenly split into a wide, toothless grin.

'He likes you.' Megan smiled for the first time since he'd arrived.

'He's gorgeous,' Josh said. 'They both are. Beautiful babies.'

'My babies,' Megan said softly. 'I'm going to adopt them. That's why I asked Charles to marry me in the first place because I thought the process would be a lot easier if there were two parents available, but…I could still do it, I think. I'm going to try, anyway.'

Josh nodded solemnly. She'd been a mother to these babies since the moment they'd entered the world. This was the unknown part of the woman he'd always loved and

understanding this bond she had with these babies only
made him love her even more.

'It would be good for them to have a father, though,
wouldn't it?'

Megan's eyes were wide. Watching him intently.

'My babies would love to have a mother,' Josh continued. Oh…help…could he put what he wanted to say into
the right words? 'You love Max and Brenna, don't you?
Enough to be their mum?'

Did she love the twins she'd left behind in Cornwall?

Did it compare with the love she had for this man, who'd
traversed the globe to find her? A love that was threatening to overwhelm her?

'Of course I do,' Megan whispered. 'They're part of
you. How could I not love them?'

'Snap.' Josh smiled slowly. 'And I've just found the part
of you that I knew was missing.' He took a deep breath.
'Come home with me, my love. Marry me. We'll both
adopt Asha and Dumi and bring them up with a big brother
and sister.'

'Oh…' The words painted a picture of a perfect future.
One that Megan hadn't even dared to dream of when she'd
put her trust in Josh's new commitment. She gave her head
a tiny shake. 'Whatever would your mother say if she found
herself a grandma to African babies?'

'She'd be thrilled to bits,' Josh said. 'You know what
she said when she was driving me to the airport?'

'What?' Josh was leaning closer. So close the babies
they were holding were able to reach out and grasp the
hand of the other. They both gurgled happily.

'She said I would be a better father if I was a truly happy
man, and a blind person could see that I was never going
to be happy without you. That I needed you. That we all

needed you. *Make sure you bring her back*, she said, *for all our sakes.*'

He leaned even closer and Megan felt herself sway towards him. Over the heads of the two babies their lips met in a gentle kiss.

'I love you,' Josh whispered. 'More than I'll ever be able to tell you.'

'Snap.' Megan's voice wobbled. Tears of joy were very, very close.

'Give me the chance to show you. Every day. For the rest of our lives. Could you do that?'

Megan could only nod. She could do more than that. She could use every day of the rest of their lives to show Josh that she loved him every bit as much. Starting right now. She closed the gap between them and kissed him again.

How tender could a kiss be? How much love could it convey? How sure a promise of the future could it seal?

A lot, apparently.

Much more than enough, anyway.

On both sides.

EPILOGUE

A BIRTHDAY PARTY for twelve-year-olds was bound to be a noisy affair.

Especially in the O'Hara household, with so many blessings in the way of family and friends.

Claire O'Hara's knees were a little stiff these days, so she moved from where she was standing on the edge of the veranda watching the game of football happening on the lawn to sink down into one of the comfortable wicker chairs.

'You all right, Claire?' Megan came bustling out of the house, a bunch of carrots dangling from her hand but paused, concern furrowing her brow. 'Is your knee bothering you again?'

'I'm just fine, lovie.' She eyed the carrots. 'Are you heading for the ponies?'

Megan grinned. 'We'll never get the girls back inside for food if I don't drag them out of the paddock. Want to come with me?'

'I went up before. You'd better take your camera. The ponies are looking very pretty with all their plaits and ribbons.'

'Good thinking.' But Megan didn't move to rush back into the house.

She wasn't looking at her mother-in-law any more, either. A tall figure had broken away from the game of football and was coming towards the house. Even from this distance Claire could see that her son only had eyes for one person right now. She could feel the connection between the two of them, getting steadily stronger with every step Josh took. The strength of that connection never failed to take her breath away.

Was it really ten years since Josh had come back from Africa and brought Megan back into their lives for good?

Such incredibly happy years.

Oh, there'd been the anxious wait about the adoption of Dumi and Asha and it had taken a while but what a honeymoon, to have gone back over there and brought the new babies home to complete their family! Claire had stayed in the farmhouse only long enough to realise what a superb twin-wrangler and mother Megan was and then, with one of those lovely twists that life could suddenly produce, she took over Megan's little cottage for her home and it was perfect. An easy walk to the lovely beach that made it so perfect for all her grandchildren to visit.

Josh had reached the veranda now and he and Megan were just standing there, smiling at each other—as though it had been only yesterday that they'd fallen in love.

'Need any help?' Josh queried.

'You're doing great,' Megan said softly. 'You and Alessandro really know how to keep a bunch of small boys happy.'

'We've had plenty of practice,' Josh laughed.

Yes. The O'Hara children's royal cousins were here for this celebration. Three little boys in the last decade and Marco, Alessio and Rocco were out there having a wonderful time kicking the football with Max and Dumi. Even better, Tasha was in the house behind them, feeding the

brand new and much longed for princess, Alandra, named
for her father.

'I'm going to round up the girls,' Megan said. 'Anna
and the others have got the table all set. How's Luke going
firing up the barbecue?'

'I'm just going to check.' Josh turned away but not before he'd given Megan one of those lingering kisses that
always made Claire's eyes go all misty. He turned back
once more. 'You all right, Mum? You're not sitting out here
all by yourself, are you?'

'No. I've got company.' Claire dropped her hand to
where she knew it would encounter the roughened fur of
an elderly companion. Crash was nearly thirteen now and
getting stiffer in the joints than she was but he was a part
of this family. So were Anna and Luke and their two children. Six year old Chloe loved to tag along in the wake of
the older girls and nine year old Ben was a keen surfer and
a best friend for Max and Dumi. As close as anyone could
get given the bond between the brothers, that is.

Claire had to blink more mistiness away as Josh and
Megan left to attend to party business. Who would have
thought that two sets of such very different twins could
blend to become such a perfect family? Eleven year old
Dumi stood a head taller than twelve year old Max already
but he had a gentle soul and the whitest, happiest smile
that brightened the lives of anyone fortunate enough to be
within range. The boys adored each other.

Brenna and Asha were completely different, too. Brenna
was a total tomboy and Asha as feminine as they came but
the two girls had also bonded as babies and now shared the
passion of ponies. How Megan found the energy to ferry
them to pony club and events was astounding given that
she had been working part time at St Piran's ever since all
the children had started school. Josh was just as amazing.

His career still seemed to be on an upward trajectory, with his skills as a consultant in such demand and a new book due to be published on setting up and running an emergency department. He still loved to work on the front line, however and somehow he found the time to be involved with the boys' football practices and matches. Somehow, Josh and Megan had found a balance. Professional, personal and parental and they could work as a team and keep everybody happy.

The noise level increased. Claire stayed in her chair with Crash at her feet as the party attendees streamed past her on their way to the food. She smiled and Crash thumped his tail as children and adults greeted him and 'Nanny Claire' on their way past.

'Are you having a good birthday, Max?' she asked her grandson.

'The best,' he said, pushing his mop of black curls back and grinning at her. Heavens, but he was the spitting image of his dad at that age.

And so much happier…

'To be sure,' Dumi added with a cheeky grin and the Irish accent he'd perfected to make his grandmother laugh.

It never failed.

Claire was still smiling as the excited troop of girls began to appear from where they'd been dressing up the ponies.

Behind them, she could see Megan. And Josh.

Walking hand-in-hand.

She lost sight of them for a moment, as the girls swept past but then she saw them again. All by themselves for a precious moment, in the garden of their home, with the beautiful backdrop of Penhally Bay sparkling blue in the sunshine.

They didn't see Claire watching them.

How could they, when they both so intent on kissing each other?

With an effort, accompanied by the happiest of sighs, Claire got out of her chair to make her way inside and join the happy gathering of her family and friends.

Life was good, so it was.

* * * * *

LET'S TALK
Romance

For exclusive extracts, competitions
and special offers, find us online:

f facebook.com/millsandboon

🐦 @MillsandBoon

📷 @MillsandBoonUK

Get in touch on 01413 063232

For all the latest titles coming soon, visit
millsandboon.co.uk/nextmonth

MILLS & BOON

THE HEART OF ROMANCE

A ROMANCE FOR EVERY READER

MODERN

Prepare to be swept off your feet by sophisticated, sexy and seductive heroes, in some of the world's most glamourous and romantic locations, where power and passion collide.

HISTORICAL

Escape with historical heroes from time gone by. Whether your passion is for wicked Regency Rakes, muscled Vikings or rugged Highlanders, awaken the romance of the past.

MEDICAL

Set your pulse racing with dedicated, delectable doctors in the high-pressure world of medicine, where emotions run high and passion, comfort and love are the best medicine.

True Love

Celebrate true love with tender stories of heartfelt romance, from the rush of falling in love to the joy a new baby can bring, and a focus on the emotional heart of a relationship.

Desire

Indulge in secrets and scandal, intense drama and plenty of sizzling hot action with powerful and passionate heroes who have it all: wealth, status, good looks…everything but the right woman.

HEROES

Experience all the excitement of a gripping thriller, with an intense romance at its heart. Resourceful, true-to-life women and strong, fearless men face danger and desire - a killer combination!

To see which titles are coming soon, please visit

millsandboon.co.uk/nextmonth

JOIN US ON SOCIAL MEDIA!

Stay up to date with our latest releases, author news and gossip, special offers and discounts, and all the behind-the-scenes action from Mills & Boon...

 millsandboon

 millsandboonuk

 millsandboon

It might just be true love...

MILLS & BOON
MODERN
Power and Passion

Prepare to be swept off your feet by sophisticated, sexy and seductive heroes, in some of the world's most glamourous and romantic locations, where power and passion collide.

Julia James

Heiress's
**PREGNANCY
SCANDAL**

MILLS & BOON

Jennie Lucas

Chosen as the
**SHEIKH'S ROYAL
BRIDE**

MILLS & BOON

Kim Lawrence

**A WEDDING
at the
ITALIAN'S DEMAND**

Sharon Kendrick

The
**SHEIKH'S
SECRET BABY**

MILLS & BOON

Eight Modern stories published every month, find them all at:

millsandboon.co.uk/Modern